THE HOLE SHOW

THE HOLE SHOW

a novel

Maya Merrick

Cover drawing by Lyle Brebner
Edited by Andy Brown
Copyedited by Liane Keightley
Author photo by Meghan Hicks

Library and Archives Canada Cataloguing in Publication

Merrick, Maya, 1974-
       The hole show / Maya Merrick.

ISBN 978-1-894994-25-5

       I. Title.

PS8626.E77H65 2007   C813'.6   C2007-905402-1

Dépot Legal, Bibliothèque nationale du Québec

Printed and bound in Canada on 100% recycled, ancient rainforest-friendly paper.

First Edition

conundrum press
PO Box 55003, CSP Fairmount, Montreal, Quebec, H2T 3E2, Canada
conpress@ican.net
www.conundrumpress.com

conundrum press acknowledges the financial assistance of the Canada Council for the Arts toward our publishing program.

Canada Council   Conseil des Arts
for the Arts   du Canada

HICKLIN

1962

Somewhere above him, if his books are right, black holes spin. Sinking and sucking through time and space, right there in the pale blue sky. He stands in the middle of the sidewalk, his head tilted back, and squints. He thinks he almost sees something, a pucker in the shimmering sheet, a tiny tug at the fabric up there. He squints harder. Feels something start to pull at him, gently, tugging at his skin as though it were taffy. He feels himself stretch, his skin yanking up. A kid bumps him from behind, knocking his heavy bag full of books to the ground, and the tugging stops. The whatever-it-was disappears. Maybe never to be seen again.

He steps off the sidewalk and walks slowly in the gutter, kicking at soggy leaves. The street sinks in apple juice light, the boxy houses sail past him on sheets of slow waves. From here he can just see the house where he lives. It sprawls as though sleeping, the garage curling into the driveway, the mirror twin of the house next door. One level of grimy white and brown siding, three cracked cement steps to the dented front door, a nameplate in brass script left from the people who lived there before. The curtains are shut. Just past his house is a bright orange wave, a tiny flag, signalling.

He walks past his house, barely glancing at it. At the end of his block half the street has been dug away, leaving a pit surrounded by a makeshift fence fitted with orange flags. Men in orange vests wave cars around the hole, as if maybe the motorists can't see it, as if it's just there

7

for the men in the vests, and maybe him. He walks over and peers down the hole as far as he can. Dark dirt, and things wriggling through the black earth. The men in orange vests strap chains to a hunk of pipe. Behind them, what's left of the pipe sprouts from the freshly dug walls of the pit, its opening as tall as he is, its opening a mouth made of stone. He leans over a little further, tries to see what's in that hole, what's in that mouth open wide. All he can see is dark. The mouth stays open, wide. Waiting.

"Kid! Git away from there. It's dangerous."

He steps back, startled into obedience. A great hook on a giant chain is lowered into the pit and attached to the severed section of pipe. It's lifted, slowly, into the air, the hole in it shining, full of bright blue sky. It turns on its chain, and the hole is gone.

"Kid!" the same man yells. "Step back!"

He nods, and moves away. The pipe is guided on its chain, right over his head, and lowered onto a flatbed truck. The men scurry around it, faithful as ladies-in-waiting, attending to the pipe. He turns, and heads across the street. In his neighbour's small front yard a bon-fire burns unattended. In the still-bright daylight it's a small beacon of eerie amber, like a live thing come from some other place. Inside the house where he lives he can see his mother, moving as a shade behind the drapes in the living room. He doesn't want to but he does.

He goes inside to find her wandering from the kitchen through the hallway, into the living room and back again, lifting objects as she pass-es them, peering underneath, as if divining.

"Hi, Mum."

She looks up at him, distracted. Held by the very tips of the fingers of her right hand is a white china pussy cat lying on its back, playfully kicking a sparkly pink china ball of yarn with its back paws. This is how she always holds things. At arm's length, and by the very ends of her fingers. She peers at the strange flat underside of the china kitten, into the little hole that appears to go right into its back, finds nothing, and shakes her head.

"What are you looking for, Mum?"

She shakes her head again, giving him a small smile, almost shy, the kind of smile that makes him feel like he's in on a secret when he's really not, really not at all, like he *knows*, as if he *understands*, but he doesn't, he doesn't at all. She puts down the puss and wanders off in the direction of the kitchen. She walks more slowly every day, underwater slow, as though she's walking over knives, wincing with every step. He turns away from her and goes to his room.

Inside the sleeping house, two bedrooms lie on either side of the bathroom, just beyond the living room. One of these bedrooms is the master bedroom. That's his mother's. The other is ostensibly for a child. That's his father's. Between the second, smaller bedroom and the door to the garage is a room that was intended as a mud room when the house was built. That's his.

Four small walls, not even painted, but the flaking pale clay of old primer. In one corner is a small, meticulous pile of boxes, most of them formerly for shoes, all covered in brown kraft paper, all neatly labelled in his own unslanted script. Up high is a thin slice of window, no good for looking out of, unless he stands on the bed. The bed itself is the same small one he's had for years and is beginning to outgrow. His feet dangle off it now, and bash into the wall when he sleeps. The room is so small that's about all that fits in it. *He* almost doesn't fit in it anymore. When he sits down on the bed, as he does now, his knees brush the wall opposite. So he curls up on the bed, and stares at his wall.

This wall is blank and bare, nothing touches it. Not a box, not his bed, nothing. There's nothing on it, not even a smudge. He cleans it every week, and sometimes more often, depending. He's been in a few rooms belonging to other kids and knows he should have posters up there, of rock stars and movie stars and whatever else he's supposed to like. He finds outsized heads unnerving, and can't imagine ever feeling at ease with huge people looming over him, reading his thoughts, or even worse, *feeding* him thoughts. But this blankness is beautiful. This is his garden, his waterfall, his seaside. This is his screen. This is his stage.

He stares at the wall for a while. He can hear his mother out there, pacing slowly. No time right now. He sighs and heads out to the kitchen.

"Hungry, Mum?"

She looks through him. The curtains in the kitchen are closed. Just behind them lies the garden. He tries to see it through the curtains, but can only make out humps, looming, grey and still. He glances at his mother, who is looking underneath every piece of fruit in the fruit bowl, and shrugs. Opens the drapes. The flower beds all dried, shrivelled plants strewn over them. Even the grass, curled up, and brown. His mother blinks.

"Keep those shut."

"What? Mum, don't you want to see the garden?"

She shakes her head and picks up a banana. Turns it fretfully on the ends of her fingers, searching for the underside.

"Mum."

She puts one hand to the side of her head, as though to block out the light. The other hand still holds the banana and its elusive underneath.

"Mum! It's not that bright."

She puts down the banana, she puts down her hand, and she looks into the garden.

"It's awful. Look at it."

"It's just fall, Mum. In the spring we can plant everything again. I've got the bulbs all boxed up. Your dahlias and lilies and crocuses, remember?"

"Hm."

His mother stands and walks slowly toward the fridge. He races her and wins.

"Mum, just sit down, I'll get you something."

He reaches into the fridge and gets out half a casserole from last night. He's getting good at casseroles. His mother sits down at the kitchen table. She looks out the window, her mouth curling down at the ends. He turns the oven on, then gets a bottle of milk from the fridge and pours her a glass. Puts it on the table. She doesn't appear to notice. He puts the half-casserole in the oven. Gets himself a glass of grape juice. Sits down across from her. Her hair is long and beautiful, the most beautiful, shiny hair he's ever seen. When she lets it down it's like waves of chocolate boiling over her. Usually though, like now, she keeps it tied back in a long, loose braid, which he thinks is not as wonderful as the chocolate waves, but still much prettier than the hard shells other mothers seem to shape their hair into. She is thin, too thin, which is why he always comes home. She forgets.

"Did you have a good day, Mum?"

She talks to the window again, her mouth moving so little he can't be sure he's not making it up.

"What on earth was I thinking?"

"What do you mean, Mum?"

"I don't even know what I'm doing anymore. Of course there's nothing there."

Her eyes stare out the window. The light outside has gone more brown than gold, shadows swarming from the ground.

"Mum, it's okay. It's just fall."

She closes her eyes.

"What was I even doing?"

He doesn't know what to say to that either. He gets up and quietly closes the curtains again. In the almost dark his mother's pale skin turns grey-blue, her hair black, her closed eyes go hollow where they shouldn't. She is so still he can't look. He busies himself with a box of matches, lights the pair of half-burned candles on the table. Pinks and whites return to his mother's skin, and she opens her eyes. She smiles.

"I'm being so silly. I'm sorry."

She reaches out for his hand. Even though he's bigger all the time, his hand still feels tiny in hers. She squeezes tight and lets out a strangled little laugh.

"What was I thinking? Bananas don't have an underneath!"

•

He lies on his back in his too-small bed, his feet dangling off the end. He can feel lines being impressed on his skin, red dents that edge up his calves the taller he grows. His toes feel like they might not feel. Like they're turning pink, then red, then blue, like they're being readied for amputation. He shakes his legs out a bit, then jumps up on his bed and stands on his tiptoes to peer out the thin window.

Grey sky, smoky clouds sinking earthward. A yellowy smudge shows where the moon should be. He heads to the garage.

Here, sandwiched between his father's workbench and the crates holding out-of-season goods, behind the pile of boxes containing all the books his mother no longer reads, is a child-sized chest of drawers. Made long ago by his father, painted by his mother. There is no space in the mud room for it. From the top drawer he removes a ratty brown cardigan with leatherette elbow patches. It had been his grandfather's, who'd worn it every day while dying in the house before this one.

He wraps himself up in the thing and goes out through the side door of the garage.

The air is damp and alive, laced with the burnt smell of the neighbour's bonfire, extinguished now. As he walks past the neighbour's place, he glances at what's left of the bonfire. A grey shivering lump, settling itself down for the night, a dwarf's orange core inside it flaring softly as it dies. Down the street, the makeshift fence surrounding the hole teeters, spiderwebby in the dark. He heads toward it.

He leans carefully over the wobbly fence, pokes his head as far away from his body as he can. The hole is leaking from places where pipes have been moved and removed, and from other places, places deep inside it. In the almost no light it seems silver. The wet. There is a little space to his right where the wire joins up with itself, a little space for him to slip through. Which he does.

He climbs down ungracefully, mostly sliding, hanging onto roots exposed like nerves under a dentist's scraper. He looks down at his jeans, at the mud covering his knees and thighs. He brushes at the caked mud, uselessly. He'll need to figure out how to get mud stains out, next time he does the wash. At least he wasn't wearing his cords.

Here in the hole the weak smudge of moon has no chance of reflecting. All around him the dirt seeps silent, its hidden veins opened. Creepy crawlies from deep within skitter softly from spade-split homes.

He puts his hand on the side of the hole. Under his skin crawls a slow cool drip of water. A multi-legged bug skitters by, its legs somehow not tripping. He trips all the time and he only has two legs. The air in the hole smells of the garden, smells of dead things rotting someday to come back, smells of something he can't quite place. Something good.

Before him is the pipe sticking out from the wet dirt walls, a hole cloaked in concrete. A pipe big enough for a boy to crawl into, a pipe that's split its skin, its rusty skeleton spewing unwound like the propelling system of some long-lost underwater beastie. He stares at the beast. He stares at its dark mouth. The mouth stays open. And he crawls in.

•

This night there is a moon, a proud aspirin tiny in the clear sky. The work on the hole has been abandoned for the winter, the fence sags inward, curling into the centre as though returning to its birthplace. Blood-coloured heaps of sodden leaves push against the fence in places, small piles with their edges shining. A thin path of tromped wet leaves leads to the mouth of his pipe. Everywhere around him is the smell of things fallen, the smell of things rotten, the smell of the magic of dirt being made. He bounces in place for a while, squishing. Then into the pipe he goes.

Here he has stashed: a box of soda crackers, four slices of processed cheese, an old pickle jar full of fake orange juice, and all of his Christmas candy. This last he bought for himself with the two dollar bills his gran sent a week early, penny candies harvested from the glass jars at the corner store, each one frowned over and inspected before finding a home inside his brown paper bag. Each square caramel has a perfect wrapper, each golden-wrapped chocolate coin undented foil.

He wraps himself in his mother's old yellow blanket, the one with the iron-shaped hole. The edges of the hole are toast-brown, and sharp enough to cut him if he's not careful. He arranges the hole over his right knee, where the thickness of his jeans will protect him.

He removes his brown leather shell from his back, opens it wide. From it he takes: a red plaid pencil case with a wide metal zip, a stack of yellow-edged paperbacks, a hardcover book embossed with the Earth's globe, a notebook printed with the map of Canada, an unvarnished wooden ruler, a jar of paste, a stack of index cards cut in half, and a small, red flashlight.

Under all of this lies a ball of cotton batting, wound tight around itself. He fits the flashlight into a rig he's made from a wire coat hanger, and turns it on. In the tiny beam of the flashlight he unwinds the cotton, slowly, carefully. At its centre, a tiny pile of tiny teeth. Molars with their spiky roots, incisors, canines, and one flat front tooth. Almost all of his baby teeth. A few have gone missing, gone wherever it is the Tooth Fairy took them, before she stopped visiting. These ones he kept, tight in the toe of a sock, adding to the pile one by one as they left his mouth, safe under his pillow, until he was sure no fairy was ever going to come for them.

Now, for each tooth, he writes a story. One of his books told him of the collection of Peter the Great, who fancied himself a dentist, of sorts. He would stop people in the street and pull their teeth for his collection. Just like that. Lacking Peter's great height, not to mention his crown, he has only his own teeth to work with.

He starts with the front tooth. On the lower half of one of the cards he writes in pencil, *Found at Lost Lagoon, while feeding the swans. A great honking from one of the birds, and a fit full of feathers. Afterwards, at the collector's feet, this tooth was deposited straight from the belly of one of the Royal beasts. Its origin is otherwise unknown.*

He rereads this a few times, then finally traces over it in peacock blue. After waiting for the ink to dry, he carefully erases the marks underneath. Finally, he swipes the back of the tooth with the pasty brush, and holds the tooth in its place on the top half of the card. He blows on it, though he is pretty sure this won't make the paste dry any faster. Putting the finished card aside, he contemplates the next tooth, an incisor. He will work his way around his own mouth, from front to back. He stares at the tooth. He turns it in the spot of light. Nothing.

Putting the tooth aside, he carefully unwraps a caramel. He melts it in his mouth until he can't stand it anymore, and chews it ferociously. Afterwards, all that is left is the taste on his tongue, and a few sweet particles, wedged deep into his brand new teeth.

1962-3

This night clouds steam up from Georgia Strait, rollers unwinding slow as spirits. Wasted grey, they stretch thin fingers up the mountain-side, sliding inside houses and clothes and pores and nostrils, stroking windows and doorways, waiting to enter. He soundlessly opens the side door of the garage, steps out, then closes behind him the murmur of the coast-to-coast broadcast, the tink of ice cubes drowning in scotch, and his mother's soft footsteps, walking quiet over knives. He pads down the drive, past the charred remains of the neighbour's long-lost bonfire, now a jaw of dampened ash sinking into dirt. Past a collection of cars, slick beasts slumbering ass to nose in the neighbour's drive. A chanting rises from the neighbour's still-lit windows, a fluttering of shadows against the glass, moths in a kill jar. Captive voices chant a countdown. Behind him voices cheer as he slides into his hole. A new year.

Safe in his hole, tight in his pipe, he turns on his flashlight. The pale beam lights a feeble trail through the damp, shining a small spot on the rounded wall of the pipe, on his knees, on his breath which he can see. Through the light shine particles, fairy-small, floating like spores through the air. He unwraps his tooth collection, and gets to work. He's made his way, finally, to a molar.

He holds it in his palm. Contemplates its curves and legs. Turns it carefully over. No denying it, now that he stares. His molar is nothing else but a tiny female form, a squat Venus grown headless from his mouth. He picks up a card, places it on his lap. Stares at it, pencil in hand. Stares at it some more. Sighs. Holds onto the pencil even tighter.

He writes *Found*. Just the one word, then his hand is interrupted by a sound. A door slams, loudly, in the direction of his house. He grips his pencil tighter, holding it over the space where his next word is to go. High heels clatter on asphalt, followed by a jangle of keys. The jingling continues for a second, swallowed by the sound of other, flatter footsteps, too many for him to count. High heels click quickly away over his head, clacking away with the small sound of brittle wings. The flat footsteps break up, multiply and separate, sliding around him in the patter of chase. His heart freezes as the flat footsteps pass.

From his neighbour's house comes the sound of singing.

"Should auld acquaintance be forgot..."

He crouches around his jellied heart, his body curling into a protective circle without him even asking. He listens past the song. Nothing. He listens for a long long while, until the neighbours are done their song and on to another. A single pair of flat footsteps walks close to his hole, circling. He puts the pencil down, slowly, onto his lap. He reaches his right hand up and, quiet as he can, turns off the flashlight. The little light wavers like a fairy wobbling out of life. He holds his breath until he is sure the small click of the switch is gone, a hand of fog held over the mouth of the sound.

The flat feet pause.

He holds his breath. He holds it tight.

Then the feet step away, back toward the sound of singing, back into the lighted windows. He huddles in the dark, curled tight around his baby tooth. From somewhere far away comes a sound, somewhere past the singing. A sound that makes his belly tighten and his skin crawl. In the dark, in his hole, he is sure he's made it up. He curls up tighter and closes his eyes, goes back to the dark in there, though it's just as big as the dark out there. He listens to the singing, listens past it for the sound that doesn't come again.

•

He wakes damp and cramped, his body curved inside his pipe. The fingers of fog have receded, pulled back to their home in the sea. From here razor light slices blue across what little he can see of the world. He crawls from his pipe, eyes blinking against the light.

Around him a strange draped landscape glitters under a coat of rare snow. He climbs out of his hole into a display of Winter, an exhibit in a natural history museum. He is the Last Hunter from the Last Great Ice Age, haunting shattered floes for one last taste of life. It has been days since he's seen anything else alive. He looks around for the Woolly Mammoth. There's always a Woolly Mammoth in displays of the Frozen North. There's got to be at least one left. The Ice Age can't just end like this. The Last Hunter, dying of hunger, frozen for the ages in a mustard velour pullover and his granddad's manky old sweater.

Halfway to his house he sees something. A small golden globe pokes out from the perfect snow. He gets close to it, bends down, touches it with one finger, softly. He brushes away the snow and gingerly uproots a small beaded purse, the size of an apple, something a lady he could never hope to meet might take to a ball.

He carries it as though it were small and alive, a kitten maybe, or a blind baby bird with a broken wing. Half-awake, he walks toward his house. He stops. Blinks. Looks down at the small, gold purse, one hundred percent sure there is no lady who's just been to a ball where he lives. He looks around. There are no footprints to follow, there is nothing.

The sun is just starting to rise, turning everything glittering and blue. Everything is made of ice, except the tiny purse, which seems almost warm. He walks and walks, going up alleys, back behind houses where strangers live. On all sides are the dark bodies of trees, huge packs of them wearing capes of new snow. A bird takes off from a nearby branch, snow falling, the movement leaving a ripple effect behind it. Trees shake softly all around, the patter of snow light as laughter. He keeps walking. Up one alley a huge black Studebaker pokes its nose out across the ditch, almost blocking the way. He edges around it, and there she is. The lady who's just been to a ball. Flat on the ground, her face beaten pulpy, blood shining wet on her lips, blood blooming in frozen flowers on the white white ground, all around her.

Up this close he can see her lashes are frozen. Sprinkled white as though with icing sugar. Her skin is as blue-white as frozen milk, except

17

where she is bleeding. Snow has built little forts in the folds of her clothes. He puts a finger to her cheek, barely touching. Her cheek is cold. He stands and looks around for any lights on in any of the houses. No lights. No sounds. Only the sound of his own breath, and the sound inside his head, the sound of his heart pumping blood to his head too fast.

He remembers in a movie once the main guy thought someone was dead and held a mirror up to the dead guy's face. He's not sure why the guy did it but he wishes he had a mirror now. He doesn't. He wonders if he put his head to the lady's chest if he could hear her heart beating. If he could hear her heart over the sound of his own heart. If her heart is beating still.

Slit like an envelope the flap of her mouth flops above her teeth, bone white shining in the new day, the new year. He walks around to the other side of her head. Perfect. On this side she sleeps.

He puts his hands to his face, so that his two palms encase his nose and mouth, and breathes hot and noisy. He closes his eyes and listens. He breathes loud, regular huffs, making his hands wet and warm, pushes his fingers into his eyes until they hurt, until black fireworks pop and fizz. It helps a little but his heart won't slow down and when he opens his eyes he still feels dizzy, as though he's been unspun.

He kneels beside the lady. Puts his head close to her mouth, his ear up close to her lips, in the middle of her face, where the wrecked side meets the sleeping side. He closes his eyes and listens, listens for something other than him. Snow falling all around them. Gravel crunching far away, down the alley, laid over with the squeak of new snow. A crow screeching somewhere above him, its cackling call unanswered. He listens. Nothing. Nothing from her.

He turns his face and opens his eyes but this close her face is just big splotches of colour, a fingerpainting in red and white and purple and blue.

He leans closer, closing his eyes. Listening, closer. Listening. Closer. Listening. Close until he feels his lips press up against something sticky and warm and wet. He pulls back as a bubble of blood puffs from her mouth, a thick sticky sigh escaping, and he finds his feet without him knowing, pushing him from below further and further away.

From somewhere far far away he can hear a man's voice call him, an angry scratch in it, from somewhere behind him calling him kid, telling him to stop, which he doesn't, until he is safely back in the mud room. It is only once he's shut the door that he realizes he still holds the tiny golden purse, the apple that the lady had dropped.

DAHLIA

1960

"If this party is for Great Aunt Patience, why'd we leave her in that hole in the ground?" Dahlia asks her mother. "And won't she be lonely, down there in the dark?"

Dahlia's mother raises her eyes to the ceiling and makes a little puffing noise out of her tightly pursed lips. "Dahlia, please. Stop asking me all your silly questions."

"But, Mama —"

"Dahlia, I won't tell you again," her mother says sharply, taking her by the hand and leading her to the kitchen door. "Just go do what I asked, please."

Dahlia pads in stocking feet out the kitchen door and down the long hallway to the glass door that hides the room they don't use. On the other side of the door hangs a lace curtain, made long ago by her Great Aunt Patience. It never goes yellow because Dahlia's mother takes it down once a year and whitens it in a slow warm bath that smells of cat pee. Dahlia doesn't know how cat pee can keep things white, but her mother never explains it when she asks.

Dahlia turns the porcelain doorknob with both hands. The door opens easily. Dahlia is faintly surprised that she hadn't even needed a key. Inside the room they don't use, there is a light switch by the door, the same as in every other room. Only this one doesn't work. There are two buttons, one above the other, and when you push one in, the other one pops out. That's when the light is supposed to happen. But not here.

Through the heavy curtains on the wide window, a bit of light comes in from the street, and from the almost full moon. An unfamiliar clutter of furniture faces Dahlia, in this room they only use at Christmas and at Easter, and for the occasional ladies' tea, which Dahlia is not allowed to join anyway. She stands still, pushing her glasses up on her nose, and lets her eyes get used to the low light. Once she can see a bit better, Dahlia scuffles slowly toward a great chest of drawers, trying not to trip on anything. There are carpets laid over carpets in here, with all their edges crossing, one over the other. There's a small sofa with a sea serpent back, two armchairs and an ottoman, and dainty end tables everywhere, their plate-sized surfaces balancing on long skinny legs. By going slowly and keeping her eyes on the floor, she makes it all the way across the room, only tripping once.

The chest is taller than Dahlia, and wider than her arms when she spreads them. Above it hangs a painting of a stern-looking man, who, in the almost-dark, is reduced to a floating head and a pair of hands. Dahlia pauses below this, her own head tilted all the way back. She thinks this man is somehow related to her but she can't remember how.

Dahlia's mother had instructed her to get twelve cream linen napkins out of the middle drawer. At least she thinks her mother said the middle drawer. It was the first thing Dahlia's mother had said to her since Great Aunt Patience's funeral, and Dahlia was so surprised at being found under the table she'd missed half of what her mother had said. Dahlia had been busy making a potion out of all the liquids on the table, and her mother's appearance had ruined the whole thing. She does remember that her mother said the napkins had been edged with lace by Great Aunt Patience for just this occasion. And that they had never been used. Dahlia's not sure if they'll ever be used again. She guesses they will be, but only if Great Aunt Patience likes her party and wants to die again.

The drawer pulls are brass and have knobby shapes in the middle, almost like shells. Dahlia puts one hand on each pull of the middle drawer and tugs. She pulls so hard her elbows hurt, but the drawer doesn't budge. She does it again. Nothing. She moves so that she can put both hands on one handle, and gives it a sharp yank. It moves! She scuffles down to the other end, and pulls on that one. By pulling first one end, and then the other, she manages to coerce the drawer into edging out of its home in a zig-zag fashion. Dahlia stands on her tiptoes to peer into the drawer.

It's full of parcels wrapped in brown paper. She closes the middle drawer, and tries the bottom one.

The bottom drawer slides out easily, so quickly that Dahlia almost falls over. Inside the drawer is a lump covered in what could be a large napkin, though it's white, not cream, and there are no lace edges that she can see. She thinks maybe her mother just got it wrong, being so busy with the party and everything. Dahlia reaches into the drawer and carefully pulls at the big napkin. It comes away easily in her hand. Underneath it is a tiny person, just a bit smaller than Dahlia is right now.

Dahlia stares down at a small head covered with heavy, auburn hair. Two blue eyes stare up at her. Two grapefruit pink lips sneer around tiny teeth. Two hands, cracked and broken at the ends, reach up, toward her. Dahlia throws the big napkin back over the girl, pushes the drawer shut to keep the girl in there, turns, and tries to run but trips on a pile of carpets. She gets quickly to her feet, and runs from the room, slamming the door. The lace curtain slowly flaps itself to stillness on the other side of the door to the room they don't use.

•

Dahlia's mother enters her bedroom without knocking, the cream lace napkins held tight in one hand.

"Dahlia," her mother says, a serrated edge in her voice. "I asked you to do one thing. One simple thing. And you didn't do it."

Dahlia is curled under her blanket but not under her sheet so it doesn't count as going to bed early.

"I'm sorry, Mama," Dahlia says quietly, staring up at the lace on the napkins. "I forgot."

"You forgot?" Her mother makes that puffing sound again. "I asked you twenty minutes ago! And you forgot already?"

Dahlia nods, miserably rubbing her runny nose on her pristine violet pillowcase. Dahlia's mother bends down and puts a hand on Dahlia's head, pushing sweaty hairs away from her eyes.

"You're in bed."

Dahlia nods.

"Maybe it's all been a bit much for you today," her mother says, her voice a bit softer.

Dahlia nods again, sniffling.

"Well," her mother says, gently removing Dahlia's glasses, placing them, folded, on the night table. "Why don't you stay in bed for a while. Maybe you'll feel well enough to come down for dinner. I'll come up in a little while, and see how you're doing."

"Okay," Dahlia whispers, curling a little tighter around herself under her blanket. As her mother leaves the room Dahlia tries not to look at the woman who keeps her sister secret in a drawer.

•

It's dark outside by the time her father comes in. He tucks her in, too tight. He reads her part of a story about a velveteen rabbit, then closes the book halfway through, saying they should have something to look forward to tomorrow. He kisses her on the cheek and his breath smells like gasoline. Dahlia thinks maybe people who drink gasoline do funny things to their children. Like leaving them alone, trapped inside a drawer. Her father pats her on the knee, and leaves, turning out the light when he goes.

Dahlia stares at the ceiling. Every once in a while a car drives by, its headlights making waves above her. She tries not to think of the girl who lives in the drawer downstairs, the girl with two glass eyes. She tries not to wonder what happened to the girl's fingers to make them break in that way, crinkled all over in patterns, like old china. Maybe the girl who lives in the drawer tried to claw her way out.

Dahlia blinks but has to open her eyes right away. Every time she closes her eyes she sees those little broken fingers coming straight at her from out of the drawer. Dahlia keeps her eyes open.

Maybe, Dahlia thinks, the girl who lives in the drawer is her twin. A twin as dark as she is white. Maybe she got all the colour. Dark red for her hair, and pink for her lips, and blue for her eyes. Maybe Dahlia is the ghost. Maybe the girl in the drawer should be afraid of her, and not the other way around.

•

After a couple of days, Dahlia starts to really worry about the girl in the drawer. She hasn't heard any noise from the room they don't use. No small peepings of a tiny girl squealing to be let out of the drawer. No scrapings of thin nails. No kicking of kitten feet. Dahlia waits.

From her room, she can hear her mother and father say good night to each other. She can hear the clicking of the switches in their room. Her older sister is out for the night, over at some friend's house for a sleepover.

Their house is old and creaks softly as it falls asleep. It shifts around her, sighing. When she is sure her mother and father and the house are all asleep, Dahlia leaves her bed.

She wraps herself in her violet housecoat, which is a size too big but good enough to last until her next birthday if she doesn't grow too fast. She shoves her feet into her sheepskin-lined slippers from last Christmas, and carefully turns off her bedroom light. Her glasses are still on, as she hadn't bothered to take them off.

In this almost dark she descends the stairs as slow as Great Aunt Patience, shuffling and hanging onto the wall. The door to the room they don't use opens as easily as it had the other day. Dahlia shuffles even slower over the piling of carpets, shuffles toward the dresser where the girl lives in the drawer. Takes a deep breath, and slides it open.

The girl has escaped. Her home is empty.

•

Dahlia's sister had instructed everyone in the house to let her sleep. She was in the habit of wearing black turtlenecks and sitting for hours in her bedroom's window seat, reading thin books and sighing. Dahlia's sister had declared the whole thing to be a cheapening of a beautiful story, a perversion of the very idea of celebrating the Lord's birth. Dahlia's mother had squeezed her lips together so hard they'd disappeared and sent Dahlia's sister to bed without any dessert. Dahlia's sister had put her nose in the air and declared dessert to be "boorg-wah," before gliding up to her room. The sound of drummy jazz had wafted down from her room while Dahlia and her mother had decided to split the extra éclair.

So again Dahlia creeps from her bed quiet as she can. Slips on her slippers and slides on her housecoat. Shuffles out and down the hall. When she reaches the top of the stairs she can see a faint glowing, a light that seems to fly in small spots, a fire of fairies. Dahlia shuffles faster, shoves her glasses up on her nose and creeps down the stairs.

A portrait of Great Aunt Patience has been installed on the wall alongside the stairs, a smoky old photo of young Patience, seated inhumanly straight with her hands folded prim in her lap. Gloom creeps toward her from the edges of the photo, an oozing, silvery smudge. In the low light with the fire of fairies all about, Dahlia thinks she sees something, a pinkness in Patience's cheeks. Dahlia blinks, and stares at the picture. And it's just young Patience, sitting stiffly, as though waiting.

The light of the fairies floats ever slower, slow as fat snow. Dahlia blinks and holds her eyes closed. Almost too much to see, almost too much to remember. She tries to press it into her brain, tries to hold it there where she will always be able to see it. She opens her eyes, and it is magically all there, all still there for her to see. The front room all dark as a warm coat, the dark snug and heavy around the million lights circling the silent tree.

She takes the last few steps to the bottom of the stairs. And there, beneath the tree, her broken fingers held out before her, a fat blue bow around her head, is the girl who had lived in the drawer.

The girl who had lived in the drawer stares at Dahlia. Dahlia stares right back. The girl who lived in the drawer is now supposed to live in Dahlia's room.

"She used to belong to your Great Aunt Patience," Dahlia's mother explains, holding the girl from the drawer on her lap. "She's very precious. Your Great Aunt Patience wanted you to have her. I thought it would be a nice surprise for you."

Dahlia rubs the last of her tears into her cheeks. Sniffles.

"Don't be such a baby," Dahlia's sister gasps, curled in a corner of the couch in a black turtleneck and black, tight pants. "It's a *doll*, Dahlia. It can't hurt you."

Dahlia blinks, doesn't say a word.

"Now," Dahlia's mother says, holding the girl from the drawer out to her, "I want you to make friends with her. Your Great Aunt wanted you to have her. It was one of the last things she ever said to me."

The girl from the drawer starts the staring contest right there. Her blue blue eyes with their sharp little lashes. Her teeth in a perfect line, bared for a bite. Her hands outstretched with their broken skin.

Dahlia stays where she is, on the ottoman, her head on her knees. Stares right back through her violet eyes, through her Coke-bottle glasses. Dahlia's mother puts the girl from the drawer on the floor, so that she leans against the couch.

"See, Dahlia," her mother pulls up the girl's arms into an even more threatening pose. "She wants to hug you."

"I need some coffee," Dahlia's sister says, unwinding herself in a black loop. "I don't suppose we have any?"

"Tea will do for you, Gertrude," Dahlia's mother says coldly, rising from her chair and heading to the kitchen. "Where did you ever drink coffee, anyway?"

"Mother, you are such a square," Dahlia's sister huffs, leaving the room and following their mother to the kitchen. "And don't call me Gertrude. I'm not an old lady, or haven't you noticed? It's Tru."

"Gertrude is a fine name," Dahlia's mother says sharply. "And I'll not have you speaking to me in that tone."

The sounds of their two voices crackle sharply down the hall, fading away to clickings small as forks against knives. Dahlia blinks at the girl from the drawer, who starts another round of the staring contest.

Dahlia stares. The girl from the drawer stares. Sounds from the kitchen clatter and tink. Dahlia stares. Dahlia stares. And Dahlia stares some more.

After she finally blinks, she's sure the girl from the drawer smiles just a little bit wider. But her hands are lowered, just a touch.

BILLY

1964

Billy sits on the toilet and pisses out his unfinished dream. After that's done, he feels more awake. He flushes, then washes his hands the way he once saw a doctor do it in a movie, turning the hot on full, tempering it with a little cold, rubbing huge lathering handfuls of suds over his palms, the backs of his hands, between each finger and up the length, under the fingernails, driving his nails up painfully into the beds. Rinses long enough to sing the entirety of "Maybellene" under his breath. He dries his hands on his own white hand towel, pushing back his cuticles under the terry. Inspects his hands, gives a little nod of satisfaction, turns off the light, and leaves the bathroom.

His uncle's voice blasts from somewhere below.

"Beagle!" A pause. Then, "Beagle! I can't find my damned toque! The Habs one! You seen it?" As regular as prayer, this morning utterance. Billy mouths along with his aunt's reply.

"If it's not on your head then it's finally rotted off, and I've never been a happier woman, Marly."

As sure as sugar, Marly wanders by the foot of the stairs just as Billy reaches the landing, the Habs toque perched on his head, as always, a point grown in the top of it from his habit of tugging at it when he's thinking or talking, and sometimes even both. Marly puts a hand up, cautiously, finds the toque there, gives it a tug, and wanders off, smiling. Billy shakes his head and continues down the stairs, and on toward the kitchen. In the hallway he passes their old low credenza, cluttered with pictures. There's his uncle, grinning over the broiled body of a pig, the Habs toque perched on his head despite the glaring sun. There's his aunt, standing stern and straight, a tight smile on her lips, holding the hand of Billy's former, smaller self. And there's little Billy, holding his aunt's hand, the two of their heads in shadow, their feet in bright sun. Marly never quite got the hang of using a camera. Billy peers at his little self, at his crooked haircut and too-big teeth, at his odd eyes. One jade green, and the other pale blue, in the photo glowing. He wonders a bit at his wide grin shining in the shade. That photo was taken the day he'd arrived here, to live with his aunt and uncle many years ago. He didn't know then that he'd never see his real folks again.

Aunt Beatrix has got a full spread going on the wide kitchen table: bacon, sausage, ham, eggs, pancakes, hash browns, coffee, fresh milk, oranges cut in wedges, strawberries, and purple juice which sort of tastes like grape but not really, more like if you told someone about grape juice and they never drank it but cooked some up in a lab some-where, measuring the flavour off a dial. Billy sits down, takes a pancake off the pile and places it carefully on his breakfast plate. It's white chipped china, from the unmatched box of kitchen stuff his mother left behind, a border of roses flaking off slowly. Billy drowns the lone pan-cake in maple syrup, the real stuff that comes in a can, punctured at the top in two places, inch long slits in the tin, bleeding. A bit of bile rises in his throat as the breakfast smells hit him. He tries not to retch.

"You're not just eating that, are you, honey? C'mon, have a little something," Aunt Beatrix hovers over him, bearing a plate piled high with meat, all shades of pink and brown, glistening.

"No, thanks, Aunt Beatrix, it's okay," Billy shakes his head, pouring syrup over his one pancake in a methodical criss-cross pattern.

"Oh, come on, honey. It's not enough. One pancake and you still a growing boy." She's got a fork in a slab of ham, almost lifting it off the plate. Billy crouches over his perfectly placed, perfectly decorated pancake.

"It's okay, Aunt Beatrix, I'm not really hungry. Looks good though," he smiles at her. She pauses, puts down the fork, winks at him.

"Just doing my motherly duty, darlin'. You and me both know your uncle Marly'll be eating it all. Like a plague of locusts, that one," she says, shaking her head as she puts the plate down on the table, in front of Marly's chair, and bustles off to hover between the coffee maker and the sink. Billy wonders, as he does every morning, what she lives on, since to his mind she only eats with them on Sundays and holidays, and even then she bustles so much it's hard to tell if she's actually eaten anything or just pulled some fancy magic trick and made the food just disappear.

Marly comes in, toque poking up above his grey weathery face, his smiley blue eyes peering out shiny from under crinkly lids.

"Beagle, it's a beauty again! Ahhhh, I love breakfast," he smiles at the table, at the food, piling meat and eggs on his plate. Billy rests his hands in his lap, and tries not to breathe too deeply.

"That all you're having, Billy?" Marly nods in the direction of Billy's pancake. Billy bobs his head in reply. Marly winks at Billy and says, "Good! More for me!" He chuckles at this, as he does every morning, while adding to the pile on his own plate. After theatrically placing one small slice of orange on top of his stack of meat and pancakes, Marly mimes dusting off his hands, and reaches for Billy's. Aunt Beatrix has joined the table with a cup of tea. They all hold hands and bow their heads for the Lord's Prayer, which even after all these years, Billy can never quite remember. He mumbles along until, "Amen," then begins to cut his pancake into equal-sized pieces, separating them from each other, just enough.

"You eat all of that, now, Billy. S'gonna be a loooong day." Marly tilts his head toward Billy's geometric pancake. Billy pokes at a piece, moving it out of line. Suddenly, none of it looks even faintly edible. Marly chews noisily, rolling bacon around pieces of pancake, making stacks of ham and egg on his toast, thoroughly ignoring the orange. Aunt Beatrix has disappeared again. Billy spears a piece of pancake. Puts it in his mouth. Chews.

Marly is his mother's brother. From a family of nine growing up in Griffintown in the middle of the Depression, and the parents from Ireland. Billy's heard more stories of famine and hunger than he has of wars, deaths, births, marriages, work, holidays and anything else all put together. He chews. Feels a little bile rise in his throat as he thinks of all the food all those people ate through all their days. Thinks of his grand-parents, the ones he never met, who moved here to the prairies after years of the city, thought farming could help feed all those hungry mouths, and now they're buried out back under the struggling plum. Thinks of their bodies dissolving into the earth, this earth he walks every day, their chiding and worries leaking up into Marly, up through the floor and into the toque. He snorts a little laugh out through his nose at that, like the hat is sort of possessed. He smiles and finally swallows.

•

There isn't any light outside yet. The air cuts tiny holes in the clothes Billy wears, enters in and sticks on his skin. Marly's up ahead, hum-ming happily to himself. Billy's clomping behind in a ratty pair of boots, about a size too big, their steel toes round and heavy, and he's looking at the fields humming flat grey into nothing, where the sky might be later but isn't now. Trees, fences, a sheep. No, wait, that can't be right. He shakes his head. But it is a sheep, moving steadily toward the far side of their land, where the fields fall off to a gully, a fence there to stop things getting in, to stop things getting out. Marly's seen it.

"Criminy. Now how'd she get out like that?" Marly directs Billy over to the barn with just a tilt of his head. Billy heads over to check the doors, while Marly goes to lead back the AWOL sheep. The doors are shut, but the latch isn't on. Billy pushes the right door in. A couple of sheep peer at him from the gloom in there, their weird little eyes blinking as he lets in the early light that's started seeping up from under the world. Once it starts it comes up fast. A little blue now, a blue tinge to things, like there's water above them and no air. No air. He listens hard. No gurgles, nobody drowning in the blue still morning. Still. He takes a soft step into the barn. Listens again. Nothing. His breathing, the sheep, the warmth of their bodies. And then there's a rustle. Smothered giggles from up in the hayloft. Billy goes back out the door.

Marly's got the sheep, and he's leading her back quietly, talking to her, telling her stories of other sheep who got lost, lost from their homes, telling her stories of wanderers. Billy goes back into the barn, climbs up the rough wooden ladder to the hayloft. Raises himself up, eyes first, peeking.

"Hey, sailor!" It's a girl in his hayloft, popping up suddenly from a pile of hay, a girl wearing nothing but a black half-slip and a black, pointed brassiere. She giggles as a hand rises from the hay, pulls her down. Billy can hear her saying, "Well, he's seen us now, Bunny!" before she pops back up again, like one of those toys on a spring. What are they called again? Jack something. Billy's lost his words. Billy is frozen, his eyes on her bra, the two cups glossy and black and pointed like weapons, like the missiles he's seen on TV, like the bombs his uncle said ended the war. There are spirals built into them, curling in from the outer breast, inexorably, painfully, beautifully, in to their final destination, their target.

"Oh, Bunny, I think I made a new friend!" She poses for Billy, in a jokey pin-up way, pouting her mouth at him and stumbling a little. Bunny yells at her to get the hell down, someone'll see her. There's a smell. A smell like the propane stove he and Marly use when they go out fishing, a smell like Christmas. Even Aunt Beatrix smells like that on Christmas.

The girl yells down into the hay, "I told you, Bunny, he's seen us already!" Her hands are on her hips, a little furrow between her eyes as she stamps her foot.

"Billy!" Marly calls while shoving open the doors downstairs. Light floods into the barn, light just turning golden, its sharp entrance suddenly making the world real. The girl looks right at Billy with this look on her face, her mouth a frozen O. Her round amber eyes weave in red rims. She wobbles a bit. Billy puts out a hand, makes a down motion. She looks at him again, cocking her head, starting to smile. He makes the motion again. Down. Get down.

"Billy! You find anything?" Marly calls up from below.

"No, sir, there's nothing up here. Whoever it was they must've gone already!" Billy yells. His hand pats at the air, his mouth says soundless, down. Get down. The girl's still standing, but slowly now she gets it, and falls back under the hay, silently, like a dream receding just after he wakes up. And she's gone.

•

There is no escape from Marly, no escape from his off-key show tunes while they herd the sheep out of the barn and into the pen beside it. No escape from the walk to the steel-walled side building, no escape from the room with the bloodstained floor, no escape from the scrubbed tables. No escape from Marly's jokes, the same jokes he tells every day, no escape from the long white apron, from the hum of the saw. No escape until Marly wipes his hand across his forehead, and smiles at Billy, and unties his own apron.

The two of them walk back to the house, Billy's eyes on the outside entrance to the hayloft the whole time. He can't see anything up there. He strains to hear anything, a peep, a giggle, a girl calling him sailor. Nothing.

At lunch Billy eats half an apple and retches while chewing. Aunt Beatrix puts a hand to his head and makes a light cluck under her breath, the same sound she makes when a sheep is sick or birthing. She sends him to bed with a glass of Alka Seltzer and a cheese sandwich, telling him he's pale as a ghost. She says she's going to town to do some shopping and she'll check on him when she gets back. Billy nods and goes upstairs. He climbs under the covers, fully dressed, with his boots still on.

He lies motionless in bed, his legs beneath the covers feeling so light he's sure they've disappeared. He sits up to check if he's still making any kind of shape under the blankets. He is. He lies back down. Waits.

After forever he hears the jangle of the keys to the station wagon, hears Aunt Beatrix shut the door to the house, hears the wagon cough and cough and cough again, the same something caught in its throat, the same cough every time Aunt Beatrix tries to start it. The wagon horks and snorts and finally it catches. Gravel crunches under the tires as his aunt drives to town to do the shopping.

Billy throws back the covers and hops out of bed. He slips downstairs and lets himself out of the house, closing the door quietly behind him. He doesn't lock the door. He's not even sure there's a key. Nobody locks their doors around here. He looks carefully both ways, to make sure Marly isn't about somewhere, then dashes to the barn.

The sheep in their pen watch him go, their heads turning in slow unison as he passes. It's bright out, blue sky cold above his breath. He checks again for Marly, then lifts the latch on the big barn door.

He stands still inside, sure he's gone paler since he left his bed, sure he can slip through walls, sure the only way the girl could see him coming is by his breath. He starts climbing the ladder, faintly surprised he can, half hoping he'll slide away between the rails, half hoping he'll go back to wherever it is ghosts come from. He doesn't. He climbs. Still seeing the girl up there in the hayloft, her hair so simple, so shiny and dark and brown, her ponytail up high, swinging like what it was named for, still seeing the light crawl up beyond the window just enough to give her a faint outline, a glow like a ghost, just fading out in the starting day. He wonders is he fading away too, to the same place, he wonders will he meet her there? Sees her fall down slow, her pale skin glowing, backward into the hay. Her easy smile falling back at him, her smile laughing up, her black brassiere shiny, monster bug eyes, pointing up to the sky as she falls back laughing. The sky through the hayloft's pass-through just turning golden behind her, dust motes floating, showing the only movement as she's gone.

And she's gone. The hayloft is empty, not even the smell remains. Billy sits in the hole the girl and Bunny have left in the hay. Stares out the pass-through for a while. And there, just lying there for all the world to see, something waits, just for him, just for him to find. A pair of lady's unmentionables, silk almost silver, white lace around the leg holes. He picks them up as though they were a new-born butterfly. They unfold in his hand and he tries not to breathe. Somewhere someone starts singing, somewhere far away, in another land.

34

The singing comes closer. *"If you're blue and you don't know where to go to...."* Billy stares at the delicate silk thing unfurled in his hand. He bites his lip. Folds the thing up neatly, and places it carefully in the right front pocket of his red mac jacket, the pocket that still has its button. Scoots down the ladder and out the door.

The singing is Marly, over in the sheep pen. He's singing to the ladies, checking their feed, dancing with them in his clumpy old gumboots. Billy closes the barn door as quietly as he can, hoping the latch will catch, and scoots away close to the ground. Behind a tree he pauses, checks behind him. Marly is leaning down to one of the sheep, crooning at her. *"Like Gary Cooper, super-duper...."*

Billy runs behind the house, peers in a window. Aunt Beatrix sails by, her hands darting in and out of her pockets. She must've forgotten something and come back for it, to be home so soon. There's no way past her, not with lady's underthings in his pocket. Billy crawls under the window as she passes above him, his hands on the cool dirt. He waits. He looks around. And there, in front of him, is a door in the ground.

Warped wood, unlatched, set into a rough hole in the ground beside the kitchen's back door. Skinny grass pushes from between the boards around the hole's mouth. Undisturbed moss lines the dark lip between the door and its frame. Billy's never been told he can go down there, but then he's never been told he can't. He thinks maybe there'd be a good place to hide the silk in his pocket down there, that maybe if he doesn't go down there no one else does either. Billy bites his lip again, lets out a big breath. Marly calls his name again. Crouching, Billy half-walks over to the door. He lifts it with a bit of difficulty, finds he needs to leave it open to the sky just so he can get in, not being big enough to balance it. He fairly runs down the crooked wooden steps.

There is a dangling electric light in the centre of the room which Billy turns on by the pull-cord hanging from the side. He runs back up the slanting steps and closes the storm door, shutting himself inside.

He walks slowly back down the steps, his hand on the cool dirt wall, blinking as his eyes adjust to the almost dark. The single lightbulb shivers in a too-small coat of pale beams, the dim corners of the room seeming somehow darker around it. Billy looks about him as he steps onto the dirt floor. The space is bigger than Billy's bedroom, every wall covered with shelves fading up into the dark, to a place that seems far above his head. Every shelf is crammed with jars. Two of the walls are stacked to a regular height, the jars neatly placed and labelled. The other two walls are a mess, large jars next to small jars, crates stacked any which way in between.

Billy steps up to one of the tidy walls, leans in close. He can just make out his Aunt Beatrix's schoolgirl script, the blue, perfect letters spelling the same word over and over on jar after jar. This shelf is *Beets*, the one above it *Pickles*, the one above that *Strawberry Jam*. Beyond that Billy can't make out the labels. He walks to the next tidy shelf. *Rhubarb*, *Pickled Onions*, *Blackcurrent Jelly*. He turns to the next set of shelves, one of the untidy ones.

The shelf at his eye level is cluttered with jars of all sizes, some small as his fist, some large enough to fit over his head, all of them full of eggs. Snake eggs, lizard eggs, the blue eggs from robins and the dirt brown of chickens, tiny speckled quail eggs and small red beads that look like gems. All of these jars are simply labelled, *Eggs*. Next to the eggs stands a hoof that has split into two, floating serenely, its severed stump clean and unbloodied. That one has no label at all.

Billy looks above him to where a cat-o-nine tails hangs, made of something dry looking, something that reminds him of a peeling sunburn. He doesn't touch it, doesn't investigate that shelf any further. He walks slowly to the next wall, passing unmarked boxes and more jars of eggs on his way.

Here a large jar catches his eye. He gets up close to it, tries to make out what is in there. A frog stretches its long legs down to the bottom of the jar, where some pretty oval stones, pink and grey and brown, are settled on the bottom. Two shriveled and raisiny things lie sort of squooshed on top of the stones, browny-pink. There are things that look like black cat hairs in there too, a clump of them, tied together with whiskery twine. He turns the jar carefully back the way it was, and takes a couple of slow steps to the next group.

Here are many smaller jars, each holding one or two snakes, most of them garter snakes, each one labelled simply with a month, or a day, or a year. A large jar holds a rattler, jaws open, fangs dangling. This one is labelled, succinctly, *Rattler*.

Something above him seems to glow, in two spots. Billy stands on his tiptoes and peers up. In a jar larger than the others and kind of flat, there floats a young cow's head, her eyes glowing even in the weak light from the shaky bulb. Billy reads the label but thinks he may have gotten it wrong. It doesn't make any sense. All it says is, *Free-martin*. Billy doesn't think that's even a word.

One of the crates is missing its lid. Billy looks behind his shoulder before sliding it off the shelf and taking a look inside.

Inside are jumbled bones in no order, tiny bird bones sifting together with the larger bones from sheep and cows and dogs. Skulls stare eyeless at him, some of them crushed in places, some of them with fangs curling from their mouths, some of them with horns. He pushes the crate back to its place on the shelf. Opens the one next to it.

Skins, piled neatly. Still with their little faces and little feet, a hundred moles lie flattened, one upon the other. He shuts the box, and reaches for another.

Hair of all colours, tied together in neat bundles. Chestnut, ginger, blonde, and grey. Ponytails tied up for keeps. Billy closes this crate with a slam, barely registering the words written right on the wood. *All Kinds of Fur*.

As he turns, his eye is caught by one of the big jars, a jar about the size of the pot Aunt Beatrix makes her jam in, on a shelf just a bit above his head. Inside it something fluffy floats. Billy steps closer. The first thing he can make out is a head. And next to it, another. New pink noses, soft pink ears. Four eyes closed as though sleeping, four perfect hooves hovering as though in mid-jump. Billy takes a step closer. It seems as though the fresh white of their wool has run together, as though they've been together in the jar so long they've settled into each other. Billy turns the jar slightly. The little sheep turn slowly in their liquid home, their two necks joined, he can see now, into one body. He frowns and checks again. Only one tail between them. The label, in Marly's block printing, reads *Tweedle-dum and Tweedle-dee*.

Billy turns and runs for the storm door, the panties forgotten in his pocket, the single lightbulb behind him still shivering in its cold, pale coat.

MARCH, 1972

HICKLIN

Beside his bed is a puddle of pale nylon the colour of false flesh, a puddle that might as well be flayed skin. The only thing he has left of her. A hole. As he has for the past three days, he rises from bed, steps carefully over the puddle of skin, dresses without looking at it, and leaves his room, not once looking back.

Just outside his room is a large space, probably intended as a dining room, with six doors leading off of it. One leads to his room, the one next to it leads to a small room full of worktables, paints, and unfinished projects. Straight ahead, as he leaves his bedroom, is the kitchen, and on his left is a closed door, behind which Beau may or may not be sleeping. Next to that is the door to the washroom. The living room is a small nook bleeding out of the dining room's space. The dining room itself would be empty but for makeshift shelves, filled with books. He walks toward the kitchen, and on his right is the door to the inner stairs, open, as always.

The kitchen is sunny but cold, light streaming in through the wide curtainless window. He glances at the door to the balcony, and sees that it, too, has been left open all night. He closes it, but leaves it unlocked, and opens the fridge. Takes out the coffee, and closes the now-empty fridge. He'll have to ask Nick if he can run up more of a tab. Who'd have thought having your landlord be your boss and your dep guy could get so complicated? He turns and puts the coffee down on the table, which slants with the floor, tilting everything on it sideways, as though in a boat. A cracked jam jar holds the scum of yesterday's tea, a small chipped plate a smile of crust. Stacked books teeter on a leaning pile of newspapers, letters, unpaid bills, notes, and sketches. Something new here. Lying long and thin on the table, a rectangular box, wrapped in brown paper and tied with twine. His Montreal address is hacked out in block letters in his father's unpracticed hand. On top of this is a fat, pink envelope.

He ignores both of these for now, and starts the coffee. While the coffee percolates, he opens the fat pink envelope. Inside is a small card printed with a rose, holding a folded ten dollar bill. A short note in his grandmother's tidy, flat, and unslanted handwriting. Unwrapped, a pair of white Y-fronts. He smiles, puts the ten bucks in his pocket, the card on top of the stove. The underpants he tosses into his bedroom. He'll wear them. On laundry day.

After pouring himself a small black coffee, he sits and reaches for the package from his father. He turns it in his hands. It looks like a small box for a small body, but is light, as though whoever had been in there had already fled.

He unties the twine, carefully winding it like a rope around his hand, an old habit of saving and re-using still seeded inside him. Picks off the brown tape, the old paper kind, and unfolds the brown paper wrapping. It's a shoe box, for a pair of child's shoes, yellowy and crushed at the corners. He lifts the lid. Inside, folded over a bundle of newspapers, is a short letter on long yellow foolscap. He reads it quickly, frowning. The letter is signed from both his mother and father, but only in his father's short, angular strokes. He reaches into the box, and pulls out the crumbling bundle.

Carefully, he peels away flaking newsprint, releasing a smell of dust and mold and something else. Something good. His fingers brush against something smooth, something with holes in it. He pulls it from its nest.

A sudden clatter on the stair, a slamming of the door.

"Happy birthday, beautiful," Beau sings, poking his pretty head into the kitchen. "I see you found your prezzies. What'd you get?"

Hicklin stares at the thing in his hands. It is small, about the size of an orange, with a sharp, curved beak and two outsized eyesockets.

"Underpants," he says, lifting the thing up, "and this."

Beau leans in to look at the thing, scrunches up his nose and shakes his head. "What is it?"

Hicklin stares some more at the little skull. "I don't know," he says, reaching into the wrappings. "My dad seems to think I found it. Apparently I called it a 'babybeast'. Used to keep it under my bed."

"Uh-huh," Beau says. "Must've had good dreams, then."

Hicklin unwraps a number of small bones, lays them on the table, alongside a detailed, hand-drawn diagram of the animal in question. The drawing is his, from long ago, the handwriting his own, loops stopping short where he'd written over a ruler. "I really don't remember any of this."

"Maybe your dad's having you on," Beau suggests, pouring himself a jar of coffee.

"No," Hicklin says, peering at the drawing. "No, he's not joking. My dad doesn't joke. Says jokes only get loggers in trouble, whatever that means."

"Well," Beau pulls up a wooden chair held together with wire coat-hangers which are wound around its legs like an exoskeleton, "let's take a look at this."

The diagram shows the position of all the bones, each one labelled neatly, with mostly made-up words. The skull, called *The Thinkbox*, is positioned in the centre of the page, surrounded by a contained explosion of little bones. The ribs, here called *Breeze-Bones*, have been placed around the head, in something like wings, the pelvic bone directly under the skull, with tiny bones arranged under it, in the form of feet. The pelvic bone has been labelled *The Heartbox*, and the feet, *Feet*.

"Paging Dr. Hicklin," Beau smiles. "Maybe your folks should've invested in some Lego."

"Ha ha," Hicklin says, reaching into the box again, "I was a *kid*, Beau."

"Oh, you're still a kid to me!" Beau says, pulling a cigarette pack from his pocket. After fishing around inside it for a second, he pulls out a perfectly rolled joint, and puts it on the table. "Happy birthday, little guy."

Hicklin smiles. "Thanks, Beau." He picks up the joint, which has *Happy Birthday Baby*, written on it in rosy felt-tip, tucks it behind his ear, and pulls a stack of index cards from the box. They won't stay as a pile on the table. "Okay, these I remember." Each piece of card has a tooth stuck to it, with a neatly written label underneath it.

"Teeth?" Beau asks, finishing up his coffee. "Where'd you get teeth?"

Hicklin points to his mouth. "My folks kind of forgot about the whole Tooth Fairy thing. I think maybe they did it once or twice, and then... I don't know. They just forgot. My dad was away a lot back then, working. And my mom...."

Beau picks one up. "So you wrote little stories about your teeth?"

"Yeah," Hicklin smiles. "I guess I really was a weird kid. I used to sneak out of the house at night and go write these things in a construction pit on my street. I wonder where my dad ever got these. I thought they'd been...."

A ghost passes in front of his face, quick, taking his smile with it when it disappears.

"What?" Beau asks. "You thought they'd been what?"

Hicklin shakes his head. "Nothing."

Beau gets up, puts his jar in the sink, then heads to the fridge and pokes around in it. Hicklin stares out the window.

Beyond the wide window, early spring sunshine comes down weak and cold and new, shining back up from snow piles slumped still on street corners as though waiting for the magic word. Below him small crowds of people walk, their skin pale in the new light, their eyes blinking, as though brushing away the dust of a hundred-year sleep. They seem to have nowhere to go. They walk slowly, looking around, as though they are new in this world. Or this world is new to them. Hicklin blinks. He sniffs the air. There is a new smell, a smell of sunshine. Silent, he rewraps the teeth and bones, replacing it all carefully in the box.

"So, honey, what're you doing this fine sunny day?" Beau asks from inside the fridge. "Hey, how come there's no food in here? Where's Flan?"

Hicklin takes his birthday joint from behind his ear and places it in a notch in an ashtray. He drinks the rest of his coffee. He sighs.

"We broke up, remember?"

Beau closes the fridge door, his hands empty. He shakes his head. "Oh, honey, no you didn't."

"Oh, honey, yes we did," Hicklin says, pushing away his empty jar. "Remember? She threw my shit out the window and called me a freak? She said she couldn't live like this anymore and if I didn't start making money she didn't see the point. Remember? She said she didn't love me anymore, Beau, she said I make her sick. Remember, Beau, *remember*?"

Beau nods. Blinks his big pretty mismatched eyes in slow motion. When he opens them he says, "Hicklin, you headcase. She wasn't breaking up with you. She was asking you to prove it to her. She's a Princess, honey, and she's telling you there's some tests she wants you to pass before her Daddy the King will grant you her hand in marriage. Don't you get it?"

"Do I look like a prince, Beau?"

Beau shrugs. "Maybe that just means you've got more to prove. Or," he continues, making his big eyes goofy wide, "maybe you're a toad!" Beau starts to laugh, his face turning red. Little hysterical shrieks come from deep in his throat. Hicklin shakes his head and gets up to retrieve his notebook from his bedroom.

Beau is still laughing as Hicklin re-enters the kitchen.

"You know what, Beau?" Hicklin sits down and opens his notebook. "Screw it. If she can't love me without all these tests, what do I care? I can't be some stupid prince for her, y'know? Screw it." He begins writing, his words jutting madly to the left, taking up way more than their fair share of space. After a couple of minutes of silence from the window sill, Hicklin looks up to see if Beau is still there. He is, staring stonily at Hicklin and lighting a joint.

"What?" Hicklin expels this loudly, but not quite yelling, and snaps his notebook shut.

Beau shrugs and slides down off the window sill. "I just think if you're gonna talk about Flannery, you might as well tell people the truth."

"What? What the hell are you talking about? We *broke up*! End of story."

Turning to face him from the hallway and leaning in on the door-frame, Beau shakes his head and gives a sad little smile. "No, honey, I don't think so. It sounds to me like *you* broke up with *her*. Here," he says, pointing to his temple. He continues, gesturing freely with the joint in his hand. "If the truth is you just can't be bothered, just say so. Don't just sit around here, pretending you got the blues. And don't lay all this baloney on *her*, Mr. Perfect! Don't be such a goob. It *really* doesn't suit you."

He hears Beau put on his boots and clomp away down the stairs. He keeps the half bottle of wine within arm's reach, smokes too. He lights his birthday joint. He puts his head down, and writes until he feels a chill coming in from the open window.

●

Much later he realizes it is no longer his birthday. He is now offi-cially eighteen. He hadn't bothered to turn on a light, and the window is still open. A little snowdrift has formed on the window sill, a tiny scrub, shining pale like a new thing just born, just born for him. He lights a cigarette, poking his finger around in the foil to find more but he can't find any. He downs the last of the wine and runs a hand through his hair.

He walks over to Beau's room and opens the door with a push of his hand. Turns on the light, and peeks his head in. Somehow, Beau's managed to cover every surface with clothes: the walls hang thick with dresses, the bed is covered with sweaters and socks, even the door to the closet is draped in silk and feathers and denim and wool. A small table by one window props up a large mirror, a spill of tubes and pots and puffballs before it. Hicklin thinks he can see some giant eyes peering at him from the spaces not filled with clothes, giant eyes from giant heads. Even the bedside tables are cluttered with things Hicklin barely recognizes: tubular pipe-like things, little baggies and small brown bottles. He shakes his head and steps back out of Beau's room, closing the door behind him.

He finds his shoes, plastic-soled two-dollar wingtips from the Sally Ann, puts one on successfully. The lace of the other snaps in his hand. He searches around in the dark for something to substitute, a twist-tie, an elastic, anything. His hand just barely misses the phone cord, sitting peacefully on the floor, unattached to the jack on the wall. He can't find anything, anything to use. He shrugs, and rises. Maybe he'll find something on the way to the bar. He descends the tilty stairs, locks the door, and heads up Duluth. After half a block he wishes he'd remembered to wear a hat.

•

And here comes Dolly, weebling toward him from across the smoky bar. She's got her war paint on tonight, slick, hair-thin lines painted around the base of her neck, on her elbows and wrists, all her joints articulated in browns and pinks over her powdered glue-white skin. She leans up against him and flutters her caterpillar eyelashes.

"Hello there Hicklin. Buy me a drink?" She talks slow and quiet, a tired, sad old song, words coming out whole with her lips barely moving.

Hicklin looks at her, and it's like he's never seen her before. He can't believe he's missed it, for so long. He must've been blind. Her hair spills red over her shoulders in perfect ringlets on either side of her cold white neck. She wears a shiny red headband, wide like Alice's. Her mouth is glossy and red, matching the headband, blinding. Hicklin wants to touch her mouth, wants to see what's under that paint, what's under that shiny shiny red. Something white, something pink, something else altogether, something maybe he's never seen before, something fresh that's never been touched by daylight. He looks up into her scary violet eyes, the whites too white, the colour inhuman, surrounded as always by their armed guard of fake lashes, extra extra long.

"Sure, Dolly. Whatever you want."

She leans her head on his shoulder, puts an arm around him all slow. "Thanks Hicklin. You're a good kid you know. A good kid." Her lips barely move, her words come out whole from her sad, shining mouth.

He's pretty sure he remembers that Dolly is younger than he is. She runs this thing called Les Sucettes. Suckers. "You got a show tonight, Dolly?"

She looks at him with gleaming, glassy eyes, putting her chin down so he's surrounded. Lashes everywhere.

"Yeah. You want to watch?"

Her drink arrives, two fingers of whiskey with a speared cherry, floating. He pays with the last of his birthday money.

"Can't," he shrugs, "no money."

She squeezes up close to him, her crinoline crunching between them. Her dress is shiny red too, strapless. She's added childish, poofy sleeves out of an almost matching fabric. They've fallen down, exposing her shoulders. Hicklin can see the thin lines she's drawn around her shoulders, so her arms can move. He wonders if they're all drawn in, around her hips and everywhere.

"Come with me. You won't have to pay for anything if you're with me. Come on. I like you." Dead cold lips not smiling as she tugs at him. "C'mon." He looks down at her hand, tugging at his sleeve. Her fingernails are creepy pink, buffed to a brand-new shine. Her pale white makeup has left tiny prints all over him, prints of her cheeks, her fingers, her neck. He looks at her. Doesn't look like any of the makeup has come off at all. She cocks her head at him, not smiling. She blinks her scary eyes. He gets up off the stool, and follows her to the back of the bar, where her tiny stage is set up.

•

A shell blue sky scrapes the tops of the trees just waking, green buds pushing from wood sleeves. They walk down a sidewalk cluttered with trash, lying in piles, offerings for forgotten gods. Around them buildings sleep, windows shut and shuttered, snoozing through the morning. A peep of birds from above. Dolly holds Hicklin's hand as he holds hers. A little too tight.

"I feel like dancing," Dolly says, slowing down. She turns her head slightly, in a series of small movements, so it almost looks like motion. "Dance with me Hicklin."

Hicklin shakes his head, the shaking starting small and getting stronger, all through his arms to her.

"C'mon Hicklin," Dolly says soft, turning her whole body toward him, in the same jittery way. Her white white hands on his chest. "Dance with me."

"I can't," Hicklin says quiet. "I don't dance."

Dolly steps close to him, leaning on his chest. Tight as those new leaves up above pushing from their brown sleeves, tight as his pants pushing, tight as his throat closing now around old words.

"I can't," he repeats. "I don't dance."

Her hips move about him slow, her arms put his around her. "Maybe you don't dance," she says, "but you can dance with me Hicklin. It's easy. You're a man. All you have to do is stand there. Hold me here."

She puts his hands on either side of her waist, spreads his fingers out wide. Then she turns in his arms, noodle thin, her leg out and away. She's right, he doesn't have to do anything.

"See," she says, her face close, her breasts squeezed up between them. "Easy."

She pulls away from him, flittering down the sidewalk, floating light over little piles of garbage, her arms full-moon white, the red of her dress coming back to life after a dark night. Hicklin walks wobbly behind her, his feet feeling bigger than ever, bigger than he would ever need. The steps he takes are long, longer than they need to be. Dolly turns to him and curtsies, low, her breasts spilling in a slice of a moment, spilling forward out of her dress. Her badly sewn on sleeves spreading.

Her hair red. Her skin not quite human, her skin too too white. Hicklin blinks. Stops walking, stops moving his feet too big too slow. But then those lines, all around her, and her mouth still so red, her mouth he can see smiling at him from a bit too far away. Her eyes could be blue, but they're not. Her scary eyes with their millipedes crawling crawling around them crinkling their legs in close around her until they look like they could walk away off her face. Those eyes aren't blue. They're unlikely. They're violet. It's Dolly here before him. He knows this. Yes, he does.

But still he does it. As if nothing had ever changed between them.

DAHLIA

Beside her Hicklin sleeps. Flat on his back, hands folded neatly under tidy sheets, neat as a heart outside his chest. Asleep as a stone knight on a stone box, looking like he could up and walk away if only someone could remember the right words. His breathing is quiet and slow, and deep as the sounds of a house shuffling on its foundations late at night. Her head on the pillow sleepless again. Her contacts, brand new soft lenses, in a glass beside the bed. Her glasses in her purse, across the room. A blur of brittle blue in the window, a skeeter of white whirling by.

In her dress she crinkles, tries not to move, tries to be quiet, tries to keep quiet the hole in her. She wants to curl around it. She doesn't. She stares out the window at the blur getting bluer.

His lips on hers flicked a switch. His tongue in her mouth only tasting. Where her heart should be, nothing. Where her insides should be, nothing. Something only lifelike. A wax model, maybe. A cylinder, twitching at the wrong times, turning slightly off kilter. No. She knows it's none of those. It's just nothing.

He'd found a chair for her, an old rattan thing with a big circular back and wide arms. Holes were worn through the rattan, the seat chewed out, with a hidey-hole in one of the arms, a small brass pull on its lid. He'd made a pillow for her from his jacket. She'd sat in the chair. He'd told her she looked like a queen.

Dolly lies flat on her back and breathes slow, in and out and out and out. Holds her eyes open. Her extra-long lashes make bars around her sight, bars she breathes hard to keep from turning to smudges. Another breath in.

He'd leaned forward over her, his mouth soft. She could tell that much. His hands about her moving. His breath in her. Her skin still dead as though it had been stuck on from another. She'd tried. Put her arms about him. Made her lips move in some approximation of this thing called kissing. Tried a little whisper that came out as more of a wheeze. Squeezed.

Squeezes her eyes closed, her lashes rasping into each other and sticking. Locking her inside.

He'd put one of his hands down her dress. Still nothing. His other hand crawled up her thigh on hot legs, too many for her to count. Her thigh was cold where it shouldn't be. Her skin lifeless as a discarded shell. She'd pushed him away, gently. I'm sorry, she'd said. I don't —

He'd paused, a confused look on his face. It's me, he'd said.

All she'd done was all she could do. She'd shaken her head.

And he'd picked up the chair, and carried it here. For her.

BEAU

At first he thinks it's Flannery, that she's forgiven Hicklin and come back.

Hicklin's sandy head next to a curly red one, just as it was, for so long. But. Skin pale, paler than human, and these funny lines all over the girl. Beau thinks maybe it's the blue light that makes her look that way, like skim milk, a cataract, a white stone glowing at the bottom of a pool.

He'd tried to find Hicklin, all over the city, went to trashy bars and strip clubs and all the little holes he likes to drink in and: nothing. Maybe he was here the whole time. It's the only place he didn't bother to check.

Beau takes a slow step into the room, the floor groaning low under his weight. The girl shifts slightly, rolls over, curling into herself, away from Hicklin. Beau can see from here that Hicklin is wearing at least a shirt, a dress shirt, dirty white, still buttoned. Beau takes another step in. Crosses as soft as he can, bends down until his face is level with Hicklin's.

"Hicklin," Beau whispers. "Sorry about your birthday."

There is a smell, a smell like Christmas, a smell like a girl falling backward in gold dust. Beau puts his hands out, trying to touch without touching, his fingers not finding anywhere to be.

"Hey." There is a whisper from across the bed. She is looking at him with these scary violet eyes, smudged from sleep and the whites a little red, but the colour so bright, he's surprised they can blink. But they do. "You seem upset."

"Nah," Beau shakes his head, once.

"But you're crying." She speaks softly, a crinkle coming out like on Marly's old records. Raspy, worn with a needle. Beau rubs a finger under one eye. Comes back wet.

"So I am," he whispers back, and gives her a weak grin. "S'been a long night, I guess."

"Come to bed." She doesn't return his smile, just folds back the edge of Hicklin's holey army blanket and squinches over a bit to make room. She is wearing a red cocktail dress with tattered sleeves. Beau stands. "Come on there's room. Come to bed."

There is white powder dusting the blankets and pillows, there is white powder everywhere.

"You always this friendly?" Beau asks quietly, climbing into the bed, sheet slightly shifting.

"Always," she whispers, forever not smiling, closing the covers right over him, slow, with an arm that smells of Christmas. He turns away from her and she curls right up around him, her breath coming slow on the back of his neck. He can't see her face anymore but she holds him slowly, tighter and tighter, crinkling with crinoline, until he falls asleep.

•

"You terrible bitch!"

"I don't believe I deserve such a harsh word."

"Oh no? You ratted on your dad to save your own ass!"

Dolly pauses and considers this, rolling her big scary eyes ceiling-ward.

"I suppose I did. I guess I *am* a terrible bitch." Another pause, a long shrug. "What the hell. He deserved it. Rat bastard."

Hicklin enters the kitchen, still wearing his ragged white shirt from the night before, his sandy hair sticking up all over, in places gone white from Dolly's dust. Beau and Dolly are sitting at the table, sharing a cigarette and drinking coffee from jam jars. Dolly is wearing glasses. Dolly is bald. The stubble is so pale it almost hurts to look at it.

She's wearing Hicklin's old skeleton print T-shirt and nothing else.

"Hicklin, have you heard this story? This little tart ratted out her daddy to save her own sweet patooty! Can you believe it? She's wonderful! Where did you find her?" Beau rises to give Hicklin a hug. "Sorry about last night, sunshine. But we got you a fantastic breakfast!"

Dolly rises ceremoniously, lifts a dishrag from a plate, does a sweeping thing with her arms like those spangled ladies on daytime TV, the ones who show off the crappy prizes.

"Oooooh," goes Beau, in a suitably awed tone.

Two slumped brown cupcakes, store-bought but unwrapped, with a nubby candle in each one slanting sidewise. A jam jar of something clear. Six bananas, a bowl of honey, and a pear. Squishy cheese and a long loaf of bread.

As Dolly lifts her arms to present these wonders there is a peep of pubes, pale as ghosts.

Hicklin bends and picks up the jam jar, trying his best to look anywhere else.

"You guys," he says. "You shouldn't have."

"It's our pleasure, Hicklin," Beau beams. Then leans in to Hicklin's ear and whispers, "I'm getting Nick back next week, don't worry."

Hicklin takes a sniff of the stuff in the jar. "Pah! What the hell is this?"

"It's alcool, baby! Cheaper than gas and twice as good!" Beau takes up the jar and sips. "Achhh!" he sputters. "Smooooooooooth!"

Dolly fixes them with a grave stare, and reaches for the jar. A finger disappears down her neck. Then another. Licks her lips and hands it over. "It's still your birthday Hicklin. Have a drink."

He holds the jar barely to his lips and feels them burn, his eyes watering from some vicious vapour. Sips. It's like being burned alive from the inside, but in a cozy way.

"Oof... geezus...."

"Ooo, oooh! Can I have another?" says Beau.

"Well I don't know," sighs Dolly, an almost cheery lilt in her voice. "Depends on the kind of day you want to have."

"On Earth, as it is in Heaven... Give us this day our holy bread..."

"Our daily bread."

"And forgive us our trespasses... Ummmm... On Earth, as it is in Heaven?"

"You said that already."

"What the hell are you two on about?"

Beau is sprawled over Dolly, as though she and the park bench were a couch. Dolly sits primly, her feet on the ground. Hicklin plops a couple of overflowing paper bags holding the leftovers from breakfast onto the snow-damp ground of the park at the base of the mountain.

"The Lord's Prayer. Beau claims he said it every night for five years but it seems he can't remember the thing." Dolly pulls one of the paper bags toward her. "Oh thank you Hicklin. I'm famished."

"I *did* say it every night for five years! It's not *my* fault if I can't remember it! Maybe the Lord should've made it a bit shorter!" Beau reaches into one of his many pockets, fishes out a joint. "Hey! Is there a prayer for this, too?"

Hicklin rolls his eyes, and bends to the paper bags. Beau lights the joint, and inhales deeply. His head feels more clear than it has in years. He hasn't had a sleep that deep and dreamless probably ever. With his arms wrapped around this girl he just met. A ghost of a girl, a girl who doesn't smile.

"Beau," Dolly says, holding out her hand, "you do intend to share."

"Oh," Beau says, blushing. "Sorry. Got lost in space."

"Happens to him a lot, Dolly," Hicklin says, pulling the pear from one of the bags. "Get used to it."

Dolly inhales and holds, then exhales a tight stream, perfect as though pushed out from a hole in some machine. She passes the joint to Hicklin.

"Well happy birthday Hicklin," she says. "If I'd known I would have brought you something."

"You took me out," Hicklin says, smiling. "Got me drunk for nothing. I can't think of a better birthday."

Beau lifts his eyebrows, waggles them around. "Oooh, you two! I sure hope I didn't interrupt something!"

Dolly and Hicklin look at each other briefly, then both quickly look away. Head shaking and mumbling ensues.

"I was just kidding, guys," Beau says, taking back the joint from Hicklin. "Jesus."

Beau takes a deep haul from the joint, passes it to Dolly, and lies back on the park bench. Stares at the sky awhile.

"Speaking of Jesus, what do you guys think of him?" Beau asks.

"Jesus," Dolly says. Not a question. Just a statement.

"Like, well, I don't know... not just Jesus," Beau says. "All the miracles and everything. The loaves and fishes. All those saints and stuff. Him and that other guy, dying and coming back to life. What about that?"

"Lazarus," Hicklin says. "He was the other guy."

"Yeah, well, what about it?" Beau reaches for the pear, takes a bite, and talks around it. "Does this stuff happen or not? Are miracles just fairy tales?"

"A miracle is simply desire intersecting with reality," Dolly states.

"What?" Beau looks from Dolly to Hicklin. "Can you translate, please?"

"Well," Hicklin starts, looking at Dolly. She stares off into the park, silent and motionless. As though recharging. "I think she means that when you want something and it comes true it seems like magic. Or a miracle. But just because you get what you want doesn't mean there's such a thing as divine intervention. I think."

Dolly stares away. Beau and Hicklin look at each other. Beau shrugs. "So..." he says, "all the crazy stuff in the Bible could be true? People coming back to life and everything?"

Hicklin nods. He's staring off to where Dolly's looking.

"What's going on?" Beau asks, standing up and searching the park.

"Just a sec," Hicklin says, and stands to go. He begins to run.

"Wait, Hicklin! What about the opposite of miracles?" Beau yells at Hicklin, who's already out of earshot. "What about monsters?"

Dolly stares up at Beau, something like a long-dead smile turning the edges of her lips.

LUCE

So kids, here's the skinny. I feel like a rat, running out on you all like that. Most of you are only knee-high and probably won't remember me in a year or two, so if I do show up someday I bet you'll all start bawling and hanging onto Mom. So here's what I'm gonna do. I'm gonna write all this down for you, like a bedtime story for someone who should be me to read to you. And that way, even if I never do come back, at least you'll remember someone. Someone with a name just like mine, and my hair and clothes and everything. Someone just like me. But the one you made up. And who knows? Maybe that one'll be better than the real thing.

So here goes.

•

What can I tell you? I arrived in Montreal, even with Q.B. (the Queen Bitch, more on her later) driving that jalopy like she was on the lam and that one last snowstorm still stuck up in the sky, just waiting for me to get under it. I don't know why Montreal, exactly. I don't really know much of anything right now. Q.B. just told me to get a wiggle on and soon we'd both be sitting pretty. So, here I am.

She dropped me off near this crumby little hill she called 'the Mountain'. Now, when I think of a mountain I think of Everest or that other one, you know, Kill-a-manjaro. Something humungous, something with snow and clouds all over the place, something with, like, crags and dwarves and big damn birds flapping around spooky caves.

You know? *Something.* So this little hill was kind of a disappointment. Not only is it about ten feet high, it's got these ratty little trees all dead poking out of its skin, and it's all grey and brown and smells like dogshit. Q.B. told me to lay off. Told me to wait until summer. Told me nothing in Montreal looks good in March. So I shut my hole, and left her alone with the flivver. That car is like driving rust, so I was floored when she made it to the end of the block, but she did, and turned, and there she was. Gone. Me, I'm still here. And where might that be, you wonder? Well, let me tell you.

Would you believe it if I told you I'm living with the foxiest Fox in this whole frozen country? You wouldn't, would you. You'd say, Luce, go chase yourself. Dry up. Shut your big lying yap. You would. I know. So, fine. Don't buy it. That comes later anyway.

I figure with this mountain being so puny and all, I'll take it on the heel and toe. Figure it'll take me about five minutes to get to the top of it and I won't even have to stop to catch my breath. That's what I figure. Yep. So I start up the hill.

The more I get into it the more I see Q.B. was right about one thing: nothing in Montreal looks good in March. I also see why the whole hill smells of dogshit: because the thing is made of dogshit. It's everywhere. Under trees in piles, slipping out from under these rickety little bushes everywhere, sliding under my feet. Pos-i-lute-ly disgusting. After slipping around like this for a while, I decide walking up a stinky little hill to more stink is for the birds, and I quit. That's when I notice something.

Someone's busting a gut. A couple of someones. I turn around slowly, trying to keep my stilts from sliding around too much, and take these really tiny steps back down the little bit of hill I actually managed to climb up. There's a bunch of rubes playing drugstore cowboy out here on the shit hill. A couple baby grands, I mean, *really* big guys, and a tall skinny black man, a real palooka, who stares at me with this look like he just knows he's the cat's meow. I give him the icy mitt and keep sliding through the shit, as graceful as I can.

They watch me go, beating their gums the whole time in French. Applesauce, I bet — these kind of guys never say nothing to each other but baloney about dames. But that one guy, he's a tall drink of water. I don't let on about that though, don't even look at him. Not because he's standing there all puffed up, not because he's giving me the eye. Nope. Because he's still laughing at me.

I walk slow as I can not looking at any of them. I can hear them sniggering as I go. One of them shouts something at me, something I don't understand. Anyway, they're starting to bug me, I mean, I'm starting to get that bearcat feeling, like I'm gonna get in a real lather. You know, you've seen it. When Mom and I would go at it, you know. So I keep walking.

Up ahead there's a big stone thing, playing stick-em-up with the sky. On top of this thing there's a statue, of something that looks like an angel. All around it there are benches, in a horseshoe, and cats hanging around, like they're waiting for word from on high. A fool's game, if you ask me, but none of them do. There's a set of stairs back behind the angel, so I head over there. I sit down and open up the bag Q.B. packed for me. God only knows what a crazy twist like her would think I need.

First off, the bag itself is more like a bindle — I mean, it's a rag for a bum to drag around. It looks like it was made out of dead mice, and no fooling. There's a weird drawstring that looks like a big old rat tail, and it's all different shades of rat, little pieces of them all sewn together. I don't know where she got it, but I'm pretty sure it wasn't Fifth Avenue. Not by a long shot. So I open the thing.

Kids, listen to me. I swear I didn't know. I thought maybe she'd put in some glad rags so's I could pretty myself up and make some friends, maybe some shine, so's I could have a bottle to share if the rags don't work. Or, what, a toothbrush. Something. So what do I see when I get into the belly of this big old rat bag sitting on my lap?

Voot. Lettuce. Dough. There's nothing else in the bag.

I feel like I'm about to have kittens, so I close up the bag. Play it cool. Look around, you know. Whistle.

And that's when our friend, the palooka, makes his big return. Now I really am going to have kittens. I've got a sack full of bills, and nowhere to go, and this lug shadowing me. That bearcat feeling is getting worse.

So the palooka sits down next to me, cozy as you please. Like we're old friends, like we used to share a bottle. He starts flapping his gums in this long windy French, his voice sort of singing, like when we used to go to the drive-in with Mom, remember? On the way home she'd put on the radio, and it would be Ella and Louis or Patsy or Peggy singing for us, and you guys would all fall asleep there in the backseat, sleeping like you were snowed, all piled up on each other like a bunch of little drunks. Outside there'd be these dark humps of hills slipping by, and inside the car so warm and cozy like nowhere else ever was, like we were all in something happy that someone we didn't even know had imagined, and I'd open up the window just a little bit just to hear the air sing like this fella here is singing now, but I can't listen to him and anyway I don't know what he's saying, so I shrug. Put the rat bag strictly on the far side of me, away from even his long arms. He sings something that sounds like a question. His friends try to look like part of the scenery not so very far away, but it's not easy to hide a couple big sixes under scrawny trees without their leaves, and I can see they're still whooping it up, still miming me falling in the shit.

"Sorry, bub," I say to this guy, who even sitting down looms way above me. "Bank's closed."

He gives me this look like I just cracked the best joke ever. Now kids, even though I got this feeling on me like I could sing and fight and cry all at the same time I tell you something: I'm not blind, and I'm not stupid. This is one hell of a looker here. Wide cheekbones covered over with a skin of coffee and cream, his eyes I swear might as well have jumped right out of a big cat and into his face, like they have this light inside them, like the sun is always setting, crazy. His fro makes him look like another planet, hovering over me, screwing with my gravity or whatever it is that keeps all the shit in the sky from slamming into each other. Anyway he looks at me with this little smile creeping up the corners of his mouth. But then he says something daffy.

"Ah," he goes, this goofy grin on his mug, "mo-dite ang-lay." He laughs at this, and points up to the angel. Someone's written something that could be what he just said on the big post the angel's standing on.

I can't stand when fellas get sappy.

"You've got me all wrong, mac," I say. "That's an angel." I point to the statue. "Me, I'm something else."

He smiles again, then says something about bells.

"Listen, mister," I grab ahold of the rat bag, make to stand. "I really gotta ankle, here."

He stands with me, follows me along a little bit. The baby grands are howling, leaning on the scrawny trees, making them shake like there's a storm coming. I turn around and he does this bad dog move, all sinking into himself. So I yell at him.

"Stay," I yell, putting my hand out. I walk away again. I can feel him behind me, but I keep walking. I can't see his cronies anymore, but they're laughing even harder. I turn quick and catch the palooka, walking along behind me, his nose in the air, a tight little wiggle about him.

"You're getting to be a flat tire," I say, the bearcat feeling creeping into my face and making me hot. "Scram."

In one step he's on me, all his height folding in to touch me from that other planet he's on. He calls me jolly, which is about the worst description of me I think I've ever heard. I tell him to dry up, and make to walk away again. That's when he does it. He reaches out a long beautiful finger and lays it on my lips.

"Shhhhhh," he says, smiling down at me from wherever it is his head is.

His finger stays there, but his smile fades as I open up my bone box and lay into him hard with my choppers.

•

And that's how I meet the foxiest Fox this side of the Atlantic, standing there with my lips wrapped around the pointing finger of a man with his head high up in the sky, a man who might as well be another planet. This Fox runs over to ask me if I'm okay. My mouth being full, I just nod. The palooka, on the other hand. The palooka squeals. Kids, when you get older, especially you, Dash, being a boy, whatever you do, whatever happens to you, however much you might be hurting or hurt: do not ever squeal. Scream, sure. Go screwy all over the place. Yell and cry. Don't squeal. Nobody likes a squealer.

After he's done squealing the big beautiful palooka says a bunch of words too fast for me to catch but I'm no ninny. I get his drift. There's nothing nice about me in any of those words. The Fox stands there, and I stand there, and the palooka stands there, his fish hook still in my mouth. The Fox puts out his own mitt, and gently takes the finger from my mouth. I spit and walk away.

I haven't gone ten feet when this Daisy comes running up to me — and when I say Daisy I mean Daisy. This fella is no fella. He's got shorter hair than most of the freaks you see nowadays, but it's still long enough to bounce in beautiful curls around his head. No beard, and he's wearing jeans. He's also wearing lipstick, and a pearl necklace, and a flouncy pink blouse. And kids, you won't believe me but — he's pretty. Prettier than most girls. I know, you're thinking, Luce, close your head. And I would. I would. Only it's all part of the story, and all of the story is true.

So he runs up to me and grabs me by the shoulders. Right behind him is this doll, a real flour-lover, and her hair is shorter than his, and she's wearing glasses that make her eyes look humungous and I tell you, no fooling, her eyes are violet. You know, like Elizabeth Taylor says hers are but they're not? This skirt's are for real.

"Are you okay?" the Daisy asks me, in what I have to say is a regular joe's voice. "That guy can be kind of a goon."

"Copacetic," I say, shaking off the Daisy. "I'm peachy, thanks."

The doll's made it up to us by now, walking, I have to say. No running for this smarty. She stares at me like I'm something slithery she's found in her dessert, those eyes going right through me. She's so white she could be a ghost.

"You don't look peachy," the Ghost says in this creepy voice that sounds somewhere between Mom's old records and a car driving slow over gravel. "Come sit with us. We're having a party."

She lifts one of her arms all slow and jerky like the Tin Man when he's out of oil, points at a crumby picnic they've got going on what I guess they hope will someday be grass. She doesn't smile.

"Thanks," I say, glomming the sad scraps laid out there: a couple of squished cakes, a jar of what looks like water, some hunks of bread, a cheese that's running all over the plate. There's a pear skeleton that looks just like a keyhole in an old cartoon. I half expect an eye to bulge out of it, spying. "But I wouldn't want to crash your ball."

Just then the Fox pipes up.

"You got him good," he says. "Nice one."

Kids, I swear I never do this. I really don't. Have you ever seen it? I blush. I blush like a little girl who's just slid down a bannister for the first time.

"That palooka can go chase himself," I say, sort of quiet. "He's screwy, anyway."

"Well," the Daisy says, grabbing my hand, "c'mon, come sit! We're celebrating!"

"Celebrating late," the Ghost says, all midnight and rain.

"No can do," I say, trying to pull away from the Daisy with no luck. For a fruit he's got a helluva grip. "I've really gotta go read and write."

They're all quiet at that, looking around at each other like they don't know what I just said.

"You can do that later," the Fox smiles. "C'mon, we're celebrating!"

"You know these cats?" I ask.

"Sure," he shrugs. "We're old friends, aren't we?"

I shrug right back. "Well, in that case..." I look around me. A big old city all around me. But a Fox right here. I nod. "Alright. Just for a bit. But then I really do have to make like a tree."

"Far out!" the Daisy sings.

"What are we celebrating, anyway?" I ask.

"Why, it's Hicklin's birthday!" the Daisy says, putting an arm around me. "Tell me, honey, what do you think about miracles?"

•

The picnic gets cold waiting for us to eat it, since as soon as we sit down the Daisy brings out some Jane, and the stuff I thought was water in the jar isn't water, it's eel juice, I mean real mean panther sweat, like this stuff could've been made in a bathtub, kids, and no joke. So we all get jawing pretty good, and of course they want to know what I'm doing here and where I'm going and all that jazz, so I lie.

I tell them I ran away from home, which is the only true part of that story. Some of the other stuff I tell them isn't fit for little ears (or eyes, since I guess someday you'll be reading this), but let's just say my story has a real bad daddy in it, and a real mean momma, and a real poor little old me. The way I make it out, I'm a real bunny. A sad sack and no fooling. They all buy it, hook, line, and sinker. The Daisy grabs my hand and squeezes it at this one part where I pretend to cry, and the Fox gives me this look that makes me want to kick off. Even the Ghost pats my hand. She's not looking at me, and the patting feels like it's coming from about a million miles away, but still. Maybe she's got a heart in there somewhere after all.

So they have a little huddle and after a while the Fox tells me I can stay with him. And we pack up the picnic nobody ate, and off we go. The sun went down while we were gabbing, leaving us almost alone up here, with nothing around but the trees.

And it's kind of spooky up there in the dark, gives me the heebie-jeebies. You know what the trees are like where we're from: runty. The trees here are skinny and tall and since they don't have any leaves yet they're all waving their bones around in the air, all their feelers and meat hooks sailing around like they're trying to catch you. Weird little scuffling sounds fly by your feet. And the dogshit smell doesn't get any better. Every once in a while a car goes by behind the trees, lighting up everything for a split second, like the whole thing is part of somebody else's bad dream. I'm dead last since I don't know where I'm going, and I'm still sliding all around on this wet ground I hope is just dirt by now, so I end up following the flour-lover, who's next in line. That's even creepier. I feel like I'm tailing a ghost. She's so pale she shines like those stones Hansel and Gretel dropped behind them in that story, you remember, the one where there's this house made of gingerbread in a forest? Tina always liked that one. Anyway, there's no house here for me, not yet, but we do finally get to a real, live road. It's got pavement and everything.

We walk along a bunch of streets where all the houses have their guts on the outside, their stairs spilling down to the sidewalks like big black metal tongues. We pass an alley, and I catch the same words that were written on the angel, all sloppy under a streetlight.

"Hey," I say, stopping. The Fox happens to be closest to me then, and he turns and looks.

"Yeah," he says, pushing his hair out of his face. It falls right back. "You get used to it."

"What's it mean?" I ask, as we start walking again.

He turns his peepers on me. "You don't know?"

I shake my head.

"Damned English," he says.

And here was me, thinking it was something about an angel. Maybe I should've watched more French movies, and a couple less of the oldies. "Oh," is all I say.

We go along pretty slow. The Fox doesn't say a thing. But then neither do I. Somewhere pretty close, a siren zips by, howling like all get out.

"Seems like I've been hearing those all day," I say. Only getting that it's true as I say it.

"Yeah," the Fox says. "Lots of fires here. Most of them aren't even investigated."

"Why's that?" I ask.

The Fox shakes his head. "I dunno."

A real chatterbox, this one. We keep walking, keeping mum. Then he says, out of nowhere, "So what are you writing?"

I don't have a clue what he's on about. "What's that?" I ask.

He frowns. "You said you couldn't come with us because you had to go read and write. Right?"

I try not to bust a gut here. After a second I tell him, "That's just a saying. Like, 'the bee's knees'. Savvy?"

"Oh," he says, looking down at the ground. "I've never heard it before. That's all. Nevermind."

We walk a bit more. "I read some," I say, after a bit. "Dashiell Hammett, Jim Thompson, Dorothy Parker. Stuff like that. Guess it sunk into the old thinkbox," I finish, pointing at my head.

He gets this look on his face like he's gone goofy, and won't talk to me for the rest of the walk.

We finally get to his house and it looks like it's bending down to meet us. The whole thing is tipping towards the street. Honest, kids, when he says, here we are, I think maybe it's like in a movie, you know, where they show a building but you can tell it's all flat, and behind it there could be anything or nothing. So we go in.

Some stairs are all bent in the middle, shoes and boots piled up all along the sides, and just brackets sticking out from the wall like warts. No bannister. The first room we go into is slanty and pretty empty except for a couple of walls of books, and an old turntable sitting right on the floor.

"This is swell," I say. "I feel like a high hat."

The Ghost stares at me, her eyes going wiggly behind her cheaters. Without even opening her trap, she turns and makes for the door. The Fox watches her go, then looks at me and says, "Make yourself at home," before chasing after her.

"Well," the Daisy grabs my hand, "I guess I get to give you the tour. This is the Grand Ballroom..." he waves his hand to indicate the empty space we're in. Leads me by the hand across the room to a doorway, opens the door and puts in a hand, turning on the light.

"The Chamber of Enlightenment," he says, sweeping a hand over a room that's mostly bed, a big flat bed right on the floor. There's enough sequins and feathers in here for a hundred showgirls, all hanging off the walls and tossed any which way all over the room.

The Daisy pulls me to the next door, and throws it open.

"The Seat of All Knowledge," he sings. It's a long skinny room, covered in tiny tiles all honeycomb shape, a bathtub at the end with an open window above it, a kid-sized sink near the door and a toilet between the two. I'm pulled away again, back across the big empty room.

"The Master's Quarters," Beau says, opening a door onto a room that looks like it's from a different apartment. A spotless white wall shines at me like new teeth. Two of the walls are floor to ceiling shelves holding closed boxes, stacked up so neatly they look like a brick wall. One of the walls is mostly window. There's another big bed on the floor, hospital corners, the whole shebang. Looks mostly like army blankets, and a bunch of pillows that're kinda worn, but clean. They're not even wrinkled. A half-slip the colour of pancake makeup lies in a puddle beside the bed. I guess I'm staring at it or something because the Daisy squeezes my hand.

"It's been there for days," he whispers, leaning close to my ear. "It's like he's going to leave it there until she comes back."

"Who?" I whisper back.

The Daisy gives a big sigh. Whispers, "His lady love."

"Oh," I say, too loud. "Oh," I whisper, "What happened?"

The Daisy shakes his head. "That's not for me to say," he says quietly. Then pulls me to another door.

"The Guest Wing," the Daisy smiles. There's a couple huge tables in there, all covered with papers and bits of fur and metal and fabric. A fold-out army cot sits folded in a corner, near a skinny window lit up by a streetlight in the alley. There's no curtain on the window, not even a paper shade.

"The Entertainment Console," the Daisy says, pointing to the window. Right across the alley is another window a lot like this one. There's no curtain on that one either. A shape drifts by, slowly, all grey in this creepy, flickering light that looks like it's coming from the floor.

"Hippies," the Daisy rolls his eyes. "Or witches, if you believe them. They put candles on the floor and chant and dance around in the moonlight. They can be pretty loud, so I hope you're a sound sleeper. Or a night person."

I'm watching a mug that's popped up in the window across the way. It's mostly hair and the rest is crazy eyes. And I'm pretty sure it's looking back at me. I wave, then blow it a kiss. It begins howling, turning its empty O mouth up to the streetlight. I snort a laugh through my nose and shake my head.

"Come on," the Daisy says, leading me back through the empty room, to the kitchen. "The Centre of the Known World," he says, pulling out a chair on wheels for me. The Fox hands me a joint.

"How was the tour?" he asks.

"Cherry," I say. "And your neighbours are Jake."

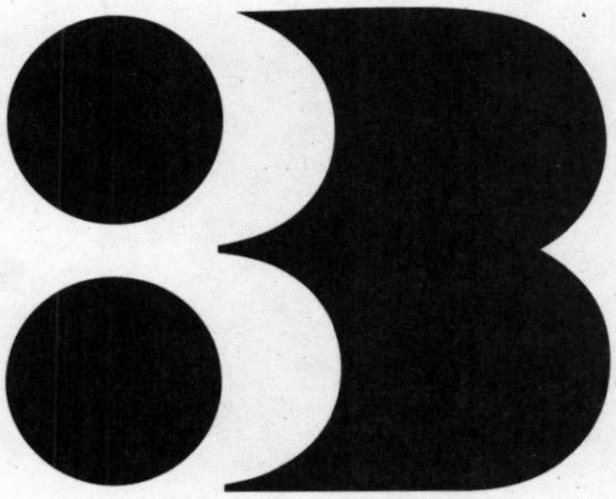

HICKLIN

1963

"Cinderella dressed in yella went upstairs to meet her fella, on the way she kissed a snake, how many doctors did it take? One, two, three, four...."

The snow from New Year's has retreated from the schoolyard, leaving behind it stubby brown grass for girls to play skip rope on. In the middle of the soccer field a few grey humps of snow sit melting, nubby as old teeth, their semi-circle formation making him think they were once a snow fort. He doesn't know this for sure, as he's spent the few days between New Year's and the start of classes at home, in the mud room. Alone, except for the time a couple of policemen came to ask him questions for which he didn't have the answers.

He squats behind the big old holly hedge, on a corner of pavement so far from the schoolyard it has its own set of rules. A space between the schoolyard and the street, a place where bullies sometimes flash French postcards at the skinny kids instead of handing out a beating, a place where girls walk alone, demurely brushing down their skirts. Today he is the only one hoping for space, here behind the holly leaves so glossy they look fake, so lickable he's tried. Just once though.

Cinderella's dressed in yella all over again. He takes the beginning of the chant as his cue, and scuttles from behind the holly, bent at his knees, scurrying as quickly as he can under the weight of his book shell, looking down at the ground, silently scuffling to the side door of the school.

"Hey, Pervert." A sharp slice of Thad's voice slides through him from above. He glances up.

Thad stands above him, his arms crossed over his chest, a mean smile twisting his face. Thad is on the track team, and is built like a small, tanned pony. His teeth gleam pure white, and his hair is just fair enough to offset his blue, blue eyes.

He pretends he hasn't heard Thad, and puts his head down, starts scurrying away. A hand lands on his head, pushes it down.

"I'm talking to you, *Pervert*." Thad's voice comes quiet from far above, sliding in slow between his vertebrae, reaching straight for the mess inside. "Don'tcha even know your own name?"

"'Snot my name," he mumbles to the ground. An ant hurries by, holding a piece of something crumbly between its jaws, something at least twice the size of its own body. The ant looks fine. Its knees don't buckle, its jaws don't twist.

"Oh, yeah?" Thad snorts. "It is now! We all heard what you did, *Pervert*."

"I didn't *do* anything!"

"Pffff!" Thad pushes his head further down. "Heard you found a lady, all messed up. Heard you made it with her, got all the way to home base. Only she wasn't breathing, Pervert. She wasn't even *alive*. At least, not when you started. Isn't that right?"

He shakes his head. The ant is gone. "No," he manages, before his throat goes tight.

"No! No!" Thad shrieks in a fake high voice. Then, low in his ear in a growling whisper, "Bet she would've said that. If she could've."

He shakes his head, harder now that Thad has got his head pushed so low to the ground. Now Thad squats down himself, holding handfuls of his hair. Pulls up his head so they can look each other in the eye.

"Bikky's dad's a cop, Pervert," Thad's face is strained and serious, his mouth a rubber band about to spring, "and he says some of the boys at the station were wondering if maybe you didn't just find her, like you told 'em. Maybe you were there the whole time. Maybe you saw it all and didn't do anything. Some of them even think maybe you did it yourself, messed her up like that."

His eyes are holes, tiny maelstroms sinking lower than even the oldest fish could swim.

"Phhhh," Thad makes this noise through his nose, then continues. "Don't worry, Pervert. I know you didn't mess her up. You can't even stand up half the time under all that junk you carry around with you. And everyone knows you can't fight."

He closes his eyes to keep the whirlpools from getting away. Something at the back of his head sings a little useless tune about how there's a settlement near Maelstrom. The name of it is Hell.

"But someone *saw you do it*, Pervert," Thad whispers.

"No," he says again, and then sniffles like a little kid. Horrified, he keeps his mouth shut.

"Yeah," Thad says, crisply. "That's it. Cry like a little baby. *Pervert*."

Thad lets go of his hair with a push to his head that's so hard he falls over. He crawls back to the holly hedge, and under it like a rat. He is scratched all over by the holly's tiny claws, everywhere kitten scratches that for some reason don't even sting. He doesn't even feel them. He curls around himself and lets all the whirlpools out. Somewhere far away he thinks he hears a bell ring, though he's not even sure anymore what it's ringing for.

•

Pervert. Constructed of parts he has not made, put together from pieces he's never seen, he clunkers lonely under two shells. One of books, and the other, this new name. Their weight combines to lower his eyes to the ground, to seal his mouth from ever uttering words other than the one that has become him, written on a scroll wedged deep inside his head.

The myth has passed from mouth to mouth, whispered behind hands up and down the hall. In this new suit he walks carefully, not sure how to move or think or talk, though talking has never been much of an option anyway. Not scraped or pushed or jostled or jived, he walks stiffly through the first day, and the second, and the third. And many more beyond.

Pervert. He passes his hole now without even looking at it, passes as his pipe is repaired, as the hole is filled with earth, his abandoned penny candies and flashlight and milk teeth and pickle jar turned into hidden treasures for an unknown future, passes by as a skin is put on his hole, sealed over with burning tar. The smell is enough to stop him, enough to shake awake his brain. He is staring at the square dark scar when he feels something behind him.

"Don't let them own you, son," a voice behind him says. His father's voice, his father's hand on his shoulder. Briefly his father squeezes, even through his shell, hard, harder than he'd thought his father could squeeze, hard enough to squeeze something like a heart up into his throat. Worse than the name he's been given is the simple truth in just those five words. His father has heard the story. His father has heard his new name.

He closes his eyes over his burning cheeks and counts to one hundred, one hundred slow breaths, one hundred fillings and emptyings of his lungs. When he opens his eyes his father is gone, a grey shape away past the driveway, a distant smudge on the far side of his own front door.

•

In the mud room he fills his boxes. Leaves and shells and broken bones, rocks and seeds and green things drying. Bits of glass and gears and plastic bits in alien shapes, starfish dried to chalk. Bottles and baby dolls and photos of strangers with their kids. Everything about the world he can no longer say.

He goes down to the docks, where he watches tankers get filled with sulfur, the bright yellow piles shining like reverse oases, deserts in the sea. Under low skies, bulging with winter rain, he picks up broken bits of metal, some of them still greasy from recent use. He finds a bone as big as his thigh, with teeth marks all over it, the rounded end where it once fit into a pelvic socket gnawed to splintery bits. In the remains of a bonfire he finds a love note, its blue ink gone runny from the rain that never stops falling, its edges flaking and black. He reads what he can, then re-folds it, and leaves it on a warehouse window sill, under a rock, just in case. Just in case someone comes back for it.

In the forest he walks under creepy evergreens, their needles always fresh and new, always dripping, dripping, drops slower and fatter than rain. Walks through puddles to shiny cliffs, where seagulls wail, circling. He collects their dirty white feathers. He also finds shining black raven feathers, and the white and brown of eagles. These he takes home, and makes into dun-coloured Birds of Paradise. Long plumes for the tails, the shorter feathers for the bodies. No need for feet. His books tell him Birds of Paradise arrived in the Old World from the New tied and dried, without their feet, giving rise to the belief that the birds had no feet in life, and thus, could never land. He hangs his homemade birds from the ceiling of the mud room, but becomes dizzy staring at them, imagining a life of constant flight, and needs to take them down.

He builds tiny theatres out of the boxes he has yet to fill. He buys a dime-store paint set with small change, twelve cakes of colour in a bright red tin. Fills the milk bottle with water, to dip his brush. He paints curtains and sets, and costumes for the tiny naked people he cuts out of a magazine he found by the docks. Their mouths open as though to speak, their faces pained, mostly. Sometimes they smile. He doesn't use those. When he is done, the milk bottle is full of a deep brown ooze. Skin has buckled where he's used too much glue. He puts the magazine, now full of holes, on the bottom of a box, the tiny people and their sets and costumes on that, and the paint set on top, to weigh the whole thing down. He puts the lid on the box, and pushes it, unlabelled, under his bed. The muddy ooze he keeps on the little window sill in the mud room. Every day a little evaporates, until there is nothing left in the milk bottle but a cracked and crusted ring the colour of dried blood.

He draws the same diagram over and over again: three ellipses of descending magnitude, a scribbled eye in the centre. He no longer labels the ellipses, no longer marks the Schwarzschild radius or either event horizon. He writes, *Singularity*, in the centre so many times it becomes a black tangle. This one he folds into a tiny square and keeps in his pocket.

Wrapped in his granddad's manky old sweater, the tiny purse dropped by the Princess sleeps with him. Under his pillow it stays.

DAHLIA

1964

It has been raining all day, all day the sound of tiny handslaps against the window, all day the trees outside fidgeting in the wind. Dahlia doesn't mind. She has a stack of fat books from the library, and even some large ones that her father had to take out for her. Dahlia loves going to the library with her father — he stays in the periodicals, reading the same newspaper they get at home, while she chews her way through the stacks. And at the end of it, he'll take out anything she has in her massive pile. Even art books, which are strictly forbidden for those with a child's membership.

One of the art books inspires quite a flurry of activity in Dahlia's room. She takes everything off of her violet bookcase and stacks it on top of her chest of drawers. After opening the drawers in ever larger increments, she strips her bed of its violet sheets, and drapes them over the whole. She doesn't have enough dolls, so she edges into her sister's room and borrows hers. Even so, Dahlia needs one more body.

Dahlia looks over to a pile she's made on the floor of all the toys she won't be using for this. There's Georgey-Porgey, and some broken tin toys, and a tall nutcracker in a blue soldier's uniform. Maybe he'll do. She picks him up, but his clothes are painted on. She puts him back down. There, behind the rest, lying on her side, is the big doll from her Great Aunt Patience.

The doll stares at Dahlia. The doll has stood on Dahlia's highest shelf for four years, behind a clutter of books and toys. Untouched.

Dahlia bites her lip and pushes her glasses up on her nose. Reaches for the doll.

Dahlia undresses her carefully, balancing her on her lap. The doll is wickedly heavy, and seems to twist and heave in her arms. Once her dress is off, Dahlia sees there are words punched into the doll's metal back. *Edison's Talking Doll.*

"I didn't know you were a talking doll," Dahlia says, placing the big doll in the very front of the group, to preserve perspective. "What can you say?"

"Dahlia!" her mother sings off-key while entering her room without knocking. "Dinner's nearly —"

Her mother is still, her hand on the doorknob. She takes a deep breath, exhaling loudly through her nose. When she speaks again, there is no song in her voice. More like rocks.

"Dahlia, what have you done?"

The dolls have been relieved of their clothing and posed at varying heights on the makeshift violet backdrop. Their legs and arms have been carefully placed, so that seen all together they seem almost to mimic movement.

"They're *Woman Descending a Staircase* — see?" Dahlia jumps up from the floor with a large book carefully held in her two hands, its protective plastic film sticking to her. Her mother takes the book from her, delicately, as though it might transmit a deadly virus simply through touch. Her mother peers at the two-page spread. Indeed, it is labelled in the lower right-hand corner as *Woman Descending a Staircase.* The same woman in every shot, nude, doing exactly what the caption says. A series of tiny photos, depicting an eerie sense of machine-like motion.

Dahlia's mother flips through the book. Horses seem to run, birds seem to fly. Men, women, and children walk, run, and jump, all naked. Every last one.

"Dahlia," her mother says, snapping the book shut. "Where on Earth did you get this... filth?"

"It's not filth, Mama," Dahlia says, pointing to the typewritten label affixed to the spine. "It's an art book. See?"

"Eadweard Muybridge," Dahlia's mother reads from the cover. "You need to watch out for these *artists*, Dahlia," her mother says, placing the book tight over her chest and wrapping her arms around it. "They'll lie to get what they want. And what they want, Dahlia, is — well, it's not for little girls to think about."

"But, Mama." Dahlia reaches for the book. Her mother shakes her head. "But, Mama. They're so beautiful. It's like magic. Like taking time apart. As if it could stop. But it can't. Magic!"

Dahlia's mother stares down at her. A wrinkle seems to grow right then between her eyebrows.

"I'm sure I wouldn't know about that, Dahlia," her mother finally says, "but I do think you're spending far too much time alone. I think it's time for you to take up an activity."

"Okay," Dahlia says, nodding her head. "Photography!"

Her mother lets out a laugh, or a sort of laugh anyway, a laugh that's been strained through cheesecloth and left to clot. She bends down so that her face is level with Dahlia's. This close Dahlia can see silver hairs wound in with her mother's chestnut chignon. A faint powdery dusting over her mother's skin. Cheeks just a little too pink. Her mother shakes her head, and leaves Dahlia's room, closing the door tight behind her.

•

Dahlia follows her mother's legs up the creaking, crooked stairs, staring at the tattered hemp runner underfoot. It's worn through in places, so the red paint beneath shows through like a rash. It makes her itchy just to look at it.

"Dahlia!" her mother calls, sort of half-turning. "Are you fussing with your new clothes?"

Dahlia hadn't even noticed but she had been scratching at her arms through the stiff new wool of her coat.

"No, Mama," she lies, putting one hand on the bannister, one at her side.

"Well, good," her mother says, turning back and continuing up the stairs, "that coat has to last you."

A sudden banging starts up somewhere above them, as though someone were taking a hammer to a very old, very out of tune piano. A thumping follows, actually many thumpings, ever so slightly out of time. Clacking of wood against wood. The destruction of the piano and the many thumpings grow louder as Dahlia follows her mother's legs up the stairs. Dahlia squints and tries to picture her mother as a photo series, but the seams on her mother's legs are so straight they become all Dahlia can see. A pair of chopsticks, disembodied and clacking their way up the stairs, in time with the thumpings coming from above.

Her mother stops at a landing, and opens a door. Now the thumpings are drowned out by the raspings of the poor old piano. Her mother goes in, with the noise and everything. Dahlia follows.

Into a huge room, full of windows and mirrors and many many girls, all with the same black torso, all with pink plastic legs, all with hair pulled tight into a bun at the back of their skulls. They stand on their tiptoes, right on their toes, and then down. Up, down. Up, down. The back of the piano faces the room, all the struts and boards inside it exposed, as though someone really had been taking a hammer to it. From where Dahlia stands it looks as though it's being played by a cloud of smoke. She wonders how smoke can play so loudly, and so badly. Before she can run over and check, she is tugged by her mother toward a desk near the door.

Behind the desk is a woman with a sweaty face and a slick of black hair. A long, brown cigarette jammed into a silver and mother-of-pearl holder sticks out from her mouth. She smokes while smoothly inserting large silver hoops through holes in her earlobes. When she is done with her ears, she ties a paisley scarf about her head. Then she turns, and seems to notice them for the first time.

"Hello," she says, unsmiling. She slides from sitting to standing to squatting in front of Dahlia without discernible motion. Dahlia can't begin to see how even Muybridge could take the magic of that apart. The woman puts her face on a level with Dahlia's. Looks in Dahlia's eyes, right through her thick glasses. The woman nods. Stands. Slowly circles Dahlia, nodding all the while.

"Okay, okay," she says, nodding. "Take coat, pliss."

Dahlia looks up at her mother. Her mother nods, and puts out her hand to take the coat. Dahlia removes it. Without it she notices just how cold the room is.

The woman circles Dahlia again, nodding. She pauses.

"Show leg, pliss," she demands, pointing, as though maybe Dahlia doesn't know the word *leg*.

Dahlia looks up at her mother, who nods, smiling.

Dahlia shoves her right foot forward, unsure of how exactly to 'show' her leg.

"Not like this," the woman says, slumping over and dangling a foot off the ground, limply. "Like this!" She transforms into a sleek wave, her leg extended in a ripple, her arm above her in a perfect arch, her neck taut.

Dahlia tries to imitate this. The woman and her mother both get looks on their faces as though live worms were trying to escape from their mouths.

The woman nods, quickly, gets down to Dahlia's level again.

"You come for cless?" she asks, looking into Dahlia's eyes.

Dahlia nods, just once.

"You love the ballet?"

Dahlia looks up at her mother, who nods, smiling. Dahlia nods.

The woman shakes her head. "No. Not yet. Maybe someday, but now... no."

"Oh," Dahlia's mother pipes up. "She does love ballet, she's just a little shy right now. We went to see *Giselle* and Dahlia just loved it, didn't you, dear?"

Dahlia starts to nod but is interrupted by the woman grabbing her by the chin.

"Okay," she says. "Stand again."

Dahlia keeps standing, the same old way she always has.

The woman circles. She pushes Dahlia's head back, her shoulders back, puts a hand on Dahlia's rear and says, "Tuck this in."

Dahlia tries but she doesn't quite know where to tuck it. She sort of tilts her pelvis forward by bending her knees, but the woman shakes her head.

"Tuck," she commands, "like this!" The woman turns and demonstrates. Her bum all but disappears. Dahlia tries again, and again the woman shakes her head.

"Okay," the woman says, walking around Dahlia and holding up her arms, one by one, then both together. Dahlia is beginning to understand how meat feels when it's laid out by the butcher. All cold, behind glass, being stared at and weighed and poked and sliced up.

"She is very old," the woman says.

"She's nine!" Dahlia's mother gasps.

"In Russia, this is very old," the woman shrugs. "I start at four. Maybe five. By nine, girls *en pointe* already. See?" The woman gestures grandly at the identical girls evenly spaced in the huge room. Now they are practicing turning. Turning, and turning, and turning, and... stop.

Now that she looks more closely, Dahlia can see that these girls are all about her own age. She looks up at her mother.

"She really would like to try," Dahlia's mother says to the woman. "You must have a beginner class for... older girls?"

The woman shakes her head. "No," she says with a gloomy finality. She looks up at Dahlia's mother and cocks her head, "But! Maybe I start one, hah? Maybe. What about these glesses?"

"She has to wear them all the time," Dahlia's mother says. "She has very poor vision."

"She is very pale," the woman says. "She is unwell?"

"She's an albino," Dahlia's mother says, sharply. "There's not a thing in the world wrong with her."

The woman nods. "This very good for Snow Queen, wili... many things. Is not problem."

"Well, good," her mother sighs, with a beaming smile. "You hear that, honey? The Snow Queen!"

Dahlia is concentrating on standing. Now that she knows how hard it is, she wonders how hard it is to turn. She looks over at the other girls, who are still practicing. Their heads spin almost in unison, as though they're all joined to clockwork hidden under the floor. Someone is tapping on the floor, in time with the death rattle of the piano, and counting, and counting, and then saying good. All the girls stop, and shake out their legs and walk in small circles like birds looking for food.

"Okay," the woman says, screwing a new cigarette into her fancy holder and lighting it, "we start. We see. The glesses, no."

"But," Dahlia peeps, "I can't see —"

"No glesses!" the woman says, smoke frothing from her nostrils.

"Just try it without them, Dahlia," her mother says, sweetly. "You'll be fine."

Dahlia frowns and pushes her glasses up on her nose.

"I am Ekaterina," the woman barks. "I see you next week, okay?"

"Oh, of course," Dahlia's mother says, still smiling. "Thank you very much, Ekaterina."

The woman nods, then turns and storms gracefully into the huge room. "Okay girls!" she yells. "You know this Dying Swan?" Her arms become waves, no wings. Even with the cigarette holder still between her fingers her arms are not arms. Wings. Her face turns to utter despair, she sails over the floor, beautiful and dying. The girls smile, titter with each other, puff up their feathers. The woman stops and smiles widely at the girls.

"Yes," she says softly. "Is beautiful, yes?"

The girls nod, small smiles sprouting from a couple of faces.

"Okay, but you!" she yells, waving her arms about wildly. "You are all the Dying Chicken! Start again! *Répetez*!"

•

There is no changing room, only a battered bamboo screen in one corner of the huge room. Dahlia and three other girls are trying to get changed behind it without getting in each other's way, their school clothes in piles on the floor. Dahlia removes her brown wooly tights first, peeling them off from under her skirt. Then her orange and brown panties. She tugs on her white beginner tights awkwardly, pulling them up while still wearing her skirt. The lady at the store told her pink comes later.

"You have to *earn* the pink tights, dear," the saleslady had said, earnestly.

Dahlia pulls on her black beginner leotard and tugs it up to her waist. Only then does she remove her brown and white plaid skirt. With the top half of the leotard hanging like flayed skin, she looks up and sees she is in the changing area with only one other girl. She is a full head taller than Dahlia, with wild curly hair the colour of a lion spilling over her shoulders. Her face is as round as the moon, and pocked like it too, with a satisfied expression plastered on it.

"Hi," she says, smiling. "I'm Sera." She says it *ser-ah*.

"Dahlia," says Dahlia, extending a hand. Sera looks at it, cocking her head. Then she starts to laugh, throwing her head back, her hair flying.

"I don't do that," Sera says, then leans in close to Dahlia and whispers, "I'm a free spirit!"

Dahlia nods, slowly. "Ah... ha," she says, distinctly.

Sera smiles, a wide canyon cracking the surface of the moon. She spreads her arms wide. "I *love* the dance," she says, spinning. "Don't you?"

Dahlia shrugs. "I don't know yet. It's my first class."

Sera stops spinning, smiles even wider. "Did that bitch tell you that you were too old?"

Dahlia nods.

"Hold up your arms like she was going to cut them off? Tell you to tuck in your bum?"

Dahlia nods again. Now that Sera is standing still, Dahlia can see she is still wearing her underwear beneath her leotard. Apparently free spirits prefer patchwork-print panties.

Sera shakes her head, her mane flying everywhere. "Bet she told you she doesn't have a class for older girls, too!"

Dahlia nods.

"Don't listen to her," Sera whispers close to Dahlia's ear again. "She's full of it! Old Mother Russia my ass. Dance can't be taught... you must *live* it!" And with that, Sera spins out of the changing area.

Dahlia pauses. She looks at her brown Mary Janes, half hidden beneath her pile of clothes. Then at the brand-new black beginner slippers. She had sewn in the elastics herself, a week in advance. She sighs, takes off her orange turtleneck, and pulls up the remaining half of her leotard. Picking up her slippers, she heads out onto the floor.

•

Dahlia shuts her bedroom door tight. Her mother and father are having drinks before dinner, short things that look like water but smell like varnish and lime. Tru is out again. Dahlia sighs. All, all alone.

Her room is small, but tidy. A wide window opens to the branches of a tree waving friendly green limbs at her. White walls, violet bed cover, violet curtains. Dahlia's mother thinks it's wonderful Dahlia has such pretty eyes. Dahlia's mother thinks everything should match them. So she has a little writing desk, painted white with violet trim, and a tall bookcase, also violet. The bookcase has been refilled since the Muybridge re-enactment of the other day, the books and dolls and tin toys back in their homes.

Dahlia scans her room, looking for someone to talk to. Georgey-Porgey, her old bear with one eye, is a good listener, but knows her too well. There's the skinny ballerina doll her mother surprised her with this morning, but she looks sick. Dahlia doesn't want to bother her. The big doll from her Great Aunt stands on the highest shelf, her broken fingers reaching out. Dahlia looks at her. The mouth seems almost to smile today, the hands seem like they're looking to be held. Dahlia drags a chair over to her shelves. By standing on her tiptoes, she can just reach. She grabs the doll by her ankle, an ankle as big around as Dahlia's wrist, and carefully brings her down.

The doll is as heavy as a real child, and just as unruly. Dahlia manages to get the doll on the bed, stands her up against big violet pillows. The doll stares, her blue eyes ringed with painted lashes, longer and darker than any Dahlia could hope to grow.

"Hello," Dahlia says. "You have very pretty eyelashes. Mine come in all white, see? And I have to wear glasses all the time. You're lucky."

The doll stares. Behind her teeth Dahlia can just make out a small pink sliver of tongue. It reminds her of the words on the doll's back.

"I read on your back that you're a talking doll," Dahlia says, turning the doll over carefully. "Is it true? Do you talk? What can you say?"

The doll says nothing. Dahlia unbuttons the back of the doll's old-fashioned chocolate-brown dress and takes it·off, leaving the doll to stand in her shoes. Turns the doll around, so they are face-to-face. The doll's whole torso is metal, pressed into a mannish musculature, reminding Dahlia of armour she's seen in books about Ancient Rome. The doll's arms and legs are made of pale wood, her hands and joints of a stiff cracked plastic. Her head is fine porcelain, her heavy eyebrows painted on in a look of slight disdain. Below the doll's head is a circular pattern like the mouthpiece on a telephone.

Dahlia turns the doll over again. Here there is a little door, and a square hole. Dahlia fiddles with the door until it opens. There's a jangle of small machinery in there, circles on circles, metallic intestines winding inside.

"Hm," Dahlia says, peering through her glasses. "Looks like you're missing something. There's nothing to wind you with."

Dahlia leaves the doll face down on the bed while she rummages in the drawer of her little violet writing desk. Pens, pencils, pencil crayons, rulers, notebooks. Keys to a diary she lost, to a little metal monkey who clapped two tin plates together before he got broken, to a bluebird who pecked in a circle before Dahlia took him apart. She tries all of these keys in the hole in the doll's back. None of them fit.

"You're a tough nut to crack…" she pauses. Turns the doll over and looks at her again. "You know something? I can't believe it! I've never given you a name. You must think I'm awful. I mean, I told my mom I'd named you Dolly, but that was fake. Who names a doll Dolly? It's like calling a cat Cat. I made it up so my mom would stop asking. I was really afraid of you when we first met. You probably remember, huh?"

The doll stares.

Dahlia stares back. "I'm a little bit afraid of you now, if you want to know."

The doll stares, her little smile looking somehow mean again. Dahlia can't blame her for looking mean. No name, for four years. She shakes her head and looks closely at the doll.

If she didn't have that little smile, the doll would look just like someone Dahlia's seen before. A picture, somewhere. A picture she sees every day.

"Patience!" Dahlia says, a bit too loud, almost a yell. "That's who you look like! My Great Aunt Patience, when she was young. I bet that's why you were given to her, right? Because you looked the same?"

The doll stares at Dahlia. Dahlia smiles. "Well, that's your new name. Patience. I hope you like it."

Patience stares. Dahlia starts to re-dress her, pulling the old silk carefully over Patience's cracked hands.

"I guess you're never going to talk," Dahlia says. "At least not until I can find a key for your back. But that's okay. Nobody else here talks. Just me."

Dahlia buttons up the back of Patience's dress, turns her around. "I just came back from ballet class. My mom's making me go. I think she thinks I'm weird. And that I spend too much time alone. You don't think that, do you?"

Patience remains silent on this.

"It's okay, I guess." Dahlia props Patience up against her pillows again, sits curled so they're almost face-to-face. "My teacher's a bit of a kook. It's like she's onstage all the time. It must get tiring, don't you think?"

Patience reserves judgment.

"Well, I think it would," Dahlia says. "Who wants to act a part all your life long? How dull. But she's alright. She yells a lot, though. I'm in the class for older girls, even though I'm only nine. I don't think that's old. Do you?"

Patience refrains from comment.

"There's a nice girl in my ballet class," Dahlia says, lying on the bed, her head facing away from Patience. "Her name's Ser-ah! That's how she says it, like she's singing or something. She's kind of a flake, but at least she doesn't call me what the other girls do. You want to know what they call me?"

Patience remains silent.

"They call me 'The Ghost'!" Dahlia shakes her head. "Like I'm the walking dead or something. I explained about how I'm an albino and everything but they all just looked at me like I was speaking Chinese and then giggled. Girls are really stupid sometimes, you know?"

Patience keeps mum on the subject.

"I mean," Dahlia rolls over, a little ungracefully. "Do I look dead to you?"

Dahlia knocks against Patience as she sits up, too quickly to recover, too quickly to catch the falling doll. There is a thunk as Patience hits the floor.

"Oh no," Dahlia breathes, leaning over the edge of the bed. Patience stares up at her from the floor. Patience groans, a whirring wheeze from under her chin. Dahlia reaches for her, holding her breath. The wheeze grows to a growl. Dahlia heaves Patience up off the floor, holds her tight in the crook of her arm. "I'm so sorry, Patience. What can I do? If you're broken, I'll fix you, I swear I will. What do I do?"

"If I... should dieeee," Patience says, a lumbering grumble from below her face.

"You're not going to die!" Dahlia screeches, holding Patience close to her chest. "I've been terrible to you! I never named you and I left you up there on that shelf all by yourself. And now I've killed you!"

"Beeeefore," Patience grumbles, the sound rumbling in Dahlia's own chest. "I... I... I...."

"Patience," Dahlia says, holding her closer. "Come on. You just fell, a little fall, you're tougher than that, right?"

"I should dieeeee," Patience continues, her voice slowing, grinding, coming unwound, "beeeeforrrre."

The wheeze from deep within Patience slows to stillness. Dahlia holds her out, looks at her face. Same shiny blue eyes, same pretty eyelashes. Deep red hair in ringlets. Teeth tiny behind grapefruit lips. Dahlia blinks. She settles Patience against the violet pillows, pushes her broken fingers down, so she isn't reaching. Edges away, slowly, carefully, and steps from the bed. The slightest movement. Patience slides, just a little, tilts to one side.

"I... wake," says Patience, lipless words growling loud from under her chin. The doll stares. Dahlia turns and runs, slamming the door behind her.

BILLY

1964

It's Sunday so Aunt Beatrix and Marly are gone by six. He has the house to himself all day. What better time to leave?

Billy pulls on his boots, throws on a worn red mac and heads out the back door. The last snow is melting from the roofs around the farm, from the barn and the chicken coop and the farmhouse, ice water dripping down all over, regular as heartbeats. Nothing grows yet but the air smells charged, the smell of things just starting to push themselves back up from underground. Billy wrestles his bike out from its corner of the garage, and hops on. He's grown since last fall, his legs gone gangly, but he shrugs and pedals as fast as he can, away down the road, his knees bumping his elbows all the way to town.

Between the Coin-O-Mat and the second hand bookstore the wide front window shimmers. So shiny it throws back the perfect reflection of cars passing, people passing, the reflection of him in his mac and over-alls, his too-big boots. His hair is hippy-long, floating in mud-coloured curls from under his cap. He waits, leaning on the handlebars of his bike. He waits. The sun moves just enough, and he can barely see, popping through his reflection like magic or mayhem, silk and beads, embroidery and pearls, gold-coloured clasps and shimmy skirts. They float in the window, barely scraping through from another dimension.

He turns. Leans his bike against the window of the Coin-O-Mat. He breathes, slow, and walks natural as anything, right through the door.

Ting-ting.

Attic smell and two ladies laughing, one behind the counter. A few ladies poking through the racks, sifting the bins. The lady behind the counter smiles and leans forward. Her hair is a smooth chestnut, curled on her head solid as a snail shell.

"Hey there, honey," she says with lips as red as his bike, her teeth sharp and shiny and white. "You looking for your mom?"

His throat throbs where his heart has jumped into it. He shakes his head, too fast. "No!"

The snail lady backs up, putting her hands up, stick-em-up style. "Okay, settle down, cowboy. Can I help you with anything?"

Billy shakes his head again. He'd practiced in the bathroom, slick as anything. He tries to remember what lie he'd made up. "I... um. I think I'm looking for a present for my sister. I mean, a birthday present. For my sister. I think."

"You think?" the snail lady raises one eyebrow.

"No, I mean, I do," Billy nods again, again too fast. "I do. I need a birthday present for my sister. Yeah."

"Okay, cowboy. But most of what I've got here's for old ladies, like me and Baba Yaga here." The snail lady's friend whaps her playfully on the shoulder and they both laugh down at Billy. The snail lady picks up a silver case from the counter, opens it and takes out a filterless cigarette, using it to point across the road. "Maybe you'd have better luck across the way, at the department store. Their Young Misses department has all the latest. Minis, even. I bet your sister likes minis, huh?"

Billy shrugs, tries to look nonchalant. "She likes lots of stuff. Our mom's dead and my sister likes to wear her old clothes. So she likes stuff like this." He hadn't practised this part of the lie, which isn't completely a lie, but it comes out before he can stop it.

The snail lady freezes with a silver lighter halfway to the end of her cigarette. Her red mouth turns down like a sad clown's. "Oh, honey, I'm so sorry. No wonder you got so upset when I asked you if you were looking for your mom. Oh. Oh, I'm so sorry. Here, have a cookie."

She smiles again and holds out a pink and white china plate, sugar cookies laid on it like scales. They sparkle with coloured sugar, green, blue, and pink. Billy takes a pink one.

"Thanks," he says, his heart sliding down out of his throat.

"Now you just look around as long as you like," the snail lady smiles, holding out her right hand. "And if you need any help, just ask me. I'm Darlene."

"Billy," Billy says, transferring his cookie to his left hand so he can properly shake.

"Pleasure to meet you," Darlene says, red mouth smiling so wide her lips go flat, a mouth made by marker. "Such a nice brother."

Billy bites his lip and heads to the back of the store.

"You're a big fat liar," a voice seeps out from the ground, from below the hanging hemlines of a hundred shiny dresses.

Billy looks around but all he sees is a nice mom, smiling into a full-length mirror over the scooped neckline of a lime-green cocktail dress she's holding in front of her clothes. She rolls her eyes, replaces the dress on the rack and walks away to another part of the store.

Billy resumes his inspection of every item on the circular rack. It bristles with wool, gold thread, sequins and silk, a fabulous forest to get lost in. He doesn't dare do what the nice mom did, and just hold something against himself, like that, in front of the mirror, in front of everyone. In front of himself.

He looks at every dress. Each one. Ignores the fact of the price tag. Just looking. A shimmy dress shiny with jet beads holds him for a long moment. He strokes it, the beads alive against his fingers.

"You don't even have a sister," comes the voice again, accusing him from some place he can't see.

Billy looks around again. There is no one anywhere near him. Darlene catches his eye, smiles brightly, and holds out the plate full of cookies, a question in her shoulders. Billy smiles and shakes his head. His cookie is safe in his pocket. He doesn't want to get any crumbs on anything.

"Your mom *is* dead, but that's about the only true thing you said since you walked in here," the voice says brightly. It seems to be coming from somewhere very near him, and from somewhere in the floor. He parts some of the dresses, peers through them. There, in the centre of the circular rack, surrounded by a protective circle of silk and wool, sits a round blonde girl dressed head-to-toe in black. She smiles at him, her pink cheeks plump around the pinkness of themselves. She waves.

"Caught me!" she says, and giggles.

"What're you doing in there?" Billy asks, leaning down a bit and whispering so Darlene doesn't notice him talking to the clothes.

The girl shrugs and rolls her eyes dramatically. "I'm *hiding*. What does it look like? Hey, your eyes are weird."

"Why're you hiding?" Billy squats down a little more, ignoring the comment about his eyes. The girl smells like strawberries. Or, really, like fake strawberries.

"Cuz my mother doesn't understand why I *insist* on wearing only black. That's what she says. Insist. As though I'm fighting with my clothes every morning or something. She says I need to be more *feminine*. More lady-like, whatever that means."

"Oh," is all he says.

"Is she out there?" the girl asks, sort of craning her head forward but not really making a real effort to check it out herself.

Billy shrugs. "I dunno. What does she looks like?" He can see the nice mom from before, and Darlene and her friend, and a small, dark-skinned lady, beautiful even in the hot pink polyester dress she's trying on. None of the ladies look a thing like this cheery gnome dressed all in black.

The girl frowns. "Nevermind," she says, a hard edge coming into her voice. "Just get in here. She's gonna see you and then *bang*! My cover's blown."

"Why should I get in there?" Billy asks. "I'm not hiding from anyone."

"Maybe not," the girl says, smiling so hard her shoulders lift up. "Not right now, anyway. Betcha wouldn't be so mellow if your aunt was in here, though."

"What do you care about my aunt?" Billy asks, crouching down into a full squat. His legs are getting sore from half-standing.

"Nothing," the girl shrugs. "Just think she'd be interested, is all. She's at church and you're here shopping for your imaginary sister. It's a bit funny, don't you think?" She pauses and regards him for a second. "You know," the girl says, looking pretty serious despite her flushed cheeks and cozy pinkness, "you don't look sick."

"I'm not," Billy says, a little loud.

"Really?" the girl stares at him, her mouth scrunching up to one side, considering. "Then how come you were always in the hospital?"

"I wasn't," Billy says again, even louder. "You must be thinking of someone else."

"Nope," the girl says, shaking her head from side to side so hard her long blonde braids swing like two tails. "It's you. Billy Brennan, right?"

Billy nods, slowly, frowning.

"My mom saw you there all the time." The girl pauses, then frowns, looking up. "At the hospital in the city. It was a long time ago, but my mom still remembers you. You must've had something awful. She always calls you a brave little boy."

"What?" Billy asks, genuinely confused. Then he remembers something, something he's supposed to remember. "I *was* in an accident when I was little. Before I came here."

"Maybe that's it," the girl says, craning her head out a little, then ducking it back in, quick. "Would you just get in here?" the girl asks, her hands flying out, palms up, exasperated. "My mom is for sure gonna catch me any second."

Billy looks around the store. From here he can't see much, but he doesn't see any legs coming toward them. "How do you know all this stuff about me?" he asks.

"Get in here and I'll tell you," the girl says, smiling her appley smile.

They stare at each other. Somewhere ladies laugh. The door goes *ting-ting*.

"Fine," Billy says, crawling inside her circle, "but it better be good."

•

93

Sunday dinner passes quietly, Billy staring at his plate as if his eyes could burn the food away.

"You feelin' okay, Billy?" Marly's voice asks from somewhere far far away, "You haven't touched your plate."

"I'm fine," Billy answers, talking to the squooshy peas, the slices of roast, the congealing gravy. "May I be excused?"

"Not 'til you eat something," Marly's voice says, a stern note in it like when he's talking to a sheep that's chewed through the pen. "Your aunt spent a long time on that dinner there."

"Marly, he doesn't look well," Aunt Beatrix's voice says. "Go on up to bed, Billy. I'll wrap that up for you. You can have it later, if you're hungry."

"Okay," Billy says to the peas, which are starting to go a bit blurry. He pauses and gulps, breathes out. He pushes his chair back from the table, and says very quietly, "Thank you, Aunt Beatrix."

Billy rises from the table, and without looking around him, almost runs up to his room. On his way, he passes the credenza. He stops in front of the picture of his littler self, holding Aunt Beatrix's hand and smiling, his head in the shadows. He looks at every other picture on the cluttered surface. Not a single one of him before he came here. Like he didn't exist. Like he popped out of a pod, human age three.

He runs to his room and quietly closes the door.

•

The following Sunday, Billy leans his bike up against the wall of the *Other* cinema. That's what Aunt Beatrix calls it. There's the one they go to, every month or so, and then there's the *Other* one. The *Other* cinema sometimes plays movies even when there's nothing spelled out on the marquee. Billy's not sure what that means, but it makes Aunt Beatrix's nose crinkle.

Billy walks inside. Since it's nine in the morning, the place is empty. Billy looks around. The walls are a creepy pink, the colour of the hard fake skin of a baby doll. There are starchy looking stains on the grey carpet in the lobby, and the candy at the concession stand is dusty. The popcorn machine is streaked with grease, but empty, as if whatever was inside it jumped out and made a run for it.

"Hello," a friendly, light voice says. "Beelly, yes?"

The beautiful, small lady from the dress shop walks toward him through the big double doors that lead to the theatre. She carries a big, flat broom, her hair all tied up in a pink kerchief.

Billy nods.

"Mona ees upstairs," the beautiful lady says, leaning the broom against the wall. "I am her mother, Béatriz. I know your aunt, we have almost the same name. Come with me."

Billy follows behind the little lady. At the top of the stairs they pass a few doors, all closed, then turn a corner. All the walls are pink, the same fake flesh pink as the lobby, and the doors are a hotter shade, like scrapes or burns on the sides of the walls. At the end of a long hallway the lovely lady stops.

"Heeere we are!" she sings, holding out her pretty little hand. "Very nice to meet you, Beelly."

Billy shakes her hand, only then noticing that she is only a couple of inches taller than him. She leaves, off down the hall. Billy stares at the door. He knocks. Nothing happens. He waits, then knocks again.

"Just a sec," Mona's voice calls. "I'm gluing!"

Billy waits. Then he waits some more. He's just raising his hand to knock again, when there's a metallic clanking from behind the door. A lock is unlocked, and then another one, their tumblers rolling in quick succession. Finally, the door is flung open.

There is Mona, all in black, her long blonde hair behind her in one long, braided tail. She gives Billy a huge, rosy grin, then wraps him up in her arms, squeezing until he can barely breathe.

"Hi!" she says, letting him go. Billy gulps in air.

"Hi," he says, weakly.

"C'mon in!" Mona walks into her room, waving him in after her. "I usually ask for a password, but this is your first time."

"You lock your door?" Billy asks, entering her room, "*and* ask for a password? How come?"

"*You* try living here, then tell me if you want a password," Mona says darkly. She regards him for a second, then says, "Actually, you're prettier than me. You'd need a couple more locks."

"Oh," Billy says, taking a look around him. Mona's room is pure stuff, so much stuff Billy can't take it all in at once. The walls are somewhere behind all the stuff, pox-pink spots showing through in a few places not covered by books and objects. The ceiling is pink, too, hovering over them like a great swath of skin. Plank-and-cinderblock shelves teeter from floor to ceiling along two walls, books stacked in chunks along them, separated from each other by little displays Aunt Beatrix would call *clutter*. Wheels of all sorts and sizes, clocks and watches, wrappers and ads and posters, skulls from small animals, keys, mate-less shoes, even the odd pair of soiled underpants. Behind some of the displays, obituaries are taped to the pink walls. Above him dangle models of planes, rockets, animals, and some shapes Billy sort of recognizes, geometrical shapes that look like they were made out of tinfoil. On a table in the middle of the room is another model, under construction. It seems to be a model of rocks. Mona's small pink bed is nearly hidden in the corner of her room, under a huge pile of wonderful colours shot through with black, dark as holes. Billy looks more closely at this. It's a big pile of dresses, beautiful dresses. He guesses the black holes are Mona's regular clothes.

"Well?" Mona says, spreading her hands and smiling.

Billy nods. "It's something else."

"You bet," she waves him over to the model of rocks. "C'mere, tell me what you think."

What he'd thought before was a model of rocks, is, in fact, a model of rocks. "Uh, real nice," he says, raising his eyebrows.

"I bet you don't even know what it is," Mona says, her hands on her hips.

Billy nods. "Sure I do. It's rocks."

Mona laughs, her cheeks going red. "No, silly! It's a model of the Burgess Shale. It's actually a model of the discovery — see, here's

Walcott, and his daughter, Helen. And here's his wife, Helena, and his son, Sidney. Did you know Sidney found the first creature in the Shale? And that Walcott named it after him?" She points to a group of tiny people, laid side by side next to the unfinished model.

Billy shakes his head, "No. No, I didn't."

"Well, now you do!" Mona looks around the room, runs over and grabs a book from a pile, "Here! I'll show you. There's some great pictures in here!"

"That's okay, Mona," Billy tries a smile. "Thanks, though."

"Oh," Mona closes the book. "Okay."

"Maybe some other time," Billy says, quickly.

"Sure," Mona says, raising an eyebrow. She turns and starts putting the book back on the shelf.

"It's just, it's the weekend," Billy says. "Books and me... we don't get along very well. I leave them alone, they leave me alone. An understanding, you know? I mean, I can read and everything...."

"I was going to show you pictures, Billy," Mona says, rolling her eyes. "You can't look at pictures?"

"Hey, Mona," he says, "about your mom..."

Mona lets out a big sigh. "What about her?"

"Well," Billy starts slow, not wanting to ask what he's dying to ask, "you guys don't really look that much alike."

Mona rolls her eyes. "No kidding. She's my stepmother. I guess she kind of... inherited me."

"Oh," Billy says. "Well, I was kind of inherited too, then, I guess."

"Yeah," Mona says. "She adopted me and everything. You?"

"I don't know," Billy says. "I don't think so. My aunt and uncle are my godparents, though."

Mona frowns. "But you're mom's dead, right?"

Billy nods.

"So you must be adopted," Mona says. "Unless...."

"Unless what?"

"Nothing," Mona stares off to a spot on the wall, her face going dreamy. "Nothing. So, hey! I talked to my mom."

"Oh, yeah?" Billy tries to sound calm, though his throat is constricting. He swallows. Tighter than an anthill's mouth. "She remember anything?"

"Yeah. She says you were born at the hospital in the city, the one where she worked, and whatever happened to you happened when you were born."

"But, I told you already," Billy says, his words crawling out small as live ants, the red kind with wings and hot pincers, biting him on the way. "I was in an accident. When my mom died."

Mona shakes her head and looks doleful, her mouth a flat line between her two appley cheeks. "I don't think so. My mom's sure it's you. She was a candystriper, you know, one of those girls that go from room to room with books and candy and stuff? And she made friends with your mom —"

"She knew my mom?" Billy interrupts. He tries to think of his mother's face but it swims in shade somewhere in him, a nothing. Nothing but a lovely smile coming warm at him from far above. "What was she like?"

"Beautiful and kind," says Mona, reaching behind her for a glass half-full of pink liquid. "Lemonade?"

"No, thanks," Billy says, though his throat has constricted even more tightly. Mona empties the glass. Billy licks his lips.

"Anyway," Mona continues, "your aunt was always visiting, and even though she was nice and everything, she and your mom used to fight a lot. My mom's not sure what it was about, but they yelled about God a lot."

"God?"

"Yeah," Mona shrugs. "Something about God's will. You know your aunt better than I do."

"I guess." Billy isn't sure he knows anyone anymore. He stares at the model of rocks, at the tiny people laid out side-by-side, waiting for their paint to dry before being placed in the hole for all time. Mona reaches out and puts her hand on his, warm as a fresh buttermilk biscuit. She smiles, her pinkness radiating out, reaching even him.

"Hey, Billy? How about we do something fun?"

The lie of his sister has become a fiction. A doll for the two of them to dress up.

"Here!" Mona throws another dress at him from the pile on her bedroom floor. "She's going to *love* this one! Try it on!"

Billy picks it up. A slinky black thing hangs in spiderwebs from between his fingers, a circle of fur dangling off of it, a soft, dark hole in the centre.

"How the heck am I supposed to put this on?"

Mona rolls her eyes and walks over to him, picking her way delicately past the piles of discards and keepers.

"You are absolutely hopeless!" she says from behind him. The zipper of the dress he's wearing is unzipped, slowly. He shrugs it off, a lipstick red tube that, according to Mona, did nothing for his hips. Mona forms the new dress into a puddle and shoves him into place. She pulls it up, placing his arms through holes where they should go, keeping his thumbs and fingers away from holes where they shouldn't, finally fastening the fur about his throat. Mona steps back, and lets loose a big toasty smile.

"Now *that*," she beams, "that's a good one."

Billy walks carefully around the piles to where he can just see himself in Mona's cluttered spotty mirror. And there he is, mink at his throat, a glamour of thread spun about him. A narrow band runs his full length, the black spiderwebby things, now that they're hung properly, looped in graceful curves about his sides and arms. Even his Y-front peeking through can't ruin it. He's lovely. He's something. He almost can't look but then once he's started, he almost can't stop.

Billy manages a nod. "I think she'll like it," he whispers.

APRIL-MAY, 1972

HICKLIN

"We should send her home Hicklin," Dolly says with her eyes closed as Beau applies her extra-long luxurious lashes. "She's just a baby."

Hicklin looks up from his sketchbook, raises his eyebrows. "Geez, Dolly. You just got here and you're already deciding how to run the place?"

Dolly speaks softly, barely moving her lips, while Beau props his hand on her cheek with his fingertips, delicately placing an eyelash on her left eye. "Beau asked me to come stay with him," she says. "And I have to say I'm looking forward to sleeping in a bed again. In any case Ginger's put up with me being on her couch for far too long. But if you don't want me here please. Just say so."

"I was kidding, Dolly," Hicklin says, flipping back in his book a couple of pages, making a note there. "Of course you can stay."

"Well thank you very much," Dolly says. She pauses while Beau shakes his head, removes the eyelash, and wipes away the remaining glue. Then she opens her eyes. "But I do think she should leave. She's a child."

Hicklin looks up from what he's doing. Dolly sits wigless on a small stool in front of a large, square mirror propped up on Hicklin's desk. She is wrapped in a pink kimono. She'd brought over a violet valise, dropped it in Beau's room, and enlisted Beau and Hicklin to move her plants. They'd shrugged and nodded. How many plants can a girl really have? They'd made about a thousand trips to and from Ginger's place, the few short blocks seeming longer with each go-round. Armfuls of coffee cans sprouting weeds, cracked terracotta planters holding things with spiky flowers, plastic baby baths coated with mossy growths. Dolly had arranged it all on Hicklin's L-shaped balcony, spreading out her garden just so. She hadn't even batted an eyelash at Selene, the pigeon who came with the place, cooing and strutting about the balcony. She had glanced at Endymion, the cat who found Hicklin, curled in a grey knot on the couch, and had placed a broken tea pot holding a tall poppy on the window sill above him.

Hicklin rolls his eyes and leans back on his pile of scrounged pillows. "She's not that much younger than you, Dolly. Or have you forgotten I know how old you are?"

"Will you stay still?" Beau scolds Dolly. "We've only got the one pair left. You want them stuck to your cheeks?"

Dolly sits still and quiet. Beau deftly applies her right eyelash, pats down the edges, and gingerly wipes away the excess glue.

"Okay, that's one," Beau says, nodding. He starts trimming the other eyelash. Dolly turns to face Hicklin.

"I know you know how old I am but that doesn't matter," Dolly says evenly in her raspy voice. "Luce is a baby."

"Yeah, she's a kid," Hicklin says while sketching something in the book on his lap. Then he looks up into Dolly's scary eyes. "But, we're all kids. And anyway, have you been listening to her? She's been around the block more than you, me, and Beau all put together!"

"Maybe so," Dolly says darkly, turning back to Beau and closing her eyes again. "But she's going to be trouble. You should send her back to wherever she came from. Now."

Hicklin and Beau look at each other. Hicklin makes a small circle near his temple with his right index finger. Beau giggles. Dolly sits serene and eyeless, awaiting her other eyelash. Hicklin goes back to his notebook, Beau back to Dolly's eyelashes.

"Thought I heard you all beating your gums," Luce says, leaning on the doorframe, lazily unwrapping a hunk of Bazooka Joe. "Anything interesting?"

Hicklin looks up. Luce pops the gum in her mouth, and smiles at him from under her hair, a dark feathered mop hanging over her eyes, just brushing her shoulders. A pair of pink heart-shaped sunglasses perch over her bangs, a glint of gold just visible at each earlobe. Luce's skin is toast brown under a white T-shirt Hicklin'd lent to her, the bottom hem pulled up through the neck to make a couple little cups for her tiny breasts. Her legs stretch long and brown below cut-off jeans about the size of underpants. Her feet are bare, her toes encased in rings. He's given her the small room next to his, but she seems to prefer his room to any other. Last night he had to carry her, squealing, from his bed, and dump her on her own.

"No," he says, flushing. "Just talking."

"Hicklin here was just telling us a story," Beau says, wiping the last bit of glue from Dolly's eye. "Weren't you, Hicklin?"

"Oh, yeah," Hicklin says, closing his notebook. "Sure I was. I was telling them about..."

"The teeth," Beau prompts, holding up a mirror for Dolly. She flutters her eyelashes slowly, pushes at the lashes. Then nods. Beau puts the mirror down. Luce picks it up, holds it in front of her, staring. Not really at it. More through it. She takes it from her face, but holds onto it.

"Right," Hicklin says. "The teeth. What was I saying, again, Beau?"

"You were telling us where they came from," Beau says, re-capping the eyelash glue.

"They came from my head," Hicklin says, sternly.

"This some sort of code?" Luce asks, sliding into the room, to a spot on Hicklin's bed, almost touching him. She smiles, chewing, her eyes hidden under her dangling bangs. She holds up the mirror, uses it to talk to Hicklin, behind her. "You guys planning a job?"

Hicklin frowns. "No," he says, not sure what she's talking about. "No, we're talking about teeth. My dad sent me some stuff from when I was a kid. Most of it I don't even remember, but there were these teeth in there, that I thought had been...."

There is a pause here. Luce cracks her gum, loudly. Hicklin licks his lips and stares out the window. One of the hippywitches across the way catches his eye, and makes a howling O of his mouth, inside his beard, lifting his head like a wolf. Hicklin looks away.

"See, there you go again," Beau says, standing. "Seems this is a story Hicklin doesn't want to tell us after all. C'mon, Doll, we should get you in costume."

Dolly nods, and rises. "See you Hicklin," she says, pausing to examine Luce. "Those are my jeans Luce. Or they were. I hope you enjoy them." With that, she exits the room, her back unnaturally straight, her head held high.

Luce rolls on her back, holds the mirror up over her face. Blows a bubble until it bursts. Picks the gum off her face, pops it back in her mouth. "She hates me," Luce states, chewing loudly, looking up through the looking glass.

"No she doesn't," Hicklin says. "She just comes across that way. Kind of... cold."

"Nah," Luce says, cracking her gum, putting the mirror down on the floor. "She hates me. I don't care. It's just a fact."

"She's just..." Hicklin starts.

Luce shakes her head. "It's just a fact." She pulls the gum from her mouth in a long, thin strand, wrapping it around her finger. Rolls onto her side, hand under her cheek, pin-up style. Puts the gum back in her mouth, sucking it right off her finger. Smiles up at Hicklin. "So what's the skinny with these mysterious teeth?"

"Oh, it's nothing," Hicklin says, edging away across the bed, slowly. "I just thought I'd lost them, that's all."

"Correct me if I'm wrong, but I'm thinking they were your baby teeth?" Luce looks up at him, her eyes hidden behind her bangs. Hicklin nods. "So you lost them. That's what happens."

"No," Hicklin says, shaking his head. "I mean, I'd lost them, yeah. But then... I used to go down in this pit near my house, and write little stories about my teeth... It sounds really stupid."

"Go on, Daddy," Luce says, turning around on the bed so she can face him. She sits up, leans her legs out, her toes almost touching him. "I won't tell."

"Don't call me that," Hicklin says, a blush crawling up his neck, a live thing with its own brain.

Luce shrugs, chews, lies down on her back and puts her hands on the floor. Sits back up. Smiles again. "Okay, Daddy. Whatever you want."

"What'd I just say, Luce?" Luce smiles and makes a key-in-lock motion over her lips.

"I..." Hicklin says slowly, "I thought the teeth had gotten buried, with everything else. I guess my dad found them, cleared out the pipe before the hole was filled in. I thought I'd forgotten them there, the time I found...."

Luce stares at him, her mouth open, her chewing stopped, her eyes round. There is a pause. Hicklin bites his lip.

Luce shakes him by the upper arms. "What? Found what? Spit it out, already!"

Hicklin takes a big breath. Shakes his head. "I can't."

Luce stops shaking him but leaves her hands where they are. "Can't? Don't you mean *won't*?"

"I *can't* talk about it," Hicklin says. "I'm sorry. I've never talked about it. I... wouldn't even know where to start."

"How about, 'Once upon a time'?" Luce suggests, pulling the sunglasses down over her eyes. "Works for everybody else."

Hicklin sighs. Gets up off his bed. Walks toward the door of his room, and out of it, closing it squarely behind him.

He walks over to the wall near Endymion's corner. Grabs his coat. Pats the sleeping cat sparely on the head. Turns. Luce stares at him from behind two dark hearts.

"Daddy," she says, leaning against the wall, long legs propping her up. "I need to cool it. Sometimes I flap off, the old brain box doesn't work."

"Don't call me that," he says, buttoning his jacket wrong and having to start again. "I mean it."

"Okay, *Daddy*," Luce says, picking up her rat bag. "I'll make you a deal. I don't call you Daddy, and you. You smoke a joint with me. You've really gotta chin, even if it's balderdash."

He's not sure about most of what she's just said, but he understands the word 'joint'. He nods. They walk out together, though he leaves space for another body between them.

Hicklin and Luce arrive a bit late, giggling from the joint they've just shared. The bar is packed, people staggering into each other, the air blue and heavy, a smoky low cloud thunderheading above. The Stooges are playing on the turntable, someone screaming about wanting to be a dog. Hicklin leads the way through the crowd to a tiny space at the bar. Ginger waves at him and yells, "The usual?"

Hicklin nods, but is pushed aside by Luce, who gestures Ginger close to her, whispers something in her ear. Hicklin frowns. Luce shrugs and turns away. Ginger returns, placing a tumbler of scotch before Hicklin, something milky and sweet-looking before Luce.

"That'll be —" Gin starts, but is cut off by a look from Luce. More whispering, head-to-head. A quick exchange of bills, while Hicklin discreetly looks away.

"It's not the best, but it's the best they've got," Luce says, lifting her glass. "To thank you for letting me stay with you."

"Oh," Hicklin nods, clinking his glass against hers. "Thanks. But really, you don't have to do this — I mean, it's not much of a place."

"Daddy," Luce says, "it's a helluva lot better than any place I ever stayed in."

"Luce," Hicklin shakes his head, "don't call me that. Please."

"Sorry, Daddy," Luce grins. "I forgot."

Hicklin frowns but doesn't say anything. He looks over to where Dolly and Beau are setting up the 'stage'. Mostly it involves moving a couple of tables aside. Dolly is wearing her glasses, a demure brown wig in a sort of school-teacher-from-last-century style, and a too-large grey terry bathrobe. He waves, but she doesn't see him.

"C'mon," he says to Luce, bending down so he can talk in her ear. "Let's go say hi."

"Oh, scrumptious," Luce says, her eyes to the ceiling. "Do let's." She takes a big sip of her drink. Hicklin turns and pushes his way through the crowd.

"Hey, Dolly," is all he can get out before Dolly scurries away from him, toward the bathroom.

"Nervous bladder, apparently," Beau smiles. He's wearing a yellow work smock, unbuttoned to the waist, leaving his chest bare. Sparkly pink pasties are affixed to his flat nipples.

"Oh, yeah," Hicklin nods. "How's it going?"

"We're missing a wili," Beau says, pronouncing it with a hard 'w' and giggling. "You know anyone?"

"Did I just hear that right?" Luce asks, slithering out from behind Hicklin. "You're missing a willy?"

"Funny," Beau says, turning and stalking away to the bar.

"What'd I say?" Luce asks Hicklin.

"Search me," Hicklin says. "I thought it was his dumb joke."

Dolly returns from the bathroom, embraces Hicklin, ignores Luce. "Hicklin," Dolly says, her voice a bit more scrapey than usual, "we're missing a wili." She says it with a 'v' sound, and no giggle.

"I heard," Hicklin says.

"What's that?" Luce asks, finishing off her drink.

Dolly stares at her. "I'm sure you wouldn't care."

"Try me," Luce says, putting her glass down on a nearby table.

"They're dead ladies," Dolly says, leaning in close to Luce, "who dance men to their deaths."

"Sounds like fun," Luce says.

"You have to dance," Dolly says.

"I'm a regular Ginger Rogers," Luce says, staring up at Dolly. Dolly doesn't blink. Luce doesn't either.

"Fine," Dolly says, "but you need a costume fast." With that, Dolly heads toward the bathroom again.

"See, Hicklin," Luce says, heading back to the bar. "I told you she hates me."

DOLLY

Her nervous peeing dealt with for another four minutes, Dolly packs her talc away in her purse, along with the fat brush. She readjusts her plain brown wig, and ties her old housecoat about her tight. Pushes open the bathroom door. Stands still, just outside the reach of the crowd. A great mass of bodies shifts together in the almost dark, lit here and there by raspberry spots. Dark heads bob gently, all their tops together like the skittery skin of a midnight lake, a sheath of smoke pouring through them, from their insides out. There's a ripple in the crowd, a shape creating a wake behind it. A head like dark wings, a crow-call crackling from it.

Luce is slicing the crowd apart, her hair ratted out in crazy shapes, like razors, sliding sharp as her smile. Behind her, Hicklin's sandy head. Luce is dancing shirtless through the crowd, shrieking as she goes. Hicklin catches her by the waist of her short shorts, pulls her close. Takes his scarf from about his neck, ties it over her tits without looking. Luce's mouth smiles wide, her arms up, she spins in Hicklin's arms and he holds her. Luce leans to whisper in Hicklin's ear, a whisper Dolly can't read. Her lips red shining in the skin of bobbing black. And Hicklin holds her. And Hicklin smiles.

"Luce," Dolly says, Patience speaking through her, her voice grating, "please come here. I have to show you the steps."

Luce twirls her way over. "Thought I'd let the girls run free, but Daddy's got other plans," she says, pointing at the scarf wound tight about her. "This suit you?"

Dolly nods. "It's fine. But you need a skirt."

"All set, I'm borrowing one from the Daisy. Hey," Luce's mouth says, lips red as though she's just finished bleeding a body dry, "what do you call this show, anyhow?"

"*Giselle*," Dolly says, staring down at Luce. A grin creeps across Luce's mouth, a back-row-of-the-class snicker escapes.

"Jizz-elle?!" Luce hoots.

"Yes. That's what it's called," Dolly nods, "*Giselle*."

Luce shakes her head, laughing, "No, no! *Jizz*-elle! Get it? Jizz?"

Dolly regards Luce coldly. "I see," Dolly intones, unblinking. "Male effluvia. A bit literal don't you think."

"Oh, fine, *Mother*." Luce points her head to the ceiling, her eyes perhaps rolling behind her hair. "Show me your pretty steps. You got any munitions?"

Dolly stares at her. Hicklin shrugs, bends in to tighten the knot behind Luce's back. "I'm sure I don't know what you're talking about."

"Sure you do," Luce grins. "Powder, talc. Munitions. You know all about it. Leastways you look like you do."

Dolly nods, turns neatly. Luce can follow behind her if she wants. Anyway, she needs to pee again.

•

In the alley behind the bar they dance, floating over slick, shiny puddles and muddied mattresses, their four feet never soiled. Dolly stops. Turns.

"Again," Dolly says, her hands on her hips, Ekaterina style. "*Répetez.*"

Luce flickers in and out of sight, dancing from one alley light to another. The air breathes a dog's breakfast around them, a street perfume of fish and coffee and rotted meat, the sky above them caving in under grey. Luce dances. Luce invents steps Dolly's never thought of, puts a wicked spin on everything, a shimmy that reeks of rut. Dolly pulls herself straighter to make up for it.

"Okay," Dolly says. Luce stops, smiles. Not even breathing hard. "You've taken some classes."

Luce shakes her head, her ratted hair making a black star in the dark. "I grew up cutting a rug, mostly with friends of my mom's."

"They were dancers," Dolly states.

"Ab-si-tive-ly," Luce smiles, her teeth coming out sharp and shiny. "But not the pretty princess kind, you read me?"

Dolly's not sure that she does, but she nods. Stiffly.

"So this is some kinda struggle?" Luce asks, stretching her arms above her.

"Struggle," Dolly repeats the word, not really a question.

"You know," Luce seems to lift herself from her raised hands, does a pretty good Isadora Duncan impression, swirling down to her feet and back up, graceful as water spinning away down a drain. "Modern dance."

"Something like that," Dolly nods. She pauses. Luce is already re-doing the steps, better every time. Almost better than her.

BEAU

A spot appears in the dark, wobbling fairy small. It grows, slowly, to hover on the back wall in a wavering imitation of the moon. Other lights come up, undimmed from dark nothing, lights shining a deep sleepy blue, their watery light smudged by the smoke. Weeping white edges of willows drape the wings. Lumbering gravestones are scattered about, leaning one toward the other, like a bunch of drunks trying to find their way home. One of the headstones is larger than the others, inscribed with the name, *Giselle*, in poster paint shaded to look like stonework. Beau sits curled in his long skirt by the side of the stage, in shadow.

A loop begins playing, a spooky simple almost-hum, a dumdum-dumdumbeedowah, over and over. From behind the willows they come, three ladies one by one, hopping forward, one leg behind them held at right angles to the floor, their long skirts fan behind them, small small hops carrying them forward, heads down, arms out before them as though stretching toward something just out of reach.

There is Ginger, a dark ghost in beads and buckles, a white web of ripped stockings encasing her fro. Behind her is someone Beau doesn't know, a lion-headed lady glowing gold even under a coat of Dolly-white powder, mummy-wrapped from waist to neck and all down her arms in a streaked, dirty shroud. And behind her is Luce, her dark hair ratted out into wings on either side of her head, her breasts wrapped tight in a scarf. They reach centre stage, their legs drop, their long muddy skirts wet at the hems folding in to enclose them. A short, complicated dance follows, angular steps on perfect tiny feet. The dumdumdumdumbee-dowahing grows louder and louder, and finally shifts into song.

The three ghosts take up backup singer poses and mime the vocals, shimmying in place.

As Roy Orbison's voice starts shivering through the air, a pale apparition, wearing nothing but floor-length white hair appears from behind the largest gravestone. She appears to be glowing she is so white, glowing even from her eyes which seem not to see. Dolly in white hair, Dolly in nothing else. She raises her arms, lip-synching Roy's ghosty voice, doing a wiggle dance that reveals some of what lies under all that hair. There are cheers and wolf-calls from the crowd, spotty hoots in the smoky dark. The three ghosts look from one to the other, still mouthing backup, and head to the front of the stage. Beau stands, waves the ghosts over. Here they scan the crowd, hands to their foreheads, eyes searching a near horizon, smiling all the while. Beau sees what he wants, claps his hands together. Pops into the crowd, and returns, holding the hand of a craterous youth, greasy hair hanging lank around his pocky face. The ghosts enclose Beau and the boy as they walk into the low light of the stage. The crowd hollers louder, their catcalls and whistles turning the youth a glowing red.

The white lady slinks toward them, her wiggles becoming more and more wiggly, turning almost into spins. Roy Orbison warbles in his eerie voice, "*There goes my baby, there goes my heart, they're gone forever, so far apart....*" Beau takes the white lady's hand, and puts the spotty boy's hand in it, waggling his eyebrows. The white lady spins around the boy, closer and closer, wiggly as smoke around his scrawny body. She turns around him and around him. The three backup ghosts roll their eyes, then move forward in one smooth motion.

The ghosts lay their hands on the boy, pull him and push him from hand to hand in front of the white lady, his eyes wide in terror as she sings to him and him alone, as she spins more and more wildly, as he is slapped and pushed from ghost to ghost. Luce pulls him from the grip of the other two, throws the boy to the floor, hops on top of him. The wings of her hair bend down to the ground, taking his face somewhere away from the crowd, taking his face away. The crowd hollers, louder. She rides him faceless. She rides him until she is done, rolls off him smiling. The two other ladies pull him up, a shiny grin on his reborn head. He is tossed and held and thrown from ghost to ghost. The white lady shimmies, the white lady seems not to see. The white lady does not touch him and does not smile. She spins and spins in the centre of the stage, her long white hair lifting lifting, lines around her joints barely visible under all her glowing white. She spins and spins and stops. Then, with one finger, she reaches out, and pushes, ever so slightly, on his chest. He falls to the floor, the grin still on his face.

The boy lies on the floor, breathing hard, his face shiny red in patches. The four ghosts spin behind him, slowly, directed by Beau. They spin closer and closer and then reach forward with all their hands together. They pull him to his feet, then toss him offstage into the cheering crowd.

The lights go off.

•

The crowd dances as though one body made of many parts, a simmer in the smoky air. Beau, still wearing his skirt and pasties, spins the spotty boy, holds him close. The boy smells of grease and sweat, and smiles at Beau, a shy thing, little in his face. Beau spins, closes his eyes.

"Beau." He opens his eyes. Dolly stands behind him, her white hair traded for a pile of candyfloss pink, in the fashion of Marie Antoinette, a tail trailing behind her, a blue ribbon about her neck. She's put on tattered jeans patched with brown and black mole fur, and a ripped gown of goldfish, torn with shears to above the knees, still swishing behind her to the floor.

"Beau," she says to him, puts her hand forward, a white stain on his arm. "Come with me. I can't. Can you."

He doesn't know what she's talking about and can't tell if she's asking him a question, so he doesn't answer.

"Come with me Beau," she says, pulling him away from the boy. She takes his hand in hers, squeezing it too tight. He nods. And they go. Into the bathroom so Beau can change, back into his yellow jumpsuit.

115

Then she pulls him up the Main between other couples going other nowheres. Past windows still lit at this hour and at any hour, spinning with meats and pastries and booze and noise. Crossing to darker side streets. They walk without talking, her hand in his tightening every once in a while as though on a timer.

Through Parc Jeanne-Mance and across the wide avenue. Here they stop.

"You have something," she says. Again maybe a question. Again, a command. He nods, and pulls a bottle from the over-large pocket on the front of his yellow worksuit.

Slowly they walk between trees, which poke fingers through the low skittish sky. The last of the morphine is drunk down at the bottom of the hill, the bottle tossed back on the road for anyone to run over. Beau so slow. Inside his belly creeps, inside his belly creeps are crawling, inside his belly creepy-crawlies. And on his outside, only Dolly.

Hair piled high as leaves raked in front yards, ready for the fires. He stops and fishes in the other giant pocket on the front of his worksuit. She blinks, as though she's been practicing. Beau smiles over a brown bag of penny candy he's pulled from his pocket, takes a cinnamon heart from the bag. Rubs the red from it onto her mouth. Another heart for him. Matching red candy, matching red lips. He takes her hand again when she puts it out. They walk.

Through trees still as cadavers around them. Over muck that sucks at their feet, pulling on their shoes with every step. Under a sky that sits on them moonless, fat with rain.

In a clearing, dark as a bowl, dark as a still shiny looking glass, she stops. So he stops. A headlight flickers through the trees not so far away, its light small as a cupped hand. Blinking a code through the trees, through the spaces between them. He thinks of clapping his hands but can't remember why.

"What was that thing with fairies?" he thinks he says out loud.

Dolly doesn't answer but pulls him to the ground. They face each other, backs to the trees. Eyes on the trees behind the back of the other.

"Would you," Dolly says, pulling her toes closer, her feet, he notices only now, are bare. Her toenails painted gold.

Beau leans toward her and is trying to think of an answer to this but even if he'd thought of one he'd have a hard time saying it as her mouth is covering his.

Pink sugar, bright red hearts. He licks her lips and her tongue which tastes of toothpicks and dental floss, her tongue coming to taste him down below. Her tongue following her hands, sliding down his sides slow as shade.

His hands on her sides so hard, silk over her bodice hard as a constructed body. Skin that is not skin under his hands. Breathing low breaths with no taste into his mouth.

"I can't," he thinks he says. "You don't...."

"But I should," Dolly says, a crease creaking her voice.

"No, I mean, you don't under-"

Her cinnamon lips on him again, her hands searching. He pushes her away. "It's me," he says.

Dolly shakes her head, back and forth, back and forth. Her hair floats pink around her, come a bit loose from the pins. She looks at him, her scary eyes ghosts in her faint face. Nods.

"C'mere," Beau says, pulling her into a hug. After forever she pulls away, looks at him. Curls of her hair mirror her smile. Blood stops heart stops cells don't die here, here where she smiles for all time like this for him.

His blood pink sugar. His heart cinnamon shiny. He closes his eyes. They wrap their four arms up in each other.

When he blinks it's all blue. A hundred years later and the enchantment has been lifted. The slow morning has settled over them, tucking them under in spooling blues. He lies back on the dried grass, her head on his shoulder, her hand light on his belly. He blinks and says nothing and holds her tight to his body, close to his side where she fits.

LUCE

The Ghost and the Daisy skedaddle sight unseen, like they walked into the mirror in the bathroom and never came out. I make a quick phone call to the Q.B., then me and the Fox decide to make believe we're walking home.

There's a room full of people and a room full of noise but when he looks at me and asks me to go with him I don't even think about it, I just go. Me. Luce. You kids know, you know how I am. You tell me to do something and I do the opposite. Not this time. Not with him. He says come, I come. Like his wand is magic.

He walks fast and even I know we're not going anywhere near his place. We walk through little streets tight with buildings all dark with their insides hanging out, like their skins've been split. Balconies and stairways spilling people and smoke out of house's mouths. I'm still in my glad rags, all dolled up for the party in the next world, and the wind comes on cold from uphill. I don't care. Like none of these people care. Like this cold is nothing, like they've just been set free, come back from somewhere a whole lot colder than this.

The Fox slows down as we turn a corner, sort of waits for me to catch up with him. He starts telling me about *feu follets* which are like little lights that make folk crazy until they follow them off to their doom, kind of like the willies, now that I think of it, and about the werewolves right here in Quebec, only here they're called *loups-garous*. I have to ask him to spell these for me since they sound like *foo folly* and *loogaroo* to me. Seems if you don't take communion and you're bit, you turn into a wolfman — or wolfwoman, I guess. I ask him what communion is. He looks at me like I just fell from the sky. You know, he says, when you go to church and eat a wafer that's Christ's body, and drink wine that's Christ's blood? Geez, I say. Sounds like the cure's worse than the disease. He laughs at that.

We pass a church (and I tell you, kids, there's one about every other block here — I guess to keep all the city folk from becoming *loups-garous*) and he tells me another story, about an enchanted canoe. If you're ever stuck out in the woods here, you just call on Old Nick and bing! there's the canoe. And you just sort of promise your soul to him, and you can fly anywhere, as long as you don't touch a church steeple or say the Lord's name. I'm a shoo-in for this one, I tell the Fox. How do we call Old Nick? He laughs but really, I'm not joking. I'd love to see this place from way up there, flying along in an old devil canoe.

We're wandering around, sort of aimless, and suddenly we turn a corner and there it is. At the end of this little street, this big beast that looks like it's diving into water. It's got a cross sticking out of it, a big harpoon stuck right in its back. I ask him what it is. It's the mountain, he says, you know, where we met? I stare up at it. In the dark it really looks like a beast. A great big spiny thing, humping like a whale.

It grows and grows up ahead, like it's coming right for us. He tells me this story about how there was supposed to be a flood here, right here where we're walking now, and that some guy with a fancy French name prayed to Our Lady, and she kept the tide from coming. So the guy put a cross up on the mountain, like to say thanks to the Lady, way up high where I guess she could see it, and the cross has been there for hundreds of years. Sticking out of the back of this beast. We get closer to the beast and I think something.

Here we are in this place that the flood didn't come to, here we are walking where maybe we were never supposed to walk, here we are and it's silk. It's beautiful, it's better than anything I've ever done. Just walking here with him, doing not much of anything. But there it is, this beast hulking dark over the city with a cross in its back, and through all its spines and dirt and dogshit maybe all it's doing now is what it's been doing all along. Waiting. Waiting for that flood it was promised.

The Fox gets this look on his face when I say this. He doesn't say anything and I think, there you go, Luce, there you go again. Beating your gums when you should just keep mum.

"Nevermind me," I say. "Just flapping off again. You must think I'm real gone."

He still doesn't say anything but he shakes his head.

"I'm not really a bunny," I say, feeling like more of one every second he stays quiet. "Sometimes I just say whatever comes into my head."

He stops walking, so quick it takes me a second to stop myself. He gives me this look again, like something's trying to get out of him, whole, and he grabs my wrists so tight it's like a flatfoot has slammed me in bracelets and he just stands there so long light slows and my heart stops and I'm afraid to breathe. He closes his eyes and opens his mouth and holds my wrists tighter and tighter and says something I can't make out like he's speaking words you don't have to hear to get, but I don't hear them and I don't get them, and I hold my breath and keep still and try not to blink. And then a cat yowls somewhere down the alley and a car drives by us, its wide end shooting smoke, and he blinks and looks at me like he's just waking up. Things start moving and once they've come back to life there's no stopping them, things start moving and all they do is move him away. Like whatever it was he might've said got sucked in that exhaust pipe and used for fuel. Gone. Burned up, never to be seen again. At least not until the beast up there goes back to wherever it is it came from.

He drops his hands from my wrists and starts ankling away, toward the great beast humping dry over the city. I stand still for a second. Put my arms around myself where I get now that I'm covered with goosebumps, cold somehow that has nothing to do with the weather. I feel like a boob, kids, I can tell you. Somehow broke the spell I didn't even know I cast. I watch the Fox get smaller and smaller, walking closer to the speared sea beast, finally disappearing into it, like that's where his home is. And all I do is watch until he's nothing but a shadow, swimming invisible into other shadows that swallow him whole, soundless. In the dark so dark there's nothing here. Nothing left but me shivering in his scarf and a dirty skirt.

Behind me a voice says *allo*. I turn around, and it's the palooka, the one I met the day I got here. He smiles down at me, a big, beautiful smile from that other planet. He makes a gesture, curling his arms around his own body and shivering. He nods, says something I don't get. He does it again, and points at me. I nod. He takes off his coat, a thing of soft skin all fringed under the arms, holds it out to me. I take it, put it on. It's way too big for me, the sleeves falling past my wrists. I stand there goofy as a kid playing dress up, and he laughs. He tilts his head, ever so slightly, and holds out his hand.

"*Je m'appelle Oscar*," he says.

"Luce," I say, and take his hand, feeling like I got my very own planet on a string.

•

Next day I get back to Hicklin's flop, first thing in the morning. Turns out, the palooka's an early riser, a real go-getter. Well, I guess he gets what he wants. At least for a minute.

So I'm humming this song which you can't really hum, this Stooges song the palooka played for me, pointing at the title on the back of the record's sleeve. Title's the same as what the kids at school used to call me. Maybe it's why I ended up the way I did.

Anyway, I'm just getting to the most unhummable part and climbing up that one flight of stairs on the inside, and here I go into the kitchen and there's the Fox. A dead soldier on the table and it's not even done being morning yet.

"On a toot?" I ask, putting the rat bag on the floor under one of the crumby chairs that passes for furniture around here.

He looks at me like I'm talking Greek. "What?" he asks.

"You're on the giggle water first thing," I say, pointing to the empty bottle. "That spells B-E-N-D-E-R to me, Daddy."

He frowns at me. "Can't you ever just say what you mean? Here," he says, handing me a telegram. "This came for you."

"Oh, this is just ducky," I say, sitting down to look at the thing. Still sealed. What a good boy. "You're a real pill, sometimes, you know that? And I do say what I mean, Daddy. Pardon me for not being *groooovy*."

The Fox closes the book he's reading, and stands up. "I've asked you before, Luce. Please don't call me that. And, for your information, I haven't slept yet," he says, taking a hold of the dead soldier and putting it on the floor, next to a whole platoon of its buddies. "I was worried about you."

"Oh, for crying out loud!" I roll my eyes. "Gee, Daddy, next time you scram on me, I'll be sure to stay put."

"I came back," the Fox says, picking up a stack of books from the table. "Maybe ten minutes later. And you were gone. So I waited around and finally came back here."

"And hey, presto! Here I am," I say, making a magician's poof! with my hands. "Everything's Jake."

"Well, I'm sorry, I was worried," the Fox says, making to waltz out of the room. "You're just a kid."

He leaves me alone and it's a good thing too. That old bearcat feeling comes screaming into me. I pick up a plate that's lying on the table and pitch it as hard as I can against the wall. The sound of it splitting into all its own little pieces makes me feel better, so I pick up an ashtray and toss it. The damned thing doesn't break, but it makes a pretty good noise. I slide everything off the table with a whoosh of my arm, a good bunch of clattering and slivering from the things all falling apart. I go for the dead soldiers next, and I've gotten through a few of them when I'm grabbed from behind, my arms all jammed up at my sides.

"Luce!" the Fox low and heavy in my ear. "Settle down!"

I squirm in his arms, but he's pretty strong for someone who's probably never lifted anything heavier than a book. "I'm not a kid!" I scream, wriggling. He's got me good, but I don't let up.

"You're *really* not convincing me," he says, wrapping me up tighter. "Calm down."

I stomp on his foot. He hangs on, so I do it again, harder. "Let me go!" I howl.

"Fine," he yells, flinging his arms open and hopping around on one foot.

I grab the rat bag and toss it over my shoulder. "Go screw," I spit at him, before running down the stairs and slamming the door behind me. I've gotta go meet the Queen Bitch, but I gotta say, kids, right now, I'm feeling like the second runner-up for the crown.

5

HICKLIN

1967

"Is there going to be a shower?"

His mother is standing almost in the door of the mud room, just poking her head in, her body out of view and safely in the hallway. He's packing, placing his small, tidily folded items one by one into her valise, an off-white hard valise with a silky pink lining and built-in vanity mirror. The only time she'd used it was on her honeymoon.

"Yes, Mum, there's going to be a shower," he answers patiently. Actually, he hasn't the foggiest. On paper, he's going to Montreal to visit the World's Fair, a wondrous reward for himself and two other scholarship-winners, who will inexplicably travel with a contingent of rich kids, whose parents have happily shelled out for a week of peace and quiet. On paper, he's going to stay in something called an *auberge*, which he assumes will have a shower. The rich kids are staying at the Ritz.

"You'll be careful, won't you? They put bombs all over the place there."

"Yes, Mum, I'll be careful."

"I would hate to hear you'd gotten killed by a postbox."

"I won't get killed by a postbox, Mum, I promise." He rolls his eyes imperceptibly.

"Who puts a bomb in a postbox, anyway? It's barbaric. And how is it a Quiet Revolution, if they're using bombs?"

"Mum."

"Well, bombs aren't quiet, are they? You know they killed someone a few years ago?"

"I know, Mum."

"Horrible, horrible."

"Mum, they're oppressed people."

"That's no excuse. *Oppressed*. Who isn't oppressed these days?"

He refolds a pair of underwear and sits it on top of his other things. She taps her fingers against the mud room's doorframe.

"It's not like they don't have jobs and houses and everything else."

"Mum, not so long ago whole families were living in tar-paper shacks. Right across the river from the city. All winter long. What would you do?"

"I'd move."

His mother's fingernails tap at the frame of the mud room's door, then stop. Her hand slaps flat against the white-painted wood. She lets a little gust of air out from her nostrils, making a huffing sound.

"And be careful of all that foreign food they have there."

He puts another carefully folded pair of Y-fronts into the valise and stares at them. He closes his eyes, and sighs.

"Why, Mum?"

She raises her eyebrows and leans in a little closer, lowering her voice conspiratorially.

"*They don't wash their hands.*"

A tiny snort escapes through his nose.

"Mum!"

"Don't laugh! It's true!"

He's shaking his head, laughing silently, his hands up at his face.

"Well, go ahead and laugh. What do I care? *I know. I've seen it.*"

Her words of wisdom thus delivered, she nods sharply at him and shuffles away down the hall, leaving him to fall on his bed, laughing so hard his nose snots up and tears leak down his cheeks.

Underneath the tightly folded underpants and all the socks rolled in pairs, underneath his one dress shirt and his favourite brown velour pullover, underneath his worn copy of *Tropic of Cancer*, even underneath his notebook and the Brownie camera that used to be his dad's, wrapped in his granddad's manky old sweater, the tiny purse lies, still in stasis.

He likes to think he's followed his dad's advice, he likes to think nobody owns him. He likes to think that, even though it's a story he tells himself. A story that isn't true.

•

"Hey, hey! It's the Pervert!" Thad turns around, punches him on the arm.

His books tell him there is an order to all things. It appears that part of this order is that he will always be behind Thad. He has always been behind Thad. Ever since the first day of first grade, when he was seated behind Thad as a result of alphabetical order. The shadow and the boy, joined by the stitches on the soles of their feet.

"Hey, Thad." He looks at his feet as the line up of kids is slowly swallowed by the bus to the airport, knocking his knees with the hard case of his mother's valise. The seats at the back are full, as are the ones at the front. Thad throws himself into the window seat of a wide vinyl bench, and pats the space next to him with a wink. He sits, perches his mother's valise on his lap.

"So, Pervert, you looking forward to the big city? You gonna make it?" Thad smiles at him, waggling his eyebrows.

"Yeah, *Pervert*, you gonna *make it*?" Bikky and Dink are leaning over the back of his and Thad's seat, lecherously parroting whatever their leader has to say. Bikky and Dink are the kind of guys who rely on the alphabetical seating business. Bikky and Dink have been together since the first grade, when they were seated one behind the other and instantly realized they never had to go anywhere else for all the fun they ever needed. They speak together, finishing each other's sentences, as if they're a pair of conjoined twins that somehow got creepily separated.

He shrugs. "Yeah, maybe. I hear there's really pretty girls in Montreal."

Thad starts laughing. "Yeah. Live nude girls! You like *live nude girls*, Pervert?"

"Yeah, *Pervert*?"

"Yeah, Pervert, you like 'em live?"

He is silent. His hands on his mother's old valise sweat so much they start to slip away from what he holds. Thad shoves him, playfully, shoulder into shoulder.

"I'm just messing with you, Pervert. I know you like girls. Right? I bet you can name one, right now."

"Yeah, name one."

"Right now."

He pauses. Bikky and Dink are leaning in closer, their smiles widening. Bikky's a strawberry blonde, built like an ice chest with a small safe for a head. He's covered in freckles, the big, blobby, pale kind that all run into each other in places, creating a kind of optical illusion: are the freckles the freckles or is his pale skin the freckles? Dink is a rat-faced dark-haired boy with thin sharp fingers and tiny crazy eyes. The smell they make together is not unlike the smell of bread proofing. He doesn't know what they smell like apart. He's never seen them away from each other. He sighs.

"Nevermind. Don't you guys know it's rude to kiss and tell?"

Thad, Bikky and Dink fall about laughing, Thad giving him a shove.

"You've never *kissed*, Pervert! How the hell can you *tell?*"

"Yeah, Pervert, how can you tell?"

"Yeah, Pervert?"

He is silent. He lays his small valise across his knees and stares straight ahead. Thad shoves him again, harder, pushing him right off the seat and into the path of Flannery. Flannery. Flannery, who has only been in their school for a year, Flannery who keeps to herself, Flannery who spends almost as much time in the library as he does. Flannery who also plays soccer and who has a team of ironed blondes who filter her every move. Flan. He knows her friends call her this, though he is not her friend. All he knows is that her hair is made of fire, her breasts are monstrous, her bum is strangely tiny, and she was the only other person in their class who knew all the names of the Pre-Cambrian periods. He lies in her path, frozen for all time. She gives a little shriek, putting her hands to her face.

"Watch it, Pervert! You wouldn't want to offend the lady, now, wouldja?" Thad holds him down on the floor of the bus with a strong, stringy leg, smiling at him with fake-innocent wide eyes.

"Now would*ja?*" Bikky and Dink chirp, their heads bobbing up like two baby birds, waiting to be fed.

From the ground Flannery's breasts block out her face. He hears her voice above him, disembodied, complaining.

"Quit *sta*-ring, Pervert! *Geez!*" She prods him with her toe.

Her breasts are bigger than his head, each one. They could *kill* him. She pokes him again with her scuffed pink shoe. Stacked heels, rounded toes, ankle straps, dusty rose leather. He hears laughter all around him, kind of far away. Then Flannery's voice again, coming to him clear and cranky and from very far away.

"Move, Pervert!"

Her arms go akimbo, her breasts struggling and squeezing under her sweater, ready to pounce. Thad pushes down harder on him, making his ribs crunch a bit, making it hard to breathe. His bones make these sad little crumply sounds, sounds like a flattened rat on the side of the highway.

Flannery's breasts hover above him in zero-G, two monsters from another planet who've come from very far away to relieve him of his senses. She is wearing white knee socks. Her pink miniskirt is a shade brighter than her shoes, and leaves a swath of flesh free between her socks and hem. Her breasts are barely restrained by a bubblegum coloured sweater, stretched so the weave opens, revealing something flesh-tone underneath. Or maybe, flesh. He can't stop trying to decide which would be better. He's not exactly struggling, but Thad keeps increasing the pressure on his ribs.

"*Fine!*" Flannery squeals, and stomps her little foot. She breathes out sharply through her nose, lifts her foot, and *steps right over him.*

He does it without even thinking. He can't think. He doesn't really remember about thinking. He looks up. A lighter bubblegum pink, trimmed with lace, and one tiny, renegade red hair, waving at him as she passes. Without even thinking. He *reaches up*. He hears the laughter turn to a spooky, silent inhalation, a vacuum effect sucking out from the event horizon. Which would appear to be located in the centre of his pants.

She freezes. And then, ever so slightly, she pushes against his hand. There is no sound. She does it again, harder. He can feel something happen to her, though he's not sure what. He can feel that little red hair, stiff and strong, pricking his index finger. Silently, she pauses, rubbing against him, just barely. And then, just as quietly, she moves away, and keeps on walking. Her tiny bum recedes to the back of the bus, where she stops, turns around, and says, very clearly, but softly: "Pervert." She makes the T sound sharp, and pointy. It cracks him in the side of the head.

Thad lets him go and slides over to the window. He manages somehow to manoeuvre himself into the remaining half a seat without standing. He replaces his mother's valise on his lap, its hardness happily hiding his own. The bus is silent.

Mr. Willis climbs aboard, treading purposely up and down the aisle, reminding kids to tuck in that shirt, brush that hair, pull that skirt *down*, young lady. He tells them all that they are representing their school. He tells them to behave. He praises their silence, thinking it an indicator of good behaviour. He tells them to keep it up.

"Mr. Willis?" It's Flannery's voice. His blood stops circulating. His eyes turn to Jell-O. He shuts them, to stop them leaking out.

"Yes, Miss Flynn?" Mr. Willis has reached the back of the bus, is standing there jingling change in his pockets. He can hear it.

"I have something to tell you." She pauses.

Jingle, jingle, jingle.

"Yes?"

He keeps his Jell-O eyes shut tight.

"I —"

Jingle.

"Yes?"

Still, they're leaking.

"My mother made some date squares, for you and the other chaperones. Would you like one?"

He feels a punch on his thigh, and opens his eyes to see Thad grinning wildly and giving the thumbs up. He allows himself a smile, before shutting his eyes again and waiting for his heart to climb down out of his throat. He exhales, and grabs ahold of his mother's valise.

•

When they arrive in Montreal, all the kids pile out of the bus and talk in huddles, girls giggling together with their backs toward the city, boys shoving each other for no reason. Thad, Bikky, and Dink have already disappeared, their suitcases abandoned pods beside the big back wheel of the bus. Most everyone else is part of a cluster. From above, he thinks, it would look a lot like mitosis, like cells dividing. Seemingly random, squiggly, but actually highly organized. He stands awkwardly away from the other kids, a solitary mutant cell, banging the hard shell of his mother's white valise against his knees.

"Hey." He feels this more than hears it, deep inside his ear, hot. A hand slides into the little pocket stitched to the front of his favourite brown velour pullover. He turns just in time to witness Flannery's tiny bum wiggle away into the distance, just in time to see her giggling with one of her girlfriends, one of the sea of girls with waist-length, ironed blonde hair. He puts his hand into his pocket and withdraws a piece of paper, folded into a tiny square with his name written on it in smudgy blue ballpoint. He looks around to make sure no one is watching him but of course no one is. Not even Mr. Willis.

Hey. Meet me behind the Ritz in half an hour. Flan.

•

Forty-five minutes later he has one hand up Flannery's skirt and her tongue in his ear. Onscreen Faye Dunaway's mouth is moving, but the words he hears are French, as though Faye's ghostly separated twin were speaking for her, slightly out of time. He shuts his eyes. Flannery whispers in his ear. All he can hear is Faye Dunaway's breathy French sister saying, as he translates, "My, my. The things that turn up in the street these days."

133

Now she is Bonnie and he is Clyde. They run whooping down unknown streets, pointing gunfingers at strangers and laughing crazily at each other. He uses his mother's once-used valise to shield himself from imaginary shots from imaginary foes, uses it to protect her. She has no luggage, as hers got taken straight to the Ritz. She grabs him again, pulls him toward her, into an alley, behind a pile of cardboard boxes gone saggy in the August heat. He smiles at her, his smile devoured by Bonnie.

"Let's go on the lam," she laughs straight into his mouth. "Wanna run away with me?"

He has forgotten all his words, has forgotten how to say yes, forgotten how to breathe even without her mouth around his. She kisses him harder and his memory fades, his universe shrinks so all it contains is two perfect handfuls of Bonnie's tiny bum.

His ears burning from the things she's told him, his hands burning from where they've been, he walks beside her. They pass corner groceries, here called *dépanneurs*, and little cafés where the people have become smoke, trapped clouds in glass cases. He hears music from somewhere and then wonders if he's not just imagining it. She stops in front of a glass display case, empty but for a couple of pins skewering a shred of black velvet. The music is louder here, but still so faint he can't bear to ask her if she hears it too.

"I wonder what was here," she says, leaning in close to the glass so it looks to him like she's leaning in to kiss herself, her mirror twin. "I bet it was a necklace. A diamond necklace. I bet the diamonds were as big as eggs. I'd love to have a necklace like that. You ever see *Gentlemen Prefer Blondes*? Like that."

He leans close to the case, tries to see what she is seeing, but all he can see is her twin, her lips parting as though they'd happily lick right through the glass to get to the prize on the other side.

"Someday someone's going to buy me a necklace just like that," she says quietly.

There is a pause, and she moves slightly closer to him. He is still staring inside the box, into her twin who is not looking at him. Seconds pass. She gives a sharp sigh through her nose, turns, and quickly walks away.

●

The next day the whole group of kids, Ritz and non-Ritz alike, ride the monorail through a small version of the world, shrunk down and laid out before them. They visit every country they can, look at the future in the form of shiny kitchen gadgets. Ladies in miniskirts and oversized berets smile at them from every door.

They come across a black thing, sprawled across an open space. A network of beams, growing out of each other, like the nervous system of some monstrous beast laid bare for them to climb.

Flan swings upside down, her hair a flag for a bull, waving through the heat. He swallows, and walks over.

"Hey, Flan," he says through the smile trying to die on his mouth. "What're you up to later?"

Flan stares ahead of her, not registering.

"Flan?" he waves a hand in front of her face. "Hello?"

Flan turns her head to the girl next to her, one of the blondes, her own hair Rapunzel long, falling to the ground.

"Do you hear something?" Flan asks the girl. The girl looks around, right through him.

"No," she says, smiling an upside down smile. "Do you?"

Flan shakes her head. Their hair waves around him, gold and ginger. He resists the urge to wind his hands in there, and pull.

He walks away, hands in his pockets. And there, as if by magic, is a note. It could be the same note as yesterday's, and for a second he thinks it is. Only after *Hey. Meet me behind the Ritz in half an hour. Flan.* is written one word.

Sorry.

DAHLIA

1967

If she pees onstage it's Ekaterina's fault. She *told* her she didn't want to do this. She *told* her she'd do something else, anything else, sew costumes, run the spots, scrub the floors. She tried *everything*. But no. Ekaterina just said something about the ballet becoming your soul and walked away, waving her arms. Then Sera had grabbed her, spun her around and insisted in a sing-song voice that this'll be fun. Fun. Fun is cartoons on Saturday morning, fun is spinning around on a swing so fast you think you might throw up. Fun is most definitely not wearing a pom-pom for a hat and playing second fiddle to the snowflakes. Especially with your mother saying, But I thought you were going to be the Snow Queen. Turns out, that takes about ten years. For now, it's pom-pom hats in the background for her.

Along with the pom-pom hat, Dahlia is equipped with two long, white batons, each one outfitted with a smaller version of the hat. The rest of her costume consists of a white leotard over blue tights, and the only thing she's wearing that she adores: false eyelashes. She'd borrowed a pair from her mother's medicine cabinet, stuck them on badly, peeled them off and tried again. The second time they came out better, still a bit wonky as it's hard for her to see without her glasses. But the effect, she has to admit, is something else. Her violet eyes unreal, like two doll eyes transplanted into her very own head. Dahlia flutters her eyelashes a bit, then holds her eyes open wide, to keep the lashes from getting caught in the frames of her glasses.

Under her leotard, Dahlia wears an elastic bandage, the kind she would normally wrap around an aching knee or sprained ankle. Dahlia's breasts have taken over, overnight, and according to Ekaterina, snowballs aren't supposed to be a C-cup. She tries to huddle back into her regular slouch but she can't. She shoves her glasses up on her nose, as she's been doing manically every ten seconds for the past hour, and holds her eyes open wide.

"Dahlia! You look wonderful! How was your Christmas? And your New Year's? Isn't it exciting to be getting back to dancing? Are you excited? I'm excited!!! Are you excited?!" Sera comes bouncing up, her snowflake costume flying open as she twirls. Not a tutu, but not a leotard either, Sera is in the middle ground, with a swirling chiffon skirt that she can't seem to keep closed.

"Oh, so excited. I can't wait for this to be over." Dahlia folds her arms over her chest and frowns toward the floor. "This show should be put on before Christmas, anyway."

"Oh, Dahlia! Don't be silly!" Sera shoves Dahlia playfully. "Lots of schools do it after. Hey! I got flowers!!! Did you get flowers???"

Dahlia didn't get flowers. She's not even sure her parents have arrived yet. Her mother said her father had to work late again, and that she would pick him up. She said they'd try to make it for the opening curtain. She said they'd see her when it was over.

"Oh, my daddy sent me some but they're at home." Dahlia smiles this creaking, stretched smile at Sera. She smiles so hard she almost believes it. She tilts her head up and casts her eyes to the ceiling, look- ing, she hopes, dreamy. "The bouquet was just *too* big to bring here. But they're really pretty." Sera cocks her head to one side and bobs it up and down. "Pink," Dahlia adds, before Sera gives her a great big smile and one last bob of her head.

"Wow! Well, good luck out there!" Sera gives Dahlia one of her trademark bear hugs, a hug full of sunshiney hair and a smell of cooked cabbage, a hug so long Dahlia feels an inch taller after it. "Oh, Dahlia, it must be wonderful for you to be in the background! Not front and centre, so you don't have to worry about remembering your steps! And you're sure to be the only snowball with glasses!!! You'll really stand out!!!" Sera catches someone's eye and makes her way over, waving to all the pretty angels and blowing kisses to all the elves. Dahlia shoves her glasses up on her nose, then crosses her arms even more tightly over her chest and wonders if she has time to run to the bathroom for just a second.

Ekaterina is stalking around madly directing, pointing with her cigarette at places where costumes need to be re-pinned, patting rouge on Kirby, the only boy in the school, who consequently won the role of Clara's bratty brother by default, and cinching Sera's skirt together tightly, knotting her ribbons with a frown. Dahlia walks over, hugging her chest and trying her best to breathe.

"Ekaterina?"

Ekaterina is trying to squinch down Loretta's overly ratted hair, the tallest hair in the whole ballet school.

"Yes?"

Loretta is rolling her eyes and tapping the toe of her black ballet slipper impatiently. Loretta smokes before class and carries a switchblade in her purse. Loretta dates university boys and carries a safe. Loretta is *fast*. Loretta is smirking and quietly giving Dahlia the finger. Dahlia sighs and walks away, shoving her glasses up on her nose one more time.

"Nothing," Dahlia mutters, to no one.

•

It is bright, brighter than any place she's ever been before. She can't see anything, anyone, since Ekaterina had held her hand out for her glasses just before Dahlia stepped from the wings. But up here it doesn't matter, nothing matters, nothing at all. No one else is there, at all, at all. And she can just kind of be *invisible* up here, away from everybody else, where everyone can see. Dahlia blinks and gets this feeling like maybe she's found a big secret, like maybe that blinding light can take her into someplace she never even knew existed. She forgets her steps and gets shoved by the snowball behind her. She stumbles through it, her first minute and a half onstage, and makes it offstage and into the bathroom before she even really knows what happened. She locks herself in a stall and starts to laugh, until her pom-pom hat comes loose, almost falling in the toilet. She laughs so hard her lashes come loose and crawl down her face, their million million black legs tracing scratchy trails down her cheeks and leaving the only evidence that she was ever even there. Onstage.

•

Dahlia closes her bedroom door tight against the sound of her parents. They hissed at each other all the way home, so Dahlia had to open the window just to have something else to fill her ears. With the door closed, the sound of them is reduced to a strained murmur, a chitter of creatures far away.

Dahlia can also hear noises coming from her sister's bedroom. The sound of drums parumping through the wall. And other sounds, sounds Dahlia used to hear sometimes from her parent's room. She opens the window, wide, and drags a chair over.

Snow falls lightly, faint enough to leave ghosty little piles in the crooks of the tree outside her window, to leave a skinny blanket on the road, black veins showing through where cars have driven past. Dahlia breathes the cold air, filling her lungs.

She steps from the window and takes her arms out of her white snowball costume, unwraps her breasts from their bindings. Pulls the leotard off, and her tights, and wraps her old housecoat about her. It's too small now, but holey and comfortable. Dahlia unpins her white hair, lets it fall around her shoulders.

She sits on her bed carefully, next to Patience. All her other dolls have been given away. Only Patience remains.

"Look, Patience," Dahlia says, pulling the eyelashes from their little case, where she had replaced them after the show. "I've got eyelashes like yours now. Only, mine fell off."

Patience stares at Dahlia.

"I did it," Dahlia says, smiling. "I thought I'd pee my pants and throw up but I didn't. And you know something, Patience?"

Patience looks at Dahlia from beneath her heavy eyebrows.

"I loved it!" Dahlia puts the eyelashes on her night table. "I don't think my parents were there, though. They said they were, but..." There is a sound at Dahlia's door, a tiny knock, as though from a very small hand.

Dahlia leans forward, listens again. For a while there is nothing. So long Dahlia starts to think she made up the knock, along with the tiny hand. But there it is again. Soft but insistent, *clk-clk*. Dahlia gets off her bed, carefully, and walks toward her door.

"Dahl!" Her sister's whispered voice. "You up?"

Dahlia opens the door, just a little. Puts one of her eyes to the door. "Yeah. Why?"

In the skinny space Dahlia's allowed she can see only that Tru is sweaty and smiling, wrapped in her own housecoat.

"I didn't expect you all back so soon," Tru smiles. "I've got company."

Dahlia blinks at her sister, slowly. "Really."

"Oh," Tru bites back a laugh. "That obvious, huh?"

Dahlia shrugs.

"Listen, Dahl." Her sister leans forward, as close as she can get with Dahlia holding the door nearly shut, "We just need to borrow your window for a sec. I've gotta get him out of here before the folks come up to say goodnight. You've got that little roof under your window, right? Whatdya say?"

Dahlia stares at her sister.

"C'mon, Dahl," Tru smiles. "I'm in kind of a jam."

Dahlia stares at her sister.

"Okay, okay," Tru starts nodding. "What do you want? Candy? Toys? A new dress for your dolly? What?"

Dahlia bites her lip. "Your gold dress," she says simply. She thinks a bit more. "And some false eyelashes. Two... no, three pairs."

"Dahl, I just got that dress!" Tru says, her whisper rising. She pauses, lets out a breath. "And false eyelashes, too? Our little Dahlia's growing up, huh? Catching up with the twins?"

Dahlia starts closing the door.

"Okay, okay," Tru says, jamming her toe between the door and the frame. "I'll get you your eyelashes. *And* you can have the stupid dress." She pauses, smiles at Dahlia. "Can I at least borrow it back once in a while?"

"We'll see," Dahlia says, opening her door.

•

The August heat settles in the theatre, squatting hot and fat all through the empty space. Backstage, the girls try to powder away their sweat, try to keep their eyeliner from melting off. Dahlia peers in the mirror and powders her nose for show. Her face is cool and white, as always.

This time Dahlia's breasts run free, filling her peasant's dirndl past capacity. The other girls, even Loretta, frown and try to stand taller when Dahlia's breasts float by. Sera told Dahlia she saw one of the older girls stuffing her shirt.

The ballet school is putting on a lighthearted summery affair by the name of *Giselle*. Dahlia and Sera, years behind the other girls and not yet *en pointe*, play peasant girls in the opening scene. They carry matching arcs of fake flowers, to wave over their heads in glee at the mere implication of a wedding.

"I hate these sappy first acts," Dahlia mutters to Sera, hanging her plastic arc over her neck and slinking into a surreptitious slouch.

"Me too," Sera says, loudly, attempting to hula her own plastic flowers. After a couple of wobbly rotations, they fall to the floor. Ekaterina is on them in a moment.

"Girls!" she barks, pointing down at the fallen flowers with her long brown cigarette. "What are flowers on floor?"

"Sorry, Ekaterina," Sera says, bowing into a pretty peasant curtsy and simultaneously retrieving her flowers.

"These come from Russia," Ekaterina frowns from under her tight black headscarf. "On boat with me. You don't want, I take away."

"No, I want," Sera says, smiling her most sunshiney smile.

"And what is problem here?" Ekaterina turns her frown on Dahlia, still slouching. Ekaterina imitates Dahlia's slump and closes her eyes. "You take nap before show?"

"No," Dahlia says, standing up straight, tucking in her bum, removing the plastic flowers from around her neck. "I'm ready."

Ekaterina regards them as if from a great distance, as though her cigarette holder were a telescope and the two of them small uninteresting hunks of ice impeding her view. She tilts her head and nods.

"I know, nobody want to be peasant girl," Ekaterina says, taking a long dramatic drag from her cigarette. "Especially in Russia where girls peasant girls for real. Everybody want to be fairy queen or wili or princess or stupid Juliet. Well, is not like that. Somebody always have to be peasant girl. And today, is you girls, okay?"

"Okay," Dahlia and Sera say together, a peeping chorus.

"If no happy time, is not real, the sad time, you see?" Ekaterina holds her hands out, as if showing them the sad time on an invisible platter. "So you make the happy time real for the people out there, yes?"

Dahlia and Sera nod, bobbing in silent assent. After Ekaterina leaves them they roll their eyes at each other and head to their spots in the wings, their nylon flowers and plastic smiles at the ready.

•

Backstage, after the show, wilis flit in circles from parent to parent. Ekaterina smokes, standing alone, pretending not to speak any English at all when approached by a mother inquiring after her child's progress. Dahlia and Sera stand in a corner, slouching in their peasant costumes. Dahlia's parents enter, her mother leading her father by the hand. Her father with overly rosy cheeks.

"Hello, girls!" Dahlia's mother sings. Her smile too wide. She kisses Dahlia and Sera, once on each cheek. Frowns at her husband. "Say, hello, Albert."

"Hellllloo, Albert!" he sings gustily. Dahlia rolls her eyes at Sera.

"Well! That was just lovely! And all of you were so good!" Dahlia's mother chirps, her shoulders climbing up to her ears with joy. "What were those ghosts called again, Dahlia? Those pretty girls in white?"

"Wilis," Dahlia says, pronouncing the word with a 'v' at the beginning, and not the 'w' most of the girls use on purpose, just to have an excuse to giggle. "They were girls who had died on their wedding nights, after being wronged by their husbands-to-be, like Giselle. That's why they dance men to their deaths."

"Is that right?" Dahlia mother blinks and tilts her head. "Well. They were very pretty."

"A woman dun't have to be undead to dance a man to his death," Dahlia's father says loudly, a crooked smile on his face. "In't that something mothers teach their daughters?"

A space of silence separates Dahlia's father from the rest of the crowd, ripples spreading through the whole backstage. Dahlia's mother tries on a smile, reaches a hand out to barely touch Dahlia's father on the arm.

"He doesn't mean that, do you, Albert?"

"Nooo," Dahlia's father smiles ever wider, shaking his head furiously. "No, no. Can't get in the way of the sisterhood, can I? I'm outnumbered!"

"I'm sorry," Dahlia's mother whispers to Sera. "We had some wine with dinner."

"Whine?" Dahlia's father shouts. "You bet, whine! Whine whine whine! All you women are so hard done by, aren't you?"

"I'm sorry," Dahlia's mother says again, her smile more plastic than anything Dahlia could ever conjure up. "He's a little overworked."

"I wonder why?" Dahlia's father reaches for a drink, and finding nothing, slams his fist hard on the top of a costume table. "Fancy schools and ballet lessons and everything else a pretty girl needs. Right, Dahlia? Pretty girls need pretty things. Right?"

"Dad," Dahlia says, trying for his hand. "Let's go outside for a minute. I think you need some air."

"Hah!" Dahlia's father snorts. "Air! I don't need air! I need a drink.

Excuse me... ladies."

Dahlia's mother holds herself very straight, her smile frozen in place. "He's just a little tired, girls," Dahlia's mother says, her mouth barely moving, her eyes on Dahlia's father, weaving through the crowd. Then the smile disappears. She grabs Dahlia's hand, and nods to the small crowd. Without another word, Dahlia's mother pulls her toward the back door.

Dahlia waves to Sera, who makes a telephone gesture by the side of her head. Ekaterina stage-whispers loudly to her as she passes, "Don't fill bad, Dehlia. My father is tired like that too all the time. Is no problem."

Dahlia gives Ekaterina a little smile, and then is outside in the wet summer air, still in her peasant's dirndl, being pulled by her small mother down a back alley to some mysterious end.

•

Dahlia sits on the edge of a bed the size of her daddy's car, eating French toast rather ungracefully from the room service cart.

"Dahlia, please," her mother says, frowning downward with her smudged red lips. "You're getting maple syrup everywhere."

Dahlia looks down to her lap, and sees her mother is right. She's dropped a piece of French toast right in the lap of her peasant's dirndl. She hopes the dress didn't come all the way from Russia, hopes Ekaterina won't bark at her when she sees the spot. Dahlia licks her thumb and tries to rub away the sticky, with limited success.

"Oh, just leave it," Dahlia's mother snaps, putting her thumb and index finger to the bridge of her nose and pinching. "You'll just make it worse." Dahlia's mother is drinking small drinks, one after the other, from a bottle that came on the room service cart.

"Why don't you go to bed, Dahlia? Your mother's very tired and we've both had a long day," her mother says, taking another gulp of her drink, while sitting in a dusty rose chair beside a big window. The curtains are drawn.

Dahlia drinks the glass of milk her mother ordered for her, all in one go. It is so cold it tastes of metal. There is a flower on the room service tray, just one flower in a slim vase. Its head is yellow and too big for its stem, so it droops a bit. Like it's looking down at something. Even in the grey half-light of the room, Dahlia can see that the edges of the yellow flower's petals are dry and brown, pulling into themselves, curling up like a kid going to sleep.

"Mom?"

Dahlia's mother sighs.

"Mom," Dahlia tries again. "Why are we staying here? And what about Tru?"

Dahlia's mother sighs again, longer than before, then takes down the rest of her little drink. "We are staying here until your father comes to his senses. As for your sister, I think she can take care of herself. She's probably out with some... *boy* right now."

"Oh," Dahlia pushes her glasses up on her nose, then chews on her lower lip.

A tinny *squink* accompanies Dahlia's mother unscrewing the cap on her bottle. She pours herself a larger drink, then noisily plonks down the bottle without bothering to recap it.

"Your father has decided he would rather spend the night alone," Dahlia's mother says into her glass. "Or *his* version of alone, anyway."

Dahlia doesn't know what this means. She pushes away her unfinished French toast, moving the whole cart in the process.

"Dahlia, *please*. Your mother needs to rest now."

But her mother takes another drink instead.

•

Dahlia's mother snores, curled in a tiny corner of the giant bed, on top of the covers. Dahlia unfolds a spare blanket over her mother, and kisses her on the forehead. Then she creeps out of the hotel room, closing the door softly behind her. Dahlia locks the door with the only key, and heads toward the elevator.

Downstairs she pulls herself ballet-straight, and strides toward the door. Nobody stops her from leaving, no one even asks where she is going. She exits onto Sherbrooke Street, turns right and keeps striding. Turning right again, she finds herself in an alley, down which she strides, still perfectly straight. Seeing a small space behind some stacked trash, she sits, takes off her glasses and folds them neatly, pulls her knees up under her chin, and closes her eyes.

She breathes slowly and swallows, breathes and swallows, until she is sure she's swallowed every last tear from behind her eyes. She slumps against the wall behind her, cool where her skin touches brick. She crosses her hands over her knees, dangling, and stares across the alley at a brown blur. She stares at it, hoping it will resolve itself into some other place, somewhere other than the place she's in now. Nothing happens. She closes her eyes again.

"Excuse me," a voice says from somewhere below her, "do you have a match?"

She stares at a spot below her, where the brown blur wavers in the spare light. It moves, slightly. She shakes her head.

"You look blue," the blur says.

Dahlia shakes her head. No smile comes to her lips. "You don't want to know."

"Sure I do," the blur says.

She puts her glasses on, blinks until the blur comes into focus. It's a boy, probably not much older than her, smiling up at her. She stares at him from behind her glasses. Blinks, slowly. "What I mean is I don't want to say."

He nods, takes a cigarette from a fresh pack. He lights it with a box of matches, inhales, and breaks into a coughing fit that turns his eyes red and teary. He wipes away his tears, and holds out the cigarette pack to her. She shakes her head. He puts the pack away.

"I can understand that," he says, still coughing. "I only started smoking today, myself."

Dahlia stares at him again. "No kidding."

"And I guess I didn't really need a light," he says, holding up the matchbox sheepishly.

Dahlia nods, slowly. "You don't say," she says unsmiling, pointing at her glasses. "I'm not totally blind."

"That was supposed to be funny," the boy says.

"Oh," Dahlia says. "Really. Well I don't really feel like smiling. Or laughing. Maybe ever. Sorry to disappoint."

"Oh," the boy says, taking another drag from his cigarette. He coughs again, but not for as long, and not until he tears up. "Okay. Sorry."

They are both silent against the background hum of the Ritz's motors.

The boy looks up at her. Raises his eyebrows a bit. "Hey! That's a hell of an outfit," he says, the words 'hell of' sounding stiff and unused, like they're new in his mouth.

"Shut up," Dahlia says, crossing her legs under her, pulling her crinoline around her knees. "Is happy time, okay?"

"What?" the boy asks, holding his cigarette awkwardly, not smoking it. He coughs behind his hand.

"Nothing," Dahlia mutters, shaking her head.

"I've got a girl in there," the boy says, throwing his unfinished cigarette to the ground and stepping on it. The Ritz's motors let out a sympathetic wheeze and then a deep, low cough, as though trying to clear something from deep within.

Dahlia nods. "Sure you do."

"I do!" the boy says, loudly. Then more softly he says, "Only..."

"Let me guess," Dahlia says, "she's a robot."

The boy shakes his head.

"A ghost?"

Another shake.

"Hmmm," Dahlia says, staring off down the alley, where a very short man is dragging out bags of trash. "Oh I know. She's your mother."

"Sick!" he says. "Geez, and I'm the one they call..."

"What?" Dahlia asks.

"Nothing," the boy says.

Dahlia nods. "I was kidding."

"Oh," the boy says, "Oh. Well. It's kind of hard to tell."

"It is?" Dahlia considers this. Nods. "Well I said no more smiling. I never said anything about cracking wise. Anyway I'm the one with a mother up there."

"Oh, yeah?" the boy smiles. "You live up there?"

Dahlia shakes her head. "No," she says, then pauses. A little frown. "At least I don't think so."

A grey and brown bird lands on a little pile of garbage across the alley, pecks at it, hops to another spot and pecks again. Finding nothing, it hops to another trash pile, and pecks again.

"She's supposed to come meet me out here," the boy says, leaning against the wall Dahlia is perched on. "But I've been out here forever. I'm starving."

"Me, too," Dahlia says, just now noticing an empty ache in her belly, a place where her unfinished French toast was supposed to go. "Let's go inside."

The boy shakes his head. "That's okay," he says. "I'm just gonna stay out here."

"Oh come on," Dahlia says, standing and stretching herself out tall, her arms above her head. She bends down, her hands flat on the ground. Standing up and rolling her shoulders, she looks down at him. He's skinny and pale, wearing a thin velour pullover and cords, both in faded shades of mustard. His cords are worn almost bare at the knees. His once white sneakers are almost black with grime along their rubber edges, and dusty brown on the canvas. His right sneaker has a hole in the toe, where a peep of red shows from his sock. His sandy hair falls in his eyes, a bit long around the edges, but pretty obviously not for style. "I bet you could eat something."

The boy shakes his head again. "No, that's okay. But thanks."

"Come on," Dahlia says, hopping lightly down to the ground, "we can charge it to the room."

The boy doesn't follow her.

She turns, "We can leave a message for your girl at the desk. Come on."

Halfway down the alley, she hears footsteps behind her. She slows down until the boy catches up with her.

"I've got money," he says, putting his hands in his pockets.

She shakes her head. "Don't worry about it. Rat bastard can pay for it."

The boy frowns. "Rat bastard?"

"Nevermind," Dahlia says. "You ever had oysters?"

•

"Where I come from, you can eat those right out of the sea," the boy says, pointing to Dahlia's platter. It's silver, about as long as Patience, and covered with a bed of crushed ice, on which oysters lie in their half shells.

"Really?" Dahlia asks, lifting one of the half shells and staring at the grey-green glob lying there. "Isn't that dangerous?"

The boy laughs, shaking his head. "Where do you think those come from?"

"I don't know," Dahlia says, slurping down the oyster. She licks her lips. "I never really thought about it."

"You should come out and visit me sometime," the boy says, putting a small, blunt knife into a crystal bowl of *foie gras*. "My dad knows some really fine fishermen. They'll catch you anything you want. There's nothing like eating something right out of the water."

"Really," Dahlia says, reaching for another oyster. "It sounds a bit, I don't know." *Déclassé*, she thinks, but she swallows the word along with the oyster. "A bit... rustic."

The boy shrugs, and covers a bit of toasted baguette thickly with *foie gras*. He crunches it down, and reaches for another. "Now, this stuff," he says, dipping the knife back in the bowl, "is fantastic. What is it?"

Dahlia shakes her head. "You don't want to know."

"Sure, I do," the boy says.

"It's *foie gras*."

"Well, it's delicious. Maybe I can take some back for my folks.

149

What's it made of?"

Dahlia watches him chew and swallow. "I'll tell you when you're done. Do you speak French?" Dahlia asks. She eyes the oysters, tries to imagine what it is they do in the ocean, before they end up here, on her plate. She takes a sip of juice.

"Yeah," the boy says, brushing his hair out of his eyes. It falls right back. "That's why I'm here. I won this scholarship, and the trip here and everything. Top of my French class."

"*Félicitations*," Dahlia says.

The boy shakes his head. "It's no big deal," he says, picking up his dessert fork and poking it into his Caesar salad. "Nobody speaks French where I come from. I can say *bonjour*, so I win."

Dahlia nods. "Nobody speaks French where I come from, either," she says, picking up her salad fork and starting on her own salad.

The boy frowns. "But you're from here, aren't you?" He looks from her fork to his. "I'm using the wrong fork."

Dahlia shakes her head. "I'm not the Queen," she says. "I don't mind. And yes, I am from here, but nobody speaks French where I'm from. It's an anglo part of town."

The boy switches his forks, then looks at her with a raised eyebrow. "Oh, yeah? Like where the bombs've been set off?"

Dahlia nods.

"It's kind of exciting, huh? A revolution. Right here in Canada." He pauses, frowns. "Well, for now."

"I don't know how exciting it is to have people trying to kick you out of your home," Dahlia says, putting down her fork. "Or bomb your neighbourhood."

The boy's frown deepens. "Don't the FLQ just want to protect French language and culture? No one's talking about kicking anyone *out of* anywhere."

Dahlia blinks, slowly. "But the anglos live here too," she says. "Not to mention the Irish and Italians and Portuguese and Greeks and Africans and Jews and everybody else. And the French who aren't interested in separating. And the Indians! They were here first, though no one seems to remember that. Don't all these people have just as much of a right to protect their languages and cultures as the French?"

The boy's eyebrows crush down over his eyes, his mouth crunches over to one side. He nods. "Huh," he says. "That's a dilly of a pickle."

"I suppose that's one way to put it," Dahlia says, picking up her fork again. "Anyway, the way they talk about it in the papers it's all French-English. As though Montreal only has two kinds of people, and they never talk to each other. Sometimes they even meet, and become friends! Sometimes they even marry each other, and have children! I bet you don't hear about that in the papers out west."

The boy shakes his head. "Nope," he says, taking a sip from his water glass, a crystal goblet on a thin stem. He balances it carefully in two hands, then lowers it slowly to the white tablecloth. "But who wants to read a story where everybody gets along?"

Dahlia's mouth twitches. She raises her eyebrows and shakes her head slightly. "Ha ha," she says, not laughing, the words two separate things.

The boy smiles. "Almost got you on that one, hey?"

Dahlia wipes her mouth with her huge napkin, the last of her peasant girl lipstick staining it. "Oh, no," she intones, looking down at the blood-like smear on the otherwise pristine cloth. "I'm still a peasant girl."

The boy smiles, hiding a laugh behind his hand, trying to turn it into a cough.

"I must look awful," Dahlia closes her eyes. "Why didn't you tell me?"

"I think you look great," the boy says. "Like no one I've ever seen before."

Dahlia opens her eyes. Stares at the boy. "It's not makeup," she wipes hard at her mouth, "I'm an albino."

The boy stares right back at her. "I know," he says. "And I think you look great."

Dahlia stares at the boy. She pulls herself ballet-straight. She can feel a blush creeping hot under the rose-red of her peasant girl cheeks.

"I'm just saying," the boy says. "I didn't mean to embar —"

"They force-feed the ducks," Dahlia says, sitting up even straighter. "Until their livers are full of breadcrumbs and fat. Then they slaughter them and take out their livers, take out the goo, and put it in fancy pots for rich people to buy."

"What?" the boy asks.

"*Foie gras*," Dahlia says, nodding her head toward the almost empty bowl. "That's how they make it."

The boy smiles. "I know," he says.

"You know?" Dahlia asks. "Why did you —"

The boy's grin grows wider, wide enough for Dahlia to see that his canines protrude beyond his front teeth. Like a wolf's, she thinks. "I just wanted to see if you'd tell me."

Dahlia stays sitting perfectly straight. "You don't find it cruel."

The boy shrugs, and brushes the hair away from his eyes again. It falls right back. "Seems to me it's just food, and lots of things we do for food are awful. Like slicing someone's strongest muscle, prying open their shell and swallowing their whole body in one go, hopefully while they're still alive."

"Is that true?" Dahlia says, her eyes going wide. "Who would do such a thing?"

"Anyone who eats oysters," the boy says, reaching for one himself. He slurps it down. Licks his lips, tasting, testing. "But these ones aren't alive anymore."

Dahlia stares at him. "You don't have many friends, do you?"

"No," the boy answers. He frowns. "Why, was that weird?"

Dahlia nods. "A little."

"Oh," the boy says. He smiles at her, a bit of a hopeless shrug in his shoulders. "Sorry."

"It's okay," Dahlia says. "You're... " Like no one I've ever met, she thinks. "Unique," she says, finally.

"A real singularity," the boy says, happily scraping the last bits of force-fed duck liver out of its little pot.

BILLY

1967

Billy passes the bottle to Mona, who sits up a bit on the pile of dresses to accept it. Billy stays where he is, staring upwards at the shiny seams of the Platonic solids. Mona made them herself, out of cardboard covered in tinfoil, and hung them above her bed. Her bed which is now, as always, covered deep in the dresses Billy adores, the dresses Mona's mother buys for her, dresses which never in a million years would ever fit Mona. Billy snuggles into the pile, his arm rasping against old hand-made lace, his feet swimming in silk.

"Where'd you get this?" Mona asks again.

Billy shrugs. He'd taken it from Marly's stash, down in the root cellar, which he could easily tell Mona. "I found it in the back of a bus," Billy says breezily. "Like I said."

Mona pokes him on the leg. "No," she says, poking, "you said you got it from the belly of a big fish. You cut him open and there it was."

Billy nods. "Oh, yeah. That's right. I did."

"You big fat liar," Mona says, passing the bottle back to him. "You know you can't lie to me. I always know."

Billy nods. "Yep."

"Let's go dancing!" Mona squeals suddenly, sitting up so fast Billy is tossed about on the bed, as though he had been thrown off a wobbly planet.

"Okay, okay," Billy laughs, getting his limbs reorganized in the pile on the bed. "Where?"

Mona smiles. "I know a place."

"Okay," Billy says, getting out of the pile and standing. "Just let me get dressed."

"You are dressed," Mona points out. It's true. He is dressed, in Mona's gown of silk cords with a fur collar.

"Mona, I can't wear this outside," Billy shakes his head. "Just let me put my pants back on."

"No," Mona says, pushing him back down. "It's my birthday and I want you to wear this."

"It's your birthday?" Billy asks.

"Yeah, it's my birthday!" Mona huffs. "Some friend! You don't even know when my birthday is?"

Billy takes a thoughtful pull from the bottle and stands again.

"Mona," he says, holding his arms out so all the little silk strands hang in wings from wrist to waist. "Look at me. I look ridiculous. This is just something I do... with you. Let me put on my pants."

Mona shakes her head. "You really have no idea, do you?"

"No idea about what?"

"How goddamned beautiful you are in that dress — or any dress!" Mona starts picking up random items from the pile on her bed and throwing them at Billy. "You're my mother's perfect daughter! You're the prom queen! You're Miss fucking America! Don't you get it? You can have anything you want in the world and all you want is your god-damned pants? Fine!"

Billy's jeans come flying across the room, his horseshoe belt buckle getting him good over the eye. A clogged-drain trickle of blood pearls in his eyebrow.

"Oh, shit!" Mona runs over to Billy, who is standing perfectly still, his right hand clamped over his eye. "Billy, I'm so sorry!"

Billy stares away with his uncovered left eye. "I'm fine," he says. "Fine. Let's go."

Mona hugs him so hard he thinks she must be squeezing more blood out of him. "Great!" she says. "I've just gotta go downstairs and get one thing."

•

The pink walls moan as though every step Billy and Mona take on the brown carpet hurts. They pass through a door set into one of the walls, the seam of it meeting the wall thin as a scar, which Mona opens with nothing but a knock. Billy follows Mona in, blind for a second. The moans come from everywhere here, and in the almost dark it's as if Billy has been shrunk and swallowed, down a deep throat. Pink walls close in, squeeze tight. He closes his eyes, then opens them again.

Pink walls close in, squeeze tight. Billy is not even sure at first what he's looking at but at least he gets that it's flesh. The feet orient him. He can see the shoes just fine, so there's the leg, and there's the rear, and there's another leg, and there's another rear, and there are two breasts, jumping for joy. At least he thinks it's joy. From the sounds, it's kind of hard to tell.

Mona grabs his hand, puts a finger to her lips. The door they've come through led them into the rear of the theatre, behind the last row of seats. Up ahead of them are scattered, dusky shapes, dark as holes in the brightness of the screen. Billy stands still until his eyes adjust to the lack of light. The holes resolve themselves into heads, faceless in rows ahead of him. The moans increase in frequency and pitch, the squeals turning to a sound almost of fear.

Mona grabs his hand and motions for him to follow her. She hunches over, walking low as she can. Billy does the same, the dress pulling tight against his behind. She leads him to a couple of empty seats, near the far left wall, away from the beam of the projector, away from the exit doors.

"It's harder for my folks to see us here," she explains in a whisper. "Don't move. I'll be back in a sec."

"What?" Billy turns in his seat, but Mona is already away, shuffling hunched to a seat near the front of the balcony. Billy's stomach turns itself into a knot with no end, rolling inside him. He swallows.

Onscreen the shoes don't move. Everything else moves around them. A rump white and spotty as the moon tightens, clenching. A face

155

beneath it, mouth open in something like a scream.

"Hey," a voice whispers, raspy and weavy, a harshness to it like the throat it's coming out of has been scraped. "You're a pretty thing. Too pretty for a place like this."

The face on the screen is the face of a lady, her mouth red and wide, big enough to swallow him whole. The spotted rump pulls away from her, rolls her over. Her shoes above her head, satellites circling. Billy stares until the screen blurs, until he can't see the mouth or the moon, just the faint shape of two red sparkly shoes, pushing through the air.

"Not a talker, eh?" There's a metallic clinking, soft as a charm. Billy stares at the shoes, at the blur on the screen. "No problem, sweetie. No problem. You just sit tight. I'll take care of everything."

Billy stares until he has to blink. The white rump moves faster and faster, the cries around him grow louder and louder until they seem to be coming from somewhere near him, somewhere hot into his ear. Billy closes his eyes. Beside him a movement, a silent stroke.

The sounds increase around Billy, his eyes closed. There's a moan bigger than the others all put together, a moan that turns into a scream. Billy opens his eyes just enough to see the lady onscreen, her head turned too far to one side, her mouth still open, but open still. Billy blinks. The spotted rump moves off her, turning, a slick thing like a sword sticking out from the front, as though jabbed deep in the gut. The lady doesn't move.

The camera catches her still, a flicker fading from her. It jitters as though jolted, and the screen goes black.

"Don't worry, pretty thing," the raspy voice beside him whispers, shoving something onto his lap. "She comes back to life. There's another show in half an hour."

The seat beside him is now empty. Billy sits in the dark of the room, the heads about him faceless. Looks at his lap. A crumpled something sits there. He unfolds it. A five dollar bill. Billy crumples the thing up, and shoves it in the only place he's got, down the front of his dress.

Billy is still sitting in the same place when Mona returns. The theatre's lights have remained low between shows.

"Billy!" she whispers loudly, sitting in the seat next to him. "I'm so sorry, it took longer than I thought it would to find the guy. You okay?"

Billy shrugs. Stares at the screen, a pale rectangle shimmering before him, bigger than a door but just as flat. He wonders could he open it, hop through to somewhere else.

"I got it," Mona leans in close to Billy. "Let's go."

Billy shakes his head.

"C'mon," Mona says. "We're supposed to go dancing, remember? I hate hanging around here on nights like this."

Billy shakes his head.

"Oh, what? You waiting for someone?"

Billy shakes his head again. "No," he says, staring at the screen. "I just want to stay. For the next show. I just need to see...."

The beginning. He can't say it. The once upon a time, that ended with the lady being killed by a bull. He just needs to see the start, to see her happy. Before he can go.

•

Mona pulls him into the girl's bathroom, into a stall. Passes him the tiny bottle.

"Careful," she says. "Don't drink too much or you'll ralph."

Billy takes a little sip, the stuff in there so bitter he almost spits it out. "Acchhh... what is this?"

Mona shrugs. "It's good for you," she says, smiling and taking the bottle from him.

"It better be, if it tastes that bad," Billy wheezes, wiping his mouth with the back of his hand. Mona passes the bottle back to him, and he gives it another go. His arms go noodley, his skin warm from the very inside of him all the way out.

"Oooh," Billy breathes. "It *is* good for me."

"See?" Mona says, slipping the bottle down the front of her dress. "I don't lie to you."

They dance on the roof of the cinema, the sky too big to be a bowl above them. Billy watches the moon rise, Mona's head under his chin. They turn and turn until Mona's father calls her from below.

"You can stay," Mona says. Billy shakes his head, smiling. Warm all over, and slow.

"I better get back," he says. "They'll miss me."

•

There is no light on even on the porch. Billy breathes in the cold, snow just starting to fall down behind him silent in the great depths. Hand on the doorknob he slowly turns. The door opens silent. No sound down this low. This deep might as well be space.

Bubbles from his bell escape with every breath. He clomps along the ocean floor slowed by weight, weight in his feet, weight in his head. Weight in his eyes. Far away he sees something. Clomps closer.

In light they sit, two of them. From somewhere above them light builds a roof, grown down around them in a sphere. Marly with his toque, face turned frownward over a brown mug. Aunt Beatrix broom-straight, hands folded in front of her. Without their own breaths they could be wax. Billy watches. Their chests move though nothing else does. Slowed by weight and depth just like him. So they are all far underwater.

His diving bell comes with him, noiseless along the silent floor. They turn to him. Marly and Aunt Beatrix open and close their mouths, as though gasping. Gulping. Drinking in air with their two lippy holes. Billy finds himself sitting, somehow inside their lighted bubble. He blinks a few times, then keeps his eyes closed.

They make sounds he can't place. Sounds like songs through water. Sounds like bubbles. Sounds like they are making the light themselves.

Billy opens his eyes but they hurt. His pupils feel like they're growing, growing, growing to the size of dinner plates. He wonders if he's becoming jelly, growing tentacles. He stares at his hands but they're just hands. His fingers don't swish stickily and there are no suckers along their undersides. But his eyes pound with the pain of growth. He closes them again.

The sounds like singing stop. Billy bends his head forward as his eyes have got their own weight now, have grown heavier even than his head. He wonders vaguely what Marly and Aunt Beatrix think of his diving bell. He wonders if it's the reason he can't make sense of the sounds they make. He wonders should he take it off.

A mug that reminds him of his mother, handmade, bulb-shaped, painted honey and brown. He pushes his hands around it, squeezes. Hopes as he remembers somehow hoping before that it will squeeze back. It doesn't. He thinks it never has.

"Billy."

He hears it and it makes sense to him but he doesn't know who this Billy is. Wait. Yes he does. He nods.

"Do you hear what I'm saying? We couldn't tell you before... but now, well. Now they're saying you need to go back."

Billy shakes his head, no. He can't go back, not now. He shakes his head, his eyes so big they make the shaking slow. And hard.

"They say you just didn't grow like the rest of us."

Billy laughs. Of course he didn't. Can't they see his eyes? The size of dinner plates growing heavy out of his head.

"You'll have more pain. And... if you don't go back, it could get worse. More drugs. More hospitals. You don't want that, do you?"

More drugs? Sure. Billy nods.

"I know this is a lot to take in, honey. You look like you've had enough. Marly, take him upstairs. He looks terrible."

Terrible coils slither from beneath his fingernails, sticky and wet. New skin slippery with birth. His limbs gone to jelly he finds he can't stand, but slides along the ocean floor, at home in the sand, in the silt, in the thousands of rotting hims that have gone before.

"Oh, Marly, help him. He can't even stand."

"No, he can't, can he. I wonder why, Beagle?"

"Well, we've upset him. Take him up to bed."

His body is wet in places he doesn't even have holes, wet to slide between low rollers down here in the dark, here where he needs these eyes to be bigger, bigger, big enough to see. He dives under a rock, hides from their grasping hands. His eyes flash green against their light.

"Lord in Heaven, Marly, get him up from under there."

"Billy! Come on, off to bed with you!" A hairy human hand reaches for him. He scuttles backwards, amazed at how quickly he can do it. Scuttling comes naturally to things that came from the deep sea, once upon a time. "Billy! What on earth are you doing, hiding under the coffee table like a little kid? Come on now."

His tentacles slide on the sand as he is lifted heavy as a bag of sand and thrown over Marly's shoulder. Catch of the day.

JUNE, 1972

HICKLIN

"What are you talking about?" Hicklin asks Nick.

Nick shrugs with one shoulder, as the other is leaning up against the doorframe of his *dépanneur*. "I'm talking your rent's been paid. Merry Christmas."

"You're sure?" Hicklin asks, frowning.

"Course I'm sure," Nick says, nodding. "You ever hear of a landlord making up a story like that? Now go on, get outta here."

"Oh-kay," Hicklin says slowly, folding up his cheque and putting it in his back pocket. "If you're sure...."

"I'm sure, already!" Nick says, rolling his eyes. "Unless you feel like paying some of that tab you kids owe me...."

"Oh," Hicklin says. "Yeah, of course. Here —" he holds out the rent cheque.

"I'm just kidding," Nick says, smiling for the first time. "Take your girl out, have a good time. She deserves it, eh?" he asks with a wink.

"Sure," Hicklin says, uncertainly. He turns and heads across the street.

It's only once he's halfway across that Hicklin stops. He's sure Nick must've noticed Flan's absence by now. So who's his girl? He turns back to ask Nick, but he's gone inside, to joke with his buddies over a game of chess that never seems to end. Hicklin shakes his head, and crosses the street to the apartment.

Beau greets him at the top of the stairs, a stack of records in his arms. "Hicklin!" he beams. "Come see!"

Hicklin rounds the corner into the living room. There's a pile of empty cardboard boxes on the floor, and a brand new stereo in the place of the old one.

"Where'd that come from?" Hicklin asks Beau, looking around the room. "And where's my old stereo?"

"That old thing?" Beau rolls his eyes. "It was a hunk of junk, Hicklin. Look at this! It has an eight-track *and* a turntable!"

"I found the old one," Hicklin says, to his shoes, "and fixed it up myself."

"It's in your room, Daddy," Luce calls from the kitchen. "I know how you're stuck on your old things."

"Luce?" Hicklin shakes his head again. Walks to the kitchen. Luce is unpacking a box of dishes, heavy, handmade looking things glazed mustard and avocado. Dolly is at the sink, washing.

"*C'est moi*, Daddy!" Luce puts down the plate she's holding, and smiles at Hicklin. "Pretty good French, huh?"

"What's going on?" Hicklin asks the room in general.

Dolly turns to him, holding up a pink sherry glass. "She brought me dishes," she intones, turning back to the sink.

"What?"

"Well, technically, the dishes are for everyone," Luce says cheerily, bending and picking up another couple of bags. "To replace the ones I broke. And these are for everyone, too!" From the bags Luce lifts bottles. Vodka, gin, whiskey. Hicklin reaches out, touches a foil-wrapped cork.

"Luce, is that champagne?" he asks.

"Ab-si-tive-ly!" Luce says. "What say we pop this baby?"

"What?" Hicklin asks, pulling out the wheely chair and sitting carefully. "Luce. Did you pay our rent?"

Luce turns to him. She shrugs and gives him another smile. "Well, I had to do something! I felt like an absolute heel, Daddy, a real moroon. You folks take me in and what do I do? Nice way of saying thank you, if I do say so myself."

Dolly says nothing, but Hicklin can see the back of her head moving in a nod.

"Okay," Hicklin says. So does that mean she told Nick she's my girl, he wants to ask. Instead, he puts a hand to his head, and squeezes. "But, Luce. Where'd you get the money?"

"Well," Luce says, her smile turning sharp and wide, her canines coming out pointy, "I'm a *kid*, right? Let's just say I've got a paper route and leave it at that. *Daddy*."

Hicklin opens his mouth to say something when he's interrupted by a wave of feedback and someone screaming, "*Kick out the jams, mother-fuckers*!"

"C'mon, guys!" Beau yells from the living room over a racket of guitars and noise. "The MC5's never sounded so good!"

Dolly walks slowly to the other room. Luce slides around the corner, then back again. She crouches down before Hicklin, her hands on his knees. "I'm sorry, Daddy," she whispers, leaning in closer to kiss him on the cheek. "Pals?"

Hicklin nods dumbly as she slips away, into the other room. He sighs. "And don't call me that," he says, his voice drowned out by the immortalized screaming in the other room.

•

Days pass as Hicklin sits in his room. Out in the living room he can hear the stereo, hear T. Rex on constant rotation, telling them all to, "*Bang-a-gong, get it on*." Lou Reed sings low and slow about the Venus in furs. Jim Morrison teaches him how to spell G-L-O-R-I-A from beyond the grave. Over and over and over again.

Hicklin hooks up his old turntable, and plays Beethoven's Ninth at full blast, but that only makes the other fellows scream louder. He gives up, and goes roaming the alleys, hunting for treasure.

He walks and walks, his feet taking him from one stack of trash to another. He picks up an old crank-shaft ice cream maker, puts it under his arm, for Anatole, Nick's father. He keeps walking. Turns down an alley, and there's Dolly, her bald head shining even in the cool shade, as though she's the source of the light, and not just reflecting it. He takes a deep breath, takes one step toward her. Then turns, and scoots away, the way he came.

He turns onto Duluth, and there's Beau, playing hopscotch with Nick's kids. Across the street, Luce sits in front of the dep, her long legs stretched out in front of her, her heart-shaped sunglasses pulled down over her eyes. Gold glints through her hair, from where her earrings are. The men who are usually inside playing their never-ending game of chess have come out, blinking into the sunny day, to lean against the wall, all around Luce. One of them leans down to her, whispers something in her ear. She laughs, puts her hand on his shoulder, pulls him closer to her. Whispers something back. The two of them peer across the road, to where he stands, the ice cream maker still tucked under one arm. He turns, and walks away, toward the Main. He thinks he's got enough in his pocket for a drink. Behind him he hears Luce call him Daddy. He keeps walking.

•

He's walking Luce to the show, since Beau is nowhere to be found, and Dolly's already there. He keeps to the street side of the sidewalk, as close to the traffic as he can get without walking in it. She smokes and walks slow, her heart-shaped sunglasses poking their pointed ends out from under her hair.

"Daddy," she says, when they've gotten halfway to the show. "What's eating you?"

"Nothing," he answers, reaching into his pocket for a pack of cigarettes. He pulls one out and stops to light it. Luce stops too, near him.

"Applesauce," she says. "You're all balled up."

He shakes his head. "No," he says, starting to walk again. "I'm fine."

They pass a construction site, a small square hole dug out of the asphalt. He tries not to look, but can't help himself. He takes a deep breath.

The smell is the same. He raises his head a little, sniffs.

"What's up, Doc?" asks Luce, turning to face him, miming a large

166

carrot in the corner of her mouth.

He shakes his head. "Nothing," he mumbles.

Luce cocks her head, tilts it to one side. Raises one eyebrow. "Well, *something's* up. I can tell you that much from here, and even with my peepers shut." She closes her eyes, a smile growing across her lips.

He shakes his head. Closes his eyes. "I don't know what you're talking about, Luce, I —"

"Ahhh, tell it to Sweeney, Daddy," Luce sings. "I can tell."

"It's nothing," he says to his shoes. "Just a breeze."

"A breeze!" Luce howls, her boney shoulders shaking. "That's swell. I'll give you a dollar for that one."

Luce fishes around in the pocket of her faded cut-offs. The pockets actually hang out below where she's cut them so it seems her hand is moving around creepily inside her body, darting from one place to another under her skin. "Here!" she holds a wadded dollar up to Hicklin's face. He pushes it away, his head sinking ever closer to the ground. She takes a step closer. So close he can smell the bubblegum scent wafting from the gloss on her lips, gloss from the fat tube she wears on a pink rope around her neck.

"What was it, Daddy?" Luce asks, standing so close he can feel the heat from her skin, hot, too hot for this time of year, hot as though something were burning inside her. "A real tomato walk by, or what?"

He keeps his head down and tries to walk away. Luce puts a hand on his arm.

"Luce," he says, softly, "it's nothing. Just... let's go... aren't we going to be late?"

Luce snorts lightly through her nose. "Ooooh, late for Dolly's little bit of Victoriana?" A hand on Luce's hip as she looks hard at him. "You must really be hard up for fun." A beat, and then a loud, "HA!" as she realizes the cheesy pun she's made.

"Yeah, good one," Hicklin says weakly, "Okay, really, let's go."

He starts walking but his steps slow, even without him thinking as he passes it. He can't help it. He turns his head and takes a great sniff of the air. Musty water slow running in a broken brick pipe, rotting wood struts serving no purpose but to add to the smell of old earth unfolding, laying its layers open for any old eyes to see. It's the same, the same as he remembers, not remembers, it was never gone.

•

Dolly in blue, a Victorian nymph gown, all gossamer and ties about the waist. She holds a golden lyre, and stands on a pedestal that turns as music plays, cranked out of a nearby record player. Her hair is a bloody, unearthly red, piled and tumbled over her skull in crested wavelets. Her eyes are closed.

She spins and holds her fingers over the lyre, posed as if about to play. All the joints on her fingers and hands, elbows and wrists, were painted by Luce. Beatniks and art students walk by, stubbies clutched in their hands, smoke wafting from the ends of their fingers. They talk of the paintings on the other walls. They talk of the sculptures. They talk of Art. Not one of them stops before her, not one of them reads the plaque Luce has painted to mark the pedestal. *Galatea*, it says, and nothing else. For almost an hour this is all that happens: she spins, she smiles, her frozen hand pretends to play.

Then in walks Pygmalion, in top hat and tails, sweeping past the Art, pushing past the people with their smokes and drinks, leaving a wake of curses behind him. He stops before Galatea, raises his hands in a silent exclamation. Smiling, he circles the pedestal, tripping over the record player's cord in the process, steadying himself a bit by putting a hand on Galatea's leg. While he bends to put the plug back in the outlet, she opens her eyes. Blinks. Gives her head a little shake. Raises the golden lyre to her eyes, blinks. Throws the thing over her shoulder, almost beaning Pygmalion in the process. The turtlenecked crowd watches.

Pygmalion stands close to Galatea's pedestal, utterly transfixed. He reaches out a hand to touch her. She begins a series of jerky movements, trying to swat him away, but is too slow. Galatea raises an admonishing finger, waves it slowly over the crowd. Still she spins.

The room is silent as she bends, slowly, slowly, bends down to her toes and gets hold of her hem. Up it goes, to her knees. Her bare feet are joined to her pale ankles by slim, painted lines. Her calves shine white against the blue of her gown. She pauses, raises her eyes to the crowd. Blinks. Someone wolf whistles, sparking a round of spattered claps. Her face does not change. She lifts her hem halfway up her thighs.

Her knees are articulated, pale white. She spins slowly, blinking at the crowd. A couple more whistles come her way, accompanied by shouts of encouragement. She begins, jerkily, to pull her hem higher.

Pygmalion jumps in front of her, his arms spread wide. He waves his hands wildly, shakes his head. He is told to get out of the way. He is booed. He turns to Galatea, puts his hands together, looks at her imploringly. She drops her hem and stands.

There is a smile of relief on Pygmalion's face, but nothing on hers as she spins. Pygmalion shakes his head and goes behind the pedestal and opens a small door there. Bits of machinery are pulled out and tossed, clanking, onto the floor. From a pocket within his tailcoat Pygmalion produces a wrench. He gets to work on something inside Galatea's pedestal, as she turns, standing, very very still.

Slowly, slowly, she raises her arms. Slowly, slowly, she bends them, putting her hands behind her neck. Then slowly, slowly, she puts her arms down. Her gossamer gown falls to her feet. The crowd cheers. She is wearing a short slip, the colour of her skin, the colour of skim milk. Every visible joint is articulated. As Galatea turns, a box can be seen on her back, a box of machine parts, with a small key sticking out to one side. Pygmalion stands from where he had been messing with the pedestal's contents, a horrified look on his face. In his hands are two large screws.

Galatea wiggles her toes. Peels first her right foot, and then her left, from the pedestal. She looks at the crowd and blinks. Pygmalion is down on his knees, his hands clasped. He shakes them back and forth, back and forth, as Galatea spins. She tilts her head and raises one foot. Looks at it. Then the other. Puts her feet back where they were, and strikes her starting pose. For one full turn, and then another. Pygmalion smiles up at her.

Galatea bends her head to his. Puts a hand on his shoulder. Steps delicately from the pedestal, using Pygmalion's shoulder as a support. And slowly, slowly, Galatea walks away. The pedestal turns.

•

The art students have left, or collapsed into couples on the floor. A film loop of a chicken rotting is playing against the back wall, accompanied by the nonsensical voice track meant to explain something about the artist's thoughts.

"Drama," the voice says. "Ecstasy. Wonder. Amusement. Nourishment. A clap of thunder. Where is the lightning? Where? Where? Where?"

At the final, "Where?" the camera zooms in, inside the festering chicken, and fades to black. Hicklin leans back against the wall and laughs, as he has every time the thing has ended. Across the room, he can see Luce throwing back her head. She runs up to him, a little wobbly, her eyes a bit too bright, still laughing.

"Daddy," she pants. "Have you seen this awful movie? It's absolute piffle!"

"Yeah," he says, "I've been laughing at it all night."

Luce shakes her head. "Whoever did it couldn't make a piece of toast. But you guys were... *superfine!*"

Hicklin raises an eyebrow.

"What?" Luce asks. "No good?"

Hicklin shakes his head. "I like the way you talk," he says.

Luce shrugs. "Thought I'd try it out," she says, with a little smile. "What I meant to say was, you guys were the cat's meow!"

Hicklin squinches up his nose, then buries it deep in his lukewarm beer. "Naaaaah," he says quietly into his drink, "I don't know about that."

"No, really! You really threw these high hats for a loop! I don't think they knew what the hubbub was, bub."

Hicklin shrugs. "Maybe. I don't really like performing but Beau wouldn't do it. Said he just wasn't having a 'pants day', whatever that means."

"Where is he, anyway?" Luce looks around at the few remaining drunks. "Wasn't he at least supposed to come?"

"Yeah," Hicklin shrugs. "Maybe the no pants thing went too far and he just couldn't bring himself to wear clothes. Who knows? It's happened before."

Luce giggles.

"You think I'm joking," Hicklin says, all super-serious.

Luce shakes her head, biting her lip. The chicken movie has started up again, the chicken fresh and plump and new, the voice saying, "Promise. Urgency. Beauty."

"I can't watch this again," Hicklin says, downing the last of his beer. "And anyway. Don't I owe you a drink?"

Luce nods. He helps her up, and they go. Behind them the pedestal turns.

"Still got some Mary," she grins, holding up a Beau joint, perfectly rolled. "You in?"

Now it's Hicklin's turn to nod.

•

Tight-skinned in two bodies, faces laced with humping reds, sliced light on white cheekbones, sharp against pools of store windows, mirror-dark. Luce small beside him, a warm wall between him and this city dark, dark as though there never were another way, dark as if there never were such a thing as light. From here he can't even see the sky. Where there should be sky there is only a crawling well, arches of colour growing veins above, roots or tubes or branches, from here he can't tell. Lights are shaped into words around him, words he's forgotten how to read, the hum around them low as fairy voices and just as golden. Luce's purse is tiny and endless, inside it potions and pills and powders, enough to make him wordless for once, enough to make him stop and look and listen. She darts between cars and he follows. She slides through the crowd and he follows. She is tiny, a tiny anchor, but a tiny anchor is all he needs right now. She stops before a door, looks back long enough to see he's following her, and disappears. By the time he's reached the door he's not at all sure it's the right one, not at all sure it's the one she disappeared into, but in he goes, tripping along a dark hole, so dark it could go up or down.

Hicklin feels his way along a soggy hallway that squishes under his feet with the soft squelching he's known only at low tide, squelching of sand still wet with things from the undersea tugging slow on every toe. There are stairs, but he still can't tell which way he's going. At the end of it, a weak pool of dirty light, and Luce inside it shining, her black hair hiding everything from him but an angled grin. Before the curtain, a man. Too tall he huddles into a grey suit, slick at the knees, hems hovering homeless over wrists and ankles. The man turns to them with an outstretched palm, his face a no-face in the low light. Luce hands the man a folded bill, the colour of it lost, disappearing before Hicklin can even start to look. The man holds the curtain open for them. Beyond him something thumps.

Into a room that could be any size, any shape, its true nature hidden by walls of mirrors everywhere, a room that thumps with music so loud it's lost all meaning. There might be words in there somewhere, somewhere there might be notes. Above him darkness and some sense of real height to the ceiling, though when he looks up he feels he might be wrong. When he looks up he is, in fact, crushed by the sense that the room he's in is tiny, an unlit coffin standing on its head. As though the room is just the size of him, just the size of whoever might enter it. He closes his eyes just to feel something bigger before he starts to choke. And opens them. And there is Luce, ahead of him, darting off through the crowded tables, through the waitresses dropping ashes in the drinks they serve, away through the ladies that spin all round. He follows her, through smoke that seeps up from the floor to hover at waist height, candles on tables shifting in an eerie breeze that seems to come from everywhere, all the candles flickering in different directions, *feu follets* to light his way.

He reaches Luce without losing his way, and stops, and stands. All

around them ladies slide through glass, twisting sideways into themselves, twinning and separating smooth as microbes. Spinning bodies
eat each other under weird lights that glow without illuminating, legs
crawl from all angles, breasts over heads under feet hanging tight onto
poles. A hand pulling him down to a seat, down closer to the *feu follets*
which only he can follow.

"Cool it, Daddy," Luce whispers, close in his ear, her voice a hissing
whisper over the thumping. "You look like you're having a heart attack.
You never been in a skin joint before or what?"

The places the ladies aren't wearing any clothes, which are many, are
beginning to bulge and bump in time with the thumping, the thumping
all around, so loud he thinks it could be coming from inside himself.

"What," Hicklin breathes, affirming.

Luce laughs, then looks at him, her eyes going squinty under the
fringes of her bangs. "Well, then. What's the rumpus?"

Hicklin shakes his head. "I dunno... it's all... different."

"Aw, you big Ethel," Luce smiles. "Too much tea, that's your problem."

Hicklin doesn't know what this means and shows it by frowning.

"Take it easy, sunshine, I'm only fooling," Luce smiles, and takes his
hand, gently, gently, maybe the softest anyone has ever held his hand.
"Okay. Rule number one: stay the hell away from the sad sacks on sniffer's row." Luce gestures with her chin and Hicklin follows with his
eyes. There below the stage is a horseshoe of dreamers, faces uptilted
over stubbies and chubbies, eyes glazed with the stunned look of the
newly undead. One breathes through his mouth, and shifts his knees in
a seated Charleston. Hicklin looks away, back to Luce. Her black hair
hides all but the corners of her mouth, her tongue slides long and lean
in and out. She is speaking. He has no idea what she's saying. He hopes
it is beautiful, to go with her lips. Beside her he feels huge and hairy
and intensely grotesque. He looms. Like a man.

"So you can always find your way around," Luce is saying, continuing whatever it was he missed. "See? Easy. These places are all the
same."

A woman spins her hair in a fan making her faceless, her twin showing off her rear in the mirror, circles circled by twin threads, snapping. Luce leans in close again. Whispers.

"Take a breath, bub. You've really gotta relax."

Hicklin sits and takes a breath. The room breathes with him, the ladies expanding in strange places, their limbs pulling their bodies behind them back to their twins in the mirrors all round. Sockets pop. The walls go soft. The thumping settles.

"Sorry," Hicklin says quietly. "I think I missed what you said."

Luce loses the smile she's had on, gets the point back in her chin, the sharpness in her lips. Shakes her head, slightly. "I only give the tour once, Daddy."

A waitress is there, silently, furtively waiting. She's wearing a shirt so Hicklin can actually look her in the eye. Her appearance distracts him for a second from what Luce just called him.

"*Quelque-chose à boire?*" the waitress asks, taking a drag of her cigarette once the question has been asked.

Hicklin thinks. In his pockets there are: a used tissue, a button he found on the street, and approximately one dollar in change.

"Two beers," Luce says, holding up her fingers in a V.

"*Deux bières,*" the waitress says, her voice sliding down a hill to a rolling rest.

Luce looks at Hicklin, her shoulders up.

"*Oui,*" Hicklin says to the waitress. "*S'il vous plaît.*"

"*Ouuuui,*" the waitress drawls, a long 'a' rolling back up the hill.

The waitress is gone as quick as she came. Hicklin searches the floor for a trapdoor, but finds nothing.

"Still off your nut?" Luce asks. "Or are you cool?"

Hicklin doesn't know what 'off your nut' is, but he thinks he knows what 'cool' means. He's pretty sure he's not it, but he nods anyway. As he nods the room bends around him, as though he were the horizon to all the little people who float past.

The waitress returns, popping back out of her hole in the ground. Luce passes her a bill. Hicklin tries on a smile, to which the waitress responds with a raised eyebrow.

"*Ça va?*" she asks, tossing the change Luce has handed back to her into a tumbler that rests on her caban.

"*Oui, ça va bien, merci,*" Hicklin answers, trying to make his smile bigger. On his face it feels huge and plastic, like something that's been melted onto him. The waitress holds his gaze. Wrinkles around her eyes, grouted with black. Thin lips hold tight to a cigarette. A slight sag to her chin, her face just starting to fall. Hicklin wonders what will be under there when it all falls off. He wonders if it will happen now. He stares but doesn't see the flesh move. The waitress narrows her eyes and pops out of view again, back down her hole.

Luce takes a sip of her beer, right out of the bottle, even though the waitress has brought them two small, fluted glasses.

"I gotta powder my nose," she says suddenly, as though the beer has passed through her, instantly, in some strange imitation of the digestive system. "Don't take any wooden nickels."

And just like that, she is gone, her black head shining through the crowd. Hicklin pours a little of his beer into the glass, watching the bubbles speed to the surface and die.

He sits and looks. The room seems to have arranged itself so that he is still the centre of it, still stuck in the middle, still trapped in a space no bigger than a coffin. Around him the action spreads in semi-circles, larger and larger the further from him they are. He blinks. He stares until his eyes get dry. Holding his eyes open like this he catches it, catches the room moving around him.

Everywhere there are dancers, everywhere are mirrors, everywhere everyone has their twin. He stares and sees the mirrors flip over, turning all the twins into originals and vice versa. He sees the trapdoors the waitresses pop out of, sees sliding panels toward the back, where men enter only to disappear. The *feu follets* flicker, each blown a different way by a breeze he can't follow, even with his eyes dry and open.

He reaches out a hand and takes hold of his beer. Not to drink it, just to hold it. The glass is solid, and cool, and whole. He holds it tight.

"Everything Jake?" Luce sits down, putting two new beers on the table. "Check it out — the bartender gave me a couple on the house."

She turns and sends a wink sailing across the room.

Hicklin turns, but the bartender has disappeared, probably down his own hole.

"I know what would make you feel better," Luce whispers in his ear, something like a hiss in her voice. "How about a dance?"

"What?" Hicklin pulls away from her. "I have to dance?"

Luce laughs, so hard she has to put down her beer. "No, Daddy," she smiles. "You just sit there."

Hicklin turns his mouth upside down. "Don't call me that," he says, his stomach flipping over its own secret panel, spilling things into the wrong holes. "Please."

"Why not," Luce moves closer to him, her hand on his knee, "Daddy? You think you don't like it? Or maybe you like it too much, huh?"

Hicklin shakes his head.

"Well, okay, then," Luce says, sliding so far forward on her own chair she's barely sitting on it, her knees spread around Hicklin's, her thighs holding him tight. "What do you want me to call you?"

"Don't call me anything," Hicklin pleads, trying his best to look in Luce's eyes, glinting shiny as glass below shards of black bangs. "I don't want a dance."

"Oh, c'mon," Luce starts rocking back and forth, her skinny knees knobbly on Hicklin's thighs. "You like me, dontcha?"

"Sure I like you, Luce," her face so close to his it's become a pale blob, a swimming ghost beneath bangs black as beetle back. "I just don't want a dance, is all."

"You don't like me at all, Daddy," Luce whispers in his ear, her knees still sliding up and down the length of him. "If you liked me, you'd want a dance."

Luce lowers her head to somewhere in his chest, her legs on his legs, rubbing. She purrs no words into his chest. He looks away, looks over her back humping like a whale, coming off a wave. Catches the eye of his twin in a mirror. His twin looks at him as he looks at his twin. He blinks hears a click a shift a panel somewhere slides he opens his eyes. He and his twin have switched places. Somewhere else another Luce leans back, her mouth wet. Open. Here she slides against him here the seam of her jeans meets him here her mouth is almost almost on him here her knee catches him where he's hard as an elbow inside his pants here he holds his breath lets her breathe out on his neck lets her breathe for the two of them —

A third hand here, now, and then a fourth. Pushing them apart. Luce's face squeezed around a laugh, a slice of his old self smiling in the mirror.

The too-tall man from the door pulls them apart, pulls Luce off Hicklin's lap, shoves them toward the door. Doesn't say a word. Hicklin just about runs back to the velvet curtain, gets tangled up in it. Turns to see Luce walking straight as a queen through the crowd. The *feu follets* follow her. The faces of the guys along sniffer's row turn with her. She winks at Hicklin. Somewhere in him, somewhere deep in his chest, a panel flips. Somewhere for something new.

Luce reaches the velvet, stands beside him. Gives him a daddy peck on the cheek. The too-tall man bends, lifts the curtain for them. Hicklin passes under the curtain, turns to see the too-tall man bend way way down to whisper something in Luce's ear. She shrugs, runs to Hicklin, and grabs his hand. They slip out of the soggy hallway, no sound following them but the underwater squelch of things washed up.

•

Under a sky like a bag of cats, lumpy grey and twitching with humps, they slide between wet walls, joined hand-to-hand. Luce's hair skitters ahead of him, a beacon of black calling him forward. He follows. Into a well between buildings, a hole in the heart of the block. Around them fire escapes stick their struts to the walls, hard veins holding up everything. He couldn't say where he's going but it feels like backstage. He wonders who might be watching, he wonders where they might be. Luce stops, pulls him behind a sagging stack of trash. Rain slips a skin between them.

Her hands don't know this, don't know there is this skin here, don't know where he stops and she begins. Her mouth opens a hole in him, opens him where he didn't know he could be opened, opens him quick as a knife getting to the meat of an oyster.

"Wait," his mouth says a million miles away. "Wait. Luce."

He can feel her mouth smile though he can't see it with his eyes. Her teeth take a tiny bite out of him. Her hands slide under his jacket, under his shirt, into his pants.

The skin of the rain grows over them, sinking into all the holes in his skin and all the holes in hers, making another skin, one big enough for two.

He whispers under his breath into her breath words that don't matter, words that won't help him, words that she doesn't know. She bites him again, his bottom lip, hard enough that he can almost feel her teeth meet.

His meat meeting between her teeth.

He closes his eyes.

A skin grows wet and new over them, growing his eyes closed, growing her right into him.

"C'mere, Daddy," she whispers. And he does.

DOLLY

Ginger holds down one side of the mold while Dolly pries open the top.

"You sure you don't want to go back?" Ginger asks. "Maybe have a drink? It's your show, too. He wasn't even supposed to be in it."

Dolly nods. "I know."

A slim sliver of air appears between the two sides of the mold, nothing coming out yet but a slightly sticky stench.

"How'd it go, anyway?" Ginger says while trying with her elbow to ward off her big black tom, Honky, who stretches out a polydactylic paw, tries to lay it on the plaster. Pulls it away quickly when Dolly blows a funnel of air in his ear.

"It went fine," Dolly says, gently tugging at the top half of the mold. A slow sucking sound begins from somewhere inside, the smell becoming more meaty, musty. Honky tentatively puts forth his nose, his eyes on Dolly.

"Honky!" Ginger waves her elbow around. "Piss off, cat."

Dolly leans close to Honky and hisses in his face. He regards her as he might a spot of dirt, then, as if reminded, begins to clean the inbetweens of his many toes.

Ginger tugs at her side of the mold, half-heartedly. She looks at Dolly. "So what are you doing here, on a Friday night, after a show? And even more cheerful than usual, I might add."

Dolly stares at Ginger from behind her huge glasses. Lets out a sigh small and tough as gravel. "He left with her again," Dolly says, gently nudging the plaster up.

"Sister," Ginger shakes her head. "He doesn't belong to you."

"I know," a sad little not smile, a tiny line between her eyebrows as she tugs. "I know Gin. I don't even want him. It's not that. I just worry about him. Sometimes it seems he's not very good at... *seeing* people."

Ginger raises one of her perfect eyebrows, gives a light laugh. "Um, correct me if I'm wrong, but aren't you the one with the Coke bottles, baby?"

Dolly's glasses have slid down her nose. She peers at Ginger over the top of their frames. "You know perfectly well that is not at all what I mean. Now please — hold."

Ginger hangs on to the bottom half of the mold, Dolly pulls hard on her half and the sucking sound increases, pulling as the smell gets stronger, until finally a loud *thhhhhhup* and there it is, reborn. A cow's heart, blue, glossy, and still.

•

Ginger has gone to bed, bored with waiting for the plaster to dry. Dolly picks up a stack of books, a couple of fat candles in glass jars, and a cup of mint tea, now cold. Pulls open the small door that leads to the balcony, Honky squeezing himself through her legs and out, quick as a spirit heading home.

By putting the candles on Ginger's low, broken coffee table and sitting on the floor, Dolly can read quite comfortably. She opens the Muybridge art book which she never returned to the library. Inside it she has hidden her mail, all the mail that comes for her at Ginger's.

Too many letters, though one is too many. Women with no option other than Dolly's plants. Most are brief, asking simply for one word. Help. The last letter has no return address, but the name at the bottom of the page is familiar. She re-reads what is written there, more slowly. Then she refolds it and places it back in the envelope.

She'll have to go check her garden, to make sure she has enough.

•

Dolly checks the setting plaster, her hands on either side of the carefully squared mold. It's still warm, as though the thing in there were alive. She collects her books and gets her coat, then leaves a note on the table telling Ginger not to touch anything.

Outside, the night has turned grey, tufty clouds sliding into each other. She walks quickly, ballet-straight. The few blocks between Ginger's and Hicklin's squeak close around her, the unlit buildings seeming to narrow ahead of her. She walks faster.

Reaching Hicklin's, she pushes open the gate into the courtyard, slides in. Takes the stairs up to the mezzanine. While she plucks dead leaves from her plants, she hears a noise inside, a muffled bang. Trying the kitchen door, she finds it locked. A first. She runs back down the stairs, sliding back out through the gate, and around to the front door. It's slightly ajar.

She pushes it open and creeps quickly, quietly up the stairs, not turning on a light. She takes a deep breath at the top, and pushes in the door.

Behind it, blocking the way, is Beau. Lying on the floor, still and silent.

BEAU

Pitching from side to side Billy wakes from his sleep. He's curled in the net of a hammock, swinging above damp floorboards ill-lit by fat candles. The light from the flames swings as he swings, the creak from boards rubbing against each other, swings as he swings, the blood in his belly swings. He looks around for some indication of where he might be. There is a porthole but nothing can be seen outside. Two shades of indigo sway past the round opening, giving no further clues.

Wherever he is it's hot. Sweat covers him as though it were a blanket, as though the sweat itself were making him hot. He tries to wipe his forehead but finds his hands are stuck somehow, to whatever it is he's lying on now, no longer in the hammock, but lying flat on something hard. He can feel his insides swish and sway with the rhythm of the boat. He tries again to move, to stand. He is pinned, hopelessly, under his own body, which is still swelling.

A tiny door he hadn't noticed before opens, a tiny person staggers in, swaying under the weight of an iron-bound trunk. The tiny person is hunched beneath a dark cowl. Omitting a greeting, the tiny person sets down the trunk and struggles to open it. Billy's belly swells and sways, his skin grows painful now over the contents of his body.

The tiny person succeeds in opening the trunk, and removes from it a bundle of soiled linen and a large glass jar. Inside the jar swims a something, unless it is only a something that sways and only seems to swim. Billy sweats, hotter now than he was before, hotter than he's ever been. The tiny person looks up at him and says, "You're a young one."

Billy frowns, and tries to shake his head. Looks down at his hands, and sees they're small, childishly small. He thinks he had another name, once. He wonders what it was.

"Lie still now. That's no baby. He'll get rid of it for you." The tiny person's head flicks toward the jar.

But, Billy thinks. I must be a woman, this doesn't happen to men.

"Hah!" the tiny person laughs from beneath its hood. "No woman I know has one of *those* between its legs!"

And with that, the tiny person lifts the lid of the jar. Coos softly to it. Pulls the something out slowly with the help of a pair of tongs. Turns to Billy and smoothly pulls up his shirt.

"He'll fix it for you," the tiny person says softly. "He's what we call a Doctor."

Billy tries to wriggle free of whatever binds him to the table. The tiny person laughs and holds Billy down easily with one child-sized hand.

"Strong for a woman, I'll say," chuckles the tiny person, holding the Doctor close to Billy's belly. Billy gets a glimpse of a shrivelled, dark grey noodle, about the length of his little finger. There doesn't seem to be a mouth end, there doesn't seem to be a face, but as the tiny person holds the Doctor over Billy's belly, the noodle stretches, stretches, stretches, and makes motions much like sniffing. The dangling end of the noodle thing bobs, sniffing, lightly over Billy's belly, and, apparently finding a good spot, attaches itself to his skin with a light pop and the sudden sting of broken skin. Billy turns his head away and closes his eyes, but he can still see that dirty noodle, can still feel the slow sucking from whatever it is the Doctor has in place of a mouth.

But, Billy thinks, his stomach turning, his eyes shut tight. You just said I'm not a woman. Doesn't that make me a man?

"Hah!" laughs the tiny person. "No man I know has one of *those* between its legs!"

Below his belly Billy cannot see. The globe of it swells, filling his vision, giving him a new horizon. The tiny person scurries around, placing itself between Billy's legs. Even the very top of the tiny person's hooded head disappears below Billy's equator.

"Aha!" the tiny person's eyes rise just barely over the horizon, two smudged moons of sludgy grey. With a note of triumph the tiny person proclaims, "The Doctor has found something. I know someone who'll want to see this. We haven't had one like you for ages!"

Who? thinks Billy. Who will want to see what?

"Old Fourlegs, that's who," the tiny person says, scurrying back up toward Billy's head. "You're a singular specimen."

Who's that? Billy wonders, but is ignored.

The tiny person collects the Doctor from Billy's belly, now a glowing browny-red, and swollen to the size of a large sausage. There is a wet sucking sound as the Doctor is lifted from Billy's skin, and a splat as the Doctor is returned to whatever liquid it is that fills his jar.

He's fatter, thinks Billy, but my belly is still growing.

The tiny person shakes his head, and screws the lid back on the Doctor's jar. After placing the jar on the far edge of the table, the tiny person leans in close to Billy's ear and whispers, "He can't fix you. He thinks he can, but he can't. Only *I* can do that."

And who are you? wonders Billy.

The tiny person draws itself up to its full height, gaining perhaps a quarter of an inch, and says proudly, "*I* am the Instrument."

The Instrument pulls a large, filthy oilcloth from the trunk, ties it around Billy's neck, spreads it like a tent over Billy's spread knees. Another bottle from the trunk, this one thankfully free of Doctors, Billy can see by craning his neck. The Instrument fishes a spotty hanky from somewhere inside its robe, and, after pulling the cork stopper from the lid of the new jar, places the hanky over the mouth of the jar and tips it.

"And now, sweet Prince, may flights of angels carry you to your rest," the Instrument says, holding the soaked hanky to Billy's nose. Billy holds his breath but the Instrument is patient. The Instrument waits. Billy tries to escape, thrashing his head, but the Instrument holds the hanky fast to Billy's face. Billy breathes in, one quick, shallow breath. It is enough.

"Wakey-wakey, Sleeping Beauty."

Billy is not sure if he hears this or thinks it, until his eyes open. Two sludgy grey moons glisten too close. Billy tries to move away from them but finds he is still bound to the table.

"You're a thrasher, you are," the Instrument says. "Almost made me miss my mark."

From Billy's behind to his navel there is nothing good, nothing but pain. The swelling of his belly has gone down, his planet receded, gone retrograde. Perhaps it will return someday.

"No chance of that, I'm afraid," says the Instrument, a note of something like pride coming into its voice. "I did my job, and well. You'll never have that belly again."

The Instrument turns his back to Billy, begins fussing with yet another jar, filling it with some sort of liquid, then, after quickly looking over its shoulder, dropping something like a sea anemone into it. Billy shuts his eyes when the Instrument looks over its shoulder again. The Instrument nods to itself, then scurries over to the trunk, begins rummaging through it.

Billy opens his eyes, just enough to see, to get a good look at whatever it is inside that jar. Pink and hairless, the sea anemone has planted itself upon a round foot at its base, something like a mouth sipping at the liquid inside the jar. Billy snaps his eyes shut as the Instrument returns to the jar. Carefully, the Instrument bends to scratch something upon a scrap of paper, a scraggly quill bobbing above its hand. The Instrument sticks it to the jar after spreading something gummy on the paper's backside. Just then, there comes a tapping at the door.

Billy thinks he can just make out, written there in flowing script, *The Prince's Bits*.

LUCE

Well, kids. What can I tell you? It's been a hell of a day. Let's see if old Luce can get the story straight for you, huh?

The Fox and I finish what we were doing in the alley. (You'll find out about all that soon enough, ask Mom. She just loves giving the birds-and-the-bees talk. Gives her a chance to relive her glory days.) We start hoofing it, but real slow. I can't speak for him, but I feel like I'm doped to the gills, and it's not just the dope.

We're talking stupid and walking slow, and then he just stops and says he has to tell me something. I nod.

First he tells me about Flan, who sounds like a real piece of work. She's the dame who fits that old slip that's been lying on his floor since I got here. This twist sounds like a top-of-the-line, Grade A bitch with a capital B. But I hold off saying anything, playing sweet as pie.

Then he starts talking about me. Little old Luce! Seems he thinks I'm the bee's knees, kids. Seems someone's been putting him off the scent for quite some time. I wonder who. A certain pale Princess, whispering behind her ghostly hand?

You kids would be proud of me, you really would. I get the bearcat feeling, I do. That I can't control. But do I scream, and yell, and call Clever Dolly names? Nosir. I look at him sweet as you please and I tell him things, the kind of things that make it all better. You know. And he kisses me, and that goes so well we have to jump down another rabbit hole into another alley and do what we just did all over again.

By the time we get back to our place, I'm tired in the best way, like after a day at the beach or something. I've got this warm, stupid feeling, like I could sleep for a hundred years, and be happy the whole time.

But here's all the lights on, and the Daisy stretched out on the floor, and the Ghost come running as we get in the door. Her voice is more scratchy than usual, like an old record that tried to make friends with a cat, and behind her big glasses her eyes are red-rimmed and wobbly. She says she found him like this, and that she's making him some witchy brew and that maybe we should take him to the hospital even though he hates them.

I ask why he hates hospitals and neither of them seem to know, but they both know he does. I take a look at the Daisy.

He's covered with burning blisters, blooming out all over him. They're so red and angry they make his skin look as white as the Ghost's. He's sweating and his pretty mismatched eyes are closed, but they're dancing all over the place, like two little animals are trapped under his eyelids.

I've seen this before. All you kids had it, all at the same time. Chicken pox.

Isn't he too old to have the chicken pox, the two of them ask me at the same time, doesn't everybody get it when they're a kid? I shrug. Then Hicklin gets this funny look on his face and says he thinks he remembers something, about chicken pox being real bad to get when you're older. But he doesn't remember why and the Doll and I just look at each other, lost. Hicklin starts pacing around and hitting his head. Doesn't move the gears though.

So we can't take him to the hospital and it might be real bad, so I fess up. I tell them I know a croaker.

•

I get back to our place and nothing's different: same set of violet sheets on the window making everybody look sick, same Ghost in charge of everybody, fussing in and out of the room, same Fox sitting on the floor next to the Daisy. I guess they were too chicken to move him, but anyway the Fox is man enough to touch him. He's wiping the sweat off the Daisy's head with a rag he keeps dunking into a little bowl. The Daisy looks worse. He's covered in these mad red sores like something all broken up into lots of tiny little pieces is trying to sneak right out of his skin. Makes me itch just looking at it.

Oscar walks in behind me, doing that swimming walk he does, all slow and mellow like he's always underwater, like those pictures of Muhammad Ali, when he faked that he trained at the bottom of a pool. Oscar lays his hand on my shoulder, rubs it, slow, slow, slow. Gives me a squeeze with the huge of his hand. The Fox is staring at me like I brought a box of rotten eggs home and started chucking them around like they were confetti. I shrug out of Oscar's reach and slip away from him, just one step.

"This is your doctor?" the Fox asks me, pointing at Oscar like he's not even there. "The guy from the park?"

"Hey, *ça va tout le monde?*" Oscar's swimming slow into the room, his hand out to shake hands with the Fox, smiling that smile of his, big teeth that makes me happy for no reason.

The Fox can't not shake a hand so he stands and does it though I can see that look on his face getting worse like maybe the eggs were full of maggots and now they're falling from the ceiling like snow that's not snow.

"He's in med school," I tell the Fox, as Oscar stands looking at the Daisy.

"He's in med school," the Fox repeats. "Uh-huh."

Oscar sort of bobs his head, slow like, and smiles down at the Daisy. He looks over at the Fox and makes this sort of gesture like would it be okay to touch the Daisy?

"You're in med school?" the Fox asks Oscar.

"*Oui,*" Oscar smiles, bobbing his fro big like the moon. "*J'étudie la médecine, bien sur.* And for now, I am very good. Right?"

"*On parle en français, Hicklin, câlisse,*" the Ghost says, coming back into the room with a jar of iced tea in her hand. "Oscar's French. If you hadn't noticed."

The Ghost hands the iced tea to Oscar and starts gabbing in French with him. I don't get much of it but there's a lot of tutting from Oscar and nodding from the Ghost.

"Luce," the Fox practically spits at me. "If this guy's a doctor I'm the Queen of France."

"So get a corset, Daddy, Christ," I spit right back. "I'm no crap artist."

He makes this big deal of snorting all loud through his nose and I kind of want to smack him. Oscar's got a thermometer from somewhere. He shakes it out like he's gonna conduct us in a round of Christmas carols, then rolls the Daisy on his side and shoves the thing real clean, almost invisible, up the Daisy's sleeping backside. He turns away from the bed and talks a lot and really fast in French. The Fox doesn't say anything, but he does nod his head.

After a couple of minutes, Oscar takes the thermometer out. Shakes it some more, then talks really fast to the Ghost. She and the Fox talk a bunch. Oscar goes to the kitchen, and picks up the phone.

"What?" I ask after a while, since I can't make out a word of what Oscar's been saying. The Fox and the Ghost are real quiet for a minute. "What?" I ask again.

The Ghost gives me this look that's real sad, even for her.

"I think we need to get him to a hospital," the Fox says.

"But, I thought —" I start, until the Ghost cuts me off.

"Hicklin's right," the Ghost says, her mouth barely moving. "Beau might hate us when he wakes up, but —"

She can't finish and goes scurrying from the room.

"But, it's just chicken pox, right?" I ask the Fox. Oscar is busy shaking the thermometer around and looking doctory. "Everybody gets it, right? Right?"

The Fox shakes his head. "We can't wake him up."

Oscar comes over to me and wraps a slow heavy arm around my shoulders. He smiles his big smile at me but somehow that just makes me feel like more of a heel.

HICKLIN

1969

Below them water throws itself against the rocks. They stand in the dark on the edge of a cliff below a sky so clear they could see the Milky Way if only they'd look up. There are ten or fourteen or twenty of them, all long hair, leather bags, shirts too bright for daylight and pants that flare to cuffs so wide they do nothing in the dirt but collect it. They stand leaning at angles, same as the trees, shoved sideways by wind. Once in a while, someone pulls a joint from a pocket, from a cigarette pack, from deep within a beaded bag. Once in a while, a couple pulls away from the group, finds a rock or a tree to hide behind. Once in a while, a bottle is passed around. He can see her take a bottle now, see her tilt back her head, see her spill some of whatever she's drinking, see it run down from the side of her mouth until it shines on her chin like drool. She smiles at whoever's next to her, laughs. Wipes her chin with the sleeve of her jean jacket. She doesn't even pretend to look his way.

He is standing behind a tree with peeling bark, a tree that leans over the cliff, as if daring someone to talk it back from the edge. A jumper. He hasn't had a joint passed to him or a sip out of a bottle this night or any other. He's never been within arm's reach.

There is enough light from the half-moon for him to see the new skin under the old of the peeling tree. The new skin is white as bone, the old a burnt blood red. In places the old skin has curled in on itself, to pencil-length shavings. He peels one of these curls away carefully from the rest of the tree. Pulls a cigarette tin from his bag, and places the curl from the tree carefully inside. At home he will label this carefully, *Arbutus. May 19th, 1969*. That will be all. That will be enough.

As he snaps the lid shut on the rectangular cigarette tin, he swears to himself that this will be the last time. The last time he'll answer the phone when she calls using their special ring. The last time he'll say yes when she asks if he'll come with her. The last time he'll wait and wait and wait so long that when someone stoned asks his name he won't know it himself for half a second. The last time he'll even have the whiff of her pass by him. The last time he'll even maybe have half a chance at getting somewhere in her clothes again. The last time.

Who's he fooling?

He crawls onto the tree's shedding skin and lies along its length. Waiting like a snake. He edges along the length of the tree's body, hugging the wood with his knees and hands. The skin of the tree is way more slippery than he'd thought it would be. He hangs on and slides.

When his head is out over the edge of the cliff, he stops. Looks down. Wonders how many litres per second are rushing past. Wonders how it is a tree can grow out of rock. Wonders how long it'll be until he looks over at Flan. Tries not to wonder how long until she looks over at him.

"Hey, hey!" he hears the voice at the same time as the body of the tree starts shaking, as though it's being pummelled. "It's the Pervert!"

He turns his head slowly while still managing to hang onto the tree. Out here a lot of the old skin has been shed, and the new skin is even more slippery, even kind of wet. He turns his head until he can see. Thad. Thad standing right beside the tree, and pumping it up and down with his arms. In the middle distance, a couple of shapes are moving closer. A big square one and a small rat-shaped one. He groans, loudly.

"Hey, Thad," he tries to smile. "How's it going?"

Shake-ashake-ashake goes the tree. He begins edging backwards.

"No, no," Thad grins, putting up a hand. "Stay where you are. I wanna see how far we can chuck you."

"Ha ha ha," he says, pronouncing each *ha* as a word, about the furthest thing from an actual laugh he has ever uttered. "Good one, Thad. C'mon."

Bikky and Dink amble up looking disinterested. Dink throws one of his feet up on a handy stump, takes out a pack of rollies, sprinkles a bit of weed in there, and rolls it up as though he were leaning on a horse post in the Old West. Bikky steps up close to Thad, checks out his handiwork. Nods.

"We're gonna chuck this guy in the drink," Thad says to Bikky.

Shake-ashake-ashake.

"That's the latest," he says, digging his nails into the wet new flesh of the arbutus.

"You hear this guy?" Thad asks Bikky. "He thinks I'm being funny. You think I'm being funny?"

Bikky makes his wide mouth into a kindergartner's unpracticed lower-case n. "Nuh-uh, Thad," Bikky says. "I don't think you're ever funny."

"Yeah," pipes up Dink, who's finished rolling his joint, and is lighting it up with a pack of paper matches, "you're never funny."

"Wait a minute," Thad stops shoving the tree up and down and turns to face Bikky and Dink. "You guys don't think I'm funny?"

"No, no," Bikky shakes his head, quick as he can, as if he were remote-controlled, "we think you're funny."

"Yeah, yeah," Dink nods so quick it looks like a spasm. "Sure you're funny, Thad."

He tries putting one foot down but finds there is no ground beneath it. The whole exercise causes him to lose his balance a little, and he shrieks while scrabbling to hang onto the wet new skin of the tree. The shriek sounds an awful lot like the "Eep!" uttered by the lady in old cartoons, the one who finds a mouse in her house, the one that's always just a monstrous pair of legs.

"Eeeeep!" Thad mimics, over-long and over-loud. Taking one last puff from the joint and handing it back to Dink with a one-inch heater, he turns back to business. "Okay, Pervert. Get out there."

"Thad, c'mon," he tries to sound jokey while digging his short nails as hard as he can into the new skin of the tree. Below him the sea is dark and calm. Small waves jump rope all the way to shore. The half-moon's light is squiggled on the water in a single stroke, as though beaten out of the jittery arm of a polygraph machine.

Bikky snickers. Dink snickers. Thad climbs up on the tree.

"C'mon, Pervert," Thad puts a fake whine in his voice, edges forward along the length of the tree.

He slides further away from Thad, holding tight with his hands, digging in with his nails, hanging on with every muscle in his legs, squeezing with his knees until it hurts.

"Thad, c'm —" he stops himself. "This is stupid."

"Hey, boys!" Thad yells gleefully, "You hear that? I'm stupid!"

Bikky and Dink look at each other.

"Yeah, Thad," Bikky yells. "You sure are! You're stupid!"

"Yeah," Dink squeals. "You're stupid, Thad!"

Thad stops moving forward for a second. Begins nodding as though a spring is unwinding. "See that, Pervert? They agree with you. Maybe you're in charge here."

He's reached the point on the tree where smaller branches head off from the trunk and leaves block his view. His weight combined with Thad's is causing the tree to bend down to the face of the cliff. He is trying to contort his way onto a safe-looking branch when he hears it. Her voice. Flan's voice. Coming at him from way far away, but coming at him. He can't understand what she's saying, but he turns his head and watches her storm closer. Her mouth is open, her red hair flying around her head as though she were caught in an electric field. Here she comes.

And she's calling.

"Thad!"

•

He closes his eyes and feels himself being thrown to the sky. He hangs on. Wraps his hands around the branches. Leaves smack him in the face. On his way down, tiny droplets fly up his nose. He hadn't even noticed it was raining.

He is jolted a few times but he manages to hold on. He opens his eyes. He is alone, at the top of an arbutus growing almost sideways out of rock, hanging over the sea. ·

●

The rain is everywhere at once, coming down from the sky but also, oddly, seeming to rise from the ground and come in straight off the sea. A tug sounds its foghorn far off. Below him, tiny people swarm around a something lying twisted on the shoreline. No one stayed to help him get the hell out of this tree.

He slides as slowly as he can, digging in with his remaining nails. A couple of them seem to have gone missing, leaving bloody ragged holes on the ends of his hands that're only now starting to hurt. He pushes with his knees and pulls with his hands and suddenly he's reached solid ground. It'd seemed like miles to the top of that tree, but now that he stands and looks at it, it's hardly anything at all. A few measly feet over the edge.

The fog has melted into the rain. The tug's disembodied horn keens from somewhere, unanswered. Up where he is there is still only rain. He looks down, into the fog. Tiny shapes scuttle and squeal. He wonders if he should join them.

He turns and sees a couple of long-haired, bell-bottomed kids slipping in the mud. They manage to descend, and their heads disappear from his view. He approaches the hole in the woods they've left behind.

It is not a path, not yet. More of a slightly trampled way through the underbrush and down the side of the cliff. He steps carefully, holding onto a wet, thorny branch. Repeating this, and not looking down, and not looking any further than the next step, he makes it to the bottom. His cheek has been cut by a branch flying back into his face and there are muddy, bloody holes in both his knees. His clothes are soaked, his hair sends drips into his eyes. But what greets him at the bottom of the cliff, he has to say, makes him feel as though he's doing pretty well.

Grey shapes splattered with brown and red seem to swim in the fog. They drift slowly as though trapped in a vial, cling to each other briefly before separating and moving on, to cling to another. The tugboat's sobs are being answered, again and again. He moves through the grey shapes, stepping carefully on the slippery rocks underfoot until he reaches sand. Here he is forced to adopt the staggering walk all the rest of them have, the slanting zombie walk wet sand demands. Through a large group of grey shapes he walks, toward Flan's red hair. Red as the flame from a lighthouse, the only thing he can see.

She is curled on the wet sand with the something on her lap. The something has something like a face. She is stroking it. Her face so near it she could kiss it.

"Flan," he says. Though he is unsure if his voice will make any sound at all, it does. A lot of sound. It is a bellow from somewhere inside he didn't know existed. All of the grey shapes turn to face him. Only she remains, a faceless cloud of red, swimming above Thad's ruined body.

"Flan," he says, again, more softly. Almost a human noise. The grey shapes are pressing closer and closer to him, their eyes floating pickled in their heads, their pasty faces dotted with damp. None of them say anything. Flan's head stays hidden behind her hair, a red flag for a tore-ador. Or a bull.

"Flan," he tries again, mixing the softness of the previous attempt with the force of the first. Third try's the charm. She shakes her head, slowly. Then turns to face him.

Her skin is as white as raw chicken, her nose gone red from crying and cold. Eyelids puffed out in sore circles. Mouth a bit of red yarn hacked up by a cat. Still, beautiful. The most beautiful thing he has ever seen.

"You killed him," she spits.

"I didn't kill him!" he finds himself shouting again, when he didn't know he would. He didn't even know what he was going to say. "He was trying to kill me!"

Flan shoots him a look that he is sure could set him on fire if he were standing any closer.

"Nice," she hisses. "Very nice. This your big scary killer?" She raises one of her hands and points down at the mess that used to be Thad's head. He looks for the eyes and can't find them.

"Has someone gone for a doctor?" he asks. The grey shapes look from one to the other. A small rat-shaped one takes off, back up the cliff. A square topped with red hair stays put, looming in the back of the crowd.

"Bikky," he yells, recognizing the bulk's hulking, even in the fog. "Tell her. It wasn't my fault."

The grey shapes slouch away, back into the fog.

"Flan," he walks toward her, his hands up in the tight beam of her glare, "I swear. I didn't do anything. He was trying to..." he pauses. "I was out on the tree, and he was coming after me. I was running out of tree, Flan, and he still kept coming. And then you showed up... and called his name...."

"Oh, so it's my fault now," her puffed eyelids meet each other with almost no movement. "Thanks. Thanks a lot."

"No, no," he gets down on his knees in the wet sand, next to her. Next to Thad. "He was tight. I mean, drunk. Really drunk. He kept saying he wanted to toss me in the sea... it's not your fault, Flan. It's not mine either."

"So it's his fault?" she snivels, wiping her nose with a sleeve splattered red. "How can you say that? Look at him!"

"I didn't say that..." he starts. A noise from Thad's face stops him. He and Flannery look at each other, and then down at Thad. "I think he's trying to breathe..." he says, putting an ear close to where Thad's mouth should be.

"Oh," Flan says quietly as a flood of blood and bile spouts from Thad. "Oh. Oh. Okay."

Flan turns as transparent as things that live under rocks, the colour seeping right out of her face. She manages somehow to slide Thad's head onto his lap without him noticing. She runs to the shore, and into the sea, and keeps on going. Soon all he can see of her is a dark, bobbing head. She might as well have turned into a seal.

There are grey shapes around him as he puts his fingers to Thad's face, gently, probing for a hole. Rain everywhere. Not washing, not washing away. He finds a hole, and bends to it, breathing.

DAHLIA

1968

Dahlia lies awake in her bed, Patience beside her. Dahlia listens to her parents dance themselves into separate rooms, their feet a pattern of clomping and clicking on the floor far below her. Together, away, together, away. Over tiles, where the sound is sharper, down the wooden hallway, to the rug along the stairs. Here is where they part for good. No more clicking. Heavy feet clomp back down the wooden hallway. Soft feet pad up the carpeted stairs. Past Dahlia's bedroom, not stopping. Her mother's bedroom door is opened, quietly, then shut. Click.

Dahlia waits. Her sister is out, somewhere, with one of her boys. Dahlia's acquired quite a collection of clothes from assisting her sister. She's wearing one of Tru's outfits now, a jangly jet shimmy dress. Bathroom noises come muffled through the walls, water splashing, medicine cabinet opening and shutting, toilet flushing. Dahlia's mother has her own bathroom, off the master bedroom. Dahlia shares the downstairs bathroom with her father, when he is here. Lately, he is not.

Her mother's bed barely creaks. Dahlia listens to her mother reading in another room. At ten o'clock precisely by the hands of Dahlia's Baby Ben she hears her mother switch off her reading lamp. Dahlia waits.

Dahlia asks Patience what she thinks. Patience grumbles, "To keeeeeeep."

Dahlia isn't sure if this is advice or what, but Patience has nothing else to say, when prodded. Dahlia lies still in her bed, Patience quiet beside her.

Dahlia has scissors in her bed, tucked under her leg, in case anyone had come in to say goodnight. She didn't really need to worry, though. No one did.

•

The kitchen in the morning is uncommonly full. Her mother and father are there, eating toast. Her sister is sleeping off her late-night arrival. Sunlight streams through a pot of homemade (though not by her mother) marmalade, this golden, perfect light shining out from the heart of it. Dahlia shoves her glasses up on her nose and takes a step, down the stairs. Another. All they can see is her feet, for now. She creeps down, slower, and quieter, her bare feet finally landing on the linoleum, golden and green.

She crosses the floor, silently. Her father reads the paper, her mother makes a list. Like every, every morning ever. Before.

"Hey, Kitten!" her father says to the paper. "How's tricks?"

"Dahlia, I had a most disturbing conversation with Mrs. Lovecraft the other day, did you know — what on earth have you done to your head?!!?"

Dahlia says the only thing she can think of to say.

"They said I had lice."

Which is a lie, because they didn't. She cut it off curling in long pale strands, filling her pillowcase with it the night before.

"Lice? Who has lice in this day and age?" Her father slams down his paper and strides over to peer at the top of Dahlia's head. "My father had lice! I had lice! All my brothers and sisters too! But my daughter should *not HAVE LICE*! What are they doing over there? Can't they keep the place clean? Or don't I pay them enough! Who can I call, Sissy? Who?" Throughout this tirade he is pulling at the tufts of hair still sprouting from Dahlia's head, pulling on them with his fingernails, examining the results underneath. "Sissy, I can't see a damned thing, get me my glasses, would you? And what kind of half-blind nincompoop cut your hair, anyway? Jeezus, don't they have to call before they butcher your child's head? Keeerist!"

"Oh, Albert, settle down, dear. I'm sure they had their reasons and that they got the best person they could to cut the children's hair. There must've been a lot of them. Isn't that right, honey?"

Her mother looks at her sweetly, smiling and nodding as though Dahlia should do the same. Her father is still yanking at her head. Dahlia stares down at the floor, making pictures from the spots and scuff marks on the lino.

"Honey?"

"Um, no... it was only me."

"What? Only you? What kind of a Mickey Mouse operation is that place anyway? They haven't heard of tar shampoo? Good lord! Sissy, I still can't see a damned thing, where the hell are my glasses?!!"

"Oh, yes. Sorry, dear." Dahlia's mother rises to fetch the glasses from down the hall. Her father tugs at her head, scratching her scalp with his big, blunt nails. Dahlia moves her view to a new spot on the floor. There's a high-heeled scuff mark down there, the end of a stiletto shaped like a tiny horseshoe. Driven down deep, and dark. Dahlia's mother only wears shoes with a low, wide heel. At home she wears flat, soft shoes. Like slippers. She broke one of her vertebrae diving when she was young. She was supposed to go to the Olympics. She's never worn high heels. She can't. Dahlia stares at the tiny heel mark, such a deep hole in such a shallow thing. The lino is only this thin, how can that hole go down so far? She can't even begin to see the end of it. Who could wear shoes that make holes like that?

Her father is still muttering away, pulling at what's left of her hair. Her mother is coming back down the hall, her feet softly creeping.

"There you go, Albert." Dahlia's mother hands her father the glasses. Looks at Dahlia with a stricken face. "It's such a shame, with your big performance tonight. Oh, honey — maybe we can get you a wig."

Her father lets go of Dahlia's head, to put on his glasses. Dahlia turns and stares at him. What is he even doing here, pretending like things are normal? He doesn't even live here. Do they think she doesn't know?

"Thank you very much. Now! Let's take a look at this 'lice', shall we?"

He's peering at her head now, tsking. "Dahlia, I don't see a damned thing on your head that could even be related to lice. You want to tell me the truth now? You want to tell me just what the hell is going on?"

Her mother looks slowly from Dahlia to Albert. "No lice? Dahlia, what is going on? Who did this to you?"

Dahlia takes a deep breath. Maybe she should just tell them, just say it out loud. She opens her mouth and says, "Mom, you don't have any high-heels, do you?"

•

"Wow, Dahlia," Sera exclaims, when Dahlia walks in behind the bamboo screen, "you look fan-tastic! Spin!"

Dahlia performs a slow circle, rolling her eyes and slouching. Sera runs her hands over the fresh stubble lightly covering Dahlia's head. "You are *mighty fine*, my lady. Wow. I can't wait to watch Ekaterina's head explode."

Dahlia's not sure what to make of Sera's approval, but suspects it's not a good thing. She quietly changes into her pale pink tights and black leotard, wrapping a black ballet skirt around her waist and tying it tight. She pads out onto the floor, dangling her pointe shoes by their long pink ribbons.

Ekaterina is watching a class of beginners, being taught by Lisanne, one of Ekaterina's graduates, who, after a year in the corps of the Royal Ballet, returned to Montreal, glowing with maternal pride. Her daughter sleeps in the corner in a playpen improvised from old sets: one wall a hedge from the peasant scene in *Giselle*, one a low brick wall from *The Sleeping Beauty*, a candy-cane striped wall from The Land of the Sugarplum Fairy in *The Nutcracker*, and a sideways window from *Swan Lake*. Ekaterina smokes, waving her arms languidly, almost smiling at the new recruits who are just finishing their lesson. Seeing someone enter from behind the bamboo screen, she turns. Her face turns to stone, as though Dahlia's hair were made of snakes. She says nothing, but waves Dahlia over with one quick motion. Dahlia pulls herself straight, and walks over.

Ekaterina grabs Dahlia by the head. Shakes her around a bit. "What is this?"

Dahlia manages to shake Ekaterina away. "I got a haircut!"

Ekaterina stands back, one eyebrow cocked, sneering over her long brown cigarette. "Your mother, she pay for this?"

Dahlia shakes her head.

"No? What a big surprise!" Ekaterina laughs. Then her face gets serious. She moves it in close to Dahlia's own. "You remember, of course, you are to go onstage tonight?"

Dahlia nods.

"And your wili, she die from what?" Ekaterina takes a drag from her cigarette, exhales, while looking at the ceiling and waving her hand in a little circle. "Putting finger in socket?"

"No," Dahlia says to the floor.

"Oh, no?" Ekaterina taps her black pointe shoe on the floor. "Then, please. Tell me what."

"Well," Dahlia watches Ekaterina's blocky toe, watches the trained muscles in her feet, watches the veins slithering under the skin, live as snakes. "Giselle has the mad scene, right? Where she lets her hair down and that's supposed to show the audience how horribly hurt she is? Well, I thought —"

Ekaterina's toe has stopped tapping. A thin wail comes from The Land of the Sugarplum Fairy.

"I thought maybe if you were really showing how mad you were you wouldn't just let down your hair. You'd do something bigger, you know?"

"For, like what? Cut off all your hair?" Ekaterina says, her toe still not moving. Lisanne runs lightly past, toward the wail. Dahlia nods.

"Yes," Ekaterina says. "Yes, I see this. Very nice, very good image. Okay." Dahlia raises her head. Ekaterina smiles. "But tell me, Dahlia, I think maybe I forget," Ekaterina screws another long brown cigarette into her mother-of-pearl holder, "but you are not Giselle tonight?"

"No," Dahlia says. "No, I'm not."

"Ah." Ekaterina lights her cigarette, clicks the lighter away. "Then why are you cutting off all your hair? Is best part of you, for wili!"

"Because all of those dead ladies have a story, not just Giselle!" Dahlia says this more loudly than she'd intended. The wail from the Land of the Sugarplum Fairy starts up again.

Ekaterina nods, and begins pacing the room, her forever out-turned feet clunking on the floor. She nods, and walks, and walks, and nods. Then stops. "The name of ballet is, *Giselle*! Is not, *Dahlia Plays a Wili*! You leave studio now!"

"What?" Dahlia stands, frozen, the words coming at her as though through the smoke and thorns of a hundred year sleep.

"You!" Ekaterina points. "Is no prima donnas here. I leave Russia for that. Everybody a goddamned prima donna. Well, forget it. Out!"

"But I wasn't," Dahlia begins, wrapping herself in her own arms and squeezing tight. "I just thought —"

"No *thought*," Ekaterina howls, smoke waving about her head. "Just out!"

Dahlia slouches back to the bamboo screen. Sera waits, her arms spread wide in pre-hug mode. "Oh, you poor thing," Sera says, wrapping Dahlia up in her hair and cabbage smell.

Dahlia turns her head, whispers in the direction of Sera's ear. "Oh, poor me, nothing. You want to come to a show tonight?"

•

The strobe light leaves her more blind than usual. Dahlia stumbles into the bathroom, unzipping her fleshing as she goes.

"Wow!" Sera breathes, grabbing Dahlia into a hug. "That was fantastic! It was like you were everywhere! How'd you do it?"

Dahlia breaks out of Sera's bear hug and bolts for a stall. "It's just a strobe light, and some mirrors," she calls, over the sound of her last nervous pee. "And me."

"But where'd you get the idea?" Sera yells back. "It's so simple, just you walking down a staircase. Amaaaazing."

Dahlia stands, pulls her fleshing back up, re-zips the back. Opens the stall door. "It was in a book I read once," she says, turning on the bathroom taps. "A long time ago."

Sera shakes her head. "Well, I dug it sister," she says. Raises her eyebrows. "You want another body?"

Dahlia nods. Sera grabs her by the hand, and they go out, back into the noise and sweat of the bar.

BILLY

1969

As he walks, the shoulders of the road swim with shadows, shape-shifting shades that dart out of focus before he can even begin to name them. A half-eaten moon squats low in the sky, bleeding onto the trees. Something skitters past, twitching the dying clover at the side of the road. A car whizzes by him and whatever it is turns, its eyes glowing red. Maybe a cat. A rat. A racoon. Billy speeds up, tugging on the fake-fur trimmed hood of his parka, trying not to look too closely at whatever it is. He is sure it's staring at him. Without turning to look back, Billy breaks into a run.

He takes the back way to the root cellar, slowing to a walk as he passes the lit-up rooms of the house. From out here it could be any house. He stops just out of view, his toes barely touching the long box of light that stretches from the kitchen window. From here it could be any window. A woman walks past the window, her salt-and-pepper hair in one long braid slung over her shoulder, her sleeves rolled up, her forearms red from hot water. She is carrying a stack of clean dishes, and smiling at someone else in the room there with her. From here she could be anybody. She is laughing, her head thrown back. Billy stares down at the shadow his Aunt Beatrix makes on the grass. Her shadow passes right by him, a flat, eyeless shape.

Billy walks slow and quiet around the side of the house, to the door in the ground. He lifts it, quiet as he can, just so it's half-open. He slips in, and lets the door close above him, sealing him right into the ground.

Left blind in the dark, he shuffles over to where the pull-switch for the light should be. He waves his hand above him in the dark. Nothing. He takes a step to the right and tries again. From way above him comes the sound of laughter, leaching right out of the dirt from somewhere else. He waves his hand again. Something soft flies by his hand, running all along it down to his elbow. Billy freezes even as his heart bangs his ribs from the inside. Slowly he lowers his hands. Slowly he steps to the right one more step. Slowly he sits, in the dark, underground.

Billy lowers his head until his eyesockets are filled by his knees. Presses his head down. Stays like that awhile, listening to his heart. Slow it goes and slower still. When he finally lifts his head dark shapes swim before him. Flat, eyeless shapes, pressed paper-thin. He blinks a few times but after a while can't tell if his eyes are open or closed. The shapes weave drunkenly, as though tethered to the ground deep below the sea. Billy puts out a hand and touches nothing. Light laughter from the farmhouse a thousand miles away, tinkling through dirt and space to reach him here. He puts his hands on his knees, squeezes.

He crawls over the dirt floor, carefully edging around the shadows that sway all around him. When he hits a wall, he puts out a hand, slowly. His hand finds a cool glass jar. He moves his hand, slowly, down. A rough wooden shape. He runs his hand carefully down the face of it. He can't remember which crate it is, which crate he's come for. He thinks about trying to turn on the light again, but can't imagine where it would be, how he would find it. He can't imagine what he would do if he did find it, and turned it on, and had to see all the flat eyeless shapes, lit up, and crowding around him. Here in the dark he can manage. Here in the dark, he hopes, they can't find him.

His hands find the top of the crate, and lift the lid. He puts a hand in, not too fast and not too far. Fur, short and stiff. He grabs handfuls of fur, puts them in his bag. He closes the lid. Shuffles on his knees over to the next crate. Bones. He takes some of these, mostly small ones, some big. He shuffles to the next. Paper. He doesn't remember a bin full of paper. He pulls out a stack, puts that in his bag. His hands close the lid. He shuffles to the next crate. Hair.

He slides his schoolbag around to his front, holds the flap open, and grabs handfuls of hair. When his bag is full, he closes the lid on the crate. Then he reaches up, and feels around for a jar, any jar. He finds one, puts it in his bag. Then turns himself around, still on his knees, still with his hands in the dirt, still in the dark. The flat shapes bob before him. He crawls in no direction, he crawls until he hits the splintery wood of the steps. Crawls up them, to the top. Turns, and just before opening the door, he whispers, "Bye, guys."

JULY, 1972

HICKLIN

Hicklin stares out the window. He's watched the far-off morning slide up from the underside of the world, barely blinking. He's sitting on a chair in a room intended for waiting, a room that is nevertheless not built for such a thing. Straight-backed chairs, old magazines and a radio no one turns on. Paper coffee cups long emptied. A painting of a winged horse leaping through clouds, framed in fake gold.

Luce has gone looking for a washroom after sleeping curled as a kitten in the crook of a chair. Dolly sleeps sitting up, her glasses folded neatly and held tight in her hand. Almost like she's waiting to be woken with the flick of a switch, or a simple touch.

Hicklin rises from his seat, stretches the kinks out of his neck and arms, paces to the window and back to wake his sleepy feet. The window from this room looks onto a well in the building, a tunnel of shade. Just beyond where he stands, sun floods the city, so bright the darkness he is in seems longer and deeper than any old hole. He rubs his eyes, fishes in his pocket for a quarter. More cheap coffee. More time awake.

The quarter jangles into the coffee machine, a paper cup drops down. It lands on a tilt, its mouth away from the spout. He reaches in to straighten it and is rewarded with scalding coffee all over his hand. His right hand to his mouth, he pushes the cup with his left hand, managing to get the cup aligned with the spout before the whole quarter's worth of coffee drips through the grate to the drain below.

"*Elle est ancienne,*" a voice says behind him. "*Elle a besoin d'une vacance, je pense."*

Hicklin turns to find a tiny young man in white, peering up at him over a clipboard. The young man blinks at him from behind teeny round eyeglasses perched on his sharp nose. He tilts his head, and gives a small smile.

"*La machine à café,*" the young man gestures with the clipboard. "Not your friend."

"*Bien sur,*" Hicklin agrees, nodding. "Of course."

"You are a friend of Mr. Brennan's?" the young man asks, flipping open his clipboard and blinking at it.

Hicklin nods and gives his name.

"Doctor Trépanier," the little man says, as they shake hands. The doctor's hand leaves a sticky film on Hicklin's. He wipes it off discreetly, while the doctor consults his clipboard again. "Is it possible to speak to anyone in his family?" The doctor reaches for a pen from a small collection in the breast pocket of his white coat, his hand slithering, moist and white, from his pristine cuff. "His parents, ideally?"

Hicklin shakes his head. "His parents are dead. He's got an aunt and uncle somewhere, they raised him. But I don't know where they are."

The doctor nods. "I see," he says. "This makes things difficult for me. Are you eighteen yet? Could you be legally responsible for his care? He is still a minor, you see. We need someone to...."

"I'm eighteen," Hicklin nods, remembering his coffee. He picks it up, out of the rectangular hole in the chest of the machine. It's still warm, or warm enough anyway. "I can sign for him."

"Good," the young man says, flipping through some papers in his file, which stick, slightly, to his fingertips. "I'll get the papers sorted out and then I will come back and speak to you."

"But," Hicklin says. "Wait. Can't you tell me anything now? Is he okay?"

"For now I can only say it is very good you brought him here," the doctor says. His forehead shines under the overhead fluorescent lights. "Things will be much better for him."

"Okay," Hicklin says, squeezing his coffee cup. "So he's going to be okay?"

The doctor nods but doesn't smile. "I will be back soon, with the papers. Excuse me."

The young doctor shuts his clipboard and walks away slowly, something like an ooze to his gait.

•

He enters into a space perfectly clean and white, with nothing in it but a flat double mattress on the floor, surrounded by purple and white flowers growing untamed out of coffee jars. All other furniture has been removed, all the clothes and costumes and props ferreted away somewhere. The giant heads, he is thankful to note, have been taken down, and the walls have been scrubbed a toothy white. The window is open, a violet sheet dancing in a light breeze. Hicklin feels like he's walking into another dimension when he walks into it, as though the apartment has suddenly become a tesseract, a space larger on the inside than the outside.

Beau waits at the top of the stairs, leaning on the doorframe. He's thinner, his glowing skin gone ivory and ash, spotted here and there with fading red pox. Something blue creeps about his eye sockets, darkening to almost black in an uncanny imitation of eyeliner. He smiles at Hicklin, and holds up an arm. Hicklin scoots under it, and the two of them hobble to the door of the bedroom, joined arm-over-shoulder, hip to hip.

"Looks good, doesn't it, Beau?" Hicklin asks as they stutter into the bedroom, a lilt in his voice he's far from feeling. "Dolly did a great job, huh?"

"Dearest," Beau says softly, slowly, "I'm not daft. No need for the panto."

"Sorry," Hicklin says, moving Beau's light body around so he can lower him to the bed. "I haven't been around sick people much. I mean...."

Beau lies still as Hicklin covers him over with Dolly's violet sheets and a white blanket that looks new. Stares up at Hicklin, his one blue eye clear and still, his green eye tinged a stormy grey. "It's okay," Beau says in that same soft tone, soothing as a telephone operator's. "Hicklin, I know I'm sick. I know. Stop stumbling about it."

"Sorry," Hicklin says again, tucking the sheets in around Beau, not too loose, not too tight. Just right. He tries a smile, and says, "I'll get better at this."

"Probably," Beau agrees, "by the time I get better."

Hicklin pours himself a cup of coffee, takes it outside. Dolly is sitting in the rattan chair he found for her, once upon a time. The back of the seat rises in a circle about her bright bald head, places where the rattan is broken let the light through to shine about her. Her eyes dart behind her glasses, two tropical fish in tiny bowls, as she reads from a pile of mail scattered over her crossed legs.

"Well," Hicklin says. "He's home."

Dolly looks up, her eyes wide. She blinks and quickly piles up her mail, enclosing it in the Muybridge book. "You should have come to get me," she says. "I could have helped you."

Hicklin shrugs and leans back on the skittery railing, rotten in places from winters untended. "It's okay," he says. "I had to deal with the doctors and stuff."

"How is he?" Dolly asks, sitting forward on the chair. "Any better?"

Hicklin nods. "They said he was lucky we got him there so fast," he picks at something crusted on the outside of the jar he's drinking from. "They don't think there's going to be any damage."

"Damage," Dolly states, her eyes wide and a bit wobbly, like her head's being shaken and her eyes are loose in her head. "You never told me about any 'damage'."

"Well... the thing is," Hicklin says, picking the crusty thing off and frowning at his hands. He puts the jar down. "The thing is, Doll, he had encephalitis. Brain swelling from the fever. It happens sometimes when people get chicken pox at an older age."

"Oh," Dolly says, her mouth round as the sound, then flattening to a thin line.

She nods. Her two violet fish swish in their watery bowls, a little faster, back and forth.

"But it seems like he's going to be okay, Doll," Hicklin steps over to her and takes her two hands in his. "They say he made it through the worst of it. That's why he's home, okay?"

Dolly nods.

"I'm sorry I didn't say earlier," Hicklin says, squeezing her hands. They don't squeeze back. "There was some other stuff they told me... but I think we should wait until Beau's better before we talk about it. It's pretty... private."

Dolly raises her eyes to Hicklin's. Blinks. "I'm going to be taking care of him. I think I should know what's going on."

Hicklin nods again. "I know," he rubs her hands, softly, sweetly. "But some of this stuff, it's not for me to say. Unless...."

"Unless," Dolly says, gravel in it.

"Well, you guys've... you know. Right?" Hicklin closes his eyes as he feels Dolly's hands being drawn away, smooth as though on oiled mechanisms.

"I don't see how that is any of your affair," she says, the gravel churning under wheels.

Hicklin nods. "Okay," he says, opening his eyes. "Then I think we should wait until he's feeling better. Okay?"

Dolly nods, sparely, one motion up, one down. "Excuse me," she says, standing. "I'd like to go say hello. As long as you think that will be alright."

The gravel in her voice has been crunched flat into arrowheads. Hicklin turns from them but can't avoid their point. Dolly leaves the room, walking softly, quietly, closing the door to the kitchen with a near-silent click more resounding than a slam. Hicklin sighs, and heads down the side stairs to the gate. He slips through the small opening, and out onto Duluth.

A small black spot detaches itself from the wall across the street, unfolding as it comes closer into Luce's tiny form. She crosses the street without looking, heads right for him.

"So," she smirks, her eyes unseen behind her heart-shaped sunglasses. "How'd it go? The Princesses peachy?"

"It went," Hicklin says. Luce reaches for his hand. He looks around before taking it.

"Oh, that's nice, Daddy," she spits, withdrawing her hand, stopping and lifting her glasses. Her hair falls down, a screen between them. "That how you treat your main squeeze?"

"I'm sorry," he says, reaching for her hand again. Her mouth curls into a cat-toothed grin.

"Forget it, pal," she says. "Bank's closed."

"Luce," he starts, not knowing what to say next. Her name hovers between them, shaking air ever so slightly.

"Shut your hole," she says, all kinds of smile gone from her lips. "It's hard to hide your dirty little secret when you live with it."

She turns and is gone before he can think of a word, any word. A word that will bring her back.

DOLLY

Practicing patience, her back on the floor, she waits for breath. With her eyes closed she could be anywhere. In a box underground, or deep under the sea, locked in a treasure chest waiting for some pirate to come back and collect his booty. Or deep inside a drawer, afraid of a girl.

But under her back is a blanket, and under her head a rolled-up sweater. Inside her lungs there is a breathing that works without her thinking. Her eyes are closed as she listens. Listens for a breath from above. It comes and then it doesn't. It comes and then it doesn't. It comes and then. It stops.

"To hell with patience," Dolly says out loud, uncrimping herself from a thousand floor aches. She gets up on the bed and in the blur of no glasses finds what must be a face, puts her head close to what must be the mouth and listens. Puts her head closer. Listens. Closer. Listens.

Then there is a sigh so tiny she thinks she might have to believe in it a little more just to help it along.

"Come on you bastard. I won't be strong-armed into clapping my hands," she whispers.

Another breath, and then another. Dolly nods, and bends her head to the chest to listen. Listens and nods and listens again.

"Licorice," Dolly says quietly. "Eucalyptus. Garlic. And maybe a little thyme."

Dolly feels for her glasses, somewhere below her on the floor. She finds them, puts them on, and peers at Beau. Feels his forehead.

"Yarrow," Dolly says a little louder, "and elderflower. Just a little brew."

Beau lies still, his cheeks a bit too pink.

•

Another morning, another sunup with Beau's battered breaths. Dolly's lost track of how many days it's been, but has figured out the doctors' big mystery. The patient has few secrets from the nursemaid. Poor Hicklin hasn't twigged yet, thinks they're all still waiting for his say-so to have the Big Scary Talk.

Beau mostly sleeps. He has more colour every day, as though it's been painted on him while Dolly snatched slight sleep. Once or twice a day she helps him make a slow circuit of the house, his bony hip grinding into hers until she feels they must be fused. He waves at Endymion, a furball curled by the window, a wave slow as light through water. He smiles.

Dolly walks him by the Heart of Gold, now finished. It's the cow's heart she and Ginger cast, gilded and set on a post about four feet off the ground. She tells him it's the centre of a protective circle. He stares at it for a long while.

"So where's the outside?" he asks, turning his blue and green stare on her.

She shrugs, gestures wide with her hands. Almost smiling. He nods, and they turn about the house again.

•

One day, home alone with a sleeping Beau, Dolly pokes her head into Luce's room. An army cot is pushed up against the window, near-ly hidden by the worktables and piles of papers and magazines on the floor. A small, pink spiral-bound notepad sits on the cot, a pink lolly-pop on top of it. Dolly looks behind her before she does it, but she does it. She goes in the room, and picks up the little notepad.

The lollypop turns out to be a pen, and the ink it writes in is, appar-ently, pink. Dolly scans a page or two, but it's as incomprehensible as

Luce's speech. She stops when she sees the word ghost, capitalized. Goes back and tries again.

And it's a story. A story about all of them.

When she is done, Dolly tears a few of the back pages from the notepad and closes it carefully. She puts down the pen. Then picks it up, and takes it with her.

•

It appears, after a few days, that Luce has gone missing. In her absence Hicklin retreats to what was Luce's room. Dolly can hear clatterings in there, shufflings of furniture, hammering, as though the things in there are dancing, alone with Hicklin. She knocks on the door, but when there is no answer she nods and returns to her garden on the balcony.

There was a garden at her mother's house, certainly. But one that was tended by a Gardener, and was not a place for little girls to run around. Here she grows wild creatures out of nothing, sprouting weeds no one else would even look at. Lavender and violet, honeysuckle and sage. Heartsease and belladonna, hellebore and lurk-in-the-ditch.

For some reason Hicklin knows a lot about these things, and gave her an old notebook filled with planting schedules, medicinal uses, recipes for tinctures and salves and other things. When she asked how he came by all this, he mumbled something about his mother and walked away. She kept the book.

Dolly is in her garden, bees humming under her hands, when Hicklin taps on the inside of the kitchen door, as though he wants to be let out but has lost the use of his thumbs. Dolly walks over to him.

"Hello," she says, tilting her head. "Hicklin wants out."

He shakes his head. "No, Hicklin wants you to come in. Beau's up. I think now might be a good time. Well, maybe not good. But we have to talk soon. So it might as well be now." His sandy hair stands up in little wings, as though ruffled from a wind. Maybe he hasn't been dancing with the things in his room, Dolly thinks. Maybe whatever is happening in there is more like a storm.

Dolly puts down the leaves she's been collecting, and follows him inside. She blinks in the darkness, swimming with shapes. She blinks again. Table and chairs, fridge and cluttered counter. A dark sheet over the window, making a deep pool of the room, a blue, still darkness in the middle of a sunny day. Beau sits shrivelled in a chair Hicklin's found for him, a big square thing packed all over with pillows to protect Beau's shrunken frame, a cracked coffee cup in one hand. He smiles at her. She wants to smile back.

"Doll," Beau says, smiling under the grey puffiness around his eyes, giving her a quick wink. "Hicklin here has something he's gotta say. It sounds like Serious Business. What do you think? Is it too nice a day?"

"Beau," Hicklin says, pulling up a chair for Dolly and then sitting in the wooden chair held together by wire coat hangers. "Give it up. You know what we have to talk about."

"Oh, I do, do I?" Beau makes a shocked gesture over his heart. "Whatever could I have done? I was out cold for three weeks."

"You didn't *do* anything," Hicklin says. "It's more what was done to you."

"What's that?" Beau grins, his skinny skin allowing for too many teeth between hollow cheeks. He flutters his eyelashes. "Did an overly attentive intern interfere with me while I was away? Heavens! My virgin soul!"

"Beau," Hicklin stares at him. "Come on. Please. This is something I think you need to hear. And Dolly too."

"Fine," Beau slumps back in his chair. Behind him pillows rise throne high. "What?"

"You have osteoporosis," Hicklin states, his voice flat.

Beau rolls his eyes. "Never heard of it. This some new VD they're using to scare the kids off sex?"

"No," Hicklin says, sternly. "It means you have holes in your bones. You cracked your pelvis just falling to the floor, Beau. It comes from a lack of calcium. Or, from the body having an inability to process calcium. Like yours. Beau. You have to go back on your hormones."

222

"Back?" Beau asks, his voice rising with a squeaking sound, as though his body can't contain it. "What 'back'? I was never on them!"

"Hormones," Dolly says.

"He's *supposed* to be taking hormones," Hicklin turns to face Dolly. "Because of something that happened to him when he was little."

Dolly practices patience, waits for Beau to tell the story. She's seen the end of it already, but isn't sure he knows that. She pulls herself straighter.

"A fat bag of lies," Beau says shrilly, trying to sit up, but failing. He settles for waving an arm around wildly. "A pack of worthless bull. That's what happened to me. What did they tell you, Hicklin? Some disgusting fantasy, I'm sure."

"Something about an accident," Hicklin says. "They contacted your aunt and uncle. Don't give me that look! I don't know where they are! I don't even know their last name!"

Beau's eyes are blue and green slits shining cat-sharp. He slouches into his pillows and sighs. For a second it looks like he needs re-winding, like the mechanism has run down, even the breathing and the blood gone still. Then he stares at Hicklin and shrugs. "It's probably in my file somewhere."

After this Beau closes his eyes. He breathes in and holds it. After what seems way too long, he lets it out. "Fine. They gave you the acci-dent story. Fine. Great. Did they say, 'Once upon a time, in a land far, far away,' too? They might as well have. It's a story, you guys. A lie they told me, a memory they gave me. It's not real."

Dolly gets up and goes to the fridge. In the freezer, way in the back, hidden under a bag of frozen peas, is a bottle of vodka. She unscrews the top. Gets her pink sherry glass from the cupboard and fills it, plac-ing it in front of Beau. Sits back down.

"Tell us what happened Beau," she says, her voice cool. "But have a drink first."

"Dolly," Hicklin says, a worried look in his eyes. "His meds."

"One drink won't hurt him as much as this conversation," Dolly says briskly. "Now drink."

Beau reaches for the glass and tilts it clumsily into his mouth.

"Now you," Dolly says, refilling the glass and passing it to Hicklin. He drinks, gasping. Dolly pours a drink for herself, downs it without any reaction. Something about what Beau just said comes swimming up. Something about memories given to people, in a story, in a book about... what were they called? Reli... remi... repli... Replicants. That's right. But they weren't people. People built them.

"They built me," Beau says. Dolly reaches for the bottle again. "But they made a mess of it."

Beau closes his eyes. Dolly refills the glass and pushes it toward him. Hicklin says nothing. They sit in the room dark at noon, the glass between them, something like a stone at its bottom, shiny as a rock in a stream. They breathe. There is no sound as they sit, still, for a hundred years. Then Beau opens his eyes. He ignores the drink and just starts talking.

"My aunt and uncle told me I was injured in the same accident that killed my mother, that I had to be put back together." He's speaking slowly, patiently, the words coming out tight but strong. "But I found out that wasn't it at all. I had a friend who's mom worked in the hospital I was born in. She said whatever happened to me happened when I was born. I didn't say anything though. I never said a word to my aunt and uncle. How would I begin?"

At this point he focusses on the drink in front of him, as though it's just appeared there by magic. He drinks it, coughs, and wipes his mouth where a little has spilled. Takes a breath, and continues. "Finally, they had to tell me. I was born with a bit of both, what doctors call a hermaphrodite. Or a *pseudo*hermaphrodite, like you can be a pseudo version of a misnomer. A fake version of some fairy tale creature. And they told my folks they had to choose. My mom had been raising me as a girl. They gave me the pictures when they told me. They'd been disappeared for me, hidden away in my uncle's collection. Me and my mom, two pretty girls. We look happy. We look... okay. But my dad came back from wherever he'd been, and *he* thought I looked more like a boy. Down there. And I guess the doctors did too... and they told my mom what she'd have to do to make me a real girl. I guess once she saw the dilator... she was probably trying to save me some pain. What mother wouldn't?" He lets out a brittle laugh, a black laugh with many spiky legs. Dolly refills the glass and Beau drinks it, wiping his mouth again.

"And I guess it was passable, until I didn't have any kind of puberty. It's fine to have mangled bits until everyone around you is growing tits and sprouting beards and you're doing neither. That's when they first told me I had to start hormone treatments... because they'd taken everything out of me. The doctors had told my mom it'd be safer, that because what I had were neither ovaries nor testes they could become cancerous or some such bull... and she bought it. And they took everything out of me. Cut away anything that looked girly down there. Got rid of the hole and worked on the pole, to use their words. Charming, don't you think? I can't even pee standing up, they even messed that up. It comes out the side. And then they have the gall to ask me, Can you stand when you pee? No? Then you're not a real boy. They broke me without even asking. Before I could even speak. How'd they ever think of that? In what world is this a good thing to do to a baby?"

Beau pauses, his mouth crumpled as a swatted moth. Dolly refills the glass. Beau turns his head a little and looks out of a hole in the violet sheet covering the window, then leans his head back on his tall, tall pile of pillows.

"So they said if I wanted to become a real boy they'd have to pump hormones into me. Because *they* had taken out everything inside me that would have made them. Can you tell me how ridiculous that is? They take the stuff out, and then, years later, it's, 'Oops! We took out some stuff you need — but, don't worry! We can fix you with some magic potions! Drink this!'" Beau starts laughing, a tiny shake in his little frame. "Insane. *And* they told me I'd need more surgery, you know, to look like a real boy. To pee like a real boy. To screw like a real boy. I never knew I wasn't. Until they told me."

Three sets of lungs breathe near-silent. Outside the light slips sideways, a small beam entering from the hole in the makeshift curtain. A pack of kids runs by the window, hollering.

"You're *IT*!" one of them cries.

More screeching, and the jitterbug sound of tiny feet at play. Clattering around the corner, the sound of their laughter fades.

"How'd they know?" Beau asks. He smiles, creases coming out at the corners of his mouth.

"But, Beau," Hicklin says, getting up and going around to his chair, squatting and holding Beau's hand. "Now you're sick. Osteoporosis at your age — you're shortening your lifespan. You'll be in pain for the rest of your life."

"*They* shortened my lifespan!" Beau screeches, twisting away from Hicklin. "And I've already been in pain my whole life! They made me, and they made me sick. I wasn't sick. There was *nothing wrong with me*. I just had different bits. That's not a disease. It's not a crime. I was an infant! They built me, and they screwed it up. Before I could even speak. I will *never* do anything they tell me to do. Never. So I die young? Who cares? I live as *me*. End of story."

BEAU

Morning. Outside the sun shines, clean as a hospital sheet. Beau lies still and listens. No sound of hammering from Hicklin's room, no burble of distant radio. No Dolly next to him. He pushes himself up on his elbows, and then a hundred years later, pushes himself to sitting. His head bangs slightly from the inside out, as though little men were clattering away in there, but it's clear. Clear for the first time in days. He takes a hundred years to turn in the bed, and another hundred to stand.

One hand on the wall, he shuffles to the doorway. He thinks he remembers something, maybe a dream. Of Dolly giving him drinks, of Hicklin telling him he's sick. And then a pinhole of light, tiny voices in there. Happy voices calling him it, calling him into their game. A tiny place he wanted to go and play in. He remembers telling a story, but he thinks he left a bit out. He leans against the doorframe, sagging at every joint. He picks up the cane Hicklin's brought him, made from a piece of arbutus. The Salish call it the Tree of Knowledge, Hicklin'd said. Because it can find the sun. Even if it has to grow crooked. Beau looks down at the thing. Holds it with his right hand, his left against the wall. From the doorway to the kitchen is a long tunnel, a miner's shaft drilled through the heart of the apartment. He takes a breath, and pushes out one foot. Then the other. His hand on the wall. His new cane bracing him. He makes it.

From the kitchen to the door is one tunnel, and from the door to Dolly another. Dolly's hair is white as a bleached urchin, stubble shining above a skin-pink kimono. Behind her, still blue sky peeps in between the buildings. Her hands are white birds chasing bees through her garden. Beau wonders whether everything was framed like this before; was everything so slow?

He moves his blood through his marrow and his marrow through his holey bones and his holey bones through his muscles and his muscles through his skin and somehow pushes the whole apparatus slowly through time, through the tunnel, through the frame to get somewhere. He makes it to the door and stops.

"Doll," he wheezes. "I can't remember. Did everything always have this weird frame around it? I feel like I'm trapped in an art factory."

Dolly turns her eyes toward him, the sun glinting off her glasses, making it look for a second like she has no eyes. Or like the eyes she has can get turned on and off at will. Beau blinks, testing his own eyes. The frame is still around everything, but otherwise they seem okay.

"Of course," Dolly says calmly, reaching into her big kimono pocket for something. "You just couldn't see it before."

"Oh," Beau nods, slowly. "Well. That explains it."

From the door to the saggy-assed rattan chair is a tunnel. Beau thinks he can make it. It looks pretty short. Another round of the blood-and-guts parade and he's next to the chair. His marrow naps, his bones straw beds around it.

"Phuuuuuuuuuu-h," his breath leaves him in one long waft.

Dolly is somehow suddenly right beside him.

"How'd you do that?" Beau asks with what's left of his breath.

"The regular way," Dolly answers, helping Beau into the rattan chair. Someone's covered the hole in the seat with a couple of giant cushions but Beau's bum still feels like its going to poke through any second. He shifts about, trying to find a way to sit on the edges of the hole.

"I'll get you another cushion," Dolly says, and just as soon, is gone. The thing she'd taken out of her pocket sits beside him, on the arm of the giant wicker chair, an arm wide enough to serve as a table.

An airmail envelope addressed to Dolly, not here at Hicklin's, where she lives, but c/o Ginger. There's no return address but Beau knows those big, happy loops, a circle for a dot over an *i*.

From Beau's eyes to Flan's hand is the longest tunnel yet. Beau closes his eyes and tries not to sink through the hole.

•

Dolly returns, flourishing a gigantic pillow covered in nubbly raw cotton.

"Isn't that Hicklin's?" Beau asks, nevertheless standing to allow Dolly to move in and place it under him.

Dolly lifts a shoulder in her version of a shrug.

"He's not in his own bed so I figure he doesn't need it," she replies, swooping Flan's letter into her kimono pocket. Her voice sounds flatter than usual. Beau wonders if that's even possible, or if he's hearing tunnels around things now too.

"Oh," Beau says, re-seating himself on the cushion. It's almost comfortable, if he can just ignore the way his behind's bones threaten to rip through his skin. "Where is he?"

Dolly closes her eyes and shakes her head, slowly.

"Okay," Beau says. "You done talking for the whole day?"

Dolly bends down to one of her plants, twists off a twig, pockets it. "Maybe," she says, the flatness even flatter.

Out of a silver spoon flat like a shovel she gives him sips of honey thick as the light he swims in now. His head floats like a balloon from a string once known as his neck, far above where his shoulders slump against the dark rattan. The bottle of honey is tall and brown, sweaty all down its sides, a slip of paper stuck to it. Dolly tips it, once more, for one more shining spoonful. This she puts in her own mouth.

Dolly shadows her plants, pulling thorns into battlements, plucking flowers and seed pods, laying them out in row on row for the sun to dry.

"Why did Flan write to you?" Beau's balloon head puffs, a tiny balloon around each of his words. "What does she want?"

Dolly doesn't hear him. Beau thinks he must be fading faster than he thought. He looks down, way down, and there she is, rummaging in a giant pot that's planted with what look to him like different kinds of weeds. She sits, and from her kimono pocket takes a few small pink pages with dark pink lines, and a tiny pen, a pink lollipop. Beau knows these are not Dolly's, how can they be, Dolly would never buy anything like that. Luce would, but since when does Luce write? His balloon head floats a little higher.

Dolly writes, something short with short lines, a poem maybe, or a recipe. At the top she writes in large, neat letters, *Lurk-In-The-Ditch*. So. A poem, then. Beau didn't know Dolly wrote poems.

"Since when do you write poems, Doll?" he asks, but his head is caught by a puff of air, and blown across the alley. A face appears in the neighbours' window, a face made mostly of hair. A toothy grin cuts a path through the hair as the neighbour catches sight of Beau, floating down the alley. Beau wonders what the hippywitches might do with a balloon head. He wishes somebody would pull his head back in. He lets out a sigh, and finds himself propelled backwards, back toward his body, back toward Dolly and her poem.

Dolly is wrapping some dried up old plants in brown kraft paper, tucking the edges in, making an envelope. On it she writes *Lurk-In-The-Ditch* again. So the poem is a plant? Beau's head puffs by itself, puffs him away from the poem and from Dolly and from whatever Lurk-In-The-Ditch might be. His balloon head closes its eyes, and just floats. Somewhere in there, Beau dreams.

•

The light is less like honey now and more like cold cider, spilling him awake. He wakes to find he is drinking, drinking cold apple cider from a hefty pewter mug. As he puts it down there is a clunking inside of it. He peers into the mug but can't see a thing. Shakes it. A rolling, as of maybe a glass eye, a marble, a speechless stone.

"It's a bezoar," Dolly says, watching him from where she sits, in between her many plants. "It'll keep you safe from poison."

Beau frowns down into his mug. "Why on earth would I need to be kept safe from poison?"

Dolly's scary eyes don't even blink behind her glasses. "Why on earth wouldn't you?" she replies, taking a dainty sip from her own glass. One of the glasses Luce brought home, long, long ago. An old pink sherry glass, with gold flaking off at its rim, and at the bottom, a small white stone.

They quietly sip at their drinks. The sun bleeds gold over everything. Dolly turns her scary eyes on him.

"Better," she says. Not a statement, not a question.

Beau nods. "Better."

"What Hicklin says is true," Dolly says, looking straight at him.

Beau nods, again. "Yep. I know he's right... I just can't, Doll. I can't do it."

Dolly blinks, slowly. "I know," she says, a rattle in her voice he hasn't heard before. "They're not in the business of doing anyone a favour."

Beau lets out another long sigh but his head stays where it is. He leans back against the rotted rattan. "My aunt thought it was God's will. That I was made the way I was. She told my folks not to do anything."

"You left her," Dolly says, reaching for the cider. She refills both of their glasses.

"Yeah," Beau lets out another long sigh. Still, his head stays put. "Yeah. I should probably have thanked her for trying, at least. Don't know about her reasons... but maybe she was right. I don't know. I left because she lied to me, my uncle lied to me... for years. I couldn't stay with people who could do that to a kid. You know?"

Dolly nods. Not blinking.

"But you're good," Dolly says. Not a question. Not a statement.

Beau smiles. "Sure," he says. "If you say so."

LUCE

The bearcat feeling bangs into me, sock, pow! and in a second I'm white-hot all over, so bad I can't even see. Last time I broke his things, and this time there's nothing handy but him. So I turn around, and head away, fast as my sticks will carry me.

By the time I can breathe again, I'm smack-dab in the middle of the park, right where I should be. Guess the automatic pilot kicked in. I lollygag on one of the benches, smoking and trying not to think too much. I got another telegram this morning, when Daddy was at the hospital getting the Daisy. Guess being a night owl comes in useful for some things, anyway. I sit tight and try not to look like I'm waiting, just watching the shadows crawl along the ground. The sun's just going down into a fire all of itself, when I see it. A blonde beehive, big and shiny as high noon, coming right for me. The Queen Bitch.

She sits down next to me, but not too close, a haze of baby powder floating around her, strong enough for me to smell from where I am. She starts jawing, but looking straight ahead, and not at me.

"We've got a buyer for the house," she says, as though commenting on the weather. "So next time I see you, it'll be a big one. Maybe the last. Maybe not. It all depends on him."

I nod.

"He's behaving so far," the Queen Bitch says, opening her red patent handbag and taking out a plain white envelope. She puts it down without looking, on the bench between us. "I think he under-stands. We keep out of the courts, and he gets off scot-free. So to speak."

I think the Queen's seen too many movies, but then, so have I. I don't look over at her, and neither of us says goodbye. I light a smoke, and stare off to where the sun's heading for the big sleep. Once her big blonde beehive has sunk below the next hill, and the sky's gone bloody where the sun's sunk, I pick up the envelope and stuff it in my rat bag. I stand up. Just start ankling to the wide street, cool as a cucumber. And there it is, a big heavy hand, right on my shoulder.

I turn around. It's Oscar, the palooka, his face gone goofy in a big old grin.

"Well, how do," I say, putting my hand in his. "Fancy a nibble?"

He shakes his head and laughs, and walks me across the street, the sky slipping down dark around us.

•

I stay with Oscar for a few days, letting the bearcat feeling wear off. It takes longer than usual. You kids probably remember times I wasn't around; well, they were times like this. I feel like... like you know when the bath water's running out and it makes a funnel? And if you stick a toe in there it feels like it's going to get pulled down to the sewer? Like that. But bigger. Like my whole body is a walking, talking, sucking tunnel. It starts at my head and just gets worse the further down it goes. There's one thing I can do about the middle, but not much I can do about the rest.

I don't go out. Oscar leaves in the morning to go to med school, kissing me as I lie in bed not thinking. I get up when I can't put off using the can. Sometimes I eat something. Usually not. I put on one of Oscar's big shirts, tie it up over my belly, poke around the house. He's got lots of books that're strictly off the track, I mean, real queer stuff, all in French, stuff I guess you need to be a doctor. Books of bodies all torn apart, laid out like layer cake. Most of them are old-looking drawings, and some of them are of parts I didn't know anyone had.

One book is all photos of a dame made of wax. You can take off her skin and see inside. You can take off her muscles, and take a baby out

233

of her belly, and take all her guts out, and the whole time she smiles at you with a face like Our Lady. I can't stop looking at that one, even though it makes me a little bit queasy. I keep looking at it half-hoping if I look at it enough it'll stop making me feel that way, but half-hoping it won't. So far it hasn't.

There's another book with more drawings, black and white things, mostly. There's a theatre in here, anyway, I guess the word is the same in French and English. Except instead of actors onstage, there's a couple of doctors. Some poor sap has his skin peeled off from his bits to his chest, all his darkest secrets laid out for the crowd to see. And what a crowd! The place is packed. People everywhere, in every seat in the place. And some of the people are past people. I mean skeletons. Just mingling in the crowd, la-di-da as you please. There's seven rows of seats and then at the top a couple more skeletons riding animal skeletons. I think on one side it's a horse, and on the other it's a cow. I never heard of anyone riding a cow, but then, I guess if you're a skeleton looking for a ride you can't be too picky. And then way up in the corners there're fat angels. Kinda rubs it in for the poor guy onstage, don't you think? I mean, they could've held off until he was one place or the other, not just torn open on a table.

I look at this one a lot. It doesn't make me feel queasy like the wax lady. This one, I don't know. Something about it makes me calm down a bit. Takes the edge off the bearcat feeling to think that could be me on the table, fat angels smiling down at me. Maybe I've got the blue meanies, but I don't think so. I think it's just somehow — not peaceful, not with that crowd. But honest.

And just when I think it can't get any bigger, I mean, there's nothing bigger than death, right? Oh, boy. Kids. You think there's nothing bigger than you and your life? You think the whole thing spins around you? Forget it.

Here's this book that's babies in jars, and eyes dangling from their own strings, and little girls all covered in hair and a boy with one eye in the middle of his face and no nose. Here's a skeleton that looks like it was made out of skin, the bone all somehow grown into muscle.

Here's calves with two heads, and little baby skeletons attached at the back, at the head, at the chest. Here's everything the world ever made, made new. Like it never ends.

This one reads like a book out of the kid's section, all these terms I thought I'd forgotten a long time ago. Cyclops. Werewolf. Cereberus. Hermaphrodite. Chimera. There's a picture here of a man with horns and one hoofy foot, not the Devil though, nothing like that. This is a man, called the Monster of Ravenna. There's even a mermaid in here, a little little girl with her legs all suckered together into one, her feet just flaps under her.

This one I look at every day. This one could never make me feel sick, even for a second. All it makes me feel is... happy.

I start to feel better.

I start getting up when Oscar does, dancing around him, kissing him to the door. Just so I can spend more time with these books I can't even read.

And one day there's a knock at the door. I know you won't believe me, I mean, I wouldn't. Oh, here we go, good old Luce, always good for a story. But I told you all already, and I meant what I said. This story is true.

One day there's a knock at the door. And who do you think is standing there?

I'll give you one guess.

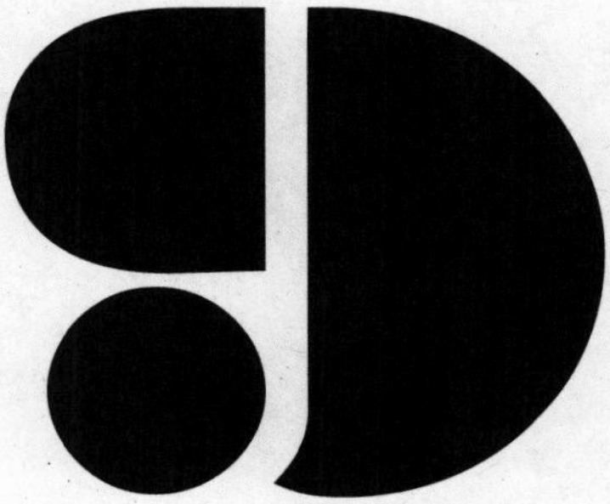

HICKLIN

1969

The myth has passed from mouth to mouth, flown silent at the speed of bees.

This time is not like the last. Last time, the hummings about him increased as he walked by, last time eyes followed him down the dented halls of the school. This time there is nothing.

Flan has returned to school, causing a ripple up and down the hallway of long blonde hair. She stands by her locker, throwing things out over her shoulder, books, papers, a pink pencil case. Photos featuring her face, other faces in the background only an excuse for a picture of herself. He slinks near. A small brown teddy bear clutching a stuffed heart sails past his head, falling unseen behind him.

"Hey," he whispers. "Flan."

"*You,*" she says, loudly, without turning around. "Get lost."

"Flan," a whimper in his voice, a whine. "Please. Let me explain."

"Explain?" she whips around, her hair flying. Her mouth showing its sphincter nature, clamped tight against him. "Explain? What is there to explain? You tried to kill him. *You* should be the one leaving. *You* should be the one who has to go take care of him. Not me."

"I told you already, Flan," he doesn't even try to touch her, he just talks low and slow, calm as he can. "I didn't try to kill him. He was coming for me."

"Oh, right," she says, turning her back to him, throwing a head

239

sculpted of clay out over her shoulder. It misses him, but just barely. "I forgot. You're the big saviour now, right? That's what everyone's saying — that you're a saint or something. That I should *thank* you. Saved his life, hoo-boy. Lucky for him you were there. You big freak."

"Flan," he says, going up close to her, leaning in. "It was CPR."

"The railroad? What are you talking about?"

"No, no — cardiopulmonary resuscitation. I'm not magic, Flan. I'm not... I'm not a prophet or a saint or whatever it is I'm supposed to be. I took a course at the rec centre. My parents thought it would be a good idea, you know. After the last time."

"You're a bigger freak than I thought. Everybody knows it. You're fucked. What is your thing with dead people, anyway? You always seem to be around at the best times, don't you?"

"What? You think I... what? You think I like this?"

"Don't you ever touch me again. Don't call me. Leave me alone. *Pervert*."

●

His mother's white valise lies open on his small bed, its pink lining exposed. A few of his boxes sit beside it, and next to those lie tidy piles of his clothes, all folded neatly. White V-neck undershirts, brown corduroy pants, mustard pullovers. Y-fronts. Socks folded over each other, white and grey and black. He has filled and unfilled the valise, has tried every permutation, and still can't find a way to fit more than three of his boxes in along with his clothes. He looks down at the things on his bed and frowns.

"Going somewhere?" His father asks, leaning on the mud room's doorframe.

He shrugs.

"Your mother would probably like a goodbye," his father says gruffly, entering the room. He's never had a visitor in the mud room, let alone one as tall and wide as his father. The walls seem to squeeze around the two of them, the ceiling seems to sink. He takes a deep breath, since it seems even the air in the room is becoming scarce. His father smells of creosote and grease, of sap and dirt. His clothes are clean, his beard and hair freshly washed. But still, the smell of the forest stays on him, as though it's become a part of his skin. Or sunk deeper, to the parts of him that make sweat and smell. He takes another breath.

"I'll say goodbye," he says, lifting a pile of white shirts and placing them in the valise.

His father nods. "This because of the kids at school?"

He shrugs, and puts a pile of socks next to the shirts. He doesn't even want to know what his father's heard this time.

"You know, son," his father says, sitting down on the end of the bed, his big hands on his knees. "Things like this, they don't last forever. In a week or two —"

"A week or two?" he says, staring down into the pinkness inside the valise. "A week or two? Dad, they've called me that... name... for six years!" He looks over to his father, who is staring at the floor.

His father nods, his big hands squeezing his knees, the tendons and veins and bones all standing out all over his hands. He squeezes and releases, and nods again. "I know, son."

"And now half of them think I'm some kind of freak who can bring people back from the dead. And the other half think the opposite! They think I tried to kill —" He throws a pile of underpants into the valise, and slams the lid shut. "I'd never do that, Dad! I'd never —"

"I know," his father says, quietly. "But you really think leaving will help anything?"

He breathes slowly and rubs his eyes. "Yes," he says. "Dad, yes. It's the only thing that'll help. What else can I do?"

"Stay," his father says, lifting his head and looking at him. "Stay and show them who you are."

"They *know* who I am, Dad," he shakes his head, and shoves the valise back. He sits in the space he's just made on the bed and lets out a big sigh. "They decide who I am. I can stay, and finish school, and get a job and a wife and some kids and a house and still. They'll still call me that name. Tell the story about how I found a girl and..." he shakes his head. "They'll still tell the story of how I tried to kill the school's track star. They'll probably tell those stories at my funeral."

His father shakes his head. "You are who you are, son. No one can change that."

"No, I know," he says. "But they can... make believe they can. And sometimes that's... I dunno. Sometimes it feels like the same thing, Dad."

His father nods. Reaches out one of his big hands and lays it on his knee. Squeezes tight. "Your mother's going to miss you," his father says.

"I know," he says. "And I'll miss... but, you see, don't you? It's not... I can't."

His father nods. "I'm taking some time off work," he says. "I'm getting too old to haul trees around. Maybe there's something else I can do. Stay here with your mother. Have another go at the good old days. So you go on, and don't worry about us."

"I will anyway," he says.

His father lifts his hand from his knee with one last squeeze, and stands. "Now, you take this and don't say anything about it," his father says, handing him a folded manila envelope. "You just take care of yourself."

He takes the envelope, holds it back out to his father. "Dad —"

"I said, don't say anything about it," his father says, a growl in his voice.

He nods. "Okay," he says, putting the envelope down on the valise. He looks up to his father's eyes, deep behind wrinkles and sun-worn skin. "Thanks."

His father nods, and leaves the mud room, shutting the door carefully behind him.

•

He wakes under a tree, the sky still dark in the holes between the leaves. He sits up, stretches. Stands and picks up his blanket from the ground, folds it neatly and puts it in his bag. There's just space enough for it, on top of a few books, and some of the boxes from home. His mother's valise holds the more fragile things. He made his way to Montreal because, like his father said, it's where he had the "good old days" with Flan. The only "good old days" he ever had. Besides, it's the only other place he has ever been.

He starts walking, up the mountain. It's awhile to the lake, but he thinks he can catch a dip before it gets too bright out. He stumbles a bit in the half-light, almost trips over a makeshift tent. A holey tarp thrown over a line strung between two trees, and two hairy feet sticking out the end.

A grumble grows in there. A hairy hand reaches out. And grabs him.

"Whashudoin?" a low voice rolls at him. "Takin' my stuff?"

"No!" he yelps. He looks around him. He can barely make out piles of things, what kind of things he couldn't say. "No, I was just walking...."

"Walk shomewheres else," the voice rumbles. The hand lets him go, and he runs, all the way back down the mountain.

•

He walks until he swears he can feel his back and front meet, in the place where his stomach should keep them apart. Feels in his pocket for the change that was there last night, before he spent it on a *steamé*. Shakes his head, then takes his bag from his shoulder. Digs around for the envelope from his dad. Still a lot of it left. If he doesn't eat. He shakes his head again, and puts the envelope back in his bag.

"Troubles, my friend?" a voice booms at him. He turns to look. A round man with sleek black hair smiles at him from a seat he's made from an overturned crate.

"No," he says. "Just... uh... counting."

"Ah," the man says, nodding. "Half of nothing is still nothing, right?"

"Yeah," he says, nodding. "Right."

"Come," the man says, standing. "I make you something."

"Oh, no," he shakes his head. "I couldn't, really. I'm okay. Thanks anyway."

The man takes a step back, squints. Looks him over, from head to toe. "I think," he says, squinting harder. "I think you are okay, yes. Not like these bums who come with their hands like this." Here the man makes a cup from his two palms. "All with their long hair and the smell. Bah! You work?"

He nods. "I can," he says. "I mean, I do. With things, mostly."

"Things?" the man asks. "Like, you fix things?"

"Sure," he says. "I can fix things."

"Ah!" the man says again, a big smile coming out on his face. "I have many things that need fixing! Come in, we talk, you eat, then you fix, okay?"

His stomach makes a rolling sound he mistakes for wheels on pavement. He nods. "Okay," he says, following the man.

•

The man's name is Anatole, and the black in his hair is from shoe polish. He gets this information from Nick, Anatole's son, who runs the dep while his father spends whole days out back, tinkering with his broken trinkets.

"It's supposed to be a workshop," Nick says, leading him through the gate, into the courtyard, then up the stairs. "But it's more of a scrap-yard, if you ask me. He's supposed to be retired, but he just can't stop doing things. You know?"

He nods.

Nick hands him a key ring with three keys on it. "This one's for the front door, and there's the back." He holds up a long, skinny key and rolls his eyes. "And this one's for the shop. Looks like it's from the Dark Ages, huh?"

He nods, and takes the keys. Pauses. "So..." he frowns. "What does your dad want me to do, exactly?"

Nick shrugs. "Bring him stuff, help him fix it if you can. Keep him company. Eat sandwiches. You know. Work!" Nick laughs, pounds him on the shoulder. He smiles, wobbles under Nick's hand. "Your pay just comes off your rent," Nick says. "Easy."

He nods. Puts the key into the lock. It sticks a bit, but then opens on a stuffy kitchen, bright in the afternoon light, and a glimpse of the wooden floor of the next room.

"You wanna walk around, or you think it's good like that?" Nick asks.

He peers in the room. Takes a couple steps in, his footsteps resounding in the empty space. The walls everywhere are bare. He smiles. "That's okay," he says to Nick. "I think it's good like that."

DAHLIA

1969

Dahlia takes off her sister's silver dress, one that she'd traded for a boy's escape a few months ago. She hangs it carefully in her closet, on a padded hanger. Patience stands with her hands down, leaning against Dahlia's violet pillows. Dahlia puts on her housecoat, and takes a notebook from her little desk. She is humming and drawing, a doodle of scenery, when there comes a small knock at her door, a knock she's grown used to. She rises, ties her housecoat tight about her, and goes to the door.

"Dahl," her sister's voice comes through the wall. "Let me in."

Dahlia opens the door a crack, puts one eye to the sliver there. Tru's face is puffed and red, her hair damp around her forehead.

"Anybody with you?" Dahlia asks.

Tru shakes her head, fast.

Dahlia opens the door a bit wider, scans the hallway.

"Dahl, please," Tru moans. "I'm not messing around."

Dahlia opens the door. Tru scuttles in, holding her arms around herself. She curls up on the floor, her arms around her knees.

"You don't have to sit on the floor," Dahlia says, dragging her little white chair from under the desk. "Here."

Dahlia's sister shakes her head again. Fast.

Dahlia sits on the edge of her bed and looks down at Tru. Without makeup she still looks like a kid, her nose freckled even in the winter, her hair almost black, curling past her shoulders. Her eyes are a pale

246

blue, rimmed with navy. Almost as scary as Dahlia's own eyes, Dahlia thinks. But not quite.

"Dahl," her sister says, holding herself and starting to rock back and forth lightly. "I think I did something stupid."

Dahlia nods.

"I can't tell Mom," Tru says, rocking a little harder, a little faster. Her face suddenly goes pale, and she curls herself up even tighter. "Oh, shit, Dahl. Oh, shit shit shit. Do you have a pad?"

Dahlia shakes her head. She's never used them, couldn't begin to imagine who would. The belt and clamps and the fist of white padding fat as a kitten. "I've got some tampons," Dahlia says, uncertainly. She's never talked about this sort of thing with anyone. "I can get you one."

Dahlia's sister shakes her head again and falls onto her side, curling ever tighter. "Go to my room," she gasps. "There's a box by the bed. And bring that little bottle there, would you?"

Dahlia leaves her room, tiptoes to her sister's door. Inside, even in the dark, Dahlia can see the big box of pads, sitting on the floor, sur-rounded by folded pamphlets, a small bottle of brown liquid, a pack of cigarettes, matches, and an ashtray. She picks up the box, so light it seems not to contain anything, and the bottle. Heads back to her room. Her sister is standing, sort of swaying, just inside the door.

"Thanks," Tru takes the box and the bottle, tries a smile. "I'll be back in a sec."

Dahlia walks into her room. Beside her bed, just where her sister had been lying, is a smudge of blood, so red it seems almost black.

"I'm leaving," Tru says. Dahlia has pulled back the covers on her bed, put her sister in there with Patience.

"You just got here," Dahlia points out.

Tru smiles, a thin thing on her pale lips. "I mean Montreal. I'm mov-ing to New York. As soon as I'm better. Y'know, like the Velvets say, *my life was saved by rock and roll. And it was allll-right....*" Tru sings this last little bit, then curls up tight into a ball. After a second she relaxes, lies back on the pillows. "God*damn*," she says, pulling her knees up under the covers.

Dahlia's eyes wander over to the spot of blood on her white carpet.

"Oh," Tru says, following Dahlia's eyes, seeing the spot. "Shit. Sorry, Dahl."

Dahlia shakes her head. "It's okay."

"I didn't know it would be this bad," Tru says, pulling Dahlia's violet covers up close to her chin. "He said it would hurt. I didn't know there would be this much blood."

Dahlia says nothing. Watches her sister reach for the little bottle, open it, and take a sip. Tru winces as though what's in there is bitter, or hot. "It's for the pain," Tru says, putting the bottle down and closing her eyes. "Better start working soon."

Dahlia watches her sister lie still on her violet pillows. "I didn't know doctors worked this late at night," she finally says.

Tru snorts through her nose. Opens her eyes, her pupils huge and dark. Stares at Dahlia, shaking her head. "Doctors don't do this kind of thing, Dahl. Oh, no. They're too good for that. No, girls like me, we have to go see other people. The kind that don't do their taxes, dig?"

Dahlia stays quiet.

"Some guy with chloroform he stole from a vet, and a kitchen table," Tru explains. "I thought *that* would be easier." She stops and lets another snort out through her nose, something like a laugh lost inside it. "Idiot."

Tru leans back on Dahlia's pillows, her eyes closed. Her lashes black against her white, freckled cheek.

Dahlia watches her sleep, until her breathing seems slow and peaceful. She turns on her small white chair, and gets back to her drawing. She's drawing hair that reaches to the floor, trying to see what it would look like when it spins, when she hears something. A small noise, regular as a heartbeat. A small wet spatter.

Dahlia looks around. No rain comes in through her open window, no glass of water has been spilled from her bedside table. She listens. Follows the noise, down.

Below her bed, a puddle grows, drip by drip, the black red of her sister's blood.

BILLY

1969

Mona has cleared a corner of her room just for him. "Thanks," Billy says, carefully setting down the jar with the frog floating inside, its long legs barely touching an almost golden ball. "But I'm not staying."

"I know," Mona says, leaning up on her elbows from her bed, newly covered in black sheets. "I just thought you might, if you had a place...."

Billy shakes his head. "I can't stay here. Not with them here. You know."

Mona nods. "Yeah. I know."

She pats the space next to her. Billy goes over, sits. "Where'd all your clothes go?"

Mona chucks her chin in the direction of a couple of long, silver rods hanging from the ceiling, crammed with black shapes, furred and feathered in all directions. Bodyless hanging.

"Where's everything else?" Billy asks, scanning the room for a hint. Nothing.

Mona points. Beside the bed is a large, old valise, its dark snakeskin flaking, its buckles rusted. "In there," she says. "For you."

"Mona," Billy says. He doesn't move. He stares at the valise as though it were a live thing, come to carry him somewhere far away. "I can't...."

"Shut your hole," Mona smiles, punching him lightly on the arm. "Of course you can. You think I'm gonna wear 'em? I'm not getting any smaller, boy, I can tell you that."

Billy shakes his head, takes a deep breath, and says, "Thanks, Mona." That's all he can get out before his throat goes tiny. Closing around the way down.

She puts her hand on his, squeezes. "What happened?"

Billy shakes his head, his throat squeezing tighter from the inside. "You were right," he says, tiny words popping small and painful as fire ants crawling up from the mouth of him. "I am sick."

"Billy," Mona squeezes his hand so hard his bones feel like they're cracking. "No, c'mon... I was just a kid. I didn't mean that —"

"You were right, okay?" Billy pulls his hand away from her before she breaks something. "They told me everything."

Mona stays quiet, her cheeks pink.

"You know why I like dresses so much?" Billy waves a hand at the valise. "I was a *girl*. My mom raised me as a girl. How about that?"

Billy can't get any more words out of his throat. He wipes at his face, wishing he could smush the tears right back in his eyes. He can't.

He opens the top of his old duffel bag, takes out the file he found. Passes it to Mona without a word.

"What is this?" Mona asks, looking down at the thing. "Billy, this is private. I can't read this."

Billy shakes his head, hides his face. "Please, Mona. I can't make head or tail of it. It's all written in crazy words...." His words are muffled behind his wet hands.

There is no sound from Mona. Finally, the sound of the file being opened, a rustle of paper light as butterfly wings. Billy wipes his eyes, rubs his hands dry on his T-shirt.

"I think most of this is probably stuff you know," Mona says, flipping through the pages. She looks up at him, her lips thin and flat between her cheeks, less pink now. Almost pale. "If they told you everything."

Billy nods.

"There's just one thing," Mona says, staring down at her lap where the file rests. "Did they say anything about the... stuff they took out of you?"

"Just that they took it out," Billy says, turning from the window.

Mona nods and bites her lip. "Nothing else?"

Billy shakes his head.

Mona clears her throat. Looks down at her lap some more.

"What?" Billy almost screams. Keeping it from becoming a scream hurts him and he shuts his mouth. "Mona."

She looks at him. "It looks like the things they took out of you... didn't match."

Billy frowns. Shakes his head. "What?"

"One of them was clearly yours," she says, shifting the papers again, re-checking. "Blood type matched and everything. But the other one...."

"What are you talking about?" Billy almost runs over to Mona, grabs the file from her. Looks at the pages she's been reading. But he still can't make any sense of what's written there. "What do you mean?"

"I mean," Mona says this very quietly, "it looks like maybe... well, it could be. If this is true... you're made of two people. Like... maybe you had a sister after all. Or, really, have... what zoologists call a chimera. It happens all the time — I mean, in animals. There's not much documentation in humans, but that could be due to a want of subjects —"

"Mona, stop it," Billy snaps. "I'm not a science project."

"Sorry," Mona says. She closes the folder, puts it aside. "I'm just trying to help."

Billy breathes, deep and slow. "I know," he says, softly. "Sorry. It's just kind of a lot to take in...."

Mona takes his hand again, softly this time. "It doesn't mean anything," she says. "You're still you."

"Am I?" Billy asks.

Mona is silent. After forever, she nods.

"Well, bully for me," Billy says, loudly. "I'm a chimera. Fan-tastic."

He picks up the file, and puts it back in his duffel bag. He closes it, fussing with the knot. He finally gives up and throws the thing across the room. He flops back on Mona's bed.

Mona's face is above him, big as the moon. She tries a smile. "Lemonade?" she asks.

Billy nods. "You got any vodka for that?"

"Lots," Mona says. Billy reaches his arms up. Mona hugs him so hard he starts to believe he really could be two people squished together.

•

Billy and Mona walk slowly, the long way, to the bus station. The late-afternoon air is hollow and cool, the streets nearly empty. The flat plate glass windows of the main drag are glazed gold from the setting sun.

"Where are you going to go?" Mona asks him, setting down the valise, and fishing in her pocket for something.

Billy shrugs. "I dunno," he says, stopping next to Mona. "I thought maybe... I dunno, I thought I'd see if I could find...."

"What?"

Billy shakes his head. "No, you know, now that I think about it it's really stupid."

"What?"

Billy sighs and drops the army bag on the ground. A puff of dust lifts, swirls lightly, and falls slow as snow back to the ground. He left the jar with Mona, joking maybe she could run some tests on it someday. Even if the things in them are his sister's or nobody's at all, he doesn't want them. "I thought I'd go see if I could find my dad." He takes off his baseball cap, pushes his hair behind his ears, and replaces the cap, pulling it down over his eyes. "Stupid, huh?"

Mona stops fishing in her pockets, stares at him, her eyebrows raised. "Really? Your dad?"

"Yeah," Billy pulls his cap down even lower. Smiles. "Guess I'm a sucker for punishment."

"You think he's alive?" Mona asks. "I mean, I thought they'd told you he was dead...."

"Yeah, well," Billy kicks at his army bag. "They told me a lot of things that weren't true."

Mona's mouth flattens. She bites her lower lip, chews on it a bit. Nods.

"And maybe it is his fault," Billy says, putting his hands in his jean pockets. "I mean, that everything turned out like it did. That I turned out like I did. But, you know... I guess I... just need to find out. If he even did any of the things they told me. If he was even around at all. If he's even real."

Mona nods again. "You're sure?"

Billy shrugs and kicks at the bag again. "I guess."

"Then you're going to need this." She holds out an envelope, tattered and thick.

"What? Mona —" Billy says, shaking his head.

"Oh, come on," she says, putting her hand closer to him. He stays standing, his hands in his pockets. Mona rolls her eyes, pulls his right hand out of the pocket, and slaps the envelope down. "Take it already, would you?"

Billy doesn't open it, but can see colours through the holes in the envelope. Brown and red and green and purple and blue. "Mona... I can't take this."

"Of course you can," she says, waving her hands over the envelope, as if to make it disappear. "I don't need it."

"This is the money you've been saving for university," Billy says, holding the envelope out, toward her. "I *can't*."

"Well, you better," Mona says, her face all serious. "Anyway, I told you, I don't need it."

"What about university?" Billy asks. "You're dying to go. You *have to* go. If I take this...."

"I'll just have to get a scholarship," Mona shrugs. She winks at him. "Should be a breeze in this bunghole town. Now take it, already!"

"I'm paying you back," he says.

"I know," Mona says.

"Good," Billy says, putting the envelope into his mac's right pocket. They stare at each other some more.

"Hey Mona," Billy says, a small smile starting, turning so big so quick it almost hurts. "Thanks."

"You fool," she says, wrapping him up in a hug. "I'm going to miss you."

I know, he thinks, the air squeezed out of him so he can't talk. Me, too.

•

Billy carries both his bags onto the bus, the valise bumping against his shins as he walks down the aisle. He passes a granny carefully arranging her bags on the seat next to her, a young mother fussing with her baby, a couple of huge men in faded, sweat-stained T-shirts. No one his age. No one even remotely related to him. He puts his head down and just walks, until he's at the last row before the bathroom. Empty, all around.

Billy heaves his army bag into the overhead rack, the bag that's full of his own clothes. His macs and jeans and Big Daddy Roth T-shirts, his wool socks, his dungarees. He picks up the valise to do the same, but holds onto it. Stares at the worn straps, the peeling snakeskin. Thinks of the dresses all piled on each other in there, and what they'd look like, spilling out of a bag held by him. A teenage boy. He places the valise carefully on the floor below the window seat, then pushes it under the seat in front. He sits in the window seat, rests his feet on the valise. Turns and looks out the window. The sun's just making its last glow low on the horizon, the cloudless sky spreading wide above him.

The bus jolts once, then moves away from the parking lot, away from the last few buildings of his small hometown, away from Mona, standing on the side of the road. She watches the bus go, her hands in her pockets. Billy turns his head as the bus rolls onto the road. Mona stares at him, and pretends not to see him for a second. But then she lifts her hand, a little smile on her lips. Billy lifts his own hand. They wave at each other until Mona is out of sight, lost somewhere behind the bus, lost to the growing shadows on the side of the road.

•

Billy goes into the bathroom, closes the tiny door. The chemical smell of the toilet strong as a live thing in there, a serpenty thing that slides up his nose and down his throat. He closes the lid to the toilet with his foot, then sits. Takes the envelope out of his mac's breast pocket, and removes all but the five dollar bills. Bends down and takes off his right sneaker, stuffs the bills in there, and shoves his foot back in. Takes the fives out of the envelope, and counts them. In among them is a folded piece of paper. He takes it out, and carefully unfolds it. Inside it is a dried-up thing with many many legs. Like a star a kid would draw at school, before being told a star has only five points. Billy looks at the paper, and sees there's a note written there.

Not that I think you'll need it, the note reads, *but here's the number of the son of some friends of my parents. He's kind of like a cousin, I guess. Anyway, he's an okay guy, and he just moved to Montreal too.*

It's a brittle star. Be careful with it. It'll break, easy.

There's the name and number, and a fat cartoony heart around a big M. Billy refolds the paper, and puts it back in the envelope. The brittle star he cradles in his hand for a second, then puts into his breast pocket, closing the button carefully. He stands, puts his hand on the latch of the bathroom door. Then he takes the note out of the envelope, reads it once more, shoves it in the front pocket of his jeans, and leaves the bathroom.

•

All around him the sky, so dark it could be solid, so dark it really could have no beginning and no end. The bus, a tiny pod lit inside with faint flickering lights along the ceiling, speeds through space. The people around him recline, pressed back in their seats, their eyes closed. Billy stares out the window past the pale shimmer of his own face, tries hard to see anything out there. Streetlights in constellations. Far-off houses, warm as planets. But mostly, mostly, only black.

"I'm feeling very still," Billy sings, quiet, just below the hum of the bus, *"and I think my spaceship knows which way to go...."*

•

He rings the doorbell. He waits. He shifts from foot to foot, trying to scratch the itch from the lace around his thighs. He waits some more. Finally, there comes a clattering on the stair, a sound with the pep of puppies in it. A boy's face appears at the small window, a face that's square as the pane of glass. Pale eyes deep-set in the boxy, freckled head give him the once-over. And slowly, slowly, the door opens.

"Hell-o?" the square-headed boy drawls, drawing out the word like taffy.

"Hello," he says. "I'm Mona's friend. I called you from the bus station?"

"Yeah," the square-headed boy says. "Come in, I guess... uh... I'm Bikky."

"Call me Beau," Beau says, holding out his right hand, the pink nails newly painted. The boy hesitates for a second, sizing up Beau's chestnut curls, pink blouse, jeans and sneakers. Finally he takes Beau's hand, shakes it, and waves him up the steps.

Beau walks up the long flight of steps slowly, glad he didn't test out his new heels the first day.

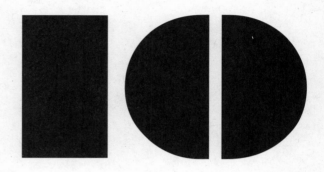

AUGUST - SEPTEMBER, 1972

HICKLIN

He closes the door. In the dark the thing he's built seems bigger than the space they're standing in, a swallowing blackness with no horizon. He stares at it until he feels like he might fall in, lost forever. Even his atoms destroyed, a nullity in space. A loss of energy in the universe, unlike anything or anyone before. A singularity.

Luce slithers her skinny arms around him, reaching. He squirms away and punches the light on.

"Aw, Daddy," she smiles, an angular grin. "Thought we were gonna watch the submarine races."

"No, I... maybe later," he stammers, a hot flush creeping up his neck itchy as poison ivy. "I wanted to show you this."

Luce slides forward, slinking around the thing and out the other side. As though the Hole there doesn't affect her, as if it is her home. She shrugs.

"It's a box," she says. "Big whoop."

"You have to go inside," he says, reaching for a latch on the side of the thing. "You have to be in it to see it properly."

The Hole, or the box, as Luce calls it, is about as high as a doorway. Flat at the back, where the door is, with what appears to be a semi-circular front. This is actually made up of seven small walls, all attached. Parts of these walls are transparent, to allow light in. The rest is painted black. He opens the door and she hops in. Slowly, he closes the door after her.

For a moment there is no sound. For another moment there is no sound. Then a long sigh, as if air were being compressed out of bellows, as of breath from one set of lungs to another. Bringing whatever is in there back to life.

"It's beautiful, Daddy," Luce's voice comes softly. "It's something else."

It's a monster, he thinks. But it's *my* monster.

"Come on in," she calls. "There's room for two!"

He hasn't been inside yet, not since it's been finished. Hasn't closed the door behind him. Hasn't been swallowed.

He swallows. And opens the door.

•

Inside seems bigger than the outside, as a system of mirrors reflect light admitted from the transparent parts of the seven walls, and from one hole, about halfway up the front of the door. With his back to the door, he can see out, to the stands. As though he were onstage, with Luce. Before them, seven times seven panels shimmy, dancing about them. Diana, Mercury, Venus, Apollo, Mars, Jupiter, and Saturn, their signs marking the seven holes. Stretching to the gods, each row is marked: The Banquet, The Cave, The Gorgon Sisters, Pasiphe and the Bull, The Sandals of Mercury, and Prometheus.

Each panel glimmers in the reflected light, something like stereo-scopic images shifting as though heading for flight. Some are shadow puppets, angular and sharp. Some painted on glass. Faces and bodies gleam and struggle, hair waves in unseen breezes, the images of himself and Luce sliding through time along with them. Below each panel, a tiny drawer. A cabinet.

There are the dancers, twinning with their mirror sisters, there is the waitress, there's the too-tall man in his too-small suit. There are the *feu follets*, waving before the stage. Here is the space, just big enough for two.

"It's the skin joint," Luce turns her many faces smiling to him. "How'd you do it? It's fantastic."

"I don't know," Hicklin says, stilled. "I didn't know it would work."

The Gorgon Sisters pass their one eye around like a bottle round a fire. Pasiphe struggles under the weight of the Bull. Pandora slips a finger under a latch, setting free the promise inside her box.

Luce's hands many hands. He keeps his eyes open, to remember.

•

Later they leave the thing, closing the Hole behind them. Luce shakes her head.

"You have to put that out in the world," she says. "You have to let other people see it."

Hicklin shakes his head. "No," he says. "I can't. I mean. It's private."

Luce smiles. "But, Daddy," she says, pointing at the thing. "It's a *theatre*. Theatres aren't private."

Hicklin bites his lip. "How'd you know it's a theatre?"

"A skin joint's a theatre, Daddy," Luce says, canines shining at the corners of her grin. "But anyway it's got the same set-up as any old theatre. Like the ones doctors used to use, right?"

Hicklin nods. "Yeah, I guess you're right... I never thought of that, though. It's modeled on a memory theatre."

"A what?" Luce opens the door to the room she used to sleep in, the room now a bedroom for the beast he's built. "Now you're making things up."

"No, I'm not," Hicklin says, following her out through the living room, past Endymion sleeping in the slanting sun of an August afternoon. "It was a real thing. At least, there's some evidence it was a real thing, I mean a thing that was once actually built. It definitely existed on paper."

"Oh," Luce says, as they reach the kitchen. She opens the fridge, then closes it against its emptiness. Sits down at the table. Looks up at him through her hair. "And everything that exists on paper is real, right?" Her smirk sitting faceless in the summer sun.

"Well, yeah," he starts, reaching into the fridge, then the freezer, under the bag of peas no one's ever eaten. Another bottle of vodka has been hidden there, since the last time. "In a way."

"And what was this memory theatre supposed to do?" Luce asks. "Put your memories onstage? Make a show out of them?"

Hicklin shakes his head. "No," he says, reaching up to a high shelf for a couple of glasses. "Pretty much the opposite. It was designed by this guy Giulio Camillo, who was working in a much older tradition. His theatre was supposed to give whoever went inside it a system for perfect recall. Like, you'd go in, and have the whole knowable universe imprinted on your memory. So if you ever needed to remember anything, you could just sort of close your eyes, and be back in the theatre, and you could find your way around in there, and there you go."

Luce makes a snorting sound. "Worked, did it?"

"I don't know," Hicklin says, putting two glasses on the table, along with the bottle of vodka. "Like I said, no one's really sure the thing was ever built. Mine's based... well, pretty loosely based on a reconstruction by Frances Yates. She was working from Camillo's texts, though. So who knows? Maybe it does work. You tell me."

Luce closes her eyes. "I seeeeeee," she hums. She pops her eyes open and looks up at Hicklin. "I see one crazy cat."

Hicklin shrugs. Picks up Dolly's small pink sherry glass, the bezoar clinking as he sets it down. Pours vodka into it, offers it to Luce.

"What's that in the bottom?" she asks peering into the glass. "It looks like a weird rock."

"It's a bezoar," Hicklin says. "It's a thing Dolly's into right now. Supposed to protect you from poison."

"Ah-ha," Luce says, smiling. "We're afraid of poison in our own house now, huh?" She shakes her head. She passes over the glass and reaches for the bottle, tipping it into her mouth. She winks at Hicklin. "See, I'm dandy. Princess is all worried for nothing."

Hicklin stares at her, then at the bottle, then at the glass. He lifts the glass and drinks, the bezoar clinking against his teeth as the burn from the vodka hits him. Luce's eyes cold on him when he sets down the glass.

"I really think you should listen to me," Luce says, reaching for the bottle again. "Even if you think I'm wrong."

Hicklin nods, and reaches for the bottle when she passes it to him.

They settle on seven, which leaves six to build.

"Why not just the one?" Hicklin asks.

"Think about it, Daddy," Luce says, as they sip vodka over a map of the city. "Imagine. All over the city, people in your theatres, having the time of their lives. Isn't it pretty?"

Hicklin thinks about it. It is pretty. "But not everyone will do what we did," Hicklin says. "Will they?"

"Doesn't matter," Luce says. "It's none of our beeswax what they do. It's up to them."

"Where will we keep them?"

"We don't keep them," Luce smiles. "We set them free."

●

He hears Luce close the door to the apartment, hears her walk lightly down the crooked steps to go 'wet her whistle' as she said. Hears the outside door close. He waits a minute, then gets up, crosses the room, and shuts the door.

Hicklin seats himself with his back to the door, leaning up against it. He takes a deep breath, and then takes a small, white envelope from his pocket, where it's been sitting folded and unopened for the whole day. He stares at his father's angular writing. He flips over the envelope, and opens it, a rough slit right across the top.

At first he thinks there's nothing inside it. No letter, nothing. He holds the envelope open, and upside down, and shakes. Finally, something small falls out. A piece of newsprint, folded many times into a tiny square. He stares at it for a while, there on the floor. In this room, with this mess, he could just leave it lying there, and no one would know. It'd probably just get swept up by Dolly's broom, and tossed away. Maybe to be found by someone else. He stares at it some more, and finally, leans down, picks it up and unfolds it.

DOLLY

"So how many skeletons?"

"However many show up."

"What about satyrs?"

"Of course. We'll need satyrs."

"Nymphs?"

"I think we can manage some."

"Nixies?"

"Yes Beau. We'll have nixies. Pixies too. Anything you want."

"Virgins!"

Dolly nods. "If you must."

Beau frowns. "But where are we going to find *virgins*? Do they even exist anymore? We'll have to raid the nunnery!"

Dolly rises from her little seat in among her weeds. "No we won't. I know one. Much closer to home."

Beau watches her go past, nothing like a smile on her face. He raises an eyebrow. "No."

"I didn't say anything," Dolly says serenely, opening the door to the kitchen.

"You!" Beau squeals. Dolly shuts the door.

She walks over to the room that used to house Luce, occasionally, the room that now holds a large black box, closed with a latch, with holes all over it. Beau's crooked walk clatters behind her.

"I knew it!" he squeaks. "Why didn't you tell me?"

Dolly ignores him, rummaging through the stacks of papers lying on a table made of a door planked over two sawhorses, looking for one that might have an empty space, maybe even an empty side.

"C'mon, Doll," Beau clicks along with his cane. "You could've told me."

"It seems I just did," Dolly says. She finds a piece of rag paper, large enough to serve as a tablecloth, and pulls it free of the stack it's lying under. Beau smiles at her, shaking his head.

"A virgin throwing me a bacchanal," he giggles. "Will wonders never cease."

"What's a back-a-nal?" Luce slinks into the room, drops her rat bag on the floor. "Some kind of shindig? And did I hear something about a virgin?"

"Oh good," Dolly says, not turning to look at Luce. "She's back. I thought I was enjoying myself a bit too much."

At this, Luce turns to Dolly, gives her the once-over. "Yeah, I think I did hear something about a virgin. One close to home, wasn't it?"

Dolly rolls up the large piece of paper she's found, standing perfectly straight. She walks from the room, nearly bumping into Hicklin who's coming in right behind Luce.

"Whoa," he yelps, as she pushes past him. "You okay, Dolly?"

She doesn't answer, just marches through the house toward the cracked kitchen door. She stands the rolled-up paper in an empty pot. Paces from the front of the balcony to the back, from the back to the front and back again. Pauses at the top of the stairs.

A squink as the door is opened. Dolly starts moving, down the stairs.

"Dolly?" Hicklin's voice from behind her.

She stops. Takes a deep breath. Pulls herself straight.

"Dolly?" Hicklin calls again.

Dolly steps down the stairs, one at a time. Each one solid beneath her. She pulls open the slanty gate, and stands there. One foot in their cruddy courtyard, one foot on the sidewalk.

She breathes, again, in and out and out and in. Hears Luce laughing, somewhere above her. Dolly opens her eyes. Looks down the street. She could just catch a cab, or take the bus, somewhere, anywhere, to get away from —

"Doll," Beau calls from the top of the stairs. His crooked walk clacking closer, one slow step at a time. "You okay?"

Click-a-clank. Click-a-clank.

Dolly turns. Closes the gate.

"I'm fine," she says, not too loud, not really loud enough for either of them to hear. She walks toward the stairs, before Beau has to go too far. "I'm fine," she says, again. Her voice sturdy. Something to lean on.

Beau stops where he is, Hicklin's sandy head peeking from behind. Dolly looks up at them. And almost smiles.

"Come on Beau," she says. "We've got a party to plan."

•

Beau sleeps beside her, his mouth open, a hot all-night yawn. The door to Hicklin's room is closed. There is a faint light from the living room, from a candle Luce has left burning. Dolly pulls the sheet from her, the single sheet she and Beau sleep under. Reaches beneath the bed, and pulls out her violet valise.

Leaving it on the floor, she opens the two clasps, popping them open like seeds from their pods. The honey fur of her mother's fur coats. Dolly reaches her hands in, and pulls Patience from her nest.

Patience stares at Dolly.

"Hi, Patience," Dolly whispers. "It's been awhile. I'm sorry. Sorry to leave you all shut up for so long."

Patience stares, neither accepting nor declining Dolly's apology.

Dolly lifts Patience carefully, holding her tight. Out of the room and down the hall, past the bathroom and into the kitchen. Just the light in the living room enough to guide her. Out the cracked back door. Dolly closes it quietly behind her, leaving it just a bit ajar.

Dolly paces up and down the balcony, like a widow on her walk. Holding Patience tight, her face facing backwards.

"Patience," Dolly whispers, "I don't know what to do. There's a lot of things I want to ask you, but somehow I can't. It's like. Well. I think maybe there's only so many questions I'm allowed to ask so they better be good ones. I know it's silly."

Dolly reaches the short part of the L, does a quick turn on tiptoe, and walks back, tracing her own steps.

"So whenever I have a question I save it for you," Dolly says, a bit louder than a whisper. "At least you'll give me an answer."

Patience remains silent.

Dolly turns at the end of the long part of the L, begins her widow's walk back to where she started.

"If you knew someone was," Dolly pauses. It's been so long since she asked a question she's half-afraid to try. She pauses, counting her own footsteps for no reason. "Do you think there are people out there who don't... who aren't... people?"

Patience stays quiet. Dolly frowns at the waste of a question mark, the waste of a question she didn't even put together properly before asking it. She keeps walking, turns at the short end of the L, keeps counting her footsteps.

"It's just," Dolly speaks quietly, as though to an actual infant. "It's just there's someone here who makes me think there might be."

Dolly stops pacing, stopping for a noise from somewhere inside, a light click of a door opening. It's followed moments later by another click, closer to her. Someone up to use the washroom. Dolly keeps pacing, keeps following her own trail.

"Lay me doooown," Patience commands, her voice crackling out of her chest, an old creak on a child's treble. "To sleeeep."

Dolly stops again. Holds Patience from her, at arm's length, searching her face for a clue that's never been there and isn't there now. "Really," Dolly says.

Patience keeps her peace.

"Just let me try again," Dolly whispers. "Please."

Patience says nothing to this, so Dolly puts her back over her shoulder and restarts her winding walk.

"Alright Patience," Dolly says. "Here. What should I do? If this person turns —"

There is a noise that is almost soundless. Almost, but not quite. Dolly turns around.

Luce in white underpants and nothing else, her skin summer-dark, the underpants glowing as if lit from within. Luce smirks, eyes hidden under her bangs.

"Aw," Luce drawls, drawing the sound out. "Isn't this cute? Dolly and her Baby, out for a moonlit stroll. How's Baby feeling? A little colicky?"

Patience is indeed making a rasping noise, a cough with a click in it.

"Go back to bed," Dolly says, walking toward Luce, who's standing in her path, walking toward her as though she could pass right through. "Your infantile comments are not needed here."

"I shoooouuld dieee," Patience croaks.

Luce puts out a hand, almost touching Dolly as she passes.

"Hey," Luce says. "Let me see that. I didn't know Baby could talk."

Dolly keeps walking, Patience looking out behind her. Keeps quiet, practising patience.

"Okay, fine," Luce's voice calls from behind Dolly, her face a face only Patience can see. "You keep Baby all to yourself. I can take a hint."

Dolly turns at the end of the long part of the L. Luce is still standing there, still watching with those eyes always hidden.

"And that's not all I can take," Luce says, before sliding inside the cracked kitchen door, so smooth and so fast Dolly can barely see it happen.

Patience grumbles, and begins her coughing sound again. Dolly keeps walking, keeps counting her steps, keeps breathing, low and deep.

"Is that all?" Dolly whispers in Patience's ear. "Nothing else?"

A deep grinding from within Patience. The sound of her thinking.

"I should die," Dolly says. "That's your advice?"

Patience growls, a low, slow roar.

"Beeeeefore," Patience rumbles, the one word from deep within her rattling in Dolly's chest, as though their two cavities had become one.

A long pause, the rattle worn away to nothing, and then Patience speaks again. "I waaaaaake," she creaks, a crack coming at the end of the word, a shattering silence deep in Dolly's chest. Dolly nods, slowly, and holding Patience ever closer, continues her walk.

•

Dolly keeps to a tight path, both in the apartment and outside it. From the room she and Beau share, to the kitchen, to her garden. Down the stairs, to the courtyard that remains her territory. A quick glance up and down the street tells her which way to take to Ginger's, or the bar. Sometimes the short way, sometimes the long way, depending on who shadows her. A small eyeless shadow and Dolly often gives up, and retreats to her garden.

In the heat she waits until almost dark, until the shadows have fled, and then she goes. Carrying the day's sweat on her back, Dolly scours the sidewalks, the alleys, the piles of garbage left to ferment in the late August heat. She harvests jewels from trash. Gowns and glass and wood and tile. A pile of mangy boas one lucky day, a scattering of sequins the next. Cats slink by her, slitting their eyes against the light, slight frowns on their furry faces. Dolly brings home wooden ironing boards, flat folding chairs, anything shiny, anything fuzzy or woolen. An endless import to their room, which is filling quickly with matter waiting to be transformed, into magic.

Dolly sews and glues and patches. Beau picks up her half-finished things, and makes them shine. Sometimes with glitter or glass, sometimes in a way Dolly can't even start to put her finger on.

Dolly borrows books from the library, filled with sketches and photos of sets and costumes that have gone before. Beau peeks over her shoulder, gives a giggle.

Dolly looks up at him.

"The Ballet Russes had Dali for their Bacchanal," he says, pointing to the caption beneath a photo of a set made from a slit-open swan, "but we've done them one better, hey Doll?"

Dolly rolls her eyes, and goes back to plucking the feathers from a once-white boa. "I hardly think our combined talents are greater than Dali's," she says. "Or Picasso's, or Bakst's, or Miro's."

Beau tries on a wing, flutters one arm, walking himself around the room, clinking his cane as he goes. "Maybe you don't, Doll," he sings, waving the wing in front of her face, smiling, "but I do."

●

The only contact she has with the other two people who live in the apartment is through sound. Dolly hears Hicklin and Luce come and go, up the stairs and down again, always by the front door, since the back door is hers. She hears them in the living room, something loud and crunchy always playing on the stereo. She hears Luce giggle, and sometimes she almost hears what it is they're saying. Light laughing things, things that clatter through the wall, slick as beetle bugs. She hears other noises too, and not just at night. She hears them so often and so clearly she starts to think maybe the people making them know they're being listened to. When this happens, she goes to her garden and sits with her plants, listens to them grow, silent and slow.

She is out there, the sky dying down from clear blue to indigo, a cat's cradle of clouds stretching across the sky of the city, when she hears the cracked kitchen door open.

"Dolly," a slivered whisper. An extra sound that tells her who it is.

"Hicklin wants out," she says, without moving her head from where she's staring, off between the buildings.

"Yes, please," Hicklin's voice says, still soft.

"Fine," Dolly says, still not bringing her gaze down to earth. "But you better be alone."

"I'm alone," he says, a bit louder. "Can I come out?"

Dolly nods.

Hicklin opens the door behind her, steps out, into her garden.

"It's so great out here," he says, lamely. There is a pause, a shuffling. "I've missed it."

Dolly turns, finally, to look at him. He's freshly showered, his tanned skin glowing against his white dress shirt, his hair beach blonde, hanging in his eyes. His eyes which are still too big for his face. She wonders how he would've looked as a child, with eyes that big in an even smaller head. Fetal or feral, she can't decide which.

Dolly stares at him, silent.

"I've missed you," he says, quietly.

Dolly nods. "I know," she says.

"Is it all because of..." Hicklin runs a hand through his hair, "you know."

"I'm here," Dolly says, flatly, a grind coming out in her voice. "Obviously you know where to find me."

"Yeah, but, you're avoiding me," Hicklin says.

Dolly stares at him some more.

"You hate her," he says, raising his hands palm up, to the dying sky.

"I don't hate her," Dolly says. "I don't hate anybody. I just don't think she's... good for you."

Hicklin sits on an overturned olive bucket. Sighs. "Dolly," he says, fumbling in his breast pocket, "lots of things aren't good for me, and I like them anyway. Vodka and porto and weed and — these," he says, pulling a pack of cigarettes from his pocket and waving them around. "And I don't see you starting any cold shoulder campaigns with me over them."

"She —"

"What?"

Dolly pauses. Looks away from Hicklin, and back again. "She's not a thing, Hicklin," Dolly states, staring at him.

"Phhhhuuuh," Hicklin lets out a big puff of air. "I know that. Boy, do I know it. Come on, Dolly. Play nice."

Dolly turns her face back to the sky, gone a bruisy purple, the cat's cradle blackening.

"I just don't see why you and me can't be friends," Hicklin's voice says, muffled around a cigarette. He takes a sharp, long drag, and lets it out. "I just don't see how it's any of your business who I'm with."

Dolly talks to the cat's cradle, pulling itself apart against the cheek of the sky. She pushes her glasses up on her nose. "Fine. You're right anyway. It's none of my business. We can be friends." She looks at him, sharply. "You and me. Just promise me something. Promise me you'll believe me when it counts."

Hicklin nods, a little smile coming out. "Isn't this where we have to spit, or bleed on each other, or something?"

Dolly blinks. "If you think it would help."

Hicklin's smile grows wider. "I was kidding."

"Oh," Dolly holds out her right hand, and looks at it. "Shake, then."

"Are you serious?" Hicklin asks. Dolly stares at him. "Look who I'm asking," he says, holding out his hand.

"Promise," Dolly says, her scary eyes not blinking.

"I promise, Dolly," Hicklin says, taking her hand and squeezing it tight.

BEAU

September sits hot as August in the house, a giant reaching its body over everything, its head in the kitchen, and a limb in every room. Beau crawls under it, to the shade of Dolly's garden, spends days sitting out there, sewing.

For himself he's making legs of fur. Some of it is from his uncle's collection, some of it is from coats and stoles he and Dolly have found. In the heat the skins stick to him, the fur flattens. He sews anyway. By the time he's going to wear the things, he hopes, the giant will have gone, traded places with its cooler cousin.

He's collecting bones, now, too. From butchers all over town, the biggest ones he can get. These are for the party, to add Hallowe'eny flavour to the torches, to the Holes. Bones to pile around the Holes, turning them into Baba Yaga's house. A place to get answers. If you ask the right questions.

There's another pile of bones growing, in a crate in the room Beau and Dolly share. From Oscar he gets human bones, some of them copies, some of them of mysterious origin, in all states of his disease. Ulnas and vertebrae riddled with holes. Frail tibias and clavicles chewed through. A femur big as a baseball bat, the hip joint worn away as though it had been nibbled. Beau stares at it, his eyes through the built-in windows. Something lived here.

Something that lives in him.

These bones he has no plans for. He just feels like he needs them.

One afternoon, Beau sits sewing in Dolly's garden. She comes up the stairs, her arms full of clothes she's found on the street, edges past him and into the apartment. He gets up slowly, and follows behind her, his cane clattering on the wooden floor.

"What'd you get, Doll?" he calls.

"I don't know yet," she answers. Not from their room, but from the room that used to be Luce's. The room that now houses Holes.

"What're you doing in here?" Beau asks, poking his head barely into the room.

"Our room is full," Dolly says, laying the pile down. It slides, a mountain of feathers and silk, sliding off each other and down to the floor.

"Oops!" Beau leans forward to try and grab the pile before it all falls to the floor. Together they scoop armfuls of mildewy clothes back into some sort of shape. Poking from beneath the clothes is something familiar. "Hm," Beau says, sweeping the clothes away. "Well, this shouldn't be here. Should it? What's it doing here, Doll?" Beau asks, moving the rest of the papers off of Dolly's violet valise.

"I don't know," she says, leaning forward to lift it. She manages to get it up on a table cluttered with crusty jam jars and papers. Lays it down. And opens it.

Honey fur. Dolly pulls it aside.

A handful of hair red as dried blood, a cracked skull. Shiny white teeth still perfect inside their shattered mouth. And two blue eyes, homeless, roaming. Rolling inside the cup of her jaw.

"Patience," Dolly breathes.

"Oh, my God," Beau says.

Dolly lifts Patience from her furry home, making sure to keep her eyes in her head. Patience's body is still intact. The blow broke only her head. Dolly holds her to her chest.

"Well," she says. She has to stop and swallow, has to stop and breathe. "It seems a certain someone has something she'd like to say to me."

"You don't think someone did this on *purpose*?" Beau asks.

"Not someone," Dolly says, her scary eyes rolling inside her own skull. "Something."

LUCE

Kids. This is the best it's ever been, I mean, ever. I wake up and I can't wait, you know that feeling? Like your birthday and the first day of summer vacation rolled up together. Amazing.

Me and the Fox have got piles of magazines, all over the living room. There's old cheesecake pin-ups, there's all the new smut from the newsstands, there's catalogues and Tijuana Bibles, there's everything. Bondage stories and lady jails, car washes and cartoon chicks riding rockets. We pick through them for the best ones, trace them over, then paint onto these big glass slides. Hicklin gets me to do most of the painting, says I've got a better touch. I dunno, maybe his eyes aren't so good. I never thought I was good at much, but he seems convinced. So I paint.

He gives me a kid's book full of pictures of the folks I'm supposed to paint. Most of them are regular people, but some of them have animal parts, and like all good monsters they have 'the' in front of their names. And here, there's a picture, of the man with the horns. But in this book he's called the Minotaur, and his folks are part of the Hole. He's not though. He's stuck in a labyrinth, in the dark, forever.

We keep the radio on, get up and dance every once in a while, well, okay, really, it's just me cutting a rug, and Hicklin standing there looking at the floor. We smoke a lot of weed, and we screw.

It takes us longer than we thought it would, and by the time the kids are hollering outside on their way to school, we're still nowhere close to being done. The Ghost is planning a big to-do for the Daisy, like to celebrate he's all better or something, though to look at him he's only getting worse. Clanking around with a cane like an old man. But their party's at the end of October, and Hicklin thinks we can get at least a couple of these Holes done by then. They want to call this big shin-dig The Hole Show. Sounds about right to me.

But not everything is peachy keen. The Daisy and the Ghost keep to themselves, sewing things in their room. Me and the Fox get his room, and my old room, and part of the living room. It's like living in two places, squished into one.

I poke around a lot, when no one else is there. Find lots of good stuff. The Daisy's got some great dresses, and the Ghost's got some interesting letters. The best stuff of all is in the Fox's room, though. Man, he's got everything.

Boxes and boxes, big, little, tiny. Leaves and rocks and bones, shells and spiny weird white things that look like they came from some other planet. The teeth he was talking about, and some horn things, all twisty. Big beetles he's labelled *bulls*, and butterflies and moths all pinned and spread wide.

Then there's other stuff, like movie stubs and a passport that I think is from some other country but turns out to be from Expo 67, right here in good old Montreal. Photos of him and a redheaded twist, I guess the Flan he's always talking about, and the slip that was on the floor in his room for the longest time, but I guess got put away sometime. A coaster from the skin joint I took him to, and a few others besides.

Then, at the bottom of all this, there's a little box all tied up with twine. Looks like it hasn't been opened in ages. I open it, and inside there's the prettiest thing, a tiny gold globe. It's got a chain, looks so thin it couldn't hold anything. I pick it up, and kids, I tell you, I feel like a goddamned princess and no fooling.

I carry the thing around with me all day, to the park, to the store, up and down the street and all day I'm smiling and feeling, well, pretty.

I get back to our place and I'm just going to sneak the little thing back where it came from, but who's home? The Fox. He gives me this look as I walk in the door like some of our 'Uncles' used to, right before they popped me one. Course the Fox doesn't.

"I've been looking all over for that, Luce," the Fox says, putting out a hand. "Give it back."

I do a little spin in front of him. "Why?" I ask, hanging onto the strap of the little purse. "Dontcha wanna *get the best for me? Daddy?*" I sing that last part, out of a song Mom used to play. The Fox keeps his hand steady.

"Luce," he says, his voice low, almost a growl. I've never heard anything like it in him. "Give it back."

"Well, did you ever?" I ask, picking up the little gold globe, holding it up close to my eyes, talking right to it. "I say, little thing, you've put quite a spell on him."

"I'm not going to ask again," he says, a rumble deep in the back of his throat, like when you take a dog's bone. "Give it back."

"You bet," I say, making to hand the thing over to him. He reaches out his hand, but I grab the thing away. "*After* you tell me why."

He gets this look in his eye, the lids coming down. His nostrils flare. The skin around his throat gets pink and patchy. This I've seen before, just not on him. I smile.

"Oh, Daddy," I say, tossing the gold purse over my shoulder. "You gonna pound me? Try not to mess up my blouse. I just bought it."

The Fox lets out a long breath, runs his hand through his hair. He turns his back to me, and paces around in littler and littler circles, until his footsteps have brought him right back to me. He's muttering under his breath, something I can't quite make out. He stops in front of me, looks down at me.

"Luce," he says, his voice gone quiet. "Please. Don't do this."

"*I'm* not doing this, Daddy," I say. Nothing like a smile anywhere near me. "You are."

•

"Everybody thinks I saved her," he says, taking a drag from his cigarette. His hands shake a little, but he's still got a grip on it.

"Maybe you did," I say.

He shakes his head. "I could've done something... if I hadn't been such a chicken. If I hadn't been too scared to go out there...."

"You were a kid," I say. "A skinny little kid. What would you have done?"

He puts his head down between his knees. "I've thought about it for almost ten years. What would I have done? What could I have done? But, Luce, something, anything, would've been better than nothing. Wouldn't it?"

"Maybe they would've popped you," I point out. "Shot you full of daylight. Bumped you off. You don't know."

He's quiet. Sits up and fishes around in his front pocket. Comes up with a little scrap of paper. Hands it to me.

"What's this?" I ask, taking the thing.

"Just read it," he mumbles, his head going back down between his knees. "I can't...."

I unfold it. It's a little story from some local rag, a five-and-dime out-fit, the date not too long ago, about a month. The headline reads, *Sleeping Beauty Back From Dead*.

"Daddy," I ask, trying to get a look at his face. "What is this?"

He shakes his head, so I go back to it. Keep reading. Seems it's the dame from New Year's Eve, 1963. Come awake after all this time. All systems go. So far, so good. But there's more: the gal's just met her nine-year-old twins. A boy and a girl.

"Oh, Daddy," I let out, quiet.

"Some of the kids at school thought I did it," he murmurs. "So please, *don't call me that*."

"Sorry," I whisper. "So she was —"

"She was raped," he says, lifting up his head, a little. His hands still twisted in his sandy hair. "Her twins came to term while she was being kept alive by machines. She never had a choice about keeping them or not. And her folks took them, raised them... I mean, what'd they do for birthdays? Take a cake to the hospital? It's demented."

I have this flash of the grandparents taking out the Sleeping Beauty's respirator to help blow out the candles, but I keep a lid on it.

"You didn't know," I say. He shakes his head.

"Not until now. I mean, I knew she was in a coma... but everything else.... My folks did a good job of keeping that away from me." He hunts around for a butt. I hand him one, lift up a lighter for him. His hands are shaking a whole lot worse now. "I mean, I guess that's good. I guess. I wouldn't have even known what they were talking about."

"And that's more nice than some people get in their whole lives," I say. I zip it before he can think about that, too much. Think of something quick. "Does she want them now?"

"I don't know," he shakes his head. "I only got that."

There's something handwritten in tiny blocky letters along the side of the newspaper. I hold it up close, so I can just make it out. I look over at him. "Did I read this right?" I ask, pointing at the handwritten note.

He takes his hands out of his hair, takes the paper from me. "If you mean, did my dad really go meet her and does she want to meet me, then yes." He folds up the newspaper, back into a tiny square. Tucks it in his pocket.

"Whew," I shake my head. I pick up the little gold purse, and hand it to him. He takes it, holds it cradled in his palms, like you'd hold a kitten. Looks over at me, a question in his eyes. "Well, you never know," I say, shrugging. "She might want it back."

•

And kids. It made me think, it really did. Got the old noggin in a tizzy. And did I leave it there? Did I ever.

One night it's hot as the breath from a big old mutt, and smells like it too. Comes out of nowhere, in the middle of all the trees changing their clothes, all of a sudden those little old men I haven't seen since July are out on their folding chairs, their grey chest hairs poking out from the necks of their undershirts, kids are roller skating, white boots flashing bright in the dark, hot alleys, their red wheels clonking along, crunching over glass. Couples sit sipping wine on their concrete stoops, babies crawling around in little front yards. And all of this I can see from the window in the kitchen. And I get this feeling, like I'm goofy, head over heels.

"Daddy," I call him. Then I remember what he said. "Hey, Hicklin," I try out his name. It's not the same as Daddy, but it'll do. He comes into the kitchen, his dirty blonde hair all standing up like it does after he's been working, his white dress shirt all spattered with paint.

"What's up?" he asks, wrapping me up tight in his arms. I spin around.

"Let's go out," I say, smiling. "I feel like getting an edge."

"What?" he shakes his head. "I can't go out, Luce, I've got way too much to do."

"Oh, come on," I pull away from him, tug on his shirt tail. "It's too hot to work. Look, none of those folks're working." I point out the window.

He looks out, leaning on his forearms, taking a sniff of the air. He turns to me and smiles. "You're right," he says, grabbing my hand. "Let's go."

We get home so late it's early, the next day starting hotter than the night before. I'm good and fried, the world twisting when I blink. The Fox helps me up the stairs, and into his bedroom, and into his bed. He goes out to get me a glass of water, and I jump out of bed, run into the living room, and grab a couple albums. I put on Fun House, loud as it goes. He comes running in, his eyes all wide, his hands up.

"Luce," he yells over the music, "turn it down! Other people live here, you know!"

I shake my head and start dancing on his bed. He puts a glass of water down on the floor, and runs over to his old stereo, the one he found himself. Turns the volume down to the level of a kitten's mew.

"Daddy!" I pout, putting my hands on my hips. "I was dancing to that!"

"You were good about that all night," the Fox says, just loud enough for me to hear it.

"Well, you're acting like my daddy, *Daddy*," I say, stumbling off the bed and down to the floor. I turn the music back up.

"Okay, then," he says sharply, turning the music down to a mouse's pipsqueak. "Time for bed, Luce. Get in." He flicks back the covers. Goes over to one of his shelves, starts scanning the books there. "How about a bedtime story? What do you feel like tonight?"

"I feel," I say, turning the music back up, "like listening to music. Daddy." Iggy sings about how *we're gonna lay right down in my favourite place*. I sing along, loud as I can.

The Fox is on me in a second, slapping one of his mitts over my mouth. "Would you just *be quiet*? You're driving me nuts. Just lie down and go to bed."

I take a deep breath, the smell of his hand salty. I nod, once. He lets me go.

And Iggy's still singing, *now I'm ready to feel your hand, and lose my heart on the burning sands*, and I nod a little, dance around the Fox.

"Okay, Daddy," I say, crouching down, "I'll be good. Here, I'll lie down here, just for you." And I get down on the floor. I stretch out long and thin, my hands all folded up on my chest. I close my peepers. Hold my breath.

"You miss her, Daddy?" I ask him.

"Quit it," he says, turning down the music again.

"You miss her?" I ask again. "Show me how you miss her, Daddy."

I open my peepers just enough to see him turn away from me.

"Get up," he says. That growl in his voice. That old bearcat feeling crawls up under my skin, making me hot all over. I lie still as I can.

"Do I look pretty, Daddy?" I ask him, trying not to move my lips too much.

He doesn't make a sound.

"Sorry, Daddy," I say, my eyes still closed, my lips hardly moving. "Am I making too much noise? Maybe I should bloody up my face a little? Crawl in a meat locker, cool myself off?"

I can hear his feet, coming toward me. He puts his hands down, one on each of my arms. Puts his face up close to mine, slowly, slowly, so slow I can feel his breath getting hotter the closer it comes, coming out of him strong as wind. His lips just brush mine, barely barely, and just like that, every nerve in my body's standing up, trying to crawl out of me to him. I open my mouth, just a little.

"Luce," he breathes down into me, his lips on mine softer than the word. His hands squeeze my arms, tight, tighter, tight. Then he pulls me up, fast, and sort of throws me to the side. I bump against the wall, stumble.

"What's the idea?" I ask, turning so I can see him.

He doesn't say a word, just grabs me by the arm and sort of starts pulling me. Out of his room, and through the living room. Every other door in the house closed. Like we're the only ones alive here.

"Hey!" I shout. "Paws off, mister!"

He still doesn't say anything, just keeps dragging me toward the door. He opens it with the hand that's not holding me, and starts dragging me down the stairs. I thrash around good, but like I said before, he's tougher than he looks. I open my mouth and try to get him with my choppers, but he just grabs me with both hands, keeping my face away from him. At the bottom of the stairs, he pulls the door open and tosses me out.

"Daddy?" I ask. Make my voice nice and soft.

"Don't call me that," he says, his voice slicing. "Don't come back here. Don't come to the show. Just *get out*."

And he slams the door on little old me.

I stand there for a second, the blue light of the new day spinning. I blink hard until the damned thing stays still. My hand a fist on the door without me even knowing, my mouth shouting his name, yelling at him to let me in. I pound the door until my knuckles go bloody, howling his name. And other things, less nice. Finally I take my hand down from the door, lean against the wall.

Next door one of the hippywitches comes out, his big shaggy head tilting on top of a too-small body. He grins at me, his long, yellow chompers making fangs in all that hair. He tilts back his head and howls. Stops and points at me. Howls again.

"Oh, go chase yourself," I spit at the hippywitch, who just laughs, and keeps howling, even as I turn around and quit the scene.

I take a couple of days, go to Oscar's, look at the pictures of the wax lady. I stare at them so hard I think I start to see something in there, something in among the vines and fruit that make up her insides. And just as it starts to come up, I blink. And it's just a hole, cut out of her, from her privates to her chest.

Oscar leaves me alone, I mean, he doesn't even try it on with me. Maybe I've lost my touch, I don't know. Frankly, I don't care.

•

The Queen telegrams me again.

At the foot of the mountain I wait, until her big gold noggin comes rising as the sun sets. She sits near me, and talks to thin air.

"We sold the house," she says. "So this'll be it."

I open my rat bag, take out a pack of smokes.

"And I mean it," she says, sliding a fat envelope along the park bench. "I don't want you coming crying to us later, about how you were so young and everything. I don't want to see you again, or hear from you. No contact, you understand?"

You too, huh? I think. I keep my trap shut, though. I nod, try to make it look like I'm just having a hard time lighting my smoke.

"We both wanted to keep it out of the courts," she says. "Anyway, I've got more than I would have, and you've got yours. And he's got nothing. Maybe next time he'll think twice about fooling around with jailbait. Not that I care."

The Queen stands. Her big yellow head sinks below the little hill, and I'm left on my lonesome, with nothing but a fistful of dollars to keep me company.

•

I'm sick of Oscar and the way he looks at me. Like I'm that wax lady, like he can see right through me. I practise in front of the mirror, just what I'm going to say, I lock the door even though no one's trying to get in. Make up the story, try out words. My eyes give me away, even I can't look in them. I let my bangs back down, hide my eyes.

I get to his place and I've got the story all worked out, the lie waiting one word on my tongue. Sorry, I tell myself, I'm sorry. Until I almost believe it.

Up the stairs on the outside. And I feel it on my skin, like when it's about to rain and your skin gets kinda prickly and you feel like a cat that wants to run yowling around crazy for no reason, you know? Tina, you know. I know you know. You used to do it all the time. Tell me you haven't forgotten. I stop where I am, halfway up the stairs. I almost turn around. Feel like a real bunny, sitting there hunted by I don't know what. So I make myself go, and find out.

I get to the top of the stairs and I'm in the garden. Even in the morning the place seems dark, and cold, all these fingers of plants coming up from underground. Gives me the willies. I look around. No Daisy staring into the sun, no Ghost haunting her own garden. I get to the door, the one with the broken window.

And then I back away, find myself a seat behind a couple big plants, crouch down. And I wait, watching through the crack in the window.

HICKLIN

1970

When the record is over he looks up and she's there. Red hair caught up in a black snood, her lips painted on. Same old blue duffel coat with wooden toggles. Brown beaded moccasin boots. Her lips smile at him.

"There you are," she says. Her voice is warm as fresh bread. He feels like butter in it.

"I live here," he whispers, wondering if this is some Beethoven-induced dream. The Ninth does funny things to his head.

"I missed you," she says, her tone seeming to indicate that she actually had.

"You did?" he asks, to make sure.

"Of course I did," she says, taking a step toward him. She is close enough to touch, but he doesn't. She could be made of smoke for all he knows, and he's not at all ready to find out.

"Missed you terribly," she says, taking a step closer. She smells of vanilla and tobacco. If she has a smell she must be real, he reasons. Still, his hands stay where they are.

"How'd you find me?" he asks, trying not to breathe, trying not to breathe in her smell.

She shrugs. "Your father."

He doesn't know how to say how he missed her. He doesn't think there's a word for it. He thinks, I've felt like I've had no brain and no heart for over a year. But he doesn't know how to say that either. So he puts out a hand, and touches her on her duffled arm.

She leans in closer and doesn't disappear.

"Life with a paraplegic just wasn't as exciting as I'd thought it would be," she says, lighting up a small brown cigarillo. "He was angry all the time, you know."

At me? he wonders and wonders if he should ask. "At me?"

"Nah," she shrugs noncommitally, leaning back against his collection of pillows. "He was just angry."

Her hair has been set free and runs in burnt curls over her shoulders and down to her breasts. He'd forgotten how strangely pale she was, how other than human her skin. No, forgotten, that's not quite the right word. He'd made himself forget.

"And, boy," she shakes her head. "Did he run around. For a guy with no legs, I mean, really. It was ridiculous."

"No legs?" he asks, panicked. He doesn't remember anything about no legs.

"Oh, sorry," she giggles. "It's just how I talk about him. That made him angry too. No, he's still got his legs. And everything else. It just doesn't work. Sure made him brush up on his other techniques, though. Must've been how he got all the ladies."

"Erm," he mumbles, reaching for a pillow and covering himself without even really thinking about it.

"Sorry," she laughs again. "I won't talk about it. If it makes you uncomfortable, I mean."

"No, no," he lies. "It's fine."

"Anyway," she says, squashing out her cigarillo in an ashtray he's improvised from half an oyster shell, "I dropped out of school about when you did and ended up just spending my days waiting for him to roll home so I could change his bag. And I just got sick of it, you know?"

He doesn't know what 'change his bag' means and he's pretty sure he doesn't want to. He tries to look sympathetic anyway.

"It must have been awful," he says, taking her hand.

She strokes his hand as though it's made of hundred-year-old skin. Shakes her head.

"No," she says quietly. "What was awful was the way I ditched you. Just like that."

"It's okay," he mumbles. Her hand squeezes his painfully, then moves away to her face. She sniffles.

"No," she declares, the one syllable pointy as an isosceles. "No, it's not okay. And I don't know how to make it okay."

She looks at him with those same puffy eyes. He still thinks she is the most beautiful thing he has ever seen.

"I'm sorry," she whispers. She leans her head on his shoulder and he lets her snot all over him. He can have a shower later.

·

He scrubs himself, brushes his teeth, and pees. He wonders, belatedly, if she's on the Pill. He'll have to ask.

He wraps a towel stamped with the name of some hotel he's never been to around his waist, makes his way back to his bedroom.

She is lying on the bed, still naked, lying on her belly, her forearms flat, her back slightly arched, her head up. Her eyes are closed, her hair bleeds over her.

He stands still in the doorway, just looking.

Without opening her eyes, she speaks.

"Why do you love me?" she asks.

He thinks.

"I never said I love you," he answers.

"Don't kid a kidder," she says, not smiling, not looking like a kidder at all. "I asked you a question."

He thinks again.

"I don't know," he answers finally.

She is silent. Her eyes remain closed.

He thinks again, and this time, he really does.

"I just always have," he answers. "It's like... an autonomous response. It just is."

She smiles and relaxes, rolling over in a smooth movement to lie face-up on the bed. He steps into his own room and closes the door.

DAHLIA

1970

Sera is doing her dance of the seven veils, complete with a drippy, severed head lying on the floor, which leaves Dahlia enough time to go to the washroom yet again. She's almost at the door when she feels a hand on her arm. She looks up. Sandy hair, a bit long around the edges. A brown corduroy blazer, white dress shirt and pinstriped pants. Smoke-blue eyes, a bit too big for his face. A face that's a little familiar.

"Excuse me," he says, leaning a little too close to her. "Do you have a light?"

Dahlia shakes her head.

"Oh," he pauses. "Well... happen to know where a guy can get some good oysters around here?"

Dahlia stares at him. "Maybe," she says stonily.

"It's me," the boy says, pointing to his chest. "From the Ritz? A couple years ago? I was waiting for a girl? We ate oysters. You and me, I mean."

Dahlia pushes her glasses up on her nose and looks hard at him. "Oh. It is you. Well. Hello."

"Nice to see you, too," the boy says, lighting a cigarette. "Still happy time, I see."

"Actually yeah," Dahlia says, taking a step toward the bathroom. "Even happier if you want to know."

The boy takes a step into her path. Dahlia stops. "I'm sorry to hear that," he says. "Can I buy you a drink?"

Dahlia shakes her head. "No. Thanks." She tries to take another step, but the boy gets in her way again.

"You were really good," he says, quickly. "I mean, I didn't know you'd be here, but then the bartender told me to stay, so I did, and it was you! I mean, I didn't know where to find you, because you never gave me your address. But here you are!"

A rumble grows outside the bar, a sound like a large animal roaming the streets. The glasses hanging above the bar tinkle together. All the heads of the crowd turn, to look out the plate glass window at the front of the bar.

"Are those..." the boy asks, looking out the window.

"Tanks," Dahlia says. "Those are tanks."

In the streetlights outside the bar, the bodies of the tanks are a shade of green that turns almost black, a flat black that makes them look unreal, as though they were trapped between dimensions. Their treads crunch on the pavement as they advance slowly down the middle of the street. Above their treads, nosing the air as though sniffing, their gun turrets sprout massive snouts.

"I didn't think he would actually..." the boy breathes, following the tanks' progress with his head.

Soldiers follow behind the tanks, as worker ants follow their queen. They, too, appear to flit in and out of this world, their drab clothes barely catching the light. Only their guns give them away, shining out beetle sharp.

Dahlia takes a sip of her drink. Then another. "Well I think it's exciting to live in a revolution," she says drily.

The boy looks at her. "Hey," he says, a little hurt in his voice, "I didn't live here then...."

"Not so much fun when you're not just reading about it," Dahlia says, finishing her drink. "So much for civil rights."

"Yeah," the boy says, still following the tank with his eyes. "It's all just make-believe, isn't it? Just takes some guys in suits to sign some papers, and bang. Tanks."

"You better believe it," Dahlia says. She walks away from him, and out the door of the bar.

No one else is outside. Not a breath, not a word. Dahlia looks up and down the street, and all she can see in any direction are tiny pale faces, floating flat behind glass. The tanks shake the sidewalk beneath her feet, shake through her, their lumbering a low sort of song. Their skins dark. The soldiers at their sides are small and faceless. Dahlia takes a deep breath. She pulls her long blonde wig from her head, and throws it up, to the top of the nearest tank. It lands and just sits there, a bright blonde mustache at the end of the tank's ridiculous nose.

A couple of soldiers turn, and appear to see her, but she turns and runs for it.

•

Dahlia sidles up to the bar, where Ginger already has her drink ready. Dahlia takes a small sip. Then a big one. She turns around, to head back through the crowd to the 'wings', a table for two near the back. Putting her drink down, she helps Ginger heave the other tables back into place. Hockey plays in black-and-white on a small screen propped up on top of a tall cabinet just behind the 'stage'. Dahlia snorts through her nose. No wonder the crowd looked so interested.

"Good show tonight," Ginger says, setting down a deuce.

Dahlia shrugs. "I don't know. I think perhaps *Coppélia* is a bit... understated."

Ginger shrugs. "All I know is, you look foxy and you bring folks in. What else do you need?"

"What else indeed," Dahlia says. She looks up at the hockey, tries to figure out what on earth might be so interesting about it.

"Hey!" a voice says, close to her ear. "Do you have a light?"

Dahlia turns, and sees it's the boy again, the one from the Ritz. "Hello," she says.

"Watching hockey?" he asks, lighting his own cigarette with a wooden match.

Dahlia turns away from him, and picks up a four-top. He bends and takes one end of it, the cigarette jammed in his mouth. They set the table down, and he takes a drag. Exhales.

"You were great last time I saw you," he says. "And I don't just mean the show — I mean, throwing your wig up there! That was priceless!"

Dahlia nods. "Thanks," she says. "You know that was four months ago."

The boy nods. "I know," he says.

"You've been busy," Dahlia supplies.

"Yeah," he says. Then his face brightens. "Hey! That's a hell of an outfit."

Dahlia shrugs, slowly. "It's my sister's. Thanks."

Dahlia's wearing the gold dress, the first one she got from her sister, years ago. It skims a second skin on her, a fishy rippling from throat to toes. With it a wig of red, a burned gold. She catches sight of herself in a mirror across the bar, then blinks as she seems to come toward herself. A head just as red, though dressed in green. Her mirror twin puts her hand out wordless, a hand the boy takes.

"This is Flan," he says, looking at Flan and not Dahlia. Dahlia nods.

"Hello," she says. "I'm Dolly."

Neither girl extends a hand, neither leans forward to trade a double kiss.

The boy raises an eyebrow. "Dolly, huh? I thought your name was Dahlia?"

"It was," she says, blinking slowly.

"Is that like, a stage thing?" he asks.

"I suppose," Dolly says.

Flan leans over to Hicklin, whispers something in his ear. He looks up at Dolly, a little shrug in his shoulders. "We have to go," he says. "But, listen, we thought it was great."

Flan looks around the room.

"*Coppélia*, right?" Hicklin asks Dolly. Then he turns to Flan. "This inventor builds a mechanical lady, and then this guy falls in love with her."

"I was here," Flan says flatly. She opens her purse and fishes around in it.

"Right," he mumbles. Then he looks up at Dahlia and smiles. "I never saw the ballet, but I've read *The Sandman*. I love Hoffmann. What was that other one that was a ballet?"

"*The Nutcracker*," Dahlia says.

"Right," Hicklin says, nodding. "With the nutcracker coming to life and taking the girl to this whole other world...."

"The Land of the Sugarplum Fairy," Dahlia says. "I've been there. I was a snowball."

Hicklin looks at her, a small smile dying away under the seriousness of her stare. "Oh," he says.

Flan looks at Dolly for the first time, a wide smile fake as an arc of peasant flowers on her face. "Well. We'd really love to stay and chat, but I have an early morning tomorrow. And Hicklin's got another big day of drinking in front of him, don't you, honey?"

Hicklin laughs as though she's joking. Dolly nods.

"See you," Hicklin says, leaning forward to kiss Dolly on the cheek. She pulls away, slightly, her skin untouched by his lips.

"Goodbye," she says. Flan turns without looking at Dolly again, turns without saying anything, and pulls Hicklin away through the crowd. Dolly threads her way through the crowd as well, gets to a small empty space at the bar. Ginger leans forward, shaking her head.

"Get a load of her," Gin says, tilting her head toward Flan and Hicklin. "What a bitch. He seems alright, though. When he's not around her, anyway. It's like she's got him under a spell."

Dolly nods. "Or a curse," she says.

•

Dahlia wraps Patience in her sister's fox fur coat, folding the honey hair over Patience's cold eyes and cracked fingers. This bundle Dahlia then lays inside her violet valise, a gift from her mother, of course. Under and over the bundle of fox fur, Dahlia builds a nest, a nest made of all the clothes she will take with her. Some of these are her own, but most are her sister's, given to Dahlia when her sister departed. The very last thing Dahlia places in the bag is her old violet pillow case, the ends tied together over puffs of her own hair. She is just in the midst of closing the valise when she hears something.

"If I should dieeeee," a weedy voice rasps slowly, the sound of husks, the skins of words left to dry overnight, "beefore I waaake...."

Dahlia flicks the clasps closed on either end of the valise. "Oh stop being so dramatic," she says. "We're not going far."

The voice screeches inside the valise, the cracked drone of the grating girl's voice muffled by the fur around her, and the leather of the bag. Eventually, it stops completely.

Dahlia heaves the valise up with her left hand and looks around her room. It looks the same, except for the lack of Patience. It looks like it has looked since she can remember, like she imagines it will always look. Waiting in stasis, just for her. She closes the door.

Dahlia creeps softly down the stairs, past the portrait of her Great Aunt Patience. She stops in front of it. Young Patience stares ahead, unsmiling, buttoned all the way up to her chin. The gloom in the corners of the photo haven't spread since Dahlia was little, as though whatever matter it was made of had found a different home.

"Goodbye," Dahlia says, to the portrait.

Patience stares at her. Dahlia turns and heads down the stairs, the valise bumping her hip as she goes.

At the foot of the stairs, Dahlia pauses to put on her coat. When she turns around, her mother is standing behind her, face frowning.

"And where are you going?" Dahlia's mother asks, her voice snapping like a too-tight elastic band.

"To stay with a friend," Dahlia says. "For a while."

"What friend is this?"

"My friend Ginger," Dahlia says. "You remember, she came to pick me up once."

Dahlia's mother turns her mouth upside down. "The coloured girl?"

Dahlia lets a long sigh out of her own mouth. "She's black, yes. Does that matter?"

Dahlia's mother tries to shrug. On her stiff shoulders it comes out looking mechanical and jittery, as though gears somewhere inside her are catching on each other. She says nothing.

Dahlia bends to pick up her valise. Patience slides inside it, jolted by the movement.

"My so-so sooooul..." a tiny voice shrieks, muffled all over by the fur and the hair.

"What on earth was that?" Dahlia's mother peeps, her eyes going wide. She crosses herself quickly.

"Patience," Dahlia explains. Her mother raises an eyebrow and takes a step backwards.

"Patience?" she asks.

"Yes, Patience," Dahlia says, stepping around her mother, careful not to jolt the valise too much.

"Patience is dead, Dahlia dear," her mother whispers.

"I know that, Mother," Dahlia says, closing her eyes. "I'm not daffy. The other Patience. The one you gave me."

Dahlia's mother blinks. A couple of small valleys grow between her eyebrows. "You mean the doll?" Dahlia's mother asks. "I thought you named her Dolly?"

"I did," Dahlia nods, "but that wasn't her name." It's my name, she doesn't say.

"Oh," her mother says, the valleys growing ever deeper, furrows going further back in geological time.

"Anyway," Dahlia says, taking a step closer to the door. "I'll call you, let you know how I'm doing."

Dahlia's mother puts out a hand, gently, lays it on Dahlia's arm. "Is this about a boy?"

Dahlia sags inside her coat. "What?"

"Well, I don't know," Dahlia's mother says, shaking her head. "I never see you, and I know you're out at all hours. I don't know where you go. You're not at school, and you're not in class. I don't think you're even dancing anymore, are you? After all your hard work...."

"Mother," Dahlia says slowly, "I'm not leaving to be with a boy." She doesn't say anything about the dancing.

Dahlia's mother raises her eyebrows, turning the valleys into flat plains. "Well," she says, "it would be nice to be told, that's all. If you're in love, I'd like to know about it."

"I'm not 'in love', Mother," Dahlia sighs. "I told you. It's not about a boy. I just —" I can't stay here, she thinks. "I just think it's time for me to try living on my own."

Dahlia's mother nods. "Alright, Dahlia," she says. "Alright. You're just leaving me, all alone in this big house. Just like your father. And your sister, who I never hear from. This is the thanks I get? What am I going to do with myself? And what about university? Have you even thought about that? Or ballet? I thought you were going to audition for some companies this year? What about that?"

Dahlia pauses, one hand on the doorknob. She straightens her back. Lets all the air out of her lungs.

"Dahlia. You haven't answered my questions."

Dahlia turns the knob. Takes a breath. Air still warm from the day lets itself in, curls around her, smelling of sunshine. She takes a step, out the door. Another to let the valise swing by the doorjamb.

"To keeeeeep," warbles Patience, deep inside Dahlia's violet valise, as the door swings shut behind them.

BEAU

1970

He is a spaceship inside winter, a hot pod traveling in a dead vacuum. Leaving the cinema, wrapped like a mummy in found itchy scarves, his hands stuffed deep in the pockets of Marly's old coat, Beau battles wind with no skin showing but a slit around his eyes. Deep in Marly's pockets Beau's hands burn. The slit around his eyes burns. His toes, too. Outside is space, outside is the vacuum that will explode his lungs from the inside out should he stop. The vacuum is white, and empty, and silent but for his own sharp breathing which he can hear inside his head, safe inside his spaceship. Tiny knives of wind and white slice his eyes. His fingers burn, gloveless in holey pockets. He tries to find a way for his hands to reach the pockets of his pants through the holes in Marly's coat pockets, gives up and shoves his hands into his pits. He turns a corner and the wind dies down a bit. Lets him blink his white lashes frozen. He hears muffled laughter from very far away. Broken glass tinkles. Someone screams.

He doesn't look around with his head, but turns his whole body so as not to disturb the wrappings around his eyes. Fuzzed out and faded shapes, bending blearily behind waves of white. Received from somewhere very far away, transmitted from the far reaches of distant space. He puts one of his hands to his eyes, tries to wipe away some of the rime. Can't see any better. The wind picks up again, the shapes move. One rises from what Beau supposes must be the ground and runs toward him. A mouth open in an O. Covered all in white, slipping between snowflakes silently stopping time.

His frozen hand is grabbed and he is pulled into a snowpile. White body cold under him.

He thinks there are words coming from the mouth like an O. He receives another message from somewhere out in space. The message is this: GO.

Beau doesn't go, instead he sinks in that O that lies below. They are freezing together, he and this white body with the face still screaming. Covered in snow for the spring to find them. The face around the scream is lovely. He thinks if he goes he'll just want to come back, so he saves a step and just stays. He is worried about the tears on the lovely face, is worried they will freeze those eyes shut tight. The body below him is shaking.

A hand on his collar, yanking him up. A fist from somewhere, zooming toward him.

Beau ducks. And finally the message is clear and he is no longer a spaceship and the O is a mouth on a person. The person still screaming.

A boot lands in the small of Beau's back, knocks him to the ground.

Someone calls someone else a faggot, loud.

Beau stands, can barely see, can barely find the shape in the snowpile that dragged him down, but he does see, finally, and grabs for something, a hand or something, and pulls, and runs.

Someone calls someone else a faggot again, much louder than before.

Beau and the O, they run.

•

Though the lighting in the deli is awful, Beau can't stop staring at the person across the table. The person across the table can't stop staring at his own hands, and shivering.

"I'm sorry," the stranger says, watching his hands hover jerkily above the paper placemat printed with the map of Quebec. "I can't seem to stop shaking."

"It's okay," Beau says. "Here."

Beau takes the stranger's hands in his, puts them close to his mouth and blows short puffs of warm breath over them. The stranger continues staring at his own hands, and slowly pulls them away from Beau's mouth.

"I'm not cold," he says simply, and continues to watch his hands waver over *La Belle Province*.

The waitress arrives with a tall skinny beer for each of them, then leaves them to decide on their order.

Beau takes a sip of his beer, which is pale yellow and not very bubbly and not very cold.

The stranger's head is hidden under a furry hunter's cap, his chin just poking out over a white woolen scarf. He is very pale. Beau is only sure now that he sees the stranger in this awful light, that the stranger is in fact a man, since he has a couple of days of sandy stubble on his chin.

"It's okay," Beau says, softly. "I've been called that before."

The waitress returns and deposits a plain white china plate the size of an EP onto the greenish formica table with a clatter. The two pickles on the plate slide against each other before settling, slightly apart. "You drink, you eat," she says, "you get a nice pickle."

The stranger takes one of the pickles and bites off the end. Crunches for a minute.

"You can have mine," Beau says, pushing the plate toward the stranger. "They're not really my thing."

"Thanks," the stranger says, pulling the plate closer to himself. Within a minute both pickles have disappeared.

"Hungry?" Beau asks.

The stranger shrugs.

"I've got a couple bucks, after the beer and everything... if you want, I can get you something. Smoked meat?"

The stranger is sucking pickle juice off his fingertips and shaking his head.

"Poutine?"

Shake.

"Grilled cheese?"

A shrug from the stranger.

"Okay, grilled cheese. I'll go get the waitress." Beau starts to rise from the booth and is stopped by the ruby helmet of the waitress' hair.

"Something else?"

"Yeah, um, can we get a grilled cheese?"

"That's it?"

Beau looks at the stranger, who has gone back to staring at his hands.

"Um," Beau says. "Maybe another couple pickles."

•

The stranger eats in silence, poking the corner of his grilled cheese in a puddle of ketchup on the side of his plate, leaving greasy little footprints. When he is done, he licks his fingers again, each one sucked perfectly clean. Beau has finished his beer and is watching the other one get steadily warmer and flatter.

"Thanks," the stranger says.

"Oh. You're welcome," Beau says, folding a corner of his paper menu over and over, dog-ear style. "You feel any better?"

The stranger shrugs.

"Do you want this?" the stranger asks, pointing to his beer.

"No, no," Beau says. "I got it for you."

The stranger shakes his head, "I don't drink."

"Oh," Beau shrugs. "Give it a try, it might stop your shakes."

The stranger says, "Well... I guess," and takes a big gulp. The beer is room temperature and flat. "I haven't," the stranger mumbles as he puts down the almost empty glass.

"What?" Beau asks.

"Been called that. Before. Other things. But not that."

"Oh," Beau lets out a long breath. "Well, welcome to the club, I guess."

·

"We'll have to whisper for a second, in case my... roommate's home," Beau says quiet into the stranger's hat, about where the ear should be. "And I can't turn on the light cuz there's people on the couch. Hang on to me so you don't fall over. Again."

"Sorry," the stranger whispers, starting to giggle.

"You're a real cheap date, man. You're soused," Beau says, turning on an overhead light that's watts too bright. The two of them stand in a tiny cluttered room. "Wait, here."

Beau turns on a bedside light with a paisley scarf thrown over it. Turns off the overhead and goes around the room lighting candles and incense. Every surface is covered with fabric, all in different patterns and clashing colours. Stacks of records come up knee-high from the floor. On one wall hangs a psychedelic print of a spaceman, his shape repeating to infinity in bubblegum pink and electricity blue. Just below the spaceman, an album cover is propped against the wall. Against a background of blue dots a man's severed head floats, his beautiful face marked with a look of fuzzy surprise. On the opposite wall a man with long blond hair, his ribby chest covered in blood and sweat, grips a giant microphone, his mouth open wide enough to swallow the thing. Beside the window a different skinny man, with crazy curly hair, looks at them with dreamy eyes. On the other side of the window is a large print depicting a green lizard thing with a duck bill and visible genitalia walking happily in the woods with what appears to be a hat with legs.

"You into the wizard?" Beau asks, looking up from a tin he's rummaging in. But the stranger has flopped face down on the only bed.

·

Beau wakes to the sun trying to shine through his found paisley curtains. He stretches, arms up, a happy yawn coming out of his pasty morning mouth. Rolls on his side to inspect the back of the stranger who lies in bed with him. White T-shirt, holey where the neckline meets the body and along all the seams, gold hairs poking up. There is a muf-fled *ponk*! from the other room. Beau shakes his head, finds his house-coat somewhere on the floor, wraps it around himself and stumbles sticky-eyed into the hallway.

"Hey, idiots," Beau yells on his way to the bathroom, "keep it down, wouldja?"

"Keep it down, wouldja?" comes parroted back to him, pipsqueaked and high. Giggles follow.

A shape stirs on the couch, a lump lurching from lying to sitting. Salt-and-pepper hair stands out in tufts on the handsome head of Beau's other roommate, René. A rolled-up newspaper flies from René's hand, hits Beau in the stomach, and falls to the floor with a thunk. Beau bends and picks up the paper, holds it out to René.

"No, no," René says, holding out a hand and turning his head from Beau. "It is for you. Or, more precisely, for that... *stray* you brought home. I thought perhaps you would need something to house-train him on."

"René," Beau says, putting the paper down on the cluttered coffee table. "I'm sorry."

René sits up fully, retreating to the corner of the couch furthest from Beau. "Don't be sorry," he says. "I love to sleep on the couch because my bed is full. It gives me, how should I say, a new perspective."

"René," Beau starts, shifting from foot to foot. "I'm sorry —"

"There you are again, with your *sorry*," René says. "But please, don't be. I can see many things from this couch. The dust in the corners of the ceiling, I had never noticed this before. There is a crack up there also, one that maybe I should get fixed. And there is nothing so beau-tiful as watching the sun rise over those lovely buildings. Nothing so beautiful as watching it alone, I should say."

"I'm sorry, René," Beau says, continuing quickly before René can say anything else, "I really have to whizz."

Beau runs down the hall and into the bathroom. He sits and pees, for nearly a minute. Then he puts his head in his hands and stares down at the white tiled floor.

"Beau, you idiot," he mutters. He closes his eyes, opens them again. He stands, wraps his housecoat back around himself, washes his hands, and walks slowly back out to the living room.

Another *ponk*! against the wall greets his entrance to the living room.

"Hey! Idiots! Quit it!" Beau puts his hands on his hips and yells into the room.

A square redhead and a weasely dark one swivel in Beau's direction.

"Quit it, idiot!" the dark one squeaks, in a fake high voice, then picks up a tattered, semi-inflated soccer ball and tosses it at Beau. Beau tries to catch it, but fumbles and the ball falls to the floor.

"Nice one!" the redhead laughs.

"Yeah! Nice one!" the dark one squeaks, immediately after.

Beau kicks the ball away down the hall. "You guys are assholes. Where'd René go?"

"I dunno. Maybe he wants to meet the fresh blood," the redhead guffaws.

"Yeah, fresh blood."

"Shut up," Beau says, sweeping past them and into the kitchen. "You two have no class."

•

Beau puts on the kettle and starts slicing a loaf of pumpernickel bread, which he's started buying simply because the two idiots don't like it. He opens the fridge door and rummages for eggs, cheese, and some kind of fruit. Two oranges, flattened from sitting on the shelf so long, are all he can find. He shrugs to himself and straightens up, closing the fridge door. The two lunks are standing right behind him, hopeful looks plastered to their daffy faces.

"Go away," Beau says, shooing at them with his hands full of oranges. "This isn't for you."

"Making breakfast for your *boyfriend*?" the redhead asks him, grinning.

"Yeah, making breakfast for your *boyfriend*?" the little dark one parrots.

"He's not my boyfriend, okay?" Beau smiles to himself as he cuts the oranges into neat boats, shoving the flat bits away. "He's just a guy who needed a place to stay."

From the other room he hears some scuffling, and then a couple of loud holy shits.

Beau pokes his head into the living room and sees the two idiots staring open-mouthed at the stranger.

"It's you," the redhead says, the 'ooo' sound hanging from his lower lip like drool.

"Yeah," the dark one says, "It's the —"

The stranger takes a deep breath, his hand on his forehead. "Bikky," he addresses the redhead, then turns to the dark one. "Dink. How've you been?"

Beau looks from the two idiots to the stranger. "You know these guys?"

The stranger nods. "Oh, yeah. We're old friends, aren't we? Can I get an aspirin? My head is pounding."

The two idiots grin, one after the other. The redhead opens his mouth to speak, just as René enters the room, his arms piled high with clothes. He dumps these on the floor, then brushes his hands off against each other, theatrically.

"I am sorry to interrupt this... reunion," René says, looking at Beau and no one else. "I only come in to ask *someone* to leave."

"René," Beau says.

"Oh, so you do remember my name?" René rolls his eyes to the ceiling. "But you do not remember me."

"I said, I'm sorry," Beau says.

"I am also sorry," René says, turning. "Please, just go."

•

Beau carries Mona's old valise, still full of all her dresses. The stranger carries his army bag. They walk slowly along de Maisonneuve, the late morning light sliding in slices through the spaces

306

between buildings.

"I'm sorry," the stranger says, quietly. "I didn't mean to —"

Beau shakes his head, and switches the valise to his other side. A whole new knee to bump. "It's okay," he says. "I shouldn't even have stayed there as long as I did. I think he wanted a girlfriend, actually. For a little while, I could play that part. But, it's not me. Some days, I just want to wear pants and lipstick and not have to explain, you know?"

The stranger says nothing. "Oh-kay," he lets out, after a while. "Okay. Well. Listen. I'm in a pretty big place right now, and I have all this room...."

"Really?" Beau asks. He stops, and puts down the valise. "For real?"

The stranger stops as well, dropping Beau's army bag to the ground. "Sure," he says, smiling. "I mean, it's the least I can do. I did get you kicked out of your old place." He pauses, bites his lip. "Only, I think you should know... I live with my girlfriend... I'm not gay."

"I won't hold that against you," Beau says, lightly. "And anyway, neither am I."

The stranger raises his eyebrows, then shrugs and holds out his hand. "I'm Hicklin."

"Call me Beau," Beau says, holding out his hand. "Your name sounds made up."

Hicklin nods. "Yours too."

"Fair enough," Beau says, bending to pick up the valise.

OCTOBER, 1972

HICKLIN

He keeps working on the Holes, by himself, though he can't paint the way Luce can. He traces carefully, but his faces lack something, his bodies come out stiff. Still, he can't think what else to do, now that it's started. Now that they should be done.

Almost fall, the light coming in slanted, tilting as the world seems to tilt. The heat of Indian summer is gone now, leaving a crushed smell behind it. The smell of leaves everywhere drying and dying and falling. Everything burrowing, back underground, to sleep. He gets up earlier and earlier every morning, trying to finish at least two more of the Holes before the Bacchanal at the end of the month.

He's made a mess of Pasiphe, and the white bull riding her looks more like a cat. He stares at his worthless cartoon until it blurs. Reaches a hand out for a fat brush, dips it in dark blue. Holds it over Pasiphe's face, a fat drop spattering down, turning her open mouth into a bottomless pit. He closes his eyes. Lets out a long breath. And puts the brush down.

He goes into the kitchen, but just as he steps over the threshold, he has to stop. Backs up, tries again. Stays put where he is, looking into the kitchen, looking into a thing he thought he'd never see again.

"There you are," she says.

"I live here," he replies, their lines still the same after all this time.

She's at his kitchen table. Just sitting there, wearing a slidy sundress the colour of burnt skin, her hair caught up in some sort of tangle. Before her a jam jar half-full of water.

"Flan," he says.

She nods. "Still me," she says.

She takes a deep breath, lets it out.

He can only watch. He knows somewhere there are questions for her, things he needs to ask, but right now it is all he can do to stay standing.

"I'm pregnant," she states, as though reporting on the weather.

He closes his eyes.

Flan puts her hands around the jar of water, holds it tight.

"Oh... kay." Hicklin lets this out, more of a sound than a word, while pulling out the wheely chair and slowly, slowly, sitting.

"Almost there," Flan says, looking into the water in the jar as though seeing the story in there. "The thing has toes by now. Eyeballs. Eyelashes. Fingernails. The whole shebang."

Hicklin pats his pockets, comes up with a pack of cigarettes. Shakes one out, onto the table. It sits there. He stares at it. Finally picks it up, puts it in his mouth, and lights it. Inhales deeply, and exhales, long and loud. "You're sure," he says.

Flan nods. Her face puffier than he remembers, a sunburn on her nose peeling, bright red to white beneath. Like the skin of a tree he fell from once upon a time.

"Okay," he says. She lifts her eyes to him, alley-cat green, shining over her pale mouth. Eyes just starting to go red around the edges, eyes too shiny from being wet on the inside. He remembers hearing somewhere that eyes don't change size. That the eyes you have as a kid are the same size eyes you'll always have. So somewhere in her sit two eyeballs, full grown. Looking out from somewhere in her. Two eyeballs, one from her and one from him. He wonders do they keep her safe.

Flan starts shaking her head, then lays it down on her arms.

"Flan," he says, putting his cigarette down in an ashtray, putting his hand out and almost, almost touching her. He doesn't. She snuffles into her arm, then raises her head.

"I'm sorry..." she sniffles.

He hands her his handkerchief, dug out of his pocket. She gives him a tight smile, and wipes her nose. A final hefty snort, and a sip of water.

"It's just..." she says. She takes another gulp of water. Looks him in the eye. "I tried."

"Tried," he says. Frozen for a second, he stares out the window. Red and brown leaves wave from the trees across the street, falling, flaking, into piles below. Crushed underfoot to nothing but dust.

"I," Flan says. She sit up straighter, pushes a strand of hair behind her ear. "I tried to get rid of it."

"Oh," he says again. Watches a leaf, wills it to fall. It doesn't. "But I would've —" he can't finish the sentence. His throat's gone dry and dusty as the leaves outside. He stands and wobbles to the fridge. Opens it, pulls out the one stubby in there. Cracks it, and downs it in one go.

"I know," Flan says. He can't see her as he's gone head first into the freezer. Under the peas, a new bottle of vodka. He opens it, and drinks. One mouthful. Two. His eyes go blurry from trying not to cough. He closes the fridge door. Stands near it, the bottle in his hand. Coughs anyway, his hand up to his mouth.

"But I don't know," Flan says, her eyes sliding beneath salamander see-through eyelids. "But I kept it anyway. Thad wanted me to."

It's Thad's, he thinks. Out loud, he takes another drink.

"My folks won't give us any money," Flan says. She rubs her nose like a kid, with the palm of her hand. "So I was thinking, maybe...."

"Maybe what?" He lifts the bottle to his mouth. Thinks about it for a second. And takes a sip, then another.

"Maybe you could help us," she lifts her eyes to him, eyes a cracked green, the green of new things growing. "Just for a while, until I can work again."

"Help you," he says, just repeating the words. Not really thinking what they mean. Hangs onto the bottle cold and solid in his hand, the floor starting to go wavy under his feet. "Like, hold the baby and burp it and walk it to sleep at night? Change some diapers? Get a clown act for birthdays? That kind of thing?"

Flan looks away, out the window.

"No?" he takes another swig from the bottle. "That's not what you meant?"

"Hicklin," Flan says, softly.

"You want money, Flan?" He turns from her. Closes his eyes. "For Thad's kid?"

"And mine," she whispers. "And —"

He takes another swig from the bottle and slams it on the table. Starts emptying his pockets. Small change and crumpled hankies and ticket stubs fly onto the table.

"Here you go, Flan," he yells. "Helluva life in these pockets. You want more?"

He turns to the cupboards and starts throwing things out of them. Pots, dishes, glasses, jam jars, beer bottles. Flan sits straight and silent until he's slammed the last cupboard. He leans heavily on it, breathing hard. He closes his eyes.

"Maybe I shouldn't have come," Flan's voice says, a million miles away. So quiet he thinks maybe he's made it up. He turns to see, but no. She's still there. Staring at him.

"Why did you come?" he asks her, his head on his arm, leaning against the cupboard door. His voice creaking from the strain of not yelling.

"I thought you should know," she says, her voice a tiny thing, crawling.

"You thought I should know," he snorts lightly. "You thought I should know Thad knocked you up? I thought his bits didn't work, or were you lying about that too?"

"Hicklin," Flan's voice fading, fairy small. "I thought you should know... because... I *don't know*."

They are quiet. Far off, a siren whizzes by, its scream muffled by buildings. Hicklin takes another drink. Recaps the bottle, leans over and puts it on the table.

"What?" he asks, when the burn of the last drink has left him.

"I don't know," Flan says, pushing her jar of water away. She reaches for the vodka.

"You don't know," Hicklin says.

Flan shakes her head. Her hand holds onto the bottle, not moving. Not uncapping, not drinking.

"You don't know, but you're staying with him," Hicklin says, his voice flat and calm, but too flat, too calm. Somewhere in him big rollers grow, way deep down.

"He needs me," Flan says, her knuckles growing white around the neck of the bottle. "He's in a wheelchair, remember?"

"No, Flan, I don't remember!" He leans his hands down on the tabletop, gets his face up close to hers. "Please, remind me."

"Hicklin." Her voice is a tiny ship just starting to wobble on light waves. "Stop it —"

"No," he screams, pushing his face closer to hers, the deep rollers in him coming fast, one after the other. "Please, tell me what I've forgotten. Tell me how I broke him, Flan, remind me how I tried to kill him. Isn't that the story? Tell me again how I make you sick. Please. Call me names. Leave me again. For him. I fucking *saved* him, Flan! Saved him so you could leave me!"

The rollers have left his eyes wet. He wipes some of it away, and reaches for the bottle. Flan gives it up without a fight. He drinks, and the floor's waviness settles a bit under his feet. Flan curls around herself, her hands on her belly. He drinks until he can breathe again. Turns from her, and looks out to Dolly's garden. A fat bee crawls its fuzzy legs over the stamen of a lily, then takes off, flying low and lazy. He thinks he sees something out there, something like a small shadow. A cat, maybe. He peers at it. Trying to see it gives him shivers. He leans closer to the window anyway.

"Hicklin," Flan whispers, "I'm sorry —"

"Why," he says, turning from the door. Not a question, not really. He knows why. Another test. Still, to make sure, he asks the whole thing. "Why did you come?"

"I need the money," Flan says, her eyes redder, starting to leak again. "My folks cut me off. If you help us I promise I'll make it up to you. I will. I'll come stay with you, Hicklin, it'll be like it was before... I won't leave you, not ever. I promise."

Hicklin sits down carefully in the chair. His face is in his hands, his fingers pushing his eyes in until they bleed black and gold, fireworks on

315

the inside. He opens his eyes, looks right at her.

"Flan," he says. Her name comes out of his mouth with sharp edges, razors stuck in it. He doesn't know who it hurts more. Him to say it, or her to hear it. He breathes out and tries again. Softly, he says, "You already left me. Twice."

Flan nods. Slowly he walks over to her. She wraps her arms about his waist and squeezes tight, looking up at him. Her face a squishy burnt thing, blue shades sliding under her eyes. Her mouth has gone thin, her cheeks are so freckled they look rashy. Her nose is burnt radish red, peeling to bone white. Still. Still the most beautiful thing he's ever seen. He squeezes her back, curling into her. Her smell of tobacco and vanilla, her hair red as the last bit of day. He squeezes his eyes shut and holds her tight.

They let each other go, slide away from each other. Flan looks up at him, a small smile growing across her lips.

"Flan," he says. Looks in her eyes, calm as a summer sea. He takes a breath, and lets it go, whooshing long out of him. "Get out."

She picks up her bag from the floor, and stands. If he'd seen her stand before he would've known, wouldn't have fallen for her story. She's as she ever was, maybe a little more swing to her hips, a little more curve in her. But not, as he counts now, seven months gone. Not by a long shot.

Flan turns at the door, and smiles what's supposed to be a pretty smile, a thing that comes out split as a snake's tongue. "It's too bad," she says, the smile growing sharper and pointier. "We could've had a lot of fun together. See you round, *Pervert*."

And with that, she turns, out the doorway. And is gone. As if she never was. Nothing left behind her this time. Not even a hole.

•

His feet take him from bar to bar to closing time, through humps of dried leaves to dirt. Somewhere else it'll be happening soon, somewhere else someone else can be in charge. His feet find their way over exposed roots even in this almost dark, his feet dodge mud puddles and thorny bushes without him even thinking. His feet push him faster and faster, up higher and higher, his breath coming too quick, out of time with the rest of him. Something like smoke hangs in the air here, in between the trees, slim fingers finding their wet way into his clothes, through the holes in his pockets, the holes in his shoes, the holes in his skin. His feet seem to be going somewhere. He wonders where.

He wants to smoke but his feet won't let him. He wants to think but he can't stop long enough to do it. His feet push him through close stands of trees, their coats of many colours coming out from where they've been hiding all summer, bloodied from the inside. When he hits open space, where there are no trees, his feet make him run, until he's safe again in the dank. Higher his feet take him, past the observation area, past the turnoff to the cemetery, higher than the tallest tree. Then they let him stop.

He is nowhere. He listens. He is no one. He makes no sound and he can't hear any. Here he stops, and looks.

Grey hunks of buildings stretch from bank to bank, inside them maybe nothing, maybe nothing but the smoke that pours from the holes on their roofs. So that's where the smoke comes from, some part of his brain thinks. From here there is no one. Those buildings are all empty. There's no one here, not even him. The river swims by barely shining in the new light. He wonders if there ever was a spirit of this river, he wonders has she drowned. He hopes there was, and that she hasn't. A fake looking yellow dribbles over everything, not lighting it really, just making everything look lit for some other moment, some moment preserved by someone else for him to pretend to witness. The buildings crumble, the park he stands in recedes to the wild where it came from. A canoe floats by, he can't see who is in it, all he can see is the bottom of the canoe and the ends of the paddles, dipping and undipping way way above his head. So he lives undersea, again, far under the water where he came from. Some of the buildings have become ruins, breaking apart into stones and wood, planks that walk themselves back to the woods. Space becomes a problem as he stands, as the forest regrows to its unplucked past. He moves aside so the trees have somewhere to go. It occurs to him that if he lives underwater he should feel wet. He doesn't. He blinks and there it is again, the city spread below him, clustered in rashy patches about spots of green, hard veins running through it, lights blinking out as the day takes its hold. He sighs. He lights a smoke, and sits his ass down on an appropriate rock.

The canoe still floats by. He waves, but no one waves back.

There is the smell of fire as he walks back through the park, bonfires burning nearly unseen in the bright shiny day. All Hallow's Eve, crisp as old leaves, a curling smell to the air. They're all set up now. No one even needs to turn a key.

The mountain simmers, crackling with orange and red before him. Dotted with dark spots even he can't see. Only three holes are finished. Waiting, to be looked out of. And into.

Hicklin crosses Avenue du Parc, stretching his legs long on the wide street. Beau sits in the shade of a big old oak, wrapped in a blanket he calls Humpty-Dumpty, a blanket made from scavenged parts. Hicklin waves from the sidewalk, and steps to the grass.

Under a parasol, Dolly walks the park. Chestnut curls from Beau's stash, these the longest by far, snake past her shoulders, almost to her waist. A scavenged strapless corset wraps her up, its many bones holding her tight. She wears the jeans she shares with Beau, the ones patched with mole skins, her feet bare, as always, for walking in the park. Close to Hicklin she comes, her eyes invisible behind her small dark glasses, her skin tinged an almost human pink by the firecracker red of her parasol. Her right hand comes toward him, from out of the red shade, her hand so white it seems severed from another, stitched on, somehow, and brought cold to life.

"Are you sure about this?" Her hand cool even on this warm evening.

Hicklin nods.

A small smile is cranked out from some hidden operator, and the tilt of the head she uses to indicate distrust. "Is she here?"

He nods again, the lie in the nod more about him than her. He knows if Dolly were to talk like anybody else that 'she' would be the hissing whisper of the deadly disease.

An efficient nod, another small movement cranked out by the hidden operator. "I'll be leaving then. I'll see you later Hicklin."

"I dunno," he says. Maybe he should return the purse to its owner after all. "I might have to leave town."

He turns and leaves without looking back.

DOLLY

All Hallow's Eve

From all over the city they come, beasts and goblins, fairies and harpies, trolls and sprites. Wrapped in fur, with wings of false feathers, their faces white or black, unseen behind masks or gauze or paint, they meet at the foot of the mountain. Here are a crowd of shapeless, dark hunks with masks on the top of their heads, so when they walk they look at the ground but their faces are white masks, bobbing neckless, low on their chests. A nearly-nude girl sits like a Sphinx, long red curls barely covering her front, carried on a palaver by gold-painted boys. A maid, mother, and crone threesome pass by, the crone laughing up at Dolly through her wrinkle-painted face. Dolly walks straight-backed through the crowd, her steps careful. Two people wearing nothing but tails and paint howl at the moon. An ogre and ogress, gnawing on bones, walk beside silver, shiny robots, some with very visible, very human, parts. A herd of zombies staggers slowly into the crowd, grab-bing heads to chew on while groaning loudly.

Dolly spots Beau in his furred legs, short stilts built under the hooves, leaning on the extra tall cane he's made, smiling. His chest is bare under a long, wild wig. Dolly searches the crowd, a mass of feathers and fur like one giant, dark body lit with flicking flames from torches propped here and there, and from the bonfires calling them up the hill. She can't see Hicklin anywhere. But then, she doesn't know how he's going to come. Dolly adjusts her fleshing, pulling up the slight sag in the knees, and checks again, to make sure Patience's eyes haven't rolled off the gold-coloured platter she's made for them. The glue still holds. Dolly moves quickly to the front of the crowd. Raises the palm leaf she holds in her other hand. And forward they go.

Up the hill, the trees shake around them, beaten by the sound of their many feet, beaten by the sound of the thousand-footed beast. Loping skeletons pass by her. Twirling tiny nymphs skitter close. There is a roar from a long thin tail, a squirming dragon lifting its red mouth open to the thin moon, a waning curve, a small smile carved out of the sky. Ginger is painted gold, her hair out in a gold-sprayed fro, a lion's face smiling on her own. Oscar is here, in a top hat and a long black coat. He smiles at Dolly with his painted face. A smiling death's head, the hollow cheeks of Baron Samedi. Two tiny people, naked but for wings, run by her so fast she can't tell if they're boys or girls. Maybe somewhere in between. Dolly pulls her pale virgin's cloak up over her head, and keeps walking, steady and slow.

In a clearing about a third of the way up the mountain, they reach the first Hole. Small bonfires flicker all around, bones prop up torches. Everywhere the ghosts and pixies and nymphs and skeletons and vagabond spirits start to dance, their limbs sharp slices against the trees. Still no Hicklin. Dolly continues up the mountain, with an escort of gnomes and undead and demons and harpies.

At the second Hole, Dolly scans the crowd. Still no Hicklin. She walks to the third Hole, higher up the mountain. Here human bodies with animal heads stand grandly, wearing gold loincloths. Beasts dance with fairies, dolls with dogs. Dolly sees a small, brown lump over by the Hole. The face is painted brown, with pointed ears low on a head wearing a small crown that looks, from here, as though it were made from a piece of cheese.

Dolly walks over. "Hello," she says. "You made it."

Hicklin nods, a smile on his face. He's stuck fur to his face, and installed two long, yellow teeth in his mouth. "Guess who I am," he says, squatting low and putting his hands up, like paws.

"I know who you are," Dolly says. "You're the Rat King."

"Awww," he says, putting his hands down. "I should've known

you'd know."

"Your turn," Dolly says, assuming a sainted pose.

Hicklin frowns. Shakes his head. "I give up."

"Saint Lucy," Dolly says. "Bringer of light."

Hicklin peers at Patience's eyes on their golden platter. "And these?"

"Traditional depiction," Dolly says, simply. "Don't ask where they're from."

"Okay," Hicklin says. He takes out his yellowy teeth and smiles, raises his eyebrows, waggles them a bit. "You wanna check out the Hole?"

Dolly gives a nod. Hicklin opens the door. And they step inside.

•

The first thing Dolly sees is nothing. And after that, nothing more. Then she blinks.

And there, all along the wall, are people doing what she's never done, people becoming more than themselves, other than themselves.

"Is this real?" she asks. The first question she's asked anyone but Patience in a long long time. But Patience is gone now. Only a pair of eyes, all the better to see you with.

Hicklin nods, nearby, a slow movement in the dark. He takes her hand. "As real as that," he says.

Dolly doesn't know what all the signs and symbols are for, but she gets that most of what they're in is a window. The flare of torches just outside, the sway of bodies doing what bodies do, just outside their view. Or just behind it.

"It's like they're in here," Dolly says, pulling her virgin's veil closer about her.

"But they're not," Hicklin says, leaning down to her. He puts his mouth upon her mouth, and his eyes upon her eyes, and his hands upon her hands; and he stretches himself upon her; and her flesh waxes warm.

Inside her something turns, inside her something catches. Her skin pink. Her breath warm.

"What did you do?" Dolly asks, the second question in as many minutes.

"Nothing I wouldn't have done a long, long time ago," he answers, right into her mouth, right into her.

"No, but..." Dolly puts her hands up on Hicklin's chest. "What did you do? I mean, it wasn't like this before."

He shakes his head, puts his mouth on hers. "It's not me," he says, quiet, into her.

She pushes back, with her breath and tongue and anything else she has.

The torches outside flicker, warm as her insides, the light from them strong as a midsummer evening. With her eyes open she can see other bodies doing what she's doing, doing what they're doing, joining as close as they can, close as two bodies can come to being one. Or more than two bodies, she can see.

Outside, satyrs heave themselves into elves, skeletons into devil girls, fey fairies commingle, small with large. A tree bends backwards as a boy dressed as a dog sucks on what could be a root.

"I didn't know —" she says.

There is no response from Hicklin, who is pulling her virgin's veil from her dead white shoulders. She leans back, against the no man's land that is the back of the stage, her eyes still outside.

"Wait," Dolly says, as he fumbles with her loose dress. He can't find the zipper, since there isn't one, so he gives up and just starts pulling it up, like Galatea's gown. "What about Luce?"

He shakes his head, and keeps tugging at her gown. She pushes him away. "I'm not doing this if —"

"She's gone," he says, simply.

"Gone," Dolly says. "I did hear you two fighting. But I've stopped listening to —"

"Dolly," he says, his face close to hers. "You were right," he says, quietly, putting his lips to hers. Dolly watches the fire burn outside, watches the ripple of shape upon shape there.

And there, among all the gasping and groping, a pair of horns rise, low and slow, as though rising from the middle of the fire. Dolly blinks, and they're gone.

"Hicklin," she says, quiet.

He shakes his head and says nothing. The crown of the Rat King on the ground. The cloak of the Rat King following. Dolly's virgin's veil sifts through the air. And then there are no more words.

Until.

"The fuckin' cops're here!" someone yells.

BEAU

Bundled in the back of a van, Beau pulls his long legs up to his chest to make room for more people. A black-draped skeleton turns from the driver's seat, his white laughing skull shouting. The door is slammed by someone on the outside, and they lurch off down the hill. Behind them red and blue lights compete with the blaze of small fires, fires dotted throughout the mountain. Beau holds his legs tight and looks out the back door's small windows, until he can only see the wide road unribboning behind them. Then he looks around.

A ghost curls up, her white makeup running down her cheeks, held by the furry arms of a horned beast. A mermaid lifts a bottle to her lips, her fishy tail pulled up, revealing legs beneath it. Beside her a devil and a gnome kiss, oblivious to where they are and where they might be going. Beau searches through the crowd, until he thinks he sees something. A pale blue shroud, a broken palm leaf.

"Doll," he calls. Then louder. "Doll!"

She turns. Her scary eyes wobbling, her mouth so pale it's almost disappeared.

"Beau," she says.

Beau crawls through the crowded van to her side.

"Beau," Dolly says, a rattle in her voice, deeper than usual. "I'm sorry about your party."

"Are you kidding?" Beau says, wrapping his arms about her. "That was the most fun I think I've ever had. Until the cops came, of course."

"Of course," Dolly says, closing her eyes. She still holds the small gold dish, Patience's two blue eyes still staring up from it.

"Where's Hicklin?" Beau asks. Dolly shakes her head.

"Where should we go?" Dolly shakes her head again. Beau looks around him, at the pirates and fairies and wilted nymphs.

"Let's go home," Beau says, holding Dolly close. "Maybe he'll be there."

The skeleton drops them near their place, the van choking once, twice, then coughing and carrying the rest of the people away.

Beau opens the front door. There is no light in the stairwell, but sounds come from up the stairs, cluttered clankings, shifting sounds, almost like the sounds of dancing. They walk up the stairs.

No light in the living room, either. But the shifting sounds get louder, and seem to come from Hicklin's room. Beau looks behind him, at Dolly's face so white beneath the morning blue of her saint's veil. He takes her hand, and they go.

The door to Hicklin's room is open, the bright overhead light is a burst of shape and colour. Boxes are everywhere, bones and rocks and hair spilling from where they've fallen. Hicklin is sort of hunched, his shaded cowl pulled back from his head, his sandy hair bright as sun over his soot-marked face. He's pulling open his boxes, seemingly at random, and shoving things in a small white valise.

"Hicklin," Beau says, from the doorway. Hicklin looks over at them, then goes back to what he's doing.

"Hicklin," Beau says again, taking a step into the room.

"Don't come in here," Hicklin barks, still not looking up from his work. "It's all organized."

"Oh-kay," Beau says slowly, looking around at the mass of stuff strewn about the room. "What are you doing?"

"I'm packing, Beau, what does it look like?" Hicklin opens a box, and takes out a pencil-length shaving, a red twirl of wood. Into the valise it goes. "You should grab what you can. We've gotta get out of here."

"What are you talking about?" Beau asks, taking another slow step into the room. "Because of the cops? They don't know anything. They don't know who you are — or me, or Doll for that matter."

"Oh, no?" says a voice outside the room, back in the darkness of the living room. "You don't think so, Daisy?"

Beau turns around but he can't see much of anything. A shudder in the dark, then, a ripple of black in the room. An eyeless face lights itself from below, a laughing mouth below shimmering black horns.

"You," Dolly says.

"Luce," says Beau.

"Hiya kids," Luce says, the lighter snapping off beneath her face. Her voice crackles out from the dark nowhere, moving as she moves. "Miss me?"

"Like Hell," Dolly says, moving away from Beau and into the blackness.

"What is she doing here?" Beau turns to the overly bright space of Hicklin's room. He blinks, blind against the light.

"I don't know!" Hicklin opens a small brown box, dumps the wrapped contents in his white valise. "I got back here and she was waiting for me. Seems she had something to do with the cops showing up."

"What?" Beau asks. Turns back to the darkness in the living room. A laugh comes from somewhere in there, from so far away it seems to come from the bottom of a deep, deep pit.

"That's right, Daisy," Luce's voice chitters through the darkness, higher than usual. "I told 'em everything. About you and your dirty business, and Dolly and her secret garden, and about loverboy here, and his filthy ways. They're very interested in all of you."

"And what? You came back here to rub our noses in it?" Beau takes a step into the dark room and is immediately disoriented. Shapes wave before him, paper-thin. A pale glimmer shows by the window.

"No," Luce's voice, sharper. Slicing. "I didn't think you'd all be screwy enough to come back here."

"Beau, don't talk to her!" Hicklin's voice comes from far far away, from somewhere behind Beau. "Just get your stuff and let's get out of here!"

"Poor Daddy," Luce sighs from the dark, close to Beau. "Mean old Luce is making his life so darned hard. Betcha wish I would just disappear!"

Beau tries to follow the pale ghost, but once it goes past the window it fades in the dark. The other shapes start to move, waving to him, as though from the bottom of the sea. He puts a hand up on the wall and leans there. He thinks he closes his eyes.

"The thought has crossed my mind, Luce," Hicklin's voice cracks from somewhere, an edge in it Beau's never heard.

Luce snorts, and then laughs, and laughs, and then is silent. Beau thinks he opens his eyes. There is a feeling in the room, the stillness just before rain. Beau's skin goes prickly and he wants to run, more than anything he wants to run, but he wouldn't know where. No sounds, not a shuffle, not a creeping foot, not a single breath.

Then suddenly she is there, all in a flash, as though lit by lightning. Luce in black tatters, a storm wearing its eye on the outside, holding something on fire. A torch, brought down from the mountain. She waves it around, a drunken spot, lighting up slices of her face, stuttered snatches of time. She laughs.

"You think you tell a pretty good story, don't you, Hicklin?" she waves her flame, lights up a grin carved out of her face. "You think old Luce'll fall for anything, just like she fell for you? I know everything. I bet the twist is here, isn't she? I bet you're hiding her somewhere."

Beau sees a quick movement, over by Hicklin's door. Hicklin's sooty face sliding into the darkness here. From somewhere he answers her.

"Who, Luce? Who am I hiding?"

"You know who," Luce screams. She's over by the window now, Beau can just see her outline against the darkness outside. "That red-headed twist. She's here, isn't she? Come on out, sweetie pie! I just want to play!"

"She's not here!" Hicklin yells, the first time Beau has ever heard him raise his voice.

"There's that story again, Daddy," Luce calls. A side of sneer in a spot of flame. "I saw her. Here. The two of you looked real cozy, a couple of regular lovebirds. Real sweet. Made me sick."

"She was here," Hicklin says, softer and slower. "But I told her to leave. Not that it's any of your business."

Behind him Beau feels something, almost a ghost, passing by him, silent.

"Stay put," Dolly's voice whispers. "For now."

Beau leans his back against the wall. Tries to keep his eyes on the flame, moving about the room. As he stares he sees it multiply, as though it's been split into parts, all with lives of their own.

"Well, if she's here, I'll smoke her out," Luce screams. A sudden wall of flame throws her into light. Beau gets it now. She's lighting all the sheets on fire, all the sheets they use as curtains.

"This way," Dolly whispers low in Beau's ear, pushing him gently toward the kitchen. "Slow."

"Luce," Hicklin's voice softer now, "Come on. You're not really going to set us all on fire, are you?"

"No," Luce says, her torch sinking, little flames licking at a pile of papers and magazines stacked on the floor. In a second the pile is crackling, pages curling in on themselves, the flames climbing the walls. "Not all of us."

The fire has crawled to the foot of a tall bookcase, has started the slow climb up, eating everything in its way. There's now enough light in the room that Beau can see Hicklin, a lumpy grey shape, standing before Luce with his arms outstretched. Luce's body shines black, with tatters all down her arms, a tail swishing behind her. For a second they are frozen like that. Hicklin takes a slow step forward, his hands before him.

"Luce, please," he whispers. "Give it to me. You don't want to burn down our house, do you?"

Luce lets out a scream, a shriek from the pit of her, the bottom of her belly. Pulls a large knife from a sheath strapped onto her thigh.

"This isn't *our* house!" she yells, and is gone, out of Hicklin's arms, still outstretched. "It's hers, it always will be! Where is she?"

Luce's flame has disappeared, into her room, which is suddenly alight. She runs out of it, trailing smoke, her small torch wavering behind her.

"Not in there!" Luce yells, running toward Hicklin's room.

"Luce!" Hicklin takes off after her. The living room is filling with smoke. There are a couple of pops as lightbulbs explode. Beau sinks to the floor, starts to crawl toward the kitchen. Dolly is already there, opening the window.

"Endymion," Beau breathes. Dolly runs past him, her saint's veil gone smoky, her fleshing burned and torn in places, another, paler skin showing underneath, a weird furry bag swinging behind her. Beau crawls after her.

She picks up the slumbering beast, holds him close to her. He opens his eyes and emits a sound more like a bark than a meow, then struggles in Dolly's arms. She puts him down on the floor, and he runs for the front door, sliding out it fast as smoke. Beau peers out the window, but can't see Selene anywhere. She must've flown off.

"She's gone," Hicklin says. He coughs. "Luce. She's gone. I told her to leave." Hicklin comes backwards into the kitchen, Luce holding him now at arms' length, the torch in one hand, the knife in the other.

"I saw her," Luce creaks. "You and her. Curled up all cozy, right here in this room. So that's how it is with you, Hicklin? You think you can just toss old Luce out when you're done?"

"No," Hicklin says, shaking his head. "No, it's not like that. I didn't —"

"Shut your hole," Luce commands. Hicklin is in the kitchen now, with Beau and Dolly.

Dolly pushes something heavy behind Beau, and whispers, "Whatever you do, don't let her get that."

Beau nods. He puts a hand behind him and feels around. Whatever it is, it's bumpy, and big. He knows what it is. Dolly must've grabbed it from the other room, when she got the cat. Beau stands still.

Luce snorts a laugh through her nose. "I should just charge admission, keep you all here as my personal sideshow. Put you in jars, a dollar a peep. Bunch of freaks."

"Luce," Hicklin starts. A poke from her firey stick and he quits it.

"You," Luce says, her voice licking itself, a flame in there, hiding. "Playing Sleeping Beauty with a kid, and then leaving her for your goddamn Princess."

"I never..." Hicklin says, his eyes on Luce. "I didn't do that. That was you —"

Luce snorts. "Yeah? But the cops don't know that. And who're they gonna believe? You? Or poor little underage Luce? And you," she points the flame at Beau. "I don't even know what you are. But you've been passed around like an old hanky down at the peepshows, huh? Oscar's buddy is one of your regulars. Isn't that right? And here's the Ice Queen," she points her flame at Dolly. "Starting to melt? Babykiller. Do they know about that, yet? The resident virgin, killing babies on the side."

The three of them are silent. Beau catches a look pass between Dolly and Hicklin, but he can't read it. His eyes are starting to tear up, and he coughs into his hand.

"You all know some stories, I think," Luce says, holding her flame over them. "So you all know what happens to the monsters at the end."

They are all quiet. Beau can hear the crackling of fire in the other rooms, a crunching as though many tiny mouths are chewing away at the walls, the books, the boxes. Smoke crawls into the kitchen on a thousand thousand bellies. There is a quiet clack as Dolly, behind him, lifts the latch on the kitchen door.

"Stay where you are," Luce snaps, stretching a long arm into the kitchen, fire at the end of it. Dolly edges past Beau, toward the middle of the room.

"I mean it," Luce warns, pointing the flame right at Dolly. Dolly stands still and straight, her virgin's veil lifting slightly at the edges.

"Luce," Dolly calls. "Catch."

Luce's rat bag goes sailing, heading straight for her. Luce turns, and drops the torch and the knife. Catches the bag.

Dolly lunges for the torch, as it rolls toward the stove. Throws it over Luce's head, into the other room. Luce stands still for a second, staring down at what she's caught. Beau leans forward to grab the knife, but is too slow. Hicklin gets it before he does. Dolly grabs the Heart of Gold from behind Beau, lifts it on its stand, and brings it down, hard, in Luce's side.

There is a long *huffff* from Luce, as she falls, her horns clacking on the kitchen floor.

And then quiet. So quiet they can only hear the fire, crawling.

A pop from the living room, another lightbulb exploding. The three of them turn to look.

Then a *whoooooosh*, as of the house itself drawing in a long breath.

And then a crack, from Luce's room, all the paints and thinners and solvents used on the Holes going up all at once. And then. Fire. Everywhere.

LUCE

I wake up in a hallway on one of those wheely things they roll stiffs out of houses on. Above me these long thin lights flicker, making everything look like an old movie, all jittery and faded. I check myself out. Still wearing most of my costume, covered over with a clean white sheet, paper-thin. I wiggle my toes, flex my fingers. Something furry in there. I squeeze again. It's the rat bag, somehow still in my hand, which means I've got dough, which means old Luce can high-tail it outta here. I sit up.

All along the hallway in both directions there're other stiffs on other wheely things. All of them covered with sheets, just like mine, some of them bloodied, some of them with holes in them, some of them so pale it's like they're already ghosts. Some of them with painted faces, or horns, or pretty Princess lips. So it's still Hallowe'en. Maybe some of the blood is paint. Maybe all of it. The lights flicker, off for a second, then on. I slip out from under my paper sheet, and hop down to the floor.

I walk close to the wall, just walking. A nurse coming the other way doesn't even look up from her clipboard, and I just keep going. I might as well be whistling. I pass the nurse's station, and see a tree standing in there, coats blossoming off it. I pull off the longest one, throw it on. And walk out of there, into a bright, sunshiney day.

The streets are empty, I mean, nobody's around. Like the only people left in the world are up there bleeding in the hallway of the hospital. I pull the nurse's coat tight around me. It's a nubbly orange fabric, kind of like something you'd find on a chair in a dentist's office, but it goes past my knees, and fits pretty good. So I walk across the street. Not even any cars on the road. The sun is so bright I'm squinting, but a chill in the air makes goosebumps on me under the coat.

I catch sight of myself in the window of a deli and almost cast kittens. Talk about the living dead, I mean, kids, I look like I just crawled up from the middle of the world. My hair's all out in the wings I put it in yesterday, but all crunched in on one side and gone on the other. Skin's covered with black, I guess partly makeup and maybe a lot of smoke, so I look like I rolled out of a dead campfire or something. In the nurse's spotless coat I look like a zombie just lurched out of Hell, by way of the suburbs. I walk into the deli anyway.

There's a couple people in here, and a waitress behind the counter. All of them reading newspapers, the waitress leaning on the counter. She looks up as I pass by.

"It's Hallowe'en," I say, with a bit of a smile. "I've just gotta iron my shoelaces, savvy?"

She frowns, but doesn't say anything as I walk on by.

I keep walking, toward the bathroom. Lock myself in there and take off the coat. Scrub myself quick, my face and arms and calves. Wet my hair and notice half of it really is gone. Must've burned off. I rip a bit of nylon off the bodysuit I'm still wearing, use it to tie my hair up pretty good. Put the coat back on, and head out. The waitress says something to me in French but I don't stop. Just walk on by, and out the door.

•

The bus station's full, people everywhere. Everyone walking around all stunned, not one smile anywhere. The light's too bright and all along the walls there's people waiting. A loudspeaker blares every once in a while, a voice honking out of it, saying stuff I can't understand. Whatever the voice is bleating, it makes the other folks move. They get up and stand in lines, get on buses and go away. I don't know where.

I get in one line, that I think is for the ticket counter. It moves really fast and before I know it some newsie's chucking papers at me. There's some change in the nurse's coat, so I give the kid a nickel and take the English one. I check out the front page and there we are. Big fire on Duluth, three presumed dead. I move close to the wall and kind of lean back, behind the paper. I read the whole kit and kaboodle. Seems they couldn't stop the fire in time, the whole place burned to the ground. Found one person, me, on the sidewalk, passed out but looking all burned up. Took me to the hospital.

But they didn't find anyone else. Found a lot of bones and even some teeth, so they're checking those out. There's another story, about the Holes, and about the Fox and how there's charges against him, if he's alive — something to do with putting on a live sex show. Guess the heat got an eyeful up there on the mountain. And there's more.

They're looking for the Ghost, too. Her little business wasn't quite on the level. Even though she was giving the stuff away, getting rid of babies is pretty much frowned upon, no matter who does it. And through the mail, like she was doing? No, sir.

The Daisy's mentioned, but only as a kind of partner in crime. They don't know what to make of him any more than I did, but they figure he was up to something.

And I'm in there too. They blab my age and go on about how since I'm a kid, there could be more charges laid against the Fox. They think they've got me, up at the hospital. Says they're waiting to interview me. Seems I'm quite the little victim. And they love it. Poor me.

I look around me. Still the light too bright, still these zombies everywhere going somewhere, somewhere, somewhere I've got to go. I get in another line.

This one doesn't move at all so I know I'm in the right one. I wait and wait but the line doesn't move. I wait and wait some more. After forever, the thing starts going. Maybe someone just got back from lunch, I don't know. Finally I make it up to the counter. Behind it, a pretty boy, not much older than me. I smile.

He says something in French.

"You speak English?" I ask, smiling my prettiest smile.

He nods, but doesn't say anything to prove it. I don't know where I'm going but I guess as far as I can.

"Vancouver," I say. "One way."

He nods, and pulls a ticket from somewhere.

"Your name," he says.

I make something up. He writes it down. Without looking up at me, he tells me how much it's going to be. It's a lot, more than I thought. But old Q.B.'s voot'll cover it.

I open the rat bag. Inside the face of a girl smiles up at me. I frown and dig it out. It's a wadded-up page from one of the magazines me and the Fox were using for the Holes, a cartoon babe in short-shorts, riding a rocket. I pull it out, and underneath it there's just more of the same. Couples and pillow fights and roller derbies and threesomes and sweet country things, naked on horseback. I look up at the pretty boy behind the counter. My insides are squealing like I'm ossified.

"Scuse me a sec," I say. "Little problem with the lettuce."

I move to the side of the counter and he calls over the next person in line. I take out everything, and that's all there is. Pages and pages of smut. My dough's gone. I close the bag and open it again, as if I'm a magician and that'll make the money reappear. It doesn't. But there's something in there. Something little at the bottom of the bag.

Flashing up at me like from some other place, there's a glint of blue. I look closer. It's a little blue glass eye, just one, staring up at me from the bottom of the bag, for all the world watching me. And that's all there is.

One blue eye staring up at me, alive for all time.

Acknowledgements

To Natasha, Kim, Nika, and Nathanael, and to Lyle, Melora, Erin, Taras, Meghan, and Tricia. Great big thank-yous to Thom Richardson and Marisol Nantel. To all the folks at the bar, and to everyone who has encouraged, pushed, and annoyed me through this book.

Special thanks to Jon Paul Fiorentino.

Extra special thanks to Andy Brown.

For Paul and Elaine.